I0561802

THINGS STRANGLED

CARLISLE CRIME CASES #5
A CHRISTOPHER SNOW & ERIN MCCOY MYSTERY

J. M. WEST

MILFORD
HOUSE

an imprint of Sunbury Press, Inc.
Mechanicsburg, PA USA

MILFORD HOUSE

an imprint of Sunbury Press, Inc.
Mechanicsburg, PA USA

NOTE: This is a work of fiction. Names, characters, places and incidents are the product of the author's imagination or are used fictiously, and any resemblance to actual persons, living or dead, business establishments, events or locales is entirely coincidental.

Copyright © 2019 by J. M. West.
Cover Copyright © 2019 by Sunbury Press, Inc.

Sunbury Press supports copyright. Copyright fuels creativity, encourages diverse voices, promotes free speech, and creates a vibrant culture. Thank you for buying an authorized edition of this book and for complying with copyright laws by not reproducing, scanning, or distributing any part of it in any form without permission. You are supporting writers and allowing Sunbury Press to continue to publish books for every reader. For information contact Sunbury Press, Inc., Subsidiary Rights Dept., PO Box 548, Boiling Springs, PA 17007 USA or legal@sunburypress.com.

For information about special discounts for bulk purchases, please contact Sunbury Press Orders Dept. at (855) 338-8359 or orders@sunburypress.com.

To request one of our authors for speaking engagements or book signings, please contact Sunbury Press Publicity Dept. at publicity@sunburypress.com.

ISBN: 978-1-62006-317-0 (Trade paperback)

Library of Congress Control Number: 2019948923

FIRST MILFORD HOUSE PRESS EDITION: August 2019

Product of the United States of America
0 1 1 2 3 5 8 13 21 34 55

Set in Bookman Old Style
Designed by Crystal Devine
Cover by Lawrence Knorr
Edited by Lawrence Knorr

Continue the Enlightenment!

In memory of Chuck Bassett

But we write unto them [Gentiles], that they
abstain from pollutions of idols, and from
fornication, and from things strangled, and from
blood.

—*Holy Bible, King James,* Acts 15:20

* * *

Yet marked I where the bolt of Cupid fell
It fell upon a little Western flower,
Before milk-white, now purple with love's wound,
And maidens call it love in idleness.
Fetch me that flow'r; the herb I show'd thee once.
The juice of it on sleeping eyelids laid,
Will make man or woman madly dote
Upon the next live creature that it sees.

—*A Midsummer Night's Dream* (II:1)

The Carlisle Crime Cases Series

1

Morning mist ghosted off the grass as the September
sun kissed the earth. Shadow strained forward, sniffing
the grass, nosing the fallen logs and leaves. A half-
dozen dogs and their handlers had converged at the
K-9 Instruction site earlier for training. Then Dispatch
called Detective Erin McCoy with a missing persons
case—a possible kidnapping. She relayed the message
to K-9 Training Instructor Corey Kauffman; he'd
ordered all hands and paws to the woods behind the
Woolworth 'store' where the vic had last been spotted.
The men, woman and K-9 officers fanned out behind the
warehouse, trekking through the rocky, wooded terrain
until the warrant cleared for the building.

A coarse, dry wind tunneled through the trees,
jigging fir needles and muscling motley leaves from their
limbs, scattering them across the ground to form a zany
quilt. Their husks skittered along the dirt path. Mac
bunched her unruly auburn curls together, restrained
them with a claw clip.

"How long has he been missing?" Kauffman asked
as his black Lab Inky shouldered ahead, nose roving a
six-foot swath to the right. Except for the wind, silence
ruled—as a breath held. No birds cawed, animals
crawled or snakes slithered. Acres of dry fallow land
stretched beyond the warehouse where the film crew
had constructed the site of Frank W. Woolworth's first
successful five and dime.

"They're not sure. Maybe twenty-four hours. The
director, JJ Reynolds, is filming the documentary in

Carlisle because he claims too many tourists mob the streets in Lancaster where the original store stood.

"Reynolds said they'd been drinking after filming, lost track of time." Shadow extended the expandable leash. In sweatshirt, jeans, and hiking boots, Mac tramped behind, trying to avoid the poison ivy and thorny patches of wild raspberry tubers. Her eyes scanned the field for broken twigs, bent or flattened grasses—any evidence that people had trudged this way, maybe dragging a body.

"Hell's bells. All of them wasted? Typical." Kauffman jogged to catch up. He wore a Redskins sweatshirt and tan cargo shorts, its pockets bulging with dog treats and granola bars. "You met the cast and crew?"

"A few, but mainly the director. He looks youngish but has grey curly hair like dust bunnies and a goatee. I left him ranting about losing his star. And a handful of actors and crew were lounging around the set waiting to shoot. Then I Googled Frank W. Woolworth."

"Who's the star?" Corey asked. "I see you're not limping anymore. Hip healed?"

"Lance Reading plays Frank W. Woolworth." Mac shrugged, trudged forward, eyes sweeping the brush and hollows. "Yes, sir, my hip's fine now; it bothers me when the barometer rises." A squawking jay fluttered in the sycamore to her left, shaking the golden yellow leaves as sparrows dodged the interloper.

"Never heard of him." Kauffman unhooked his radio, motioning to the veteran handling Brutus. "Veer further right. I think we're too tight. I'm swinging out. At this rate, we may walk to Newville!"

"I'm not familiar with him either, but Elizabeth Banks is playing his wife Jennie Creighton. You should see inside the Lancaster store replica. Plank tables decked out in red cambric line the aisles displaying sundries, toiletries, fire shovels, straight pins, and red costume jewelry. Kitchen utensils, biscuit cutters, and

2

tin pie pans are displayed in baskets. The store even contains hardware.

"My stepmother's first job was at Woolworth's—she worked behind the candy counter throughout nursing school. She's dying to see the replica, wants to watch some filming. Must be a nostalgic boon for Baby Boomers. There was a Woolworth in most towns and cities."

"Woolworth's rags-to-riches story is remarkable." Kauffman signaled again. Brutus and his handler moved out of sight beyond a clump of boulders.

"Woolworth's parents farmed, but that life didn't suit Frank. He vowed to make something of himself after a sales clerk in Watertown snubbed him and his brother when they paid for his mother's birthday gift with a handful of change. First, he worked in retail as a clerk, but he took night courses in bookkeeping and found his niche when his boss asked him to dress the display windows. The rest, as they say, is history."

"You've done your homework. I remember the storefronts; my mother shopped at Woolworth's," Corey said. "But I didn't realize that one man owned the entire chain. Never thought about it. I didn't know he lived in Pennsylvania. Thought those department-store tycoons all lived in New York."

Mac continued. "Woolworth owned five and dime stores—a big distinction in his time because average workers couldn't afford department-store prices. After he'd established several dime stores, he moved to NYC to get closer to his manufacturers. He also revolutionized Americans' shopping habits. For the first time, shoppers could browse and see the prices displayed. And he didn't quit when a store failed. Just closed the store, regrouped and tried again elsewhere. Gotta admire that—true grit." With every step, their hiking boots kicked dirt puffs into dry air.

Kauffman and Inky pulled away heading farther south.

That morning, Mac had interviewed the props buyer and manager, Larissa Latch. The five-four, persimmon-haired bundle of energy adjusted the displayed merchandise as she described the cast's Friday night celebration. "We shot the outdoor footage in Lancaster, then drove here and rented a house in the historical district for the Woolworth's exterior. Uhm, the interior's right over there." She'd pointed, led the way for Mac to see the 'dwelling,' a mock-up of the Woolworth's rented three-story on Lemon Street in Lancaster with nineteenth-century décor, simply yet tastefully furnished, cutaway walls facing the cameras.

The kitchen, wallpapered parlor, and living room lined the downstairs—a touch of red in each room, with more sedate bedrooms upstairs. Mac's eyes caught the four-poster double bed and an antique trundle bed for the Woolworth's young daughter, Helena. A massive wardrobe hung open, revealing several period suits and dresses. An open steamer trunk squatted at the foot of the bed and packing and hatboxes suggested the family was moving in.

"And after dinner Friday night?" Mac asked.

Latch explained. "Gosh. We left the restaurant, migrated to a pub around ten: Lance, Ben—who plays Frank's brother Charles Sumner; the director, JJ; myself; the camera crew; make-up mavens Tammy and Tina Wells, and the stage crew—I don't know them well. We'll shoot the store and home scenes here. After a while, someone said, 'Where's Lance?' Gee, he just up and disappeared. There one minute—" Her fingers splayed out as her green eyes widened. "Gone the next!"

"Is anyone one else missing? Perhaps he met someone?" Mac suggested. A bespeckled young man with sable hair, a receding hairline, trimmed mustache in a white shirt, brown slacks and suspenders lounged against the counter. He removed his shirt's starched collar, stuffed it in his pocket. "And who are you?"

He stood, offered a firm, dry hand. "Ben Whalen. I play Charles Sumner Woolworth, Frank's bother." His wavy brown hair had been Brill creamed in place.

Whalen answered, "Yes, the costume designer Jackie Frost and her assistant left the restaurant around nine. Said they had to get the costumes ready for today's shoot. And JJ's assistant, Rachel Stein, retired early—something about packing, going to Philly to find a boat for Woolworth's first trip abroad to buy merchandise to stock his stores."

The director paced the length of the aisle—up one, down the next, checking his watch. "All right people, looks like we're not filming now, but stay close in case we can resume later today." To Mac, he said, "I expect your detectives to find him soon. Until then, I'll be in my office." Reynolds waved his hand at the stage. "Cast dismissed until further notice."

"Did you see Reading that night?" Mac asked the fair-haired woman dressed in a long-sleeved frilly flowered blouse with a high, lacy collar and puffy sleeves over a long dove-grey skirt behind the counter.

"Yes, earlier when we were all together. I left about nine." Actor Elizabeth Banks pushed off from the counter. Her blond hair, pinned in comma curls, nested on her crown. "I better get out of costume if we're not shooting today. It takes an hour to press this outfit." She smoothed it down with her palms.

At that point, Mac had called her partner, Zachery Fields, "Need help with interviews. "A dozen people on site—warehouse just past Rustic Tavern—to interview. Shadow and I are tramping the fields behind the warehouse to search with Kauffman and the other K-9 units."

Shadow bore on, nose to the ground, following the actor's scent from his cap. She stopped to investigate, sniffing blades of grass. "Let's hope we're on a search and rescue, girl," Mac remarked more to herself, as her shepherd stretched her lead to twenty feet. Slipping a bottle of water from her backpack, the Carlisle detective quaffed half of it down. *Reading's been missing over twenty-four hours. What was the likelihood of finding their Vic alive?* Her eyes scanned the uneven rocky, terrain looking for dropped items or evidence. Spindly deciduous trees, leaves turning scarlet, pumpkin, and gold, gave way to white pine and fir, the land sprouting mounds and boulders, and then hills as they marched on. Clumps of stubby grasses and weeds clung to the knotted soil.

Surging ahead, the shepherd and Lab moved as one, stopping, sitting beneath a dying poplar. Shadow barked once, her hairs bristling. Mac and Kauffman jogged to the tree. Looked up. A young man, dressed in trousers and shredded white shirt from another century had been tied to the tree, his arms extended, legs and feet lashed around the trunk like a crucifixion. His head lolled forward, pants stained down the front. Blood had dried, congealed along the bark from his left side. Dirt dusted his dark, slightly curly hair. His comely face bore wooly eyebrows, an uneven mustache and the pallor of death. "Someone nailed him to the friggin' tree."

Kauffman whistled. "And it isn't even Easter."

"Not funny, sir," Mac said.

"I'm not joking, McCoy. Why copy the crucifixion if it's not significant?"

"OK. May be a part of the MO. So you think it's a Biblical allusion?" Mac asked.

"I'm not the detective, but it seems logical given what we're seeing."

After rewarding the dogs, Mac called it in. She fished her Powershot from her backpack and shot several photos. "Body found. We need Dr. Chen, CSU in the field behind the first warehouse on road to Newville— Rt-641. Cut him down from the tree. Yes, I know, but I can't leave him in situ. Someone must've closed his eyes." She waved latex gloves at Kauffman, snapped on her own. While she related info to Dispatch, Kauffman and several other guys sawed through the ropes with Swiss army knives and pried the nail from his side. Kauffman handed the five-inch nail to Mac, who dropped it into a glassine, labeled and dated it.

Mac looked at the fresh blood on the nail, then at the Vic. "He's bleeding! Get him down!" Laying the pale, inert form at the foot of the tree, the men stepped back. Mac felt for a pulse as Shadow lunged at his chest. The body's eyes snapped open—widened at the sight of the shepherd's forefeet on him; he gulped for air and tried to scramble away from her.

Behind them, an ambulance roared and whined, bucking over the rocky, rolling ground, rocking to a stop. Troy Hemmer's lean frame leaped from the driver's door, swung around to the rear and retrieved a stretcher. A blonde emerged from the passenger's door. They double-timed to Reading, eased an oxygen mask over his face, started an IV.

"Good girl!" Kauffman dropped pieces of the damp rope into a paper bag. Mac nodded thanks, circled the poplar, eyes canvassing the base, trunk, and limbs.

"Shadow sensed he was still alive," Corey stated as they backed away. "Sharp dog! OK, men, excitement's over. We're done here. Let's head back to the training site. Heel, Inky." He and the Lab turned back. "Oh, say hello to Chris for me. How is he?"

"Sit." Mac offered her dog another treat until the roaring in her ears died down from the shock at seeing a corpse revived. Adrenaline kicked her into overdrive. "Sure will. He lost partial hearing from that explosion last summer and experiences occasional light-headedness but won't admit it."

"Is he back at work?" Kauffman asked. "That Sims' case solved?"

"Oh, yes. He only missed two weeks in June. He's functioning!" Mac smiled, remembering her husband's insistence he return to Homicide despite lingering injuries from the blast that injured poor Mr. Mahoney. "What a chaotic case—Kelly Sims' father confessed, then Kelly admitted arguing with her husband before going to the Big Apple. On the way to the jail—" Mac interrupted herself to ask the EMT, "What's the vic's status?"

Hemmer and his partner hovered over the disoriented actor. "He's dehydrated. Nail pierced fatty tissue; he'll need a tetanus booster. Won't know more until we get him to CRMC." He ran his hands along the victim's limbs while the woman immobilized his head and neck. "One, two, three." They hoisted him onto the stretcher and, with Kaufman's aid, handed the man into the ambulance. Within minutes, they wheeled around and headed for the medical center.

Mac thumbed Dispatch. "Negative on Dr. Chen. The man's alive and en route to the hospital. Think we've found our missing actor." Ended the call. "Let's go, girl. Thanks, Corey, Inky—all of you—for helping track down our missing person. This one ended well for a change."

Several media vans rocked into view following the CSU.

"Looks like we've only just begun," Detective Zachary Fields said as he approached with the CSU. Techs covered in white jumpsuits converged at the crime scene as they fanned across the field. The youngest detective on the squad offered a cup to Mac. "Your morning mocha. The actors had scattered by the time I arrived at the warehouse. Chief said to stick to you." His stick-straight brown hair stuck out like a bottlebrush. A high forehead, rounded cheeks and lively hazel eyes in a friendly face greeted all with a smile. He wore tan Dockers and a short-sleeve blue dress shirt with Asics.

Mac smiled and accepted the coffee. "Thanks." She opened the rear of the CPD's white K-9 SUV; Shadow leaped into the cargo bay, lapped the water Mac poured into her collapsible cup. Then Mac buckled her in. "Come on. I'll take Shadow home, then head to CRMC to interview our Vic and then back to the warehouse to question the rest of the cast and crew."On the way, Mac called Sonja's office.

The CPD admin answered on the first ring. "Yes, ma'am, how can I help?"

"Will you run a search on Lance Reading, JJ Reynolds and the actors we need to interview? I'll email you the list. The victim's alive—thank God—but someone kidnapped him and tied him up, left him exposed to the elements and wildlife. Call the Carlisle hospital, find out where they stashed him. Then send a unit to guard him."

"Actors? That group that's doing the documentary on Frank W. Woolworth?" Sonja asked.

"Yes. And dig into the background of Frank Woolworth and his closest associates; I need photos so I can acquaint myself with the cast. We're in the dark about these people; there may be an attempted killer among them."

"I'm on it. I'll email you whatever I find—or call if it's something urgent. Lance Reading's a hottie."

"You know him?" Mac's voice climbed an octave.

"Know of him. He appears on the daytime soaps from time to time. OK. Gotta go. Good luck."

Turning from Lisburn into their driveway, the SUV rolled down to the bungalow. Popping the garage door button, Mac unloaded Shadow. "Be right back. Go, girl, if you need to." The dog loped a few feet away and dropped her hind end. Then Erin let her inside, checking her water dish. Nobody else was home. A note on the island read, *'Be home by lunch.'* Dad.

She thumbed one on her iPhone; call went to voicemail. "Chris, we're investigating a kidnapping and assault. Can you swing by the warehouse two buildings down from the Rustic Tavern? Think there's a doggie daycare between. The actors have an indoor stage there. Could you and Savage give us a hand? At least a dozen people to interview—one of them knows something.

"Meantime, we're headed to CRMC to interview the Vic Lance Reading, who woke up when we cut him down from the tree. Thanks. Love you." Ended call.

McCoy found Reading propped up in bed in a private room on the third floor—where the staff had put her after her hip replacement. The odors of disinfectant, bleach, and BO assailed her nose. A basket of yellow mums decorated the windowsill. A bowl of untouched soup sat on his tray table, a glass of water at hand. His eyes shut, Reading looked to be about thirty. Dusty, brown wavy hair met in a widow's peak. His wide, smooth forehead topped an oblong face. Wooly eyebrows hovered over deep-set eyes. Gaunt cheeks. A darker, rogue mustache hid his upper lip.

He blinked, rested his grayish blue eyes on her. "You're Scotch Irish."

Mac showed her shield. "Guilty as charged. Detective Erin McCoy. My partner, Detective Zachery Fields." The men made eye contact. "We'd like to ask you a few questions if you're up to it." Mac withdrew her recorder from her purse, identified herself and the interviewee, the case number, date and time.

"My great-great-grandfather was Irish," Reading said.

"How long have your cast and crew been in Carlisle?" asked Mac.

"Since last Friday. First, we stayed in a hotel, but JJ rented a brick house like the one on Lemon Street in Lancaster that the Woolworths rented. We wanted to paint it yellow—get it?"

"Yes, yellow. Do you remember what happened last Friday night?"

"Yeah, we were drinking at the hotel downtown. I remember going to another bar at a dark pub—downtown. Crowded, noisy with locals." He scrunched his nose. Cranked his bed higher. Pale and weak from his nail wound and exposure to the frigid night air, Reading reached for his tumbler of water. He looked like he'd just emerged from a 1920's ad with that walrus mustache, oblong face and lean frame.

"You know of anyone nursing you a personal grudge? You tromp on any feet during your stay in Carlisle? Insult anyone?" Mac inquired. She heard a commotion outside his door.

"Me? I'm nobody. No one recognizes me. I've been a guest on a few soaps; this is my first starring part—my breakout role! Who would want to hurt me? And as for the townies, I don't think they noticed us. New York Guild actors try to keep a low profile. Our documentary's a paean to Frank W. Woolworth's genius—his true American spirit! His determination built an empire from a dream and damn hard work. He wanted the average citizen to walk into his stores, browse, buy affordable wares and leave satisfied with their bargains."

Mac smiled at his energetic response despite his close call. "Yes, Carlisle had a Woolworth store until the early '90s. And my stepmother worked in one throughout high school and nursing school. It was her first and favorite job. She waxes nostalgic about Woolworth's and is dying to see the set.

"But I digress. Someone tied and nailed you to that tree, leaving you for dead. You're lucky a bear didn't come along and maul you. OK, does someone on the cast or crew want you out of the way? Did someone resent your getting the part?"

"A bear?" His eyes widened. He shrugged and then winced, a wind-burned hand moving to his injured side. "It must've been a prank. We try out with someone reading another part, but no one begrudged me the role." He shrugged, his bushy eyebrows arching. "I look at lot like Frank Woolworth."

"A prank is what teens do for kicks or frat boys' hazing stunts. The law calls this a crime—kidnapping and assault, perhaps attempted murder." Fields remarked, making notes.

"Why is it called kidnapping?" mused Reading. "I'm a grown man."

"Really? I—" Mac started as the door swung open, the perky Ms. Latch pushed through, a script in one hand, a chocolate milkshake in another.

The actress saw their frowns. "Oh, excuse me for interrupting. I'd explain, but it's complicated." Mac thumbed off the recorder.

"Here. Try this." Latch plopped the shake on Reading's tray table with the manuscript. "Since you look so pale and woebegone, JJ wants to shoot Frank's nervous breakdown scene." She explained to the detectives. "Woolworth's breakdown from working non-stop happened later, but we take minor liberties with the chronology. I'll just run along." To Reading, she added, "We're shooting Monday if you feel up to it. So rest up this weekend." She bussed both his cheeks and skipped out.

Fields pushed record. "Did you hear anything or anyone while you were being trussed up? How did your assailant drag and lift you into the tree?"

"I dunno. I remember voices but whispering, so there must've been two. We stumbled around, drunk. Or at least I was so I couldn't resist. Last time I drink my dinner. I don't know who would pull a dangerous stunt like that. Did you find anything?" Reading drew creamy chocolate goodness through the straw. "Umm. This tastes wonderful! Like liquid velvet."

"The CSU is still on the scene," Fields noted. "Can you think of anything else? Someone slip something into your drink?"

"We started with wine at dinner. Switched to boilermakers and margaritas later at the downtown pub. We were all punch-drunk anyhow—working twelve-hour shifts. Then someone asked for Sex on the Beach, so the women all ordered that!" He slurped up the last of the shake. "Man, I don't remember." Reading laid his hand against his forehead. "Fever. Headache." His hand dropped to his lap.

"We need to know your history, get a timeline and track down the persons who did this. You're our best lead," Mac said.

"Tell us about your yourself," Fields suggested.

He sighed. "I grew up in New York; still live there with a million other actors. I'm an only child. Can't remember my father. My mother—a paranoid manic-depressive—died when I was in film school. My grandmother's trust fund paid for college. Had my first role was in *Les Mis* when I was thirteen. Had minor roles in *Jesus Christ Superstar, Cats,* and a few off-Broadway plays." He waved his hand dismissively. "That about sums it up. Please, I'm tired." His head fell back against his pillow; his eyes closed.

Mac snapped her notebook shut, slipped her digital recorder into her purse and shouldered it. She laid a card on his tray. "Thanks for your time. We'll talk again after we've interviewed the rest of the cast, crew, and the staff at the hotel and bars. Call if you think of any detail about the attack. I'll assign an officer to you."

"Think that's necessary?" the young man asked, eyes still shut.

The door swung open again. A brunette with thick crimped hair fanning out like a pyramid strode in with a soup carton. The aroma of chicken soup wafted up. She dug saltines and a cup of pudding from generous pockets of her smock. She lowered it to the table and tapped Reading's hand. "Let's spoon nourishing soup in you." She pushed the bowl of green soup away.

Mac waved her shield. "Who are you?"

The woman with an olive complexion, close-set brown eyes, and a long nose was wearing relaxed-fit jeans topped with a clingy black jersey, exposing a roll at her midsection. Turning, she eyed Mac's shield, slid over Fields. "Rachel Stein, JJ Reynolds' assistant director." Her eyes strayed to Reading's tray table. Seeing the soup untouched, she pulled a chair over, sat down. Slipping the spoon from its plastic sleeve, she dipped it into the soup and lifted it to the actor's lips. "Open. Our documentary's slated to air on *The American Icons* around Christmas. I'm on my way to Philly to retrofit *The City of Paris* for Frank's first European voyage. And our Mr. Woolworth will eat. If you'll please excuse us, he's exhausted. Then he must rest because I plan to keep us on schedule."

Reading complied, closing his lips on the spoon.

Irked my Stein's dismissal but let it go in exchange for her cooperation later, Mac handed her a card. "We'll send an officer to guard Reading. Ms. Stein, please come to the CPD station when you're finished to give a statement before you leave town."

"We'll be in touch." Fields added to Reading as they left the cozy tableau. Riding down the elevator, she mulled over her next move. Her cell chimed 'Stand by Me,' Chris's cell. "McCoy." In the background, she heard rustling, clinking, and shuffling feet.

"Are you coming to help with these interviews today?"Snow asked. "Is this the entire list?"

"Hold on. Chris, are you at the Woolworth store?" she guessed.

"Yes. Sonja filled me in. Savage and I can interview the cast if you want to go home for lunch. The director seems agitated but relieved that Reading's alive. CSU has not returned from the field. What's your call at this point?"

"Kidnapping and assault. May bump it up to attempted murder after I talk to the doctor. Besides the cast and crew, we'll obtain statements from the staff at Comfort Suites and Market Cross Pub, since that's the last place Reading remembered being."

"Can you get a photo of Reading from the director? Make those headshots of all the actors. Fields is with me, so we'll swing by the hotel to get a list of the wait staff on duty last Friday." She waved Fields toward the K-9 SUV parked in the first row outside of the hospital, checked for traffic, hustled across the macadam as she popped the lock. Sliding into the driver's seat, Mac fired the ignition. "And we'll canvass the crime scene behind the warehouse, too."

"Roger that. Will you have time for lunch?" Chris asked. The background noise climbed a register— someone dragging something, then pinging and clinking of clanging silverware. Voices chatting.

"Yeah, I'll swing by and feed Ian. Later. Love you." She thumbed the phone icon. She caught Fields rolling his eyes at her terms of endearment and chuckled as she noticed a flush creep up his neck. "Was it something I said?"

He ignored her teasing, changing the subject. "I'm hungry. I can't think when my stomach's growling." Fields rubbed his rumbling middle. "Can't we stop for lunch? I'm OK with anything you pick." He rubbed his hand over his light brown bottlebrush and canted his eyes to his partner. His stomach rumbled again. "Please. I'll buy!"

"OK! OK! We'll stop for sandwiches. Or if you can last ten minutes, Dad will feed you. He makes something divine every day when he watches Ian. Anything from shrimp tacos to a pot of beef stew. His specialty at the Ragged Edge was a turkey special—Thanksgiving on a sandwich. Best one I've ever had!" Driving back to town, she pulled into the parking garage, found a space on the first level, and parked.

Fields hunched his shoulders and shoved out of the vehicle. "Well, I'm game. We'll come back to talk to the night shift."

"Now we're just getting a list of employees on duty last Friday night at the pub and guest list at the hotel for starters. Let's go."

2

At the bungalow on Lisburn, Ethan McCoy was spooning something creamy into his ten-month-old grandson's gaping mouth. The baby scattered Cheerios on the highchair tray. Ian poked one with his finger, picked it up and stuffed it into his mouth. Erin gave her dad a hug and tousled her son's auburn waves as she leaned over to kiss him. "Take the load off, Fields. Dad, my partner's starving. What's Ian eating?" She dropped her purse on a chair, unholstered her weapon and laid it on top of the hutch.

"Blended chicken pot pie and peas." He nodded toward the stove. "Help yourselves. The noon newscast reported your Vic survived. That's great news, for a change. If you'd rather have a sandwich, there's an Italian hoagie in the fridge."

"No, sir, potpie is great! Homemade?" Fields peered into the pan.

"Of course." Mac ladled and set a full bowl before him. She plopped a Coke down beside Zach. "If you want coffee, make it yourself," she said.

"Erin, he's your guest," her dad reminded her. Sitting, he was as tall as his daughter standing. At six-three, two-thirty, sandy hair and blue eyes, he looked more like a Swedish lumberjack than an Irishman.

"No, he's my partner, and he's a big boy. It's a Keurig! Pop in a cup." She pointed to the rack next to the machine holding a variety of k-cups.

Fields was busy spooning down potpie. "Coke's fine." He popped the lid; carbonated foam fizzed through the opening, so he hefted the can to his mouth, gulped. "Thanks! Homemade potpie. This is great!"

"Dad ran the Ragged Edge in Gettysburg for as long as I can remember; he's the chef—the best cook—in the family," Erin explained.

"Thanks, babe. Oh, Janelle called. She has Friday off. Were you able to get passes to the rehearsal?" Ethan asked his daughter.

"Not yet, but I will. We're headed back over to the warehouse after lunch to see what Chris and Savage have accomplished. The CPD Homicide Squad has a briefing at HQ at four. We can't interview the other staff at the Colonial and the pub until this evening. But I'll call tonight; let you know for sure. She's excited, huh?" she asked.

"Talked about nothing else at breakfast. Well, how often does Hollywood shoot a movie in Carlisle? The last I remember was *Witness* in Lancaster. Remember we drove down to visit the Amish Homestead and couldn't find a place to spend the night?" He took a bite of chicken. "Had to drive back home when we were done shopping; the roads were clogged with traffic."

"They're from New York, Dad. Yeah, I was disappointed that we couldn't stay in a motel! And we couldn't get close enough to see any of the shooting!" Mac said. "But you took me to the movie when it was released! Still one of my favorites—and that song is cemented in my brain! 'Don't know much about—"

"Yeah," Zach broke in. "Harrison Ford and . . ." He paused.

"Kelly McGillis," Mac continued, "And we ate at Good 'N Plenty, and you bought me new school clothes at the outlets." She plopped ice in a tumbler and poured herself a glass of water. She sat down to enjoy her smaller portion, and then wiped her hands and mouth on the napkin, turning her attention to Ian. "Thanks, Dad. Come on, big boy." Ethan unhooked the high chair strap, eased the tray back as Erin lifted the baby up and out, heading toward the rocker in the far corner of the living room to nurse him while Ethan and Zach talked about the Woolworth store.

"Oh, remember I'm leaving soon to cover a shift at Ragged Edge. Chris's mom is coming down soon to watch the wee lad."

* * *

At the HQ briefing, Chief Steve March asked each detective for an update of the day's events. "Mac, you go first, since you and Shadow were first on the scene."

She sat her water beside the Reading file and dropped into the closest chair. "When we first arrived at the crime scene, we thought the Vic was dead. His assailants crucified him. I saw no bodily movement so called it in until Kaufman withdrew the nail with fresh blood. Then we cut him down, called 911."

"I'd have preferred to see him in situ," the coroner added.

"As I said, if he's still bleeding, he's alive. He appeared dead, but when Kauffman and the others laid him on the ground, Shadow jumped on his chest. He gulped air! By then the EMT's had arrived, resuscitated him and hauled him off to CRMC. CSU arrived, canvassed the field behind the Woolworth replica set. Then my partner and I followed to interview Lance Reading—the actor portraying Frank W. Woolworth." She nudged Fields to continue.

"How did you know where to look?" asked Lieutenant Les Stuart.

"Seemed the most logical spot after interviewing several of the cast yesterday. No one reported seeing him at the motel or leave the pub where the group had congregated after dinner. No one mentioned driving."

"Thought they were staying at the house down on Pomfret," Savage noted.

"They are, but he wasn't there," Mac said, shifting her eyes to Chris's partner. Savage's PTSD flashback after the explosion while escorting a suspect to prison in their last case landed behind his desk for a month. He seemed irked, but those regs stipulated that the CPD psychologist Dr. Drummer had to clear him for fieldwork, which he hadn't done yet.

Fields reported, "But Reading claims he was too soused to remember what happened to him. He heard whispers, so at least two people are involved." He glanced at his notes, flipped the page. "He'd been tied and nailed to the tree, left for dead."

"So you think there's a religious element to this crime?" Snow asked. He combed his fingers through brassy light brown hair that needed a trim.

Fields shrugged. "Somebody mentioned it, that's all. It's one angle."

"Could be a ruse. Got any other theories?" Savage asked.

"Not yet. We don't know enough. Early days," Mac answered.

"What's your plan, Mac?" asked the Chief.

"I'm the primary?" she asked, eyebrows quirked, pulse quickened.

"First on the scene," he commented.

She outlined her immediate plans, sketched the bigger picture—crime scene, warehouse, downtown businesses, cast and crew, concluding, "We'll need all detectives on this, a uniform at the scene and one on Reading for the duration. Sonja's completing background checks. We have at least two dozen people to interview, including wait staff at the hotel and pub. Maybe CSU will turn something up. We have a five-inch finishing nail, nylon rope, and the vic's clothes.

I'll print the crime scene photos," Fields added.

"Mount them on the whiteboard," Stuart directed. The lieutenant checked the roster. "I'll assign Lee Jeffers to Reading; she's just returned from maternity leave. We'll put her in period clothing while the crew's filming so she'll be incognito. Proceed with interviews. Mac, find a reason to watch the set. Savage, you'll cover the second shift at the warehouse for the duration after you see the shrink. Uniforms can assist."

"Let's get some traction before the kidnapper tries again," March said. "We'll meet for a briefing tomorrow at nine if CSU has completed their on-site canvass, 4 P.M. if they haven't. See if the lab can rush their findings. This time, perhaps we can prevent a murder. Anything further for the good of the cause?" March scanned the room. He pushed away from the conference table. "Dismissed."

When Mac returned to her desk, she found several books, including *Remembering Woolworth's,* a bio on the 'merchant prince' and a dozen newspaper articles about Woolworth stores. She read that Woolworth was from New York. Augbury and Moore Dry goods Store hired him in 1873, paying $3.50 a week after he spent months working as an unpaid apprentice. "Imagine living on that salary!" she muttered. When his first store in Utica, New York, floundered, he moved west, plunking down $30 of borrowed money for his new store on North Queen Street in Lancaster. He called it Woolworth's 5 & 10c Store.

Paging through a six-inch folder of background checks on the principals involved, she sighed, withdrew her weapon from her shoulder holster, slid it into her bottom desk drawer. Lance Reading's headshot topped the pile. Dividing the pile in half, she handed Fields a stack as he sauntered by on his way to the break room for his coffee fix. Well into the background of a young boy with a single, unstable parent loosed in the streets of New York, she felt a presence in her office. Looked up. "Chris."

Her husband frowned. "What, no time for hello?" He skirted the desk, pulled her up against him and kissed her. She pressed against him, responding to the insistent pull, her former mentor irresistible. That scent of sandalwood. Since the explosion last summer, he'd had memory and hearing issues, but their need for one another hadn't abated. Backing her into a corner, his hand traced her body, his tongue licking her neck. The click of the door forced them to separate. Snow stepped away.

Savage stuck his head in. "Sorry to interrupt your assignation, but are you ready to roll, partner?" He glanced down at Snow's Dockers. "Or I can wait until you finish." His dark curls danced, obsidian eyes alight with delight at catching them again. "Mac, can Shadow help me patrol the warehouse nights?" His fingers drummed against the door, waiting for a response.

Blushing, brushing her bruised lips with the back of her hand, she covered her embarrassment with a few gulps of water. "Sure, but I need to accompany her, walk her through the set. We'll come over after dinner, after I've scanned the background info first—get a sense of who these people are." She strolled back to her desk, turned over another sheet: Elizabeth Banks. "See you tonight, Savage."

"Later." Savage winked and whirled out, shutting the door.

"Not until you see me first," Chris responded as he limped out, adjusting his pants.

3

At the bungalow, Erica Snow was packing up her knitting, folding the unfinished afghan into a large tote, and whispering, "Thanks for coming home early. Christopher and I are going to an American Music Theatre 'Doo Wop' concert at eight. Ian's napping. He and Pap spent several hours outside swinging and playing in the sand. About time you built him a play fort, don't you think? Speaking of the fort, the men are coming to install a stockade fence around the property next week." She bussed her son and daughter-in-law's cheeks.

"Why stockade?" Chris asked, giving his mother a peck on the cheek.

"You ask that after all that's happened here? For safety," she retorted, dusting errant strands of yarn off her slacks. The tips of her black bob swung as she moved.

"Let's change that to post and board, so we can at least see out and feel the fresh air," her son responded. "And we have six-foot lumber in the barn, so no need to buy more."

Erica sighed. "All right. I'll call to change the order." She rummaged in her handbag until she located her cell phone. "Bye, now." Phone to her ear, she breezed out the door.

Erin peeked into the bedroom to check on the baby, who lay on his stomach, his rear in the air. Now he could twist and turn; he found a favorite position—his head turned aside, one fist under his chin. She backed out, lifting off her shoulder holster and laid her pistol on the hutch. She let Shadow out; the dog gamboled around the back yard until Erin whistled her in.

As the front door whooshed shut, Chris turned to Erin, drew her in, and inhaled her piney scents, taking her lips with his, undressing her. Unbuttoning his shirt, she slid her hands up his solid shoulders, along his neck and fisted his hair. He unsnapped her slacks, pushed them down around her hips, backed her into their bedroom—falling together, locked in a tangled embrace. Working his belt loose, Erin used her feet to push his pants to the floor. Skin on skin, hands, mouths, and limbs merging, the couple connected, releasing pent-up emotions and exchanging energy. Their hunger slated, they stayed spooned together, breathless.

Chris whispered, "God, I love you."

She curled her finger around his ear, her eyes on his. "Do you?"

"As long as air is breath, breath is life and I am breathing."

"Ah." Her foot hooked his leg, hiking him closer. "Love you, too."

Shadow's cold nose shoved against Erin's foot.

"Oh, I gotta feed the dog." She disengaged her limbs from her husband's who only grunted. Pulling on knit pants, she slipped a tee over her head while dishing up Shadow's food and refreshing her water. In the kitchen, she looked in the fridge. A note on top of a casserole said, *Bake 30 minutes, top with shredded cheese.* A mixed salad sat next to it.

"Thank you, Erica. Boy, what a lifesaver," Erin said. She set the temp, pushed start and slipped the pan into the oven. Dressed again, Chris set the table. Ian yowled, the phone chirped and the doorbell chimed at once. Wheeling to catch the baby before he reached full volume, his father scooped him up and wrestled him onto the changing table.

Erin grabbed the landline. "Hello?" Arched on tiptoes, she peeped through the front door to see Savage. Shadow bounded to her side. Erin signaled sit but haltered the dog before she let Savage in. She said into the phone, "Oh, hi, Janelle." She released the dog. Reese knelt and ruffled the shepherd's neck and back, his large hands working down the dog's spine.

"Did you get tickets for us to see the Woolworth store? I have Friday off. I want to see the store displays. Did you see the set? The news says Lance Reading is recuperating. Was he injured? Did you meet him? Who's playing his wife? His sister? Any famous actors on the set?"

She smiled at her stepmother's zeal. "Not yet. Today was day one on the job. Elizabeth Banks plays Jennie Woolworth. I didn't recognize the others; they all seem so young. Tell you what. Don't know when they'll resume filming, but I'll ask for passes to observe but can't make any promises. Let me call you tomorrow."

Erin set another place setting at the table.

"Oh, Erin, you're twenty-eight; that's young! And you're eating. Won't hold you, but call me as soon as you know! I'm bursting to tell the director about my days behind the candy counter when I worked at Woolworth's, decorating Easter eggs and filling Easter baskets. Love and kisses to you all. Bye."

Chris handed Ian to Erin, motioned for Savage to join him in the kitchen. The fridge door opened; beer lids popped and fizzed.

"Hey, I love Italian!" Savage then offered to pour drinks.

"Hey, baby, what's the matter? Sleep too long?" Lately, they'd been feeding him first, nursing afterward, but she saw no harm in reversing the order, so she snuggled Ian in the rocker in the living room while she undid her bra. Another lid popped—Chris fixing Ian's dinner since the baby couldn't have baked ziti. Shadow wondered into the living room, surveyed the scene, and then turned back, sniffing the air.

"Boy, this is tasty. You make it?" Savage glanced at Chris, who balanced his laden fork with salad, garlic bread in hand.

"Mother." After dinner, Chris bundled Ian into his car seat as Erin leashed Shadow. She pushed the garage door opener, escorting the shepherd to the cargo bay while Savage hopped into the K-9 SUV passenger seat. "Wow, how do you rate? A brand-new vehicle, leather seats. If I'd known about all the perks, I'd have volunteered to handle Shadow."

Erin snorted. "That's close. I could see you with a dog!"

"Whataya mean? Shadow and I are pals, right girl?" He turned to face the caged cargo bay. The dog raised her head at the mention of her name.

"Now she's trained. You didn't have much positive to say when she was a demanding puppy." Erin backed out, palmed the wheel. Tires hummed on the road. Taking Rt-74 N to I-81, she revved up the ramp and hit sixty within seconds. Taking the College Street exit, she turned left on Belvedere, another left, and then right—drove through the intersection, hugging the left curve of 641 past the Rustic Tavern, and wheeled into the warehouse parking lot. When the door opened, Mac, Shadow, and Savage entered the Woolworth set.

Bright lights were trained toward the house, a camera following Banks while she bustled about cooing and talking to a baby. "Let's go help at the store while Daddy rests." She tugged a pink jacket on the squirming little girl. "Daddy's exhausted from buying, stocking shelves and trimming windows. When we open the store, you and Mommy will help by taking these nice people's nickels." Parking the baby on her hip and gathering a folded blanket and pillows from the bed, she hustled out of the camera's view through the bedroom door.

"That's a take." The clapboard snapped shut. "Let's call it a night. We'll start first thing Monday morning at eight. Caterer will have food on the table at seven. "Go grab dinner, have a safe weekend." JJ Reynolds rose from the director's chair, dusted his hands and turned to greet the detectives. Extending his right hand, he approached. "Thanks for your assistance. Your Officer Jeffers is with Lance as we speak. She's in period costume while on site; what a bright idea! Matter of fact, I'm making her an extra—either as a buyer or relative; she'll fit right in. Very photogenic, I might aid."

"Don't mention it," Savage said. "It's our job—to protect and serve. Any inkling yet who attacked Reading?"

Reynolds shook his head. "Surely you can't suspect any of my cast or crew? Why would they sabotage their own jobs?" Mac let Shadow sniff Reading's ball cap. The director's eyes followed Shadow as Mac led her around the cavernous space and then unleashed her. The shepherd strolled and sniffed.

Patting his pocket, Reynolds withdrew an envelope. "Here, Lance said you requested passes. Your mother worked in a Woolworth store? Where?"

"My stepmother, Janelle. Yes, in Lancaster— throughout high school, college and her nursing program. She's practically foaming at the mouth to see the replica. Haven't seen her this excited since her grandson was born. Would Friday suit? She wants to see the store and set, but watching a rehearsal or observing filming would be a special perk. Thank you." She accepted the envelope.

"I didn't just see a detective accepting gifts." Savage turned his back on her and Reynolds to watch Shadow tread along the perimeter of the building. The dog sniffed in corners, along the floorboard, and shoved her nose in boxes.

"They're not for me!" Mac said. She explained to Reynolds. "Normally, we can't accept gifts."

"Well, then, tell your chief I'll hire your stepmother as an extra. We'll have locals shop in the store and plop down nickels for their purchases." He smiled, a conspirator.

"Won't mention it at all," Mac responded. The last of the actors filed out the door, but Mac stopped her. "Miss, we need to speak to you."

The young woman turned, glanced Savage up and down. "You talking to me?" She gestured—a gloved hand to her chest as she removed the travel gloves.

"Who are you? We haven't interviewed you yet." Mac approached, flashed her shield and pulled out her digital recorder.

The actress placed her hand on her chest. "Irene Roy. I play Sidney Creighton, Jennie Woolworth's sister." Her strawberry blonde hair was roped into a loose chignon; a flawless pale face with delicate skin and too-wide aqua eyes stared into Mac's. Roy wore a navy dress with pale pink fabric roses dotting the yoke; a high lacy collar circled her narrow neck. "Not a big part, shuffling the baby back and forth, pushing the pram, but I was between jobs, so . . ."

"Were you aware that Lance Reading was assaulted, tied and nailed to a tree?" Mac eyed Shadow, canvassing the perimeter of the room big enough to house several airplanes. A range and sink behind for the lunch counter stood off to the left, which Woolworth added to his dime stores in 1910. She brought her attention back to Roy.

Savage strolled back to Mac's side, hands in his pockets, listening and observing. Roy's eyes widened as though she recognized Reese but flinched at Mac's query. She swallowed. Nodded, eyes brimming. "What sodding wanker would do something like that? Lance could've been killed. He's a sweet and kind; who'd want to hurt him?" Tears leaked down her cheeks. She groped for a hanky from her breast pocket, dried her eyes.

"Where were you Friday night?" McCoy asked.

"Driving from New York City, since on the original schedule, my part doesn't start until Wednesday. She shifted her weight from one foot to another. "Could I sit down? My feet hurt." Limping over to the set, she sat on the stage steps to unbutton her boots. "Bear, er, Ken Rogers shot footage of me on the train in Strasburg Saturday. I have my train ticket. She reached for a black satin reticule hanging from her waist, pulled the gathers loose, rummaged through it, extracted a cardboard ticket with a time stamp and gave it to Mac. Mac held up her index finger—wait, pulled a glassine from her pocket, gestured for Roy to drop it in.

"So you weren't even here." Mac glanced at the time stamp, a good alibi. "Which cameraman was with you? We'd like to see the film."

Roy winced as she tugged off her boots and looked at her bloody stockings. "Oh, my toes!" She pointed to the men clustered around a camera. "Ken Rogers. Tall guy we call Bear, straight sandy hair in a mop cut like the early Beatles. And freckled skin. I haven't even visited Lance yet. I must see how he's doing."

"I'll talk to the cameraman. I can take it from here if you want to go home," Savage said as he approached, but Mac had a few more questions for Irene Roy about the cast, crew, and schedule.

To Roy, Mac said, "And I'd like your boots and stockings. Looks like you need a bigger pair anyway." From her backpack, she produced a folded paper bag.

"You can have my copy of the schedule. I can get another one." Roy snapped it from the stapled script and proffered it. "Why is the dog here?"

"Sniffing for any traces of evidence we found at the crime scene. She won't bother you. All right, thanks for your time." Mac handed her a business card. "Please call if you think of anything else. And keep your eyes and ears open. Whoever kidnapped Reading may try again."

"I don't know anything else." Roy nodded; her brows furrowed, stepped down, back erect and padded barefoot to Wardrobe to change into street clothes. Then she'd leave the Warehouse—tired and hungry from the trip, her mind on Lance.

Mac strode over to the cluster of men—Savage and the cameraman and handed Shadow's leash and the car keys to Savage. "Excuse the interruption. Savage, I'm leaving the K-9 SUV with you, since your ride's at our place. Please keep an eye on Shadow; don't let her get out of the warehouse." From her slacks pocket, she dug out a half-dozen dog biscuits. "Reward her every time she obeys a command. Find a container for water, too. Give me a call if you need . . ."

"I got this, Mac. Shadow knows me. We're good. I'll bring her back when my shift ends. Will someone be up at midnight? Fields and Jeffers will return at 6 A.M. Then I assume you and Snow will cover while Jeffers goes to CRMC to guard the Vic."

"If no one's up, just let her in the back door." She wiggled a key off her key ring for him. Looked at it, then offered it to him.

He hesitated. His eyes studied hers for a long minute. "Are you sure? How will you get home?"

"Chris is waiting. Yes, take it. You can give it back when you're done." She dropped it into his hand. "Please leash her when we leave. She may try to follow me."

Savage nodded, approached the shepherd and snapped the leash to her halter. "Sit." The dog obeyed. Reese broke a treat in half, slipped it to her and then sauntered back to resume his conversation with the cameraman, Shadow at his heel.

Mac sneaked out the door to find Snow's Explorer. He leaned across the driver's seat, opened the passenger door for her. Mac settled in, buckled up, and glanced back at Ian, sound asleep. Leaned across the console for a kiss. "It's gonna be a late night. Let's stop for sandwiches for a midnight snack, take them home. What do you want?" His eyes turned to the road, waiting for an opening, then pulled onto the highway, headed for Carlisle.

"Hmm. We're right here: see if the Rustic Tavern will whip up us something to go. I'll take a Western shrimp salad."

"That's not a regular menu item." Chris watched her wiggle her iPhone from her pocket.

"OK, a gyro or a salad special with shrimp." She shrugged. "I'll wait."

Chris steered the Explorer into a parking space, killed the ignition, and hustled into the tavern.

Mac phoned Officer Jeffers. "CRMC released him? Got eyes on the prize?

"Yes, sir. From a distance. He and a strawberry-blonde who just arrived grabbed a corner bench at a local watering hole downtown—the Hamilton. Waitress just gave him soup."

"He should be in bed. Call for back up if you need it." Mac said.

"Not his parent, sir, but I'll give them time to eat before I escort him to their lodging. Roger that." Jeffers ended the call.

Next, she called her stepmother to give her the all-clear for tomorrow's visit to the set. "Oh, thanks, dear! I'm so excited to see it. Does it look like a Lancaster Woolworth store in 1879? Are the costumes historically accurate? Oh, you're too young to know."

"I'll let you decide," Erin answered.

"I have to finish my rounds, write my report. I'll just call Ethan when I'm done, and spend quality time with my grandson if you're working. See you tomorrow morning then. Just can't wait to see if the place is authentic!"

"Yes, ma'am. 8 A.M. Well, we're on our way home. Bye." She ended the call as her husband slid into the vehicle, extracting a round foil-wrapped sandwich, handing the bag of food to her. Unwrapped half of his and bit down on the juicy cheeseburger. "Umm."

"Yum! You can't be hungry again! You said save them for later." Erin commented, peering into the bag, seeing her flatbread gyro wrapped in foil. "I'll wait."

"I'm always hungry." Keying the ignition, reversing, and craning his neck both ways, he hesitated. "How is it your way?"

Mac peered down Rt-641. "Wait." Three vehicles passed. "OK."

Chris turned left, dog-legged under the overpass, drove straight through the intersection toward I-81 and home.

4

Crunching gravel signaled that Janelle and Ethan had arrived with the September sun strobing ribbons of light from the east, dust motes riding down the beams. Dew dotted the grass like crystals. The lighted orb drew the dew forth, which rose on its own melting.

Erin and Chris were conferring over coffee at the kitchen island.

"We'll shadow the principles on the set today. Will you go over the files of the cast and crew, see if anyone has priors? Check—well, you know what to do." Mac blushed, forgetting she was talking to her immediate superior. Her fingers braided her auburn mane into a single rope.

Chris smiled, swinging a squirming Ian up and out of his high chair. Lifting him high, and then bringing him back down with a kiss. "Yeah, babe, I got it covered. I'll call if I find any red flags."

She let her dad and stepmother in. Ethan hugged her and then made a bead for his grandson. Wearing dangling turquoise earrings, faded jeans topped with a teal T-shirt, Janelle followed suit. "Oh, I'm so excited. Does the replica look like *the* Woolworth store? Oh, well, you wouldn't remember. Come here, Ian, Nana needs a kiss. O-O! Sticky fingers." The baby reached for her, his wide smile revealing four teeth. She wet a cloth at the sink and washed his pudgy hands. "Oh, look at that adorable dimple! Looks like your dad, but you have your mama's hair. You're getting heavy, kiddo."

"I remember the one in Carlisle; it closed in '92 I think," Erin reminded her, as she dropped her holster over her shoulders, checked and slid the Glock home where it nestled under her left arm. "Let's go. Bye, baby. Be good!"

"I meant the one where I worked—before your time." Janelle gathered her sandy hair into a stubby sheaf, worked a scrunchie over it. "Imagine: filming a Woolworth documentary. All the Baby Boomers will flock to see it, especially those who remember hanging out at the lunch counter, sharing a root beer float or banana split with their dates. Aromas of turkey and fries filled the air, making us all hungry. And for those of us who worked the counters and bought their products—a return to a time when you could buy something for a dime. When I started, a turkey dinner was $1.99! Candy bars a nickel.

"I bought Noxzema, nylons, curlers, Lollipop underwear, barrettes, black composition books, pens, and other school supplies for half of what they cost at the college bookstore! And I got a ten percent discount!" Janelle concluded as they stepped out into the chilly morning.

At the Woolworth warehouse, Mac waved her shield, Janelle her pass. The guard at the door shushed them, pointing to the set. "They're filming," he whispered.

With all cameras aimed at the bedroom, the other rooms lay in shadows, the crew stayed cemetery-quiet while they filmed Woolworth's breakdown scene—taking advantage of Reading's pale pallor from his crucifixion ordeal.

* * *

A baby hiked on one hip, Jennie Woolworth carried a bed tray with a soup bowl, spoon, a folded cloth napkin and glass of tea, sat it on a side table.

Frank said, "Here, let me have Lena. Come, daughter, sit with Papa. My, you grow more beautiful each day." Reading lowered Helena to his lap, kissed the cloud of blonde curls. The baby's round blue eyes followed Jennie's movements.

"Her name is Helena, Frank," Jennie corrected. She situated the cherry wood breakfast tray across Frank's legs. Helena smacked it. Reading, plumped up by pillows in the four-poster bed, turned smudged eyes toward his wife. His pallor, matted hair and lethargic movements suggested illness. "What do you have, my dear?"

"Sustenance. Don't worry, it's not chicken but beef broth with chopped root vegetables." Retrieving the baby, Jennie seated herself in a high ladder-backed black chair with a caned bottom, settled Helena on her lap, her hand palm up; the baby patted it. "Patty cake, patty cake . . ." Jennie sang as she picked up the spoon, tested the temperature against her lip and spooned it into her patient's mouth.

"Tempting as it is to allow you to pamper me, I can feed myself. I'll try not to be a burden. This is delicious. You're a great cook, my dear. With your ministrations, I'll improve in no time, you bet." He smiled crookedly and spooned in a few more bites. Sipped the broth.

Jennie says, "May I be frank?"

Frank responded, "No that's my role." The corners of his mouth tipped up. He patted his mustache with the napkin. "Couldn't let that pass. But please continue. I value your advice, as we are partners in this endeavor."

"You cannot go on much longer doing everything yourself. You're exhausted. Searching for sites, tracking down manufacturers, buying, stocking shelves, trimming windows, clerking, selling, and accounting. Counting and stretching pennies. And preparing to open the Harrisburg store next, your mind feverish with ideas. And sleep? To bed after three, you're up with the sun. Rundown, you're prone to infection. Your body cannot endure the strain."

Frank nodded. "I've been thinking about that. Sumner has offered to manage the Harrisburg store; it'll be The Woolworth and Brother's Five Cent Store. And another man I worked with in New York, Carson Peck, offered to become partners in the Utica, New York store. We've discussed it at length."

Jennie sighed in relief. "Now, see, that's a great idea! Let them buy into the company. They'll work harder if they invest their own money. Don't forget how your cousin, Seymour Knox, waxed enthusiastic toward the concept, though he's still in Michigan but would have to move back. When you are well, let those men manage their stores, hire their clerks, and—"

"Well, I need to continue the buying, triple the wholesale orders, find more manufacturers to make more items here or go abroad to find additional stock. We're only making several dollars on a gross, so every penny counts. I need to eliminate the middlemen—the jobbers. And I must assure continuity—quality at a price everyone can afford. The Amish here are good customers; they know a bargain when they see one. We'll convince the rest of America, too. I must go to Harrisburg next week to launch the new store, help Sumner get situated, so you and the new clerk Charles can manage the store here."

Then his eyes fell on his daughter. "Oh, I hadn't thought. Will we need someone to mind Helena?" He pushed the bowl back, sipped the tea.

"I'll take her with me. Don't worry, she'll be fine. But I'll write my sister Sidney to see if she will come help." She patted her abdomen. "We'll need extra hands when this second one arrives."

"Oh, darling. My dear, that's wonderful. Little Lena will have a playmate then. "Lean over here and give Papa a hug."

Banks returned with a warm hug and kiss. He patted her stomach. "You haven't been ill?" he asked, his hand lingering.

She shook her head. "Not yet."

He frowned, considering. The camera rolled closer. "But if you would make a note of things you need around the house, I can make a list of the commodities I can sell for a nickel apiece, including seasonal items for the holidays. Like ribbon, lace, and matches."

Jennie chimed in, suggesting, "Dress patterns, teacups, strainers, spoon rests, wooden spoons, spatulas, lotion, soap, doilies, napkins, brushes and combs, rouge, hatpins, powder and diapers, rattles and toys." She paused for a deep breath. "How about office and school supplies like rulers, erasers, and the Hotchkiss fasteners? Your managers may have suggestions, too."

"Will people buy those new-fangled things? Oh my, yes! Let me write them down!" Woolworth's jotted the items in a notebook. "Good, very good. The key is volume. We'll make it, Jennie! What of these Hotchkiss fasteners?"

"Yes, it's a machine that clamps papers together by stamping and bending wire to hold them. And another new invention—don't know what they're called—but they slide up to close and down to open. They'd be so much easier than buttons. They'll revolutionize the textile industry!"

"Cut!" Reynolds barked. The clapperboard snapped shut. Warehouse lights came up. Cameras slid back. Banks walked down the stairs to the stage edge and handed the baby—to Lee Jeffers! "She's such a darling—so good!"

Reading leaned his head back and closed his eyes.

Reynolds said, "Take ten. We'll shoot the opening of the store, then break for lunch."

People herded to the tables laden with fruit, yogurt, granola bars, sandwich wraps, and cookies. Bottled water, soda, tea, and lemonade stood in galvanized tubs filled with ice. Some grabbed a banana or an apple with a granola bar. Banks and Rogers reached for the egg white and cheese wraps.

Janelle perused the pine plank tables arrayed with assorted merchandise. Leaned over to study the antique items, hands locked behind her back. "Look at these old can openers." She pointed to the two-pronged silver tools with a sharp metal tooth at one end, the turner shaped like a skate key on the other end.

"Some people don't even recognize what it is. Detective McCoy tells me you worked at the anchor store as a teen," Reynolds said from behind her.

Janelle turned her green eyes on the director and smiled. "I worked there five years part-time after high school, summers and between semesters in college. After showing me the counter and giving me instructions, the manager turned me loose. I designed Easter baskets on my very first shift. I layered shredded paper, added cello grass, then nestled little toys and candy in it." Her hands pantomimed the motions. "I decorated the Easter eggs with tiny candy flowers. Wrapped baskets in cello with a big bow, priced them, and displayed them the along the top of the glass counter. Then I weighed loose candy, poured it into little white paper bags, rang up the purchase. And *voila!* The customers, all smiles, paid me and went on their way.

"Kids came in for penny candies like little Coke bottles, gumdrops, orange circus and chocolate covered peanuts, and housewives bought fudge by the pound. Big seller-that!" She turned bright eyes on the director and spread her hands wide. "With my ten percent discount, I bought all my toiletries and school supplies at the store. *And* helped with inventory in January.

"But, of course, Mr. Woolworth didn't start out with what we sold in the sixties. Listen to me run on. I'm Janelle McCoy." She proffered her hand.

"Would you like to be an extra? We're auditioning for customers. With all your enthusiasm and your wholesome attractiveness, you'd be perfect. We can shoot your role in one day and pay you—"

"My pleasure!" Janelle extended her hand, smiling and eyes lighting up. "Just show me my mark, and I can wing it!"

* * *

Mac approached Officer Jeffers, who was wearing an ankle-length plum dress with puffed sleeves, a shirred bodice with tiny violets embroidered along the standing collar, her hair roped and gathered into a bun, stray spirals framing her face. "You look stunning! They're using your baby! She *is* beautiful, just like a Gerber baby."

Jeffers dimpled. "Thanks. Leah's the right age and such a good baby most of the time. Yes, her paycheck's amazing! I've opened a college account for her."

At that juncture, an older version of Lee Jeffers approached, her variegated blond hair threaded with grey; silver dream-catchers dangled from her ears. She wore faded jeans and an oversized red tee. "Mom, this is Detective McCoy." Jeffers surrendered the baby to her.

"Pleased to meet you," the woman nodded to Mac. "I need to get Leah home to feed her." The detective and officer watched them exit the building.

"That's neat. You can tell her one day she was a TV star," Mac noted.

"And create a drama queen?" Jeffers shook her head and then shrugged. "Well, maybe someday. For now, it's a lucky break and convenient. Excuse, me, I have to go check on Reading." She started up the stage steps.

"Think he's sleeping." Mac pointed her chin up to the man still reclined on the set, framed by the Victorian setting. "Can you give me an update?"

"On Reading? Look at him. Still recuperating, he's not able to do much. Reynolds and the rest of the cast have talked to him, asked how he's doing. That strawberry-blonde about my height and weight . . ." She paused, drawing a notebook from her pocket.

"Irene Roy," Mac supplied.

"Roy spent more time with him than the rest of the cast. They left the pub at nine, returned to the Pomfret Street domicile. Reading went to bed. Roy went out for half an hour, returned with milkshakes. I parked outside his bedroom until Officer Castle relieved me around eleven. Otherwise, his companion might have stayed the night. Yesterday, he spent the day in bed going over today's script with Banks." Jeffers nodded, pocketed the notepad.

The rest of the cast had scattered—some outside for a smoke, others dashed to wardrobe to change, and several clustered around a table laden with catered sandwiches, crudities and cookies, conversing. "I see your stepmother came along. Ah, shaking hands with the director. Bet he hired her."

Mac spun around. "What, really?"

Behind the counter, the director's assistant Rachel Stein rearranged the inventory on tables draped and tied with red cambric bows at the corners. Another person Windexed the plate glass front window while a third tidied the display of baskets holding biscuit cutters, skimmers, and police whistles. On an upended crate, an apple corer speared a real apple at the ready beside a peck basket of apples with a spray of oak leaves under it.

Her iPhone vibrated at her hip. Unsnapping it, nodding at Jeffers in dismissal—thumb up—Mac stepped outside where the cell reception was better. "Hey, Chris. What's up?"

"We have a homicide. I think it's one of the theater actors. Same as Reading, strung up and nailed to a tree. You'd better come."

"Where are you? Let me swing home, get Shadow. I'll be there in fifteen." She jogged to Janelle, deep in conversation with Stein, pulled her away. "Sorry to interrupt, but I have to go. Want to stay or go with me?"

"Oh, I'm staying. Have to report to make-up and then wardrobe. I'm the store's first customer in the next scene. Isn't that exciting? JJ wants to walk me through opening day, but I can ad lib with the counter girl because I was one. Still, I need to know my marks—where to stand." Her eyes brightened, flashing a mega-watt smile at her good fortune.

And why not? She was still comely, healthy and physically fit, her caramel hair shiny. "My overgrown pageboy is dated . . . Well, I can wear a wig."I'm not sure, but I think Banks will be the clerk who waits on me, as Lance is still recuperating. Or maybe he'll come in to sit at the Accounting Desk in back. Others will be milling around, browsing. Won't Ethan be surprised that I'll be in the documentary! Me on TV! But let me tell him, OK?"

5

Irene Roy's homicide had the same MO as Reading's assault.The assailant had tied her arms to opposing limbs. Rope circled her waist. Wind ruffled the leaves, flitting shadows over the body. The killer printed "Fornicator" across her abdomen; the victim's naked skin, tinged blue, was marbled with veins. A crimson and cream silk scarf entwined her neck; her filmed eyes gazed into the faraway. Instead of nailed in the side like Reading, someone impaled her hands and feet to the tree. Blood droplets trailed down the bark onto fallen leaves. Then her killer had used a pine branch to brush the dirt around the tree's base to erase footprints. Flies gathered, attracted by the stench. Mac swiped some Vicks under her nose, fighting nausea.

Beyond taking photos, especially the tattooed key on the vic's right ankle, Mac left the corpse to Dr. Chen, who was standing on a step stool, scrutinizing the body with a magnifying glass. Shadow sniffed the body, then nosed the ground in an ever-widening circle. Mac followed, eyes scanning the surrounding area while Snow ventured farther out—looking for signs of the killer.

Six feet into the scrub, high grasses and weeds, the shepherd stopped sat, woofed once, eyes on Mac, who had a treat ready. "Good girl. What did you find?" The ground had been disturbed. Taking a forked stick, she poked and stirred. It snagged something. Tugging gently, Mac unearthed a lacy black Victoria's Secret push-up bra, cut between the cups. Snapped a photo. Shaking the dirt loose, she then deposited it into an evidence bag. Prodding further, she found shredded lace panties. Photographed them too.

Shadow moved on, sniffing where her nose led her twelve or fifteen feet farther. Again, she signaled a find; this time Mac unearthed a broken shiny silver serpentine necklace. "Something was attached to this chain." Hunching down for a closer look at the ground and the surrounding area, Mac's eyes scanned the terrain. She snapped three or four photos of the jewelry in situ.

"You found something." Snow had doubled back to borrow the Powershot, mouthing 'thanks' and wheeled around and aimed for the trampled area behind a trio of boulders where someone had stood or laid the body down. He clicked the shutter, returned the camera to Mac, then strode west to meet Savage.

"What's a more apropos site for a crucifixion than this wind-blasted wasteland of rocks and weeds?" Black curls damp with perspiration, Savage waded through waist-high grass beyond to the warehouse neighboring the 'Woolworth store' with a dozen bays front and back for tractor-trailers to load or unload. One hand gripped an evidence bag, another his cell, calling for additional hands at the crime scene. "And Fields, track down the trucking firm who owns this warehouse. Bring a metal detector. And get a warrant; we need to canvass the inside too." He listened to Field's question. "Hell if I know; it covers several acres!"

He tramped over to his boss. "A *Cats* t-shirt slit down the middle. May be the vic's, maybe not, but we'll take it in. I need your help to load the trash barrel. It may hold more evidence. Sloppy, this time; the killer must've been in a big hurry."

Snow scratched his scruffy face. "Then why scatter the evidence all along the way? Why not just bag it and take it with him to dispose of or burn later?" If they left DNA on the Vic's clothes, under her nails or in that barrel, we'll nail them." Then he flinched at his word choice.

"Maybe the assailant panicked or the Vic fought back. Or someone interrupted them. They planned to return to gather up anything incriminating. Who would think to search this entire area?" His hand swept over the warehouses and surrounding fields, acres and acres of thin, uninhabited ground populated with mute scrub trees. "No witnesses, that's for sure."

Snow said, "Good work. We'll have the CSU swing over and grab that barrel." He unhooked his cell to give instructions. "But let's head back over there for another look. Here, I'll hand off this evidence to Mac." He eyed his watch. "Shit, it's gonna be a long day. We'll check everybody for ticks when we get home. We don't need Lyme disease yet. Let's walk along the gravel path this time."

"Poor kid. Looks so young. I've seen Hell in battle, men blown to bits, but this is just senseless. A thrill kill. Because it's similar to that other actor's crime scene, there's a pattern but what's the point? Makes ya cynical; humans are such animals." Savage wiped his face, swept his curls off his forehead with the sleeve of his shirt, dotted with briars and burrs. "Writing 'fornicator' on the body—you think a religious cult's involved?"

"With the crucifixion, it could be. Or someone wants us to think that. Could also be jealousy. If the vic's close to Reading—Why else target both?—Or someone resents the actors being here." He noticed a bug crawling along Reese's collar. "Stop, let this ladybug go back to her business." The red beetle crawled onto his index finger, then onto a nearby branch. The men trudged toward the rear of the warehouse as the sun's hot eye bore down on them.

Fields, the state police and CSU converged at the back dock at the same time. A uniformed officer climbed out of his vehicle and strode toward the loading dock where Snow and Savage were dusting off their slacks, then wiping their hands before collapsing on the wooden deck to eat the deli subs Fields had brought. From the bag, Fields dug out napkins and canned sodas, handed them out.

"Think you guys may be out of your jurisdiction," the five-nine, middle-aged state police officer remarked. Asserting his authority, he turned to the men who'd exited the second vehicle. "Spread out. Look around." In the shade of the building, he removed his hat, revealing grey stipple. His rounded face creased at the eyes, tracks ran down his nose to his mouth. "Sergeant Sean Roberts." He extended his hand. The men shook. "How about telling me what you're doing here. And tell the crime techs to stand down. We'll take that trash barrel."

"Detective Christopher Snow. We're following the evidence of our homicide, which *is* in Carlisle." Snow jerked his head right toward their crime scene. He summarized their morning, omitting the evidence they'd collected. "Where are you going to put it?" He gestured to the barrel, motioning for his team to step back but wait. He chomped down on the crisp Italian combo. Laid the wrapped sub on the napkin in his lap to pop the Coke lid.

Roberts sized up the barrel and glanced at his sedans. He scratched his head, gave his grey hat a turn. He nodded. "OK. Take the barrel to state police headquarters. We'll send it to our lab, let you know what we find." He handed Savage his card, turned as his radio squawked, and ambled back to his B&W.

The white-garbed, gloved techs loaded the round, rusty bin into the CSU van after checking for footprints and tire tracks in the dust. Then they fanned out, retracing the detectives' path to the crime scene some 100 yards east.

Snow speed-dialed Mac. "State police are on their way. Can you get the evidence we've collected to the lab now? Yes, go now. Thanks. Fields brought hoagies, so we're eating. See you at HQ later."

"We need to return to the set, get statements after lunch," Mac reminded him. Ended the call.

"Looks like we're done here," Savage observed, wadding up his trash, stashing it back in the deli bag, then into the cooler. He drew a ten out of his wallet, handed it to Fields. "Thanks for lunch. We needed fuel. Now let's stop at Massey's for shakes."

"We'll return to the documentary site to interview the cast," Snow said. They hiked back to their crime scene to secure it before heading out. Birds chirped and twittered overhead. The body had been removed. Only the ubiquitous yellow tape remained, roping off about 100 square feet, the ends dragging limply in the dirt. Their paces slowed as three white panel vans bearing TV station logos and satellites mounted on top rumbled onto the field, reporter Elena Michaels leaping from the first before it stopped.

"Shit," Savage said.

"A homicide? Have you got any leads?" Michaels approached with her cameraman, craning her neck to view the scene.

"No comment until we notify next of kin. You know the regs," Snow replied.

"Yeah. Put this in your broadcast. Crazies can bludgeon or bayonet us to death, gas or cut people to bits with AK-47s—carrion for crows. What's it all about? Only for a moment we live, but some bastard's always trying to steal it." Savage shouldered past his stunned ex.

"He waxes poetic." Snow turned, watched Savage stalk away.

Michaels slashed a hand across her neck as she turned to her cameraman. Cut. She waited for a heartbeat. Nodded. The camera blinked back on. "You heard it first on ABC: a homicide investigation at the site of the actor Lance Reading assault. A female, perhaps another of the Woolworth's documentary cast, crucified. That's my best guess at first glance. The CPD has cordoned off the area, and the CSU—in white coveralls—is collecting evidence . . ."

* * *

After booking their finds into Evidence, Mac took Shadow home, ate a quick lunch with her dad, and then nursed Ian. She left Shadow playing with Ian. Stopped at Rite Aid to print her photos. While the five-by-sevens plopped into the tray beneath the computer, she called HQ with her ten-twenty. "I'll be returning to the film site to re-interview the entire cast." She collected the stack, counting on the way to the register. "Fifty!"

"Chief called for a briefing at five," Sonja said.

"Roger that. Over, out." Mac pulled Silver into a vacant space, cut the engine. Took a moment to collect her thoughts, but the images of Roy burned her retinas: so young, so vibrant, and so vulnerable: her pale, lifeless eyes staring into the distance. She blinked. Breathed in fresh air. Blew out. Again. Counted to ten. Shook herself. Pulled on the metal door and entered the world of Woolworth.

"Take two!" the black and white clapboard snapped in front of the camera. The cameraman panned across the red and white logo, then across 'the store' where a dozen people browsed among the tables, examining the displays. In a faded black dress with her hair caught up in a white kapp, Janelle approached the clerk with a hammer in one hand, a handful of nails in the other. "Ya, I'll take des. Have thee black thread?" She laid her selections on the table. Dropped two nickels into the clerk's hands.

The young man in a charcoal suit, collarless white shirt, and bowtie smiled, took the items, accepted her coins, and bundled her items in newspaper. "No ma'am, but thread's on order. Next week. Thank you."

Janelle nodded, smiling. "*Danke*, young man. Until next week, then." She moved out of film range so the next customer could approach the counter. Young Charles ran the ten cents back to Woolworth, who sat near the back at a wooden desk. He nodded, copied the purchase in his ledger.

"We need black thread, sir," Charles said as he returned to his counter. The camera swung to another counter where Jennie waited on a farmer buying a fire shovel, tin cup, and a lather brush. Flashing a mega-watt smile, Elizabeth Banks repeated the steps. She walked the change back to her husband. Stretched out her back on her return to the counter to wait on the next customer.

"CUT!" Reynolds yelled. "Lunch break while I watch the outtakes. Stand by in case we need another take." He hopped out of his chair, strode toward the camera, but Mac stepped in front of him mid-stride. His head whipped around at the interruption, his brows furrowed.

"I'm sorry to have to report this, but Irene Roy has been murdered. We just found her. Why didn't anyone report she was missing?" she asked.

The young director with prematurely grey hair paled. He dropped his arms; his shoulders stooped. "What? NO! You're mistaken. She can't be. We're filming her part tomorrow! She's playing Jennie's sister, Sidney Creighton! No, No, No!" His hands covered his ears. "This is not happening. Who would do such a thing— and why? Why would anyone hurt"—he choked—"Irene? She's only just arrived." Reynolds thumped a fist to his chest, then covered his mouth, coughed and cleared his throat. His shoulders drooped. Reeling his emotions in, he cleared his throat and said, "Forgive me. Do what you must."

He lifted his bullhorn. "OK people, detectives are here to interview us again. It seems someone has—"

Mac laid a restraining hand on his arm. "Let us tell them. We need individual, honest information and immediate reactions. Who was the last to see her, what her routine was, latest movements, and her mood."

The metal door yawned; light rays penetrated the room as the rest of the CPD Homicide Squad bowled forward but halted when they realized the director was speaking. The squeak of back door hinges echoed through the cavernous room. Seconds later, their footfalls approaching, the Chief and Lieutenant Stuart entered from the rear exit.

Reynolds continued: "Please cooperate with the police. They want to speak to each of you. Actors, retire to your dressing rooms; crew, to your stations. Park yourselves until a detective comes around. Grab a drink or snack if you need one. Just no talking amongst yourselves!" He lowered the bullhorn with a trembling hand.

Mac followed Reynolds to the table where he picked up bottled water and stumbled into his office. Each detective approached a cast or crewmember and ushered him or her into a quiet space to relay the news that one of their own had died, that the cast may be harboring a killer. Others melted into the shadows of their accustomed places, waiting for their turns.

The actors, staff, and crew clustered in the cavern of a room afterward, gloom settling over them as the danger dawned upon them.

Afterward, Chief March instructed. "Go home. Get some rest. We may need to talk to you again. Thanks for your cooperation."

Actors and crew all turned to Reynolds who said, "No filming for the rest of the day. I need to find a Sidney Creighton." His voice hitched. "We'll start fresh on

Monday, seven to seven. Everybody, be here ready to roll. We're on a tight schedule."

The detectives motored to the station together. March announced, "OK, we missed our briefing today, but everybody report to HQ at 8 A.M. tomorrow morning so we can see what we've got and get organized. You'll be up to bat first, McCoy; be ready to make assignments. We'll put all our resources on this case. We don't want panic in the streets."

"A psychopath right-wing nut is killing actors," Savage added.

Mac frowned at him. "We don't want Carlisle residents jumping to that conclusion. There are other possibilities, so let's not label people."

"No comment to the press," cautioned Stuart.

"We've already warded off the first media onslaught," Snow said.

"At the crime scene?" barked March.

Savage nodded. "Don't worry we said the usual— ongoing investigation. Jane Doe. Will notify next of kin, release a press report later."

"You're not leaking info to your ex?" Stuart asked.

Savage's obsidian eyes glared daggers; his jaw tensed against a retort—teeth grinding his words to nothing.

Snow intervened. "Michaels is a pro who has a sixth sense about bad news. And she monitors our calls and knows our procedures. We've been at the scene and in the warehouse since dawn. We're all exhausted. Let's get home for some dinner and shut-eye."

"8 A.M. briefing," Chief March stated emphatically.

Filing out of the warehouse, Mac commented. "I've been dead before. It's not so bad."

Her husband and Savage stopped and stared at her, nonplussed.

"What did you say?" Savage asked.

She waved the notion away. "It's like floating. Your spirit leaves the body—it's corporeal after all—and just floats into the light. You become Light, that warm, creative and energetic force that girds the world and urges its growth—an awakening into the universal." She marshaled her footsteps to keep pace with Shadow and the men.

"Universal what?" Snow asked, mulling over her words, drawing his fob from his pocket to unlock the Explorer. In the gloaming, orange light rimmed the horizon, backlighting the floating clouds in a lavender haze.

"Time. Existence. The eternal." Mac answered.

Savage stood watching, his Charger several feet away. "You lost me after 'floating.'"

"You become one with the universe . . . matter returned to the cosmos." She tried again.

He shook his head. "Never mind. You missed your calling Mac. Should've been a New-Ager."

"Just relating my experience when I was shot. I even dream about it. Floating down the river, Molly Pitcher's—no, Mary Ludwig Hayes' bucket filling, pulling me along . . ." She ducked into the passenger's seat, strapped herself in as Chris folded his six-two into the driver's seat and keyed the ignition. Brittle, tired rusty leaves broke free from a Maple, drifted to the sidewalk, joining the others. "Though I feel sad that Irene didn't get to complete her journey. That someone snuffed out her life. But why?"

"That's why this job's so draining," Chris observed. "Let's go home and hug Ian."

6

Next morning, the entire Homicide squad, The Chief, LT Stuart, IT civilian guru Jay Huddleston, ME Dr. Haili Chen and Administrative Assistant Sonja Hamilton convened in Murder One, a conference room refitted for large group briefings. Zachary Fields pulled one of the whiteboards to the front while Huddleston booted the laptop for the power-point presentation. Holding a steaming mug of strong hot coffee, Savage, the last to enter, dimmed the lights. Chief March nodded at McCoy to begin.

Mac stood, addressed her colleagues. "Because of the number of cast, crew, and staff involved in the kidnapping and homicide, Jay put together a PPP from their press shots. Would the detective who initially interviewed the cast and crew members summarize each when his or her picture appears. Sonja, please jump in after each summary if we omit anything since you did the background checks. Thanks.

"We need to get out ahead of this one." Mac signaled for Huddleston to proceed. Up popped the photo of Lance Reading, head hanging, tied to and impaled on a dead tree, the rough corrugated bark a stark contrast against a gauzy grey dawn. Dr. Drummer slipped in, dropped into the nearest vacant chair.

Mac continued. "Here's what we know. Victim one, a young, relatively obscure actor playing Frank Woolworth in a documentary being filmed in Carlisle was found Saturday morning hanging on a dead poplar. Notice the blood dripping down the bark." The next photo showed a close-up of his nailed left side, the wound swollen, angry—clotted with dried blood. "He seemed lifeless when we cut him down, but Shadow jumped on his chest, startled him into breathing. You can listen to his interviews, but he's clueless about his assailant—who would jeopardize his first big break.

"He's a native New Yorker who's acted in a few of Broadway plays and TV soaps. Reared by a single parent. His father died in a racecar accident before the parents could be married—before Lance was born. His mother, who had mental health issues, worked part-time jobs, as did he during high school and college. Mother and son lived on the third-floor apartment in a Manhattan brownstone. His grandmother's trust paid for his college—he graduated summa from NYU." She paused and turned to Sonja, eyebrows quirking; Huddleston moved to his press shot.

Sonja said, "He looks like Frank W. Woolworth. Might be a coincidence, but are they related? The couple had three daughters—Helena, Edna, and Jessy, and they must have living descendants. Wasn't Barbara Hutton Edna's daughter?"

"Did Reading claim a relation to the Woolworths? We should track them down for DNA samples." Huddleston suggested. He clicked. "Here's a photo of Frank Woolworth around the same age. They look like brothers."

"Why didn't I think of that? Money could be a motive if he's a Woolworth heir, but that's a long shot." Mac frowned, distracted by Hamilton's keen observation, one she hadn't considered.

"Well, the estate was worth millions," Sonja concluded. "That's a good motive. Rumors suggested that Hutton ran through fifty-odd million in her lifetime, but you'd think the lawyers would have held a tighter rein on Woolworth's fortune."

Mac tapped a pencil against the tabletop, thinking. "OK, find those descendants, see if we can get a DNA sample—"

The next picture flashed their homicide Vic Irene Roy in situ.

Snow said, "We found Roy tied and nailed to a tree at dawn yesterday, September 10, six days after finding Reading alive. She played Jennie Woolworth's sister, Sidney Creighton. Her crime scene looks similar to Reading's but her crucifixion's different. Second, Reading wore period pants; Roy was nude. Third, both were tied to the tree with identical ropes and knots. But a rope clenched her waist *and* a scarf strangled her.

He continued, "Originally from Lancaster, she attended the Royal Shakespeare Academy in England, worked at the American Music Theater before landing a part in *Cats*, where she met Reading. Tagged along to his audition for his current role, wound up with a part herself. Five-eight, one-twenty, she was single. Parents still live in Lancaster, so we'll drive down and notify next of kin." A close-up photo of her neck showed two distinct bruises. "Dr. Chen can verify, but one line was the scarf used to strangle her; the second is an imprint of a necklace. Mac collected a broken chain matching that serpentine pattern, along with torn underwear from the crime scene. The Lab is still processing evidence."

The coroner's gaze fixed her audience on a pin— almost an accusation for jumping the gun.

"Yes. COD was asphyxiation. Her hyoid bone was broken, petechiae in her eyes; her blood vessels hemorrhaged. The nail wounds were premortem, so she suffered; the killer printed "Fornicator"across her abdomen in indelible marker postmortem. The manner of death—homicide.

"Since he survived, I didn't examine the young man so cannot confirm those similarities.

Dr. Chen continued, "Though dehydrated, Roy was otherwise a healthy young woman in her early thirties. Her nails were manicured, her hair natural—no dyes. All her own teeth—recently whitened. No abnormalities in the organs except a note wadded in her vagina." The coroner pulled out a facsimile from her pocket, reading, '*Abstain from fornication, from things strangled, and from blood.*' She had a broken femur in childhood, but it healed well. Her driver's license photo matches, but I'm waiting for her lab tests, tox screen, and dental records."

"The MO is similar, except Roy was branded 'Fornicator,' a term fraught with Biblical symbolism," Mac suggested.

"Damn it, Mac, speak English. Are these psychobabble tangents necessary?" Savage cut in. His eyes shifted to Drummer. "No offense, doc."

"None taken, but a profile helps limit the pool of suspects and delineates a pattern," Drummer said. "The FBI spent years studying criminal behavior and interviewing criminals—forming the Behavioral Science Unit."

Mac continued. "The Bible verse and COD suggest a prurient person with a rigid belief system, perhaps a Christian adhering to a strict, literal interpretation of the Bible. He's sending a message that Roy died for sin—a transgression that calls for divine justice. In Biblical times, men stoned adulteresses. Therefore, she may've been engaged in an *illicit* relationship with someone—maybe Reading. Could be the connection. It's imperative we find what was on that necklace. It will tell us more. So, the killer may be a former boyfriend, jilted lover or husband. "Sonja, could you look up the verse—"

"That's only a partial quote. It's in the New Testament: Acts, Ephesians or perhaps Thess—" Hamilton interrupted herself. "Yes, I'll look it up."

"Thanks. Fields, get a search warrant for the Woolworth warehouse and the Pomfret Street domicile to find the charm that belongs on that necklace. It may be a locket with a key opening." She nodded; Huddleston showed a close-up photo of the key tat on Roy's ankle. "And check local pawn and antique shops, too. Anything to add?" she asked the psychologist.

"You're doing fine. Strangulation and crucifixion signal overkill. It's personal. Why both? We're dealing with a killer with a short fuse or his hatred has been building over time and something triggered the rage. And taking a souvenir is typical, so the killer can relive the act," Drummer asserted. "It's the work of an amateur since he failed to finish the job with Reading."

"Who isn't angry these days?" Snow commented. "And what the hell does *'things strangled'* mean? People animals, food? Like abstaining from pork?"

"This is well beyond anger. The killer's enraged. With two victims already, there will be more because the act only temporarily assuages the rage. It's about power and control. As the rage builds again, he needs to vent. He's—sending a message he's in charge—"

Savage interrupted, "What's the diff? Mangled, strangled? She's dead. So he's a pressure cooker? The real ass-kicker is that these are not Carlisle residents!" He pushed away from the table and crossed his arms.

"And I'm not a Biblical scholar, so I cannot answer your last question." Drummer noted.

"Exactly." Chief March shot Savage a warning headshake. "They're people; it happened here. The assault and homicide must be related to the documentary. Let's move on."

Mac nodded at Huddleston to continue with the power point.

The third photo: Elizabeth Banks.

"I had her," Savage volunteered. He coughed and grinned. "No, I *interviewed* her. "The only famous actress in the cast, she's a bonafide star with movies and TV roles, like the *Spiderman* movies and *The 40-Year Old Virgin*. Married. Just wrapped *Definitely Maybe*. In this doc, she plays Jennie Woolworth, Frank's wife. Seems to get along with cast and crew and is perplexed about the kidnapping and homicide. She said they've been rehearsing and filming for three months, has three months more on her contract." He nodded at Sonja to add any pertinent background.

"She was graduated from University of Penn and The American Conservatory Theater in San Francisco. Flies home to California on the weekends to be with her family," Sonja added.

JJ Reynolds's photo materialized on the whiteboard.

"Reynolds's wrap?" Detective Fields quipped. Then he leaned back in his chair, crossed his arms, his boyish face grinning, his bottlebrush crew quivering.

"That's actually a misnomer," Sonja smiled. "Alcoa was founded by a man named Martin. This director, Jerome James Reynolds, raised the funds for the documentary by seeking people who invested $5,000 apiece. According to my research, his family rented or lived awhile in Winfield—the Woolworth's summer mansion. Hence, the interest in Woolworth. His father's an investment banker; mother's a Professor of Fine Arts at Columbia University. He has one male sibling who lives in Hawaii."

"Other than hiring the cast, crew, and staff, he admitted no prior connections to any of them except his assistant Rachel Stein," Mac noted. "He posed an excellent question: Why would anyone sabotage his or her own job or career? Besides, she has an alibi for both crimes—finding and retrofitting an ocean liner for Woolworth's first European trip to find goods to stock his stores. The boat's docked in Philly, and Rachel Stein's staging it with 19th Century décor. Reynolds cooperated—stopped filming, opened his set to us and provided free access to his people."

The Wells sisters appeared on the screen. The elder had coffee-colored hair styled in a severe bob with bangs, a stick-straight frame. Attired in black knit Capri's and a red tunic, she held a fistful of make-up brushes. Her sister, Tina frowned, a towel in one hand and cape in the other. Her chestnut hair tied into a spiky pink ponytail, a pencil stuck through it. Silver hoops dangled at her earlobes. About ten pounds heavier with rounded curves, she wore a black tee and pegged jeans. An oval mirror behind the women reflected Tammy's ramrod-straight posture; Tina's more relaxed form leaned against a cushioned barber's chair.

Stuart picked up the thread, describing the sisters' cosmetology resumes. They stuck together rather than run with the theater crowd. "They left right after dinner last Friday night to return to their Pomfret Street domicile and spent last night at the warehouse preparing for today's shooting. 'Doing hair and makeup for a dozen people, counting extras, all before 8 A.M. is no easy task,' Tammy claimed. They're quick and efficient. Voiced concern over Lance's ordeal but not devastated by the news of Roy's death. Said they didn't really know her."

Huddleston popped up Larissa Latch's photo.

"Wild red-orange hair in a longish pixie. Reminds me of Betty Boop, because 'Oh,' 'Oops,' and 'Geez' punctuate her conversation. I expect to see word balloons floating over her head!" Snow commented. "She offered no helpful information or showed any signs of guilt. She flits—either she's wired on caffeine or some other stimulant. The surveil camera at the North Gate Antiques Store caught her and Frost last Friday night buying props. Last one out of the Pub last night. The bartender escorted her back to the actors' rental on Pomfret."

"We need to interview him. Did you get his name?" Mac asked.

Chris shot her a look. "Chris Nichols. Interview's done."

Footsteps sounded in the hall. Out of breath, Officer Jeffers filled the doorway, her hair awry, one hand fisted in her long periwinkle dress with a ruched collar and puffy sleeves, lifting the skirt out of the way. "Reading rabbited!"

Detectives jumped to their feet, alert. Huddleston alone kept his seat, removing his glasses and rubbing the bridge of his nose.

Jeffers said, "No! It's OK. I think he's gone to Lancaster to talk to Roy's parents. We can track this cell number." She skirted the table to give Huddleston her cell phone.

"How do you know?" Chief March asked.

"He asked me if we found a necklace—claimed that, one, he and Irene Roy were secretly engaged! She wore her ring on it. Two, her parents live in Lancaster. So I put two and two together." She tapped her temple.

Jay nodded, returned Jeffers's phone to her. "Follow the blinking arrow."

Snow pulled a sheet of paper from his pile. "Why didn't you call it in, and then follow him?" He shook his head and glanced toward Mac, who nodded. "Come with Savage and me. I have her parents' address." He unhooked his cell phone, they stalked out. He told Jeffers, "You bring him back here."

"Code Two!" Chief March yelled after them.

Fields phoned the warrant request in.

"Sonja, call the Lancaster police, inform them of the situation. Send out a BOLO for Reading. Didn't know he had a vehicle." Mac whipped his file open. "No listing for one. He must have taken Reynolds's." Flipped to the director's page. "Here—a new red Audi, vanity plate number DRTR 33"

Sonja took the paper, speared it to her desk nail of things to do. "I'm on it." Then penned a quick post-it note to look up the Bible verse.

LT Stuart said, "I'll call Reynolds."

"And the killer knows where he's going too," Mac remarked to an empty room.

7

Mac, K-9 Officer Shadow, and Fields served JJ
Reynolds the warrants. She instructed her officers to
"look everywhere, in trunks, suitcases, make-up kits,
costumers, drawers and the actors' dressing rooms. In
every nook—storage space, clothes rack—every inch of
this place, but take care not to disturb their property.
We're looking for an engagement ring or any evidence
tied to our crime scenes—nylon rope, black magic
markers, blood, weapons, hammer, nails, a Bible with
a page torn or highlighted from the New Testament and
computer paper samples. Bag Irene Roy's belongings.
Let's go."

Grim-faced but silent, the director nodded and
gestured to go ahead, switching on the overhead lights
for the CPD.

As the officers fanned out, Mac let the shepherd sniff
the vic's scarf, unleashed her and followed a few paces
behind, letting the dog set the pace. The Warehouse's
darkness and silence hovered like an unknown,
unwelcome entity. Making a beeline for Roy's dressing
room, Shadow led her into a small rectangle with an
antique dresser, a striped second-hand armchair, and
a cot propped against the wall decorated with colorful
throw pillows. A blond wig on a stand sat on the pine
dresser. Beside it lay a comb and brush, hairpins in a
clear plastic box, and ribbons in a basket twined with
several silk scarves. Shadow sat.

"So these are Irene's?" Though the labels had been
cut off, the oblong swatches of silk had a similar

design—abstract waves in different colors—from the crimson and cream in the glassine to the sea-foam green and pink, and plum and black scarves in the basket. Donning latex, Mac opened the drawers, which revealed the usual female toiletries: tissues, curling iron, close-up double-sided mirror, cold cream, and one small bottle of perfume labeled "Beautiful." She examined underneath the drawers and behind the chest of drawers—nothing.

Officer Castle shouldered his way into the room. "Oh, I didn't realize . . . You're searching this one?" He paused, his bulk blocking the doorway. He'd put on weight since being knifed while guarding her hospital room last spring while she recuperated from a bullet wound and hip replacement. His bald pate and broad face were lightly tanned; scarce sandy eyebrows like boomerangs, he looked healthier.

"I'm not sure I ever thanked you for protecting me from that assailant," she said. Shadow slipped out of the room, nose to the ground, pressing on.

He smiled, posture erect. "Just doing my job. The assailant came at me lightning fast—gun in one hand, knife swinging in the other. Luckily, we both were at the med center. I think your CI scared the bastard off, quick thinking on his part. But the perp tried again—at your house?"

She nodded. "Now he's behind bars. The Flowers are a vicious, dangerous family. What an ironic name!

"I'm following Shadow. Go ahead, take a second look. Mine was cursory. Other than an engagement ring, diary, blood or evidence, I'm not sure what to look for, and I need to talk to the cameraman. Carry on."

Her eyes scanned the hallway for her shepherd. She heard a muffled exclamation from the next room to the left. Ken Rogers ducked out, arms up at Shadow's warning growl thrumming in her throat. "What the hell's that dog doing in my workroom?" The ten by twelve box boasted a sturdy worktable laden with cameras and equipment, a variety of lens, microfiber cleaning cloths and an Apple with monitor and modem.

"Looking for evidence. Best let her do her job. She doesn't like interruptions or loud noises. Sensitive ears." Mac pointed to her own. Rogers towered above her—fair and barrel-chested, packing at least 240 solid pounds on a six-three frame. He turned steel blue eyes on her, sizing her up.

"I have a few questions if you don't mind." Mac signaled the office chair in front of the computer, which he took. She eased her shoulder bag to the floor, which tugged at her jacket, revealing her sidearm. Perching on an upended packing crate, she slipped out her digital recorder, thumbed it on, stating the case number, persons present, date and time.

Rogers shrugged. "Fire away. I have nothing to hide." His eyes trailed Shadow's movements.

"Roy said you filmed her at Strasburg railroad last weekend?" Mac inquired.

He nodded, elbows moving to the armrests, hands dangling over the ends. "The plotline has Sidney Creighton arriving by train from Canada."

"How long were you there?" Mac asked.

"Hmm. Four hours maybe. But now we'll reshoot the entire scene with someone new. Irene had a secondary but sizeable role as her sister's helper and nanny. This far into the doc, that won't be easy."

"Do you still have that footage?"

"Sure."

"I'd like it, please."

"What for?" he asked.

"A murder investigation. There may be something helpful on that footage. We need to know about Irene Roy's past—her movements, habits, friends, family, and acquaintances. We may glean pertinent information or insight we don't have because you all are strangers to us. Do you recall anyone watching you? Or following her?"

"Oh, sure, curious bystanders collect when they see a movie cam mounted on a platform running parallel to the train. But I was too busy filming to survey the crowd if that's what you're asking." He rubbed the side of his nose, leaning back when Shadow sat beside her handler.

"No one giving you too much attention? I'm assuming Roy wore a 19th Century costume."

Rogers shook his head 'no,' and then nodded. "Yes—a navy velveteen affair with pink rosebuds—" Blunt pointed fingers to his chest. "She complained about it being hot. Took it off the minute we shot the scene."

"That didn't raise eyebrows?" Mac asked.

He smiled then. "No, she wore a *Cats* tee and Bermudas underneath."

"How long have you known her? How would you describe her?"

"A month maybe. Quiet, she usually carried a book with her. As an actor, she's a pro. She knew her lines, often prompted others before Rachel could. Didn't once refer to her script when shooting. She seemed in awe of Banks, the one actual celebrity on the set. Spent most of her time with Reading and Frost."

"Frost? Who's—"

"Jackie Frost, she's our costume director."

"Where is she? We haven't interviewed her yet."

"Haunting the local consignment and antique stores with Larissa Latch, who's looking for props."

Mac made a note to track Frost down. "Did Roy interact with others, on or off camera at Strasburg?"

"Yes, handed her stub to the conductor, who returned it, and she chatted with a couple who conversed with a stranger on the train."

"Who were they?" Mac perked up.

"Tina Wells played the wife—" Rogers stopped at Mac's quirked eyebrows.

"Yes, well, we're on a tight budget. Her 'husband' was an extra—hired on the spot because he had a handlebar mustache. Young, thin, looked the part. Tina lent him a broadcloth shirt and applied makeup. People were more curious about that process than Irene. Personally, she's reserved—animated only around Reading. They were engaged, you see."

"Oh, the cast knew that?" Mac wondered.

"I don't know. I knew it because I asked her to remove her necklace for filming, but she refused, just tucked it inside the neckline of her dress. She told me she never takes—took it off—not even in the shower."

"Did you see the ring?" Mac asked.

"I did. It's a canary diamond, third-carat I'd guess, in a Tiffany setting."

"Know a lot about rings, do you?" The detective commented.

"No, but my wife's has a similar setting."

"Oh, and where is she? Here? I don't remember meeting Mrs. Rogers."

He laughed outright. "No, she's in New York—an actress in *Phantom*."

"*Of the Opera*? Oh, that's my favorite play! I love 'Music of the Night,' and "All I Ask of You," well, all of it. Whom does she play? Would I recognize her name? It's not Mimi—"

A wide, natural grin lit his eyes. "No, she's older! The bossy one."

"Minnie Driver?"

"No, that was the movie."

"Sorry to digress. Can you tell me if Roy ever mentioned anyone at that site—former boyfriends or enemies who threatened her?"

"No, nothing like that. We're focused on our jobs. I don't think either of us could describe anyone else there, except the cast and crew." He rifled through disks until he located the one he wanted and extended it to her. One word printed on the clear case: "Strasburg."

"Thanks. Did someone interview you and ask where you were last Saturday and Sunday?"

"Yeah, a Detective Fields. I caught an Amtrak to New York. I have two kids, ages ten and twelve, who like Daddy's Sunday morning pancakes and a day in Central Park, a matinee or movie." He scribbled a phone number on a post-it note and stuck it to the disk case. "That's my home phone."

"You don't use film anymore?" Mac thumbed off the recorder, stood to leave. Shadow clambered to her feet, her shoulder against Mac's knee—separating her from the stranger.

"Yes, we do but I doubt you have the equipment to view it with. We also use digital."

"Thanks for this and your time. If you learn anything about Reading's kidnapping or Roy's death, please give me a call." She laid her card on the table and followed Shadow out the door.

"Let's take a potty and lunch break, girl." Mac rolled her hunched shoulders to ease their tightness.

Out front, Latch was fussing with the façade of the Woolworth store, shaking out the awning. A red and white sign over the door announced 'WOOLWORTH'S 5 and 10c STORE' across the doorframe and again overhead. American flags flanked the doorway. Woolworth displayed housewares and other goods—including metal and wood washboards—in front of the store while plate glass windows revealed more drygoods inside. Wrought-iron railing marched across the second-floor windows—then nothing lay beyond the facade.

No 'LIGHTS! CAMERA! ACTION!' today. Lights flicked off behind her. Other officers moved on to the Pomfret Street rental, but Mac headed home where lunch and Ian waited. Loading Shadow into the cargo bay of the

K-9 SUV, Mac's iPhone chimed, so she fished it from her purse. "Hey, Chris. Find him?"

"We did—at Irene Roy's parents' domicile. We took him into protective custody, notified Arlene and Robert Roy of their daughter's demise. Notifying next of kin is always gut-wrenching but worse when we have to mention 'murder.' They're devastated but answered our questions. They don't know who might want to harm Roy. Kept asking, 'Why? Why?'"

"Learn anything important?"

"They gave us her unopened mail and a small package addressed to Irene, plus a recent photo album, some playbills, and programs of shows she was in. Had eight years of ballet, music, and theater. They identified those they knew but didn't recognize any of the stage actors. They seemed fond of Reading, thanked him a number of times for telling them. Their son, Rob Jr. is a musician and magician on a Royal Princess cruise ship. He's flying home from the next port of call. Find anything of note?"

"Not at the warehouse. Cameraman Ken Rogers gave me a copy of the footage he shot at Strasburg of Irene, rather Sidney Creighton, arriving. He didn't notice any nefarious or suspicious characters lurking about but admitted being too focused on filming to see much else. Someone could've been following her, so we need to look at it.

"I sent the officers to search the rental on Pomfret, but Shadow and I are going home for lunch. I'm famished. Has anyone interviewed a Jackie Frost?"

"The costume designer? I think Savage did. We'll grab a bite in town. Jeffers is escorting Reading to HQ. I'll meet you back at the station in three hours. I have to deliver evidence to the lab first. Bye. Love you. Kiss Ian for me."

"Love you more. Briefing's at four-thirty. Bye."

Thumbed end. Aimed the SUV toward York Road,

passed Mayapple, wheeled left onto Shughart until she hit Lisburn, turned right and drove to the intersection. Then straight through and left into their tree-lined drive. After wolfing down a grilled shrimp taco that Ethan prepped while she nursed Ian, Erin pushed herself away from the table. "No, baby, no shrimp for you. Thanks, Dad. That wrap's amazing. What's in the aioli?" She rinsed, dropped her plate into the dishwasher while Ethan boosted the baby into his arms.

"Ian, come to Papaw. Garlic Caesar dressing, mayo, and horseradish—my own concoction. We're going out to swing, little man. If he naps, I'll throw something together for dinner." Ducking, McCoy sauntered out the back door, his left arm cradling Ian before Erin could thank him for minding the baby.

8

By the time Mac had finished viewing the Strasburg Railroad DVD, Jeffers reported in. Motioning her to sit, Mac asked, "Reading's here?"

"Yes, sir. Protective custody; I put him in a holding cell, ordered a bowl of soup from Scalles. Didn't have much to say on the return trip, but he's broken up about Roy's death. I let him stew—figured you'd want a go at him." She crossed an ankle over her opposite knee, jiggled one Asics-clad foot. She toyed with the teal laces. "And I'm taking a three-month leave of absence from CPD because Reynolds hired me for Sidney Creighton's part, paying me twice what I make now. I can't turn it down."

"Why would you? Congratulations! This could launch a new career for you!" Mac's forefingers and thumbs framed an imaginary marquee. "Leanne Jeffers wins an Emmy for her debut TV role!"

Lee smiled at the hyperbole. "No, I'm returning to the force, but either way, I would have to go with the acting troupe because of Leah! And she gets $100 for every fifteen minutes she's on camera. She's playing every child as a baby! What an opportunity!"

"What about your husband? Will he agree to your absence?"

Lee's muscles stiffened as she straightened. "There is no husband. My fiancé walked out when I told him I was pregnant. We'd been engaged for a year, lived together for two, so . . . He isn't participating in her life or paying child support. Luckily, my parents help me—in more ways than one. But with this gig, I can save enough money to stand on my own two feet!" Her eyes radiated with determination.

"You can go after him for child support," Mac said.

"No, my pride won't let me." Jeffers shook her head defiantly.

Mac stood, offered her hand across the desk. "I'm sure you'll do a fine job. With similar features, you could pass for Banks' sister. You're very photogenic. I don't blame Reynolds in the least. Have fun. But I want to spend a half-hour with Reading before our briefing, so excuse me. Report to the Chief and HR, but no leave of absence necessary. I'd appreciate you're sticking close to Reading, so you'll still be working for CPD too."

Jumping to her feet, Jeffers shook Mac's hand. "Thank you; I appreciate that. See you." Out in a blink, her footsteps padded to the Chief's office.

Sliding her Glock into the bottom desk drawer, Mac snapped her shield to her belt, grabbed her recorder and cell and marched down to the holding cell. Waiting until the officer unlocked and opened the barred door, she stepped in talking to Fields. "Come to holding for an interview." She thumbed the phone icon and slipped the iPhone into her pocket.

Reading was sitting on a cot, head in hands, staring at the linoleum.

"What the hell kind of stunt are you pulling, Reading? You got a death wish? Slipping away from your police escort could have gotten you killed! Or did you forget that your kidnapper and Roy's killers are still at large? They could have followed you, run you off the road or who knows what?"

He glanced up, his clothes rumpled; red-rimmed eyes bruised from lack of sleep and mourning, his skin a lighter shade of pale. "I wanted to tell her parents myself. I didn't think of anything else."

"That's our job! As next of kin, they have to ID her body."

His head fell back into his hands; his body heaved.

Mac paced. "Look, OK. We're all sorry for your loss. It's a shock, I know, but we have to find who did this. We need your help because your troupe's not from around here. Why didn't you inform us you were engaged?"

His shoulders hunched. He sighed, shuddering with the effort. "We were trying to keep it under wraps until we completed filming. Reynolds claimed it's better PR for the film if I'm single."

Mac motioned for the officer to bring her a chair, which she turned around, straddled, her recorder in one hand, waiting him out—a technique she used often. Remaining silent until he made eye contact. In a softer tone, she asked. "How long have you known her?"

"Three years. We met on the set of *Cats*. She's so fluid and graceful. Even her feline features made her perfect for her part in *Cats*." He smiled wistfully. "We hit it off right away. She's quiet, a listener—a nurturer, eager to please and help others. Always a book or script in her hand. She'd had eight years of classical ballet training but didn't make NYCB. That upset her—she was disappointed and depressed. So she turned to Broadway and found her niche.

"She came along to the Frank Woolworth auditions because we wanted to be together and landed the sister's role. Fit in well and got along with most of the cast. Plus, we're filming in different locales. We go to England and Germany where I'm to shop for merchandise. We were to marry once filming wrapped in New York when the Woolworths moved to Brooklyn."

"And before that?"

He shrugged. "Early on, she worked at The American Music Theater singing and dancing—some acting. And her crystal voice—a pitch-perfect soprano." He stopped, shaking his head and mussing his hair. "Why? Why would anyone hurt her? What did she do?"

Mac ignored his questions because she had no answers. "During that time, did she have arguments with anyone? Did a former boyfriend threaten her? Were either of you in long-term relationships before meeting each other?"

His eyes strayed to the door as Fields entered. Mac sat. Letting silence work.

"Nobody serious. Actors' lives are always in flux—moving, auditioning for parts, going on the road or joining other venues. Hooking up, breaking up. Even going to Hollywood or touring. People make their entrances and exits. The higher they climb, the bigger the egos. I spent a few months at Allenberry and other dinner theaters. Like I said, she was at AMT."

"What about former lovers?" Fields joined in.

He looked askance. "Don't we all have them? I was in a relationship for a year with Kimberly Bow before I met Irene. But she left me."

"Who's Kimberly Bow? Did Irene have a prior relationship?"

"Kim is the *Cats* set designer. Irene dated Martin Bishop for a while."

"Another actor on *Cats?*"

He shook his head, rubbed his eyes with the heels of his hands. "Stage manager."

"The one time I talked with her, she used British rather than American idoms," Mac noted.

"She's a graduate of the Royal Shakespearean Company in London."

"Wow! Some creds!" Mac whistled.

"Like me, she's not a celebrity, not a threat to anybody—"

"Someone hated her because her death was not pleasant or quick. How about former roommates? Did

someone else want the Sidney Creighton part? There
has to be a reason someone lashed and nailed her to
that tree. Maybe to get back at you, since they failed to
kill you."

Reading bowed his head and wept.

"Wow, Mac, that's harsh. Ease up." Fields laid a
hand on Reading's arm. "Sorry, my partner wants to
catch the killer."

Reading's eyebrows shot upward; his eyes teary; his
fingers worried his mustache. "Thanks, man. I didn't
think about that! The cast and crew get along well
enough. The only question marks are the Wells sisters.
Well, Stein's a pain in the ass, cracking the whip, but
she keeps us on track. I knew JJ and Rachel before
signing on to Reynolds's project. Three months into it,
we're just gelling."

"Any dust-ups at the Pomfret Street house? Any
hotheads among you? Sometimes strange bedfellows irk
someone, or egos get in the way. People hold grudges.
Grudges fester," Mac stated.

"Then the killer's temper explodes," Fields added.

Reading shook his head. "No volatile actors or drama
queens. The only bankable star is Banks, pun intended.
We all adore her. If we ask her, she gives us tips but isn't
bossy like Rachel. We all get along for the most part."

"What about Ben Whalen?" Fields asked.

"What about him? He's young, a neophyte." Again,
the negative headshake. "He mostly keeps to himself.
Spends a lot of time reading, researching Charles
Sumner at the Lancaster library and historical society,
pouring over old pictures and memorizing his lines.
Trying to get his role right. After hours, though, he' a
cut up." Reading smiled then.

"Reynolds?" Mac kept throwing out names for him
free associate.

"JJ?" Reading leaned back against the wall, drawing
his knees up. "He's been working on the Woolworth

documentary for years—selling it to TV means a network will air it—find an audience and . . ." He crossed his fingers, "and maybe even launch careers. I can't conceive of anyone doing anything so vile. I thought my assault was a prank. Nobody was trying to kill me or they would've. I offered no resistance. I was tanked." Shaking his head, his mouth dropped. His chin trembled. He blinked hard. "Why Irene, not me?"

"And the killer may try again. Would you like to talk to our counselor?" Mac stood, stretched and motioned for the officer to open the door. "Dr. Drummer's a good listener. And I assigned Officer Jeffers to you until we close the case."

"No, thanks. Sorry, I'm no help. Maybe her parents can."

"Can you describe the engagement ring? Where did you buy it?" Fields asked.

Reading rubbed his index finger over his ring finger. "At Jared's. A third carat canary diamond in a Tiffany setting engraved with my initials, a heart, and then her initials." He smiled then. "I couldn't afford a bigger one, but Irene's fingers are thin and she's small-boned. She thought it was perfect."

"What did your parents think of her?" Mac lobbed a last test.

"Mine? I have no living parents." His brows tightened, marking parallel lines between. "Thought I told you that. My father died in a car crash before I was born. Never knew my grandfather; my grandmother's a hazy memory. Her photos are beautiful. My mother passed when I was at NYU. I don't see how my past helps."

"Sorry, but homicides have histories; a murderer isn't born, but formed from childhood trauma and usually knows the victims," Mac explained. "We need to cull everyone's background to find the thread that leads us to the killer. We've interviewed dozens of people, sifted through all your resumes and backgrounds—CPD has a lot of information flooding in at once, so I haven't heard all the interviews. Who interviewed you the first time?"

"You two at the hospital." Reading pulled a loose thread from his jeans. Wound it around his finger, frowning, eyes downcast, studying the blue string, his thoughts elsewhere.

"Thanks for your time. In case you remember anything else, here's my card." Mac stood, stopped and pocketed her recorder, folded the chair and handed it to the uniform waiting outside the bars.

Reading laid her card beside him on the cot, brushed his fingers along his mustache. "How long are you going to keep me locked up? Don't I get a lawyer?"

"Until Monday when shooting reconvenes. You're in protective custody, not under arrest. I assigned Officer Jeffers to your detail. She goes wherever you go. Don't wander off alone anymore.

"Tell the officer when you get hungry; he'll send out for supper." The detective clutched her cell phone, sliding the door open and glanced at her watch. Speaking of . . . Jeffers approached carrying a to-go bag. Mac smelled soup. "Officer Jeffers, escort Reading to the set Monday and for the duration until the filming's complete."Shutting the door a with metallic clang, Mac left him, his head in his hands, elbows propped on knees, staring at the floor.

She had five minutes to pop into the restroom and break room for a soda and snack before the briefing.

9

CPD Headquarters buzzed with officers checking out, others reporting to duty. Phones rang, the copier gargled and coughed. Mac decided on coffee and one of Sonja's brownies. First one in the incident room, she found the interview box, read the labels, and picked "Frost, Jackie' and 'Reading, Lance,' slotted the first into the office recorder. She snapped it off five minutes later when the Chief and LT Stuart entered the room, ubiquitous mugs in hand. Savage, Fields, and Snow followed. Chris winked at Mac, nodding. Officer Jeffers entered last, feathering fingers through her hair—crimped from being pinned up. She carried a bottle of water, dropped down across from Mac.

Sonja entered toting a stack of stapled reports and scattered them around the table at each seat. Hearing the front door open and the office phone ring, she whirled out of the room. Stuart strode on daddy long-legs to the whiteboards, where he'd listed the principles' names, photos, and pertinent info.

Chief March stood, tapped his pen on the table. Savage sneezed. Fields fumbled for his notes. Snow scanned the report on Roy. Mac mentally rehearsed her summary. Dr. Drummer and Jay Huddleston filed into the room, taking seats. Huddleston booted up his laptop.

Chief announced, "All right. Here's the situation. Lance Reading booked, but your quick work secured him; he'll be in protective custody until Monday. Jeffers, as you are now a cast member on the Woolworth documentary, stick to him like a permanent. Now, we need reports. Mac?"

"Ken Rogers described Roy's engagement ring. Sonja's getting a photo of a facsimile for us. The jeweler engraved the couple's initials—a heart between his and hers, so we can trace it. Savage, check all the pawnshops from here to Lancaster—NYC and Philly, too." She slid a photo across the table to him of a key inked to a slim ankle. "Also check online for tattoos matching the one found on Roy's ankle. We might get lucky, find the artist. My guess is that the key tat goes to a heart or locket, which we may find on the killer or in his possession. Reading has no visible tats, but you might check that too since he's down the hall.

"Huddleston, run background checks on Kimberly Bow and Martin Bishop—both former lovers of Reading and Roy, respectively. See if their schedules coincide with the Woolworth actors or if any were in close proximity to Carlisle. Could be jealous lovers' revenge, though Reading denies that.

"Nothing of value turned up in our search except nylon rope backstage—though that's available everywhere—from hardware stores to Wal-Mart. I found several silk scarves of the same brand and pattern used to strangle Roy in her dressing room. We're still waiting on lab and DNA reports; the first found two distinct blood types on her tee—hers is 'A' and the other, maybe the killer's, is 'O.'

"Jeffers, since you're on the set, get a DNA sample from each cast member and crew ASAP. See if any are 'O' blood type. Keep a log of their comings and goings. Let's put Greg Castle on the tail of anyone suspicious who's paying too close attention to Reading or Roy's case. I'd also recommend that Reynolds hire a private security firm."

March agreed. "Yes, we can't put all our resources on a film cast and crew when we need to protect and serve

Carlisle residents. Though we have no other current homicides—just a B&E at M&T Bank and an assault in front of the Hamilton restaurant last night. Snow, any clues from the interviews?"

"No, sir. We've verified the principles' alibis, checked security cameras and interviewed the Colonial and Market Cross Pub personnel. Viewed the tapes from cameras at the Warehouse and the Pomfret Street rental, inside and out. If the killer is among them or tries to attack Reading again, we'll know it. Problem is no one seems to have a motive; they've only known one another for several months.

"AFIS kicked out Reynolds and Reading; both have DUIs. The cameraman Rogers has prints on file for simple assault in 2000, and he's former military. One D&D on Ben Whalen, but being drunk hardly rises to murder. And this murder was personal. The Bible verse tells us so." Snow read from his notes. "Acts 15:20; 'But we write unto them that they abstain from pollutions of *idols,* and from *fornication* and *from* things strangled and *from* blood.' Dr. Chen found a fragment of this verse, wrapped and wadded in plastic, in the vic's vagina.

"Roy's parents gave us their daughter's photo album, as well as some insight into her personality and past. One sibling, a cruise ship entertainer, we'll question after the funeral in Lancaster this Friday. Mac, Fields, Savage and I will attend. Jeffers will accompany Reading, cuffed if necessary.

"We'll question them again to identify the people in the album, talk to the actors Roy worked with, especially in *Cats,* where both Reading and Roy worked prior to this job. But so far, the killer has eluded us," Snow said.

"Anything to add to the cause, Doc?" March turned to Drummer, as LT wrote key words *Bible verse—motive* on the whiteboard.

"Too early to profile—other than to reiterate that strangling *is* up close, personal, and emotional—the killer's angry. The murder, premeditated. The Bible verse points to an illicit affair, the MO, but the crucifixion is contradictory—or at least mixing metaphors because Christ was innocent."

"But the other two beside him weren't," Mac interjected.

"True, and, as Mac said earlier, the killer's familiarity with the Bible suggests a Christian conservative who believes in a literal interpretation and an Old Testament philosophy. But I'm not comfortable conjecturing on so little," Drummer admitted, removing his wire-rimmed glasses and pinching the bridge of his nose.

"I got the 'eye-for-an-eye' reference, but you lost me on the rest, doc," Savage admitted.

"And the killer wanted to inflict pain by nailing her feet to the tree premortem," Snow added. "That's pretty vicious."

"And thus punish her for her sins," Mac added.

"*Fornicator*'s an arcane expression," Savage observed. "Could the killer be a father figure like a judge or priest—"?

Mac's eyes widened, surprised.

"What? I know big words, too," Savage winked at her.

"Or executioner," Fields commented. He chewed a hangnail. Quaffed down his brownie in one bite, chased it with coffee. Reached for another one. "Thank God for Sonja—what a cook!"

"Has any evidence come back from the lab?" LT Stuart asked. "If she had skin under her fingernails, we'd have DNA evidence to run through CODIS and our Forensic Index to see if the killers had any priors."

"And maybe prints to put in the AFIS database," Fields said.

"I'll check and then email you," Huddleston volunteered.

"Snow, you and I need to talk with Roy's parents again, have them ID every person in every photo in that album. Jeffers will be with Reading. Let's go over the interviews again; I haven't heard Jackie Frost's. And Rachel Stein's a no-show for her interview," Mac noted.

"The Costume Designer left the party early. Spent most of the weekend at the Warehouse getting costumes ready; her assistant's Kirk McCall. Kid's quick with a needle and thread. He was stitching a hem as we talked. Latch went to Northside Antiques for props for the house." Savage rummaged through the file, pulled a headshot of Frost and McCall, pushed them across the table for Mac to see.

"She's a pixie like Tinkerbell!" She left unvoiced her reaction to McCall—so thin he looked cadaverous, his dirty blond hair pulled back into a stumpy tail. "They don't look strong enough to have lifted Reading up into a tree. Still, let's see if the lab will rush any of the evidence we sent. Roy's funeral is Friday. Get back to me as soon as you have any solid leads."

Savage lips thinned at her tone. He pushed back from the conference table, fingers drumming one the arms of the chair, waiting for Chief's dismissal.

"You know your assignments. Get on with them. Briefing tomorrow, same time, same station. Dismissed." Chief March sidled over to the whiteboards to assist LT Stuart with bulleting the timeline. On the second board, he posted the cast and crew's photos using arrows to show connections to the victims.

"Hey, guys, come back. You're gonna want to see this CNN newsfeed." Huddleston turned the monitor around; the detectives clustered about. The camera panned over a ship bobbing in the water, *City of Paris* painted in white against the black hull. On the move, the camera bounced along in another boat, approached but was stopped by a burly man.

"That's far enough, buddy. Don't contaminate the crime scene."

A reporter offered his mic. "And you are?"

"Special Agent in Charge of Customs in Philadelphia, Bill Fleisher."

The camera panned across to the captain's cabin. Against the door, a body clad in underwear was nailed to a door. Crimpled long black hair screened the face, too distant to identify.

SAC Agent Fleisher shoved his palm to the camera lens. "Have the decency to turn back, stop filming until we ID the victim and notify next of kin." A commanding presence carrying over two hundred pounds of muscle, the SAC agent's five-foot-eight burly body blocked the view. The camera panned to the reporter; her hair whipped in the breeze off the water.

"Folks, you saw it here first! A homicide just discovered! We assume the victim belongs to the Frank Woolworth documentary crew. Someone nailed her to the cabin door of the *City of Paris,* the ocean liner the 'merchant prince' boarded to buy merchandise for his new dime stores! We talked to the ship's owner, who confirmed renting it to one JJ Reynolds, the documentary director. This is Dana Lewis, NBC. More on the six o'clock news!"

"That's Rachel Stein!" Fields pointed at the screen.

"We need to call SAC Fleisher," Mac said. "Apprise him of our homicide."

"Because now we have a serial killer," Fields added.

Snow unhooked his cell to make the call to SAC Bill Fleisher.

Mac nodded. "Take Savage. Fields and I will cover Roy's funeral.

10

In the bare-bones funeral home, Irene Roy's white casket was draped with a spray of scarlet roses. Mourners dotted the metal folding chairs; her parents, brother and Lance Reading were seated in the right front pew. Jeffers sat behind him. Behind them, the cast and crew of the Woolworth documentary—all dressed in black. On the left side of the aisle, a cluster of young adults whispered among themselves. Farther back, a dozen looked on in stunned silence. Their lean looks and aloof hauteur suggested New York—women simply attired in variations of Chanel's black sheaths, one wearing a fitted jacket, the men in black sport coats or vests over espresso t-shirts and slacks.

"Amazing Grace" emitted from speakers. In the vestibule, the funeral director greeted the Carlisle detectives with a tight-lipped nod at their late arrival—motioning them toward the guest book, closed the double doors, spun on his heel and strode down the chapel aisle, stepping up to the podium. Mac jotted down her name, surveying the list while Fields snapped a photo with his cell phone.

The words of the eulogy washed over Mac as she kicked herself for not attending the viewing; people often displayed genuine emotions at an open casket and left mementos like photos and trinkets. But, upon reflection, the perp probably kept the engagement ring, which he'd ripped from the vic's neck. Hyper alert, she remained standing at the rear, watching faces for any tells in behavior like the smug satisfaction of revenge.

Sitting behind the New York contingent, Fields scanned the crowd for a locket tat that the vic's key might fit—a hard task since it might be hidden from view.

At the podium, her brother Rob mentioned several childhood anecdotes: sloshing through the rain with his sister and flying kites on a vacation at Ocean City when he wouldn't return to the water because of a jellyfish sting. When he had the measles, Irene read *The Wizard of Oz* to him, and then they watched the movie together. "Our feelings are raw because a heartless murderer wrenched Irene from us—her lovely life snuffed out at thirty-five. For her, there will be no more sunrises or sunsets to marvel at. No more plays or acting. There'll be no marriage or children or grandchildren.

"I hope the cops catch whoever robbed her and us of her future, put him behind bars or send him to the electric chair—and to Hell." He nodded, resumed his seat, his cheeks red with heat. The attendees stirred, murmurs rose like locusts to feed his anger.

The preacher stepped up to make amends. "I've known Irene for twenty years, and such a tender soul would forgive her attacker. Yes, she was taken from us in the bloom of youth. Emotions are raw, but let's celebrate her life . . ."

Finally, a tall, athletic-looking woman stood, walked to the podium, unfolding a piece of paper with trembling fingers. She smoothed the sheet out, cleared her throat; tears leaked from the corners of her eyes. Her sandy hair was razor-cropped at chin-length. Cornflower-blue eyes flashed once at the audience then lowered. Her midnight blue suit bore shiny black satin lapels. "My name is Cassidy Kline. I grew up with Irene; we were close until she left for college and then studied abroad. I knew her when . . ."

Mac perked up, pulled out her notepad and waited. Perhaps this person would tell her who resented Irene, enraged enough to murder her, shame her by labeling her 'fornicator', strip her, nail her to a tree and leave the damning Bible verse. Signaling to Fields, she pointed to the speaker. They would interview her at the parents' wake later.

A frightened shriek rose from the young women in the middle. "A snake!" Several hugged legs to their chests. Reading and Mrs. Roy hopped from their seats as the funeral director tried to calm the crowd. Fields slid into the aisle peering under seats. "Please remain seated! It may be harmless. I see it!" He leaned out of view. "Got it!" Lifting it by the head and along the black 'S', he held it aloft. "It's just a harmless black snake!" Only the unflappable New Yorkers and Irene's dad remained seated. The funeral director had fled through the rear doors, perhaps to corral the attendees and line up the cortege.

Smiling but shaking his head, Fields strode up the aisle. "Let's go. I'll let him out when we get to the cemetery. He sidled up to Mac, offered his hip. "You drive. Could you tell who let the snake loose?"

She dug the keys from his pocket. "No, but get a photo of it before you let it go. I suppose this is the killer's or an accomplice's stunt to signify Roy's 'sin' of sleeping with Reading—or others—without marrying first."

"How do you figure?" Fields held his quarry at arm's length.

"A snake in the garden? It's an allusion to Genesis, a symbol for Satan's temptation of Eve and the subject of Milton's *Paradise Lost,*" Mac claimed. "Don't you know the story?"

"Vaguely." Her partner nodded. They climbed into the CPD's unmarked Bronco. Mac switched the ignition, pulled up to the rear of the dozen vehicles already lined up. Someone dropped a magnet anchoring an American flag onto the hood, a black flag on the other side. Following the hearse, the cortege passed the cemetery where a former Molly Pitcher reenactor, Margie

Hawthorne, was buried. Also from Lancaster, she's been murdered at the Old Carlisle Graveyard, lashed to a cannon and her daughter kidnapped. Mac shook herself from the reverie, pulled to the verge behind the other vehicles so Zach could free the snake.

Dusting his hands, he reached in the back for the camcorder to film the attendees from a discreet distance. Mac leaned against the vehicle, warmed by the sun perched overhead, cumulous cotton balls dotting the cerulean infinity.

Real and artificial yellow, gold and orange mums— sprays and autumn wreaths on stands decorated rows of granite tombstones, statues, and flat plaques. Mac focused on Cassidy Kline, then Lance Reading and the documentary's cast, culling their faces for guilt or glee, for any anomaly out of character with the scene unscrolling before her. Forming a serpentine line, the mourners tossed a rose or a handful of dirt into the yawning grave; then they peeled away, following the script. The preacher committed the body to the earth, consoling the grieving parents, an arm around each shoulder. Reading and the brother stood aside.

Fields strolled back to the Bronco, a thumb up, chest-high, letting her know he caught every face but shook his head—he found nothing suspicious.

Mac raised her brows, tilted her head, shrugged, and then climbed into the vehicle. Next stop, Roy's parents' house. She had Roy's album; she'd have names by the end of the day. Slipping her iPhone from her purse, she dialed Chris.

After three rings, the call went to voicemail.

"I hope you're meeting with SAC Fleisher and compiling a file on Rachael Stein. We're en route to the Roy residence, should wrap up here and be home by dinnertime." Next, she dialed her dad to check on Ian. When Zach dropped into the passenger's seat, she ended her call, followed the cortege out of the cemetery.

11

Snow and Savage arrived in Philadelphia too late to
see the body in situ; the ME had already taken it away.
At the shipyard, a scaled-down version of the ocean
liner, *The City of Paris,* roped off with crime scene tape,
rode on the waves that lapped the quay. Sandpipers
tripped along the edge; seagulls with plaintive cries
glided along the current. The Aker Philly shipyard
crane clanged as it clanked cargo onto the wharf.
Anchored ships farther out bobbed on the waves. Others
waited for a tow to the harbor. Tourists strolled along
the shops that once boasted a bustling Navy Yard. A
uniform guarded the boarding ramp. He frowned as they
approached.

"Carlisle Police Department, Homicide," Snow
reported, flashing his shield. "We need to see the crime
scene and then talk to SAC William Fleisher."

The uniform shook his head. "Sorry, no can do.
You're way out of your jurisdiction. My orders are to
admit no one." He tilted his head to the ship. "Our
CSU already canvassed the vessel." He blocked the
plank leading up to the ship. "Report to Special Agent
Fleisher's office at Customs." He pointed the direction
they'd just come from.

"We have an appointment with Agent Fleisher, but
we're inspecting the crime scene first." The detectives
shouldered past the guard while he sputtered and dialed
the SAC. His muffled voiced droned into his phone.

They padded past the lower deck—formal ballroom,
dining room tables draped in white damask, then up the

stairs to the third deck near the bow. Blood had dried where it dripped on the floorboards. A gap yawned at the captain's quarter's doorway. Snapping on latex and paper booties, they entered the cabin on the starboard side. Nothing seemed out of order in the interior: polished wood—the space staged: captain chairs with red velvet cushions, a small desk, built-in sofa, sleeping berth, and storage. A compass lay next to a flat map on what looked like a drafting table under the porthole.

Stein had stacked a pile of scripts on the desk for the crossing, Woolworth's first European voyage in February 1890 to purchase stock for his stores. Names written in the upper right corner in a tight, neat script: Frank, Charles (his young assistant), guest importer B. F. Hunt, Jr.; Reynolds would hire extras—the captain and crewmembers—on the spot. No mention of fellow passengers.

Snow and Savage strolled along the forecastle, and then inspected the wall-papered ballroom and dining room, tables set with china, silver and crystal glasses. The top deck hosted private cabins with double beds and plush furnishings. Lower decks revealed rows of built-in bunkrooms, a water closet tucked between each pair. Inside, a pull-chain over the throne dumped waste into the Atlantic.

"The vessel's seaworthy but not huge. Solid. Functional. Reminds me of the *Titanic*." Savage tested the light fixtures, checked the captain's larder. Think the cast and crew will sail across the ocean?"

"I think the ships were built during the same era. The original was twice this size with three masts and smokestacks. But no, Reynolds will use this replica for close-ups, superimpose the original using computer animation to depict the nineteenth-century New York City harbor. Pilly's just closer and more convenient for the film crew. I guess they'll film the 'voyage' in the Delaware Bay, and then fly over the pond to film his first stop in London. But it's definitely not going anyplace now it's a crime scene.

"Get photos of the scene. I'll look around the stern and promenade decks; you cover the bow. Then let's see if the Customs agent will cooperate and coordinate his case with ours." After a cursory check, he found nothing of value. He held the Reading and Roy files, sliding sideways as a feisty wave tossed the ship against the quay. A queasiness grabbed his stomach; dizziness followed. He grabbed the doorframe. "I need to get off this ship." He gagged at the fishy, oily water, hot clanging metal odors, and the hum of tourists didn't help either.

"Vertigo? Know how it feels. I'll finish here," said Savage. His coffee eyes roved over his boss. He reached out a steadying hand. "From that concussion last May." Snow disembarked and sipped cool water in the unmarked while Savage completed his inspection.

Gulls screeched and scavenged. After winding around the labyrinth of the shipyard, they located Fleisher's office—a white shoebox with papers, folders, and a landline on his wooden desk, a gentleman's sepia lithograph from another era on the wall behind the desk. Case file boxes were stacked three deep against the left wall in front of a row of filing cabinets. A computer and combo printer/fax rested on a credenza. The Carlisle detectives took the two visitors' chairs across from the desk. "Coffee, gentleman?"

"No thanks. Portrait of Vidocq?" Snow gestured to the photo.

"Ah, and how do you know the founder of the French Brigade de la Surete?" The Special Agent asked, tipping his fingers together.

"A guess. My wife says he's mentioned in James Joyce's short story 'Araby' as an author of a sexually suggestive memoir—a clever criminal turned detective."

"She would be right. The first detective of the world's first detective agency." Fleisher leaned solid shoulders back in his chair. "So how can I help the Carlisle, Pennsylvania detectives? What's your interest in our dock case?"

"Christopher Snow and Reese Savage. We had an attempted murder and a homicide with the same MO—two members of the Frank W. Woolworth documentary cast, Lance Reading and Irene Roy. The assistant director, Rachel Stein, was last seen at the warehouse during filming before coming to Philly to stage *The City of Paris* for Woolworth's trip. Has a ME completed the PM?" He laid the folder in front of the Special Agent.

Fleisher shook his head no.

"Why, may I ask? We like to sit in on it, if we may."

Another negative shake of the bearded man's head.

"Why not?" Snow asked.

"Because luckily she's not dead. Her family was worried that she didn't return home last night, so they drove to the shipyard, heard a commotion from the ship—interrupted the assailants, and scared the amateurs off. Called nine-one-one, shot off a flare. By dawn, the reporters had converged. Usually, I ignore them, but I had to back them up."

"But the news photo—" Savage began.

"Yes, EMT's advised us to leave her on the door—less blood loss. They removed the door, took her to the hospital where she's in surgery, unconscious in guarded condition, but keep that under wraps." He scanned the contents of CPD's file. Tapping the headshot. "You ID'ed her correctly, so the cases must overlap. I'd like to keep this. You have a fix on the killers?"

"Our lab reports aren't all back yet, but persons unknown targeted our homicide Vic and labeled her a fornicator, tied and nailed her to a tree and strangled her. Her killer took her engagement ring as a trophy.

We found a broken necklace at the crime scene. The first assault victim, Lance Reading, Roy's fiancé, also survived. The MO points to punishment and retribution."

"They tossed her clothes in a trash bin at the warehouse next to the film set," Savage added. "The Bible verse left in her body and the crucifixion suggest Christian conservatives—or the killers want us to think that but . . ."

"It's personal, given Roy's strangulation." Fleisher finished. "That's overkill. Has your Criminal Investigation Assessment Unit sent a profiler?"

"Since the Pennsylvania State Police are working with us, we have access to the CIAU," Snow said. "Our psychologist says it's too soon to form a profile until we have more evidence—or at least the lab reports. We haven't notified the FBI yet." His phone pinged a text message. He unhooked it from his belt, glanced at his cell. "Detective McCoy reports that someone attending Roy's funeral let a snake loose during the eulogy." He shook his head in disgust. "Apparently, another sin symbol. Looks like the same MO."

"Would we be able to visit the patient?" Savage asked.

"Her location and condition are confidential, NTK only."

'We need to know," Savage said.

"Doctors allow only family in ICU." He picked up the receiver, talked with his Crime Scene tech. "Can you fax a prelim of your findings from the Stein crime scene?" A pause while he listened. "Yes, that one. Thanks." Ended the call. "But let's see what our guys found."

Within minutes, the fax machine hummed; the printer spit out several pages. Agent Fleisher scanned them, then made copies, handing them to Snow and Savage. "They perps left rope, duct tape, a black ski cap, and a black marker. Smudged shoe prints in the oil on the deck. No fingerprints, so they wore gloves. Left the Vic in cotton granny underwear. Dark smears—likely her own type B blood—on her panties. Blood on her palms and feet, her own, I presume." He shook his head. "Lucky that she had family in the area. Any connection to the other Vics besides this Woolworth documentary? We're talking the dime store merchant?" He threaded his fingers together across his portly girth.

"That's the connection. We're still investigating but have no persons of interest at this point. Detectives McCoy and Fields are in Lancaster delving into Roy's past. Her fiancé, actor Lance Reading, claims to have no living relatives, but we're running background checks. Our Homicide squad, extra uniforms, and the State police are assisting, but we'd appreciate your help—sharing information."

"And they've crossed state lines," Fleisher smiled. "I'm a federal agent, so you'll also have Quantico's resources. You have VIDCON or SKYPE?"

Snow nodded. "Wouldn't be Lionel Howard or Isola Perez, by any chance?"

Savage cleared this throat. "Ah, no. Think they're working in D.C. on another case. You have someone in mind?"

"Our psychologist's good, and like I said—" Snow reiterated.

"PA State Police's CIAU. Well, yes. We can definitely coordinate." He heaved over two hundred pounds up, checked his watch. His salt and pepper beard branded him more a seafarer than FBI. "Why don't we go to lunch? I know a good place, and then we can stop by the hospital and check with Ms. Stein's doctors. You like oysters?"

"No, sir, but we like seafood, yes. Thank you." Savage said as they stood.

Snow added, "And I need to inform Mac, the lead on this case."

Fleisher reached for his suit coat, motioned them out the door. "I'll drive."

"We need to return to HQ for a 5-P.M. briefing," Savage commented.

* * *

At the hospital, the detectives followed the Special Agent down a dark hallway with closed doors. They smelled disinfectant mixed with a tinge of ammonia. At ICU, they observed their patient through the plate glass.

A gash in her forehead was clotted with dried blood. A blanched face framed by black crimped hair lay against a white pillow; her lips were parched and cracked. Her eyes were closed and hands bandaged. White sheets and a thin blanket covered her body. A washed out blue hospital gown gaped open, revealing an unmarred neck.

Savage whispered into his boss's ear, "Looks like someone from the Adamms Family."

"Tsk, tsk, detective," Fleisher commented as a surgeon in scrubs strode up to them. "How is she, doc?"

"She's alive. We stitched her head wound, repaired nerve damage to in her proximal and middle phalanx—"

"English, please, we're cops," Savage requested.

"Hands and feet. Butterflied the defensive wounds on palms and wrists. Blunt force trauma bruised her occipital bone and the back of her skull. Her assailant must have socked her, then slammed her head against a hard surface." He fisted his hand and threw an imaginary punch.

"Solid wood door?" Fleisher filled in.

"Hmm. Yes. That would do it. See the red marks on either side of her soft pal—mouth?" He pointed to his own.

"She was gagged." Snow nodded.

"That and she has a bruised kidney. She's on a morphine drip. We administered a tetanus booster."

"Someone beat her. Are you getting this, Reese?" Snow asked.

Savage held up his digital recorder and nodded without speaking.

"I'll send you a report," Fleisher noted. "She'll be under awhile?" he asked the doctor, who nodded.

"Check back in forty-eight hours when we move her to a private room."

Fleisher pulled out his cell. "Steve, I need you to guard a Vic." He dictated instructions. "Keep it on the QT; no radio transmissions.

"Doc, keep her ID, condition, and location quiet. No press releases. Please inform me if she wakes up. She may be able to describe her assailants."

"Plural?" the doc asked.

"That's what her relatives reported."

"Thanks . . ." Snow read his nametag. "Dr. Allen." He then turned to Fleisher. "Can we speak to them?"

"Come along. They're in the visitor's lounge." Fleisher led the way.

Two tanned young men with olive complexions, wide foreheads, and trimmed beards were pacing past each other. Tousled dark curls grazed their flannel shirt collars; long sleeves were rolled up to their elbows. Mud and blood splotched their jeans. The father slouched against a vinyl chair, head back, eyes shut; his grizzled grey crew, beard, and rumpled clothes smelled fishy.

Fleisher approached. "Mr. Stein, boys. These men are Carlisle Homicide Detectives Christopher Snow and Reese Savage. They want to speak to you about Rachel."

The senior Stein opened bloodshot eyes. "Why?"

"We have a homicide in Carlisle that's connected to Rachel's attack," Snow explained.

"How do you know?" One of the young men asked as he squared his body to theirs. Though the shortest, his muscled forearms suggested repetitive physical exertion. "I'm her brother, Samuel." They shook hands, but worried lines creased his forehead. The other young man, a head taller with deep-set brown eyes and a blunt nose approached. "This is my cousin, Rueben."

"Did you know about the Frank Woolworth documentary that JJ Reynolds is directing for a TV program?" asked Savage.

The cousins nodded, lowered themselves to chairs, eyes roving from the Special Agent to the Pennsylvania detectives.

"Rachel works for Reynolds," said her brother.

"Let's all sit down, gentlemen," Agent Fleisher gestured to the empty chairs.

"We have a few questions," Snow stated as he lowered himself to an orange plastic seat. "Did you see the assailants?"

Rueben shook his head. "Black shadows in the dark."

Savage asked, "What about height, weight, clothing—how they moved, any detail at all?"

Sam nodded. "The six-footer had broad shoulders, the other was shorter and leaner. They wore black clothing head to toe. The shorter one dropped a duffle bag."

"We couldn't see their faces—ski masks," his cousin added.

"Why would they harm Rachel?" asked the dad. "Who are these people?"

"Good question, sir," Agent Fleisher answered. "We aim to find out."

12

McCoy felt time oozing from her pores, slipping
away as she collapsed on one of the conference chairs
in the Incident Room, her mocha steaming in front
of her. Fighting fatigue and frustration—and the fact
the assailants in this case attacked with impunity.
Threading her fingers through her unruly curls, she
perused the whiteboards in the Murder Room. Sipped
her coffee. Three Vics: two assaults, Lance Reading
and Rachel Stein, and one homicide: Irene Roy. Doubts
swarmed around her, but she beat them back. Thoughts
darted in, details swam about.

Let the living live. Focus on Roy first. Thirty-five,
strawberry blond hair framed an oval face, a long neck,
and a dancer's build, her bare body pearlized on a tree,
against a foggy backdrop. Arms extended, hands and
feet nailed to the tree. Remembering the punch of the
bullet that shattered her hip, Mac shuddered at the
thought of the long spikes slamming through skin,
muscle, and bone. The searing pain, telegraphed along
the nerves. Blacking out.

"What would make someone do that?" She reread
the posted Bible verse, highlighted 'idols,' 'fornicate,'
'strangled,' and 'blood.' "Judgment, punishment, and
execution for sleeping with Reading? Jealousy must
be the motive." She studied Lance Reading's photo,
arms, and feet *tied* to a poplar, a nail piercing his side.
"Deathly pale but he survived his *punishment,* so was
his sin forgivable?" she wondered aloud. "Or is the old
double standard still at work here?"

She posted the photo of Rachel Stein that Huddleston had captured off the news alongside her publicity headshot. "Female Killed at Philly Shipyard: SAC William Fleisher had no comment until notifying next of kin."

The incident room door swung open as the Homicide Squad filed in, followed by Chief March and Lieutenant Stuart, IT guru Jay Huddleston, psychologist Dr. Gerard Drummer, Coroner Dr. Haili Chen, and blogger and media liaison Officer Tanya Storm. Missing was Officer Lee Jeffers, with the Frank Woolworth cast guarding Reading—lest someone make another attempt on his life.

March rubbed his hands together as he took his accustomed seat at the head of the table. "Ladies and gents, let's get to it. Snow, you and Savage summarize what you learned in Philly yesterday. Then Dr. Chen, any insights from Stein's doctor's report would be helpful, and Mac, you and Fields can finish with any info gleaned from the funeral." He sat, his chair puffing from his weight.

"First, the Special Agent in Charge agreed to share lab findings, reports, and new developments. Said we can use Quantico's lab. Second, Stein is *alive*, recuperating from surgery and wounds inflicted by her assailants. Plural. They must have caught her leaving the ship.

"Family members came to her aid. The men reported the attackers wore black, including ski masks.It was too dark to get a good description. Though smudged, we have a print, which I lifted and sent to Huddleston. Ship's wiped clean. But they left the tools of their trade behind." He handed the LT the list of items, which Stuart bulleted on Stein's whiteboard.

"The SAC also notified the FBI, though the state police's CIAU will send us a profiler. We weren't able to interview Stein, but she can give us a better description of her attackers when she wakes up. She's in guarded condition and under guard at the Naval hospital there, info we're to keep in-house for obvious reasons."

Dr. Chen cleared her throat. "Ms. Stein's wounds are extensive. You all have copies of the report, so I'll just say she fought back and endured a savage beating. The damage to her dermis, nerve, tissue, the ulnar extensor of the wrist—"

"Doc." Savage coughed, his obsidian eyes challenging. "Lay terms."

"The damage to the muscle supporting the back of her ulna—arm bone—wrist, hands, and phalanges are extensive. She's facing several months of pain and therapy—both physical and mental. Neither is within my realm of expertise; mine is with the dead. Dr. Drummer?"

"Yes, I'd agree. Such a beating would traumatize anyone. She will experience an entire range of emotions like survivor's guilt, angst, nightmares, even PTSD: Savage, you could speak to that."

"But I won't other than to say it's a living hell."

Mac swallowed the pain and added, "Speaking from experience, I'd say she could suffer prolonged periods of depression; fear could develop into panic attacks or phobias, like agoraphobia or claustrophobia. Doubt and 'what-ifs' become constant companions. She might spend days lost in a mental fugue. Perhaps I'd better interview her for a description of her assailants, but I'd suggest we focus on Roy since Stein's case is Fleisher's. Yes, the cases are related; yes, attackers are likely Roy's killers, but—"

"And I concur because Stein's not in our jurisdiction," March interjected. He pointed to Roy's board. "So do we have anything new on Irene Roy's case?"

Fields reported. "According to the lab, we have DNA— skin from Roy's fingernails, oil of lavender on rope with pieces of heliotrope, poison ivy and dead grass caught in fibers. We have type 'O' blood, a partial print but no match in AFIS, so the perp has no priors. Roy's was type A. And from her clothes, DNA, sweat—Roy's, and saliva—someone else's. One shoe print is a size ten."

"Size nine on the deck shoe print," Huddleston said, checking the photos from the Philly crime scene—his pale blue eyes alert behind his Lennon glasses. He pushed them up the bridge of his nose. "So let's say, these guys are six foot and five-nine."

"Alcohol level point two and stomach contents—undigested shrimp scampi would put Roy's death earlier—around ten or eleven—rather than later," Dr. Chen said. "Also, her body was not in full rigor mortis when I examined her in situ."

"Savage, find anything on her engagement ring?" Mac held up the photo of a facsimile: a third-carat canary diamond in a white gold Tiffany setting.

He finished his coffee. "Not at the pawn shops from here, Lancaster or New York City or online sites like eBay, Etsy, or Pinterest." He grinned at her raised eyebrows. "The killer likely kept it as a trophy. I'll be amazed if you find it at all. Did you photograph everyone's hands at the funeral?"

"No, Fields captured the faces, but I looked. Speaking of photos . . . Roy's parents gave me these."

Mac pulled an eight by ten from the folder and passed it around. Eight teens in all: back row standing, front kneeling. Each person, dressed alike in tutus, tights and toe shoes, had her name written across her body. A second photo—a candid of a birthday party—some of the same faces, gathered around the birthday girl, Irene Roy, a shy smile, eyes sparkling, reflecting the sixteen candles catching the red-gold highlights in her hair. Again, a spidery hand had written names on each girl. A third showed five girls posed by a pool, each with feet dangling in the water. Left hands curled around the pool's edge, right hands hidden behind one another's backs. Shoulders touching, wet hair slicked back. The fourth photo, of Roy in cap and gown standing between her parents, with NYU emblazoned on a flag opposite the American flag.

Three girls appeared in every photo: Irene Roy, Rachel Stein, and Jackie Frost. Noreen Ahmed, the pixie at the poolside, smiled from the ballerina photo. Cassidy Kline attended the pool party and sat beside the pool but was not in the other shots.

"Were these women at the funeral?" asked Snow. "Well, except Stein."

Mac nodded, then shook her head. "Not Ahmed. Kline gave part of the eulogy. Seemed grieved at Roy's demise."

"She's a big girl," Savage observed. In every photo, Kline was the tallest—big-boned with a swimmer's broad muscular shoulders. Wet hair could be light brown or dark blonde. Frost and Roy had similar lean builds and long legs; both attractive, both smiling. Frost's figure was almost tomboyish; Roy's aspect more feminine. Ahmed's dark complexion, coarse black hair, and petite body set her apart from the rest. Wide black eyes stared at the camera. "We can eliminate Ahmed. She doesn't fit the description."

"Wow, she's hot!" Fields observed from across the table. "I'll take her."

Mac ignored the comment. "Let's do background checks on all to cover our bases. So, we have our work cut out for us. Whoever has an ax to grind, his or her resentment goes back to their childhood. So we need to widen our search. Bring each of these women in for questioning. I'd ask why none of them said they knew her when. What are they hiding?"

"That's a damn good question, Detective," March commented. "Let's find out. But first, anyone have anything to add to the good of the cause?" No comments; eyes perused the photos sliding around the table.

March concluded, "Let's find these ladies; bring them in. I'll have Sonja locate Kline and Ahmed's current addresses. Snow and Savage, bring all in at the same time. Don't want them comparing notes. When you get the call, Mac, go visit Stein. Fields and Huddleston, comb through all the reports, post anything we missed on the boards. Stuart?"

"Yes, sir. I'll call Special Agent Fleisher and the state police for a profiler to work with Dr. Drummer. Send Roy's clothes to the lab in Quantico, see if our guys missed anything."

The Chief nodded, thumb and index finger rubbing his chin. "Dismissed."

13

The call pinged at 8 A.M. the next morning. Mac stood in her underwear ironing cotton Dockers, pressing out the wrinkles as if she could press the wrinkles out of her life. Launder her past mistakes; start over. Pay more attention to the moments before the pearls slipped away; listen to her body. A tear dropped, hissing on the hot iron. Another hit; the iron spit onto her slacks. *I'll never have another daughter.* She tried to shake off her self-pity because often the doldrums followed with fatiguing regularity; she couldn't afford the distraction.

While the Snows were dressing for work, Erica arrived to tend to Ian's breakfast mess: oatmeal and applesauce matted his hair. Cheerios dotted the mat under the highchair. The ten-month-old squeezed a slice of banana with glee, the pulp oozing between pudgy fingers. Plucking a wet wipe from the packet on the counter, his grandmother held Ian's wrist and wiped the hand. "Ooo. Ian. You're supposed to eat your food, not squeeze it. Or wear it!" Erica chuckled. The baby obligingly plopped the sludge into his mouth. "Here, give me that sticky hand, buster!"

Shadow weaved among the adults. Outside, an airgun spit nails into their new fence. Mac canted her head toward the fencing. "The noise makes the dog nervous. I fed her and let her out. Savage is stopping by to pick her up, take her to the Woolworth warehouse. They're filming the grand opening!"

"OK. I've got Ian. Watch, he'll smudge your blouse," Erica swiped the tray with a dishcloth. "Oh, you little minx. You need a bath." She turned him facing out, so she could wipe his face, marching to the laundry tub in the mudroom.

Mac checked Fleisher's TM: "Stein eting brkfst. Will talk." She punched Fields' number. "Meet me at the bungalow. We're going to Philly. Sure, you drive." Then she called HQ. Slid her Glock into the shoulder holster. Donned a hunter green cotton jacket over pale blue blouse and navy Dockers. She slipped into her sensible navy wedges, lugged her purse off the side table in the living room, and kissed her husband and baby a good day.

"You'll corral those women for interviews?" Erin asked.

Chris answered, "I will." He trotted to the laundry room. "Bye, Mom. Let me smooch Ian first."

Fields drove up, braked, and leaned across to open the passenger door. Two cappuccinos rode in the cup holders. Handing over the Stein folder, he explained, "I was at Sheetz when you called. Yours is the first one."

"Thanks, Zach. What's this? Nice!" her hand caressed the butter-like beige leather.

"A 2007 new-to-me Nissan Murano. Only 12,000 miles on it! GPS. Go ahead program it; punch in the street address. You want voice, press this button." He tapped the console button.

"Let's wait until we're near Philly. Think we can manage the Turnpike until then. Thanks for the coffee. I didn't get to finish mine; it's a madhouse in there: Snow, baby, dog, and mother-in-law." She sipped, savoring the rich brew, leaning against the luxurious leather seats.

"Can't even imagine doing this job with a family. It seems so chaotic these days." Fields clicked his tongue as swung the vehicle onto Lisburn, heading for Rt-15. "It's a full-time job managing me."

"Our life *is* controlled chaos, but we do what we can," Mac said. "It's hard to keep a schedule with this job.

And our parents help big time with Ian. Otherwise, we'd be bonkers. Being single is easier in some ways."

His boyish face gleamed. "Damned straight! Nothing to negotiate. No arguments, no drama. No one's nagging me to do something I don't want to do. I come and go as I please. Just peace and quiet at home. If I want theater, I can go to the movies." He eyes canted to hers as he punched a knob. Pearl Jam bled from the speakers. "No offense."

Mac shook her head. "None taken. I was single until twenty-eight. Hadn't planned to marry until . . . Well, never mind." Opening the Stein folders, she reviewed the facts while the tires hummed, picking up speed as they passed through the Turnpike tollbooth.

"You had to," Zach commented. She frowned at his bluntness. "Just saying."

"OK," Mac said after a ten-minute lull, "This is how we'll handle the interview . . ."

❉ ❉ ❉

Rachel Stein looked like a raccoon; her bruised eyes, cut lip, bandaged forehead and hands signaled a vicious struggle. Her body, a bulge under the covers, was wired to the usual IV and monitors that beeped intermittently, reporting her vitals. Sunlight slipped through the closed blinds slats. "You should see the other guys." But her espresso eyes remained serious.

Detective Fields chuckled as he showed his shield. "Good for you—a fighter who lived to tell the tale. I bet you feel like a Mack truck ran you down. Let's hope you collected evidence." The Philly CSU had already clipped her fingernails, collected hair samples and fibers from her clothes from Friday night's attack. "Did you recognize your assailants?" He drew up two chairs, settled on one. Mac perched on the second holding a digital recorder, calling off the case number and persons present.

Stein nodded; she remembered them. "There were two; they wore black, and ski masks covered their faces."

"Any notable facial features? Fields asked. "Skin dark or light?"

She shook her head no. "It happened fast, though it felt like forever. It was dark. Backed against the cabin door, I punched back, scratched, gouged and kicked one in the groin. Really pissed them off." She looked at Mac, swallowed hard. "They had a black gym bag—tools: hammer, nails, zip ties, rope, and duct tape. I fell over it when one of them punched me in the kidney. They slammed me against the cabin door . . ." She winced, turned her bandaged hands over.

Mac nodded. "The police recovered the duffel bag at the crime scene. Did you recognize their voices?"

Another negative head shake. "They whispered. One was low, raspy—masculine. A smoker? But I pulled one's hair; it felt like straw—coarse and dry. Bleached, I think. I could see it was dirty blonde. But they pried it out of my hand when they nailed me to the door." She winced, blinked hard several times. "I fainted."

"Could you smell anything distinctive?" Fields leaned back, patient.

"Besides decayed fish, oil and water? I don't remember." She shut her eyes. "Yes, peppermint. And their leather gloves stank. One covered my mouth until the other taped it shut."

"Can you identify the odor?" Mac leaned forward.

"Like rust. Copper or iron." She scratched her forehead with the tips of her fingers. "Blood? Oh, no, I'm going to be sick." Mac jumped up, grabbed a waste can and held it until Stein quit heaving. Zach sprinkled water from a pitcher over his handkerchief and gently patted the woman's mouth, handing her a glass of water.

After drinking and taking several deep breaths, she said. "They're the same ones who killed Irene and attacked Lance?"

The detectives nodded. Mac conceded, "Looks that way. We think Irene was the principal target. No one told us you guys have a history." She showed her the photo of the teens by the pool. "Did she have any enemies? Think back."

Stein gazed at the photo. "Not that I know of. You know teenage girls. Catfights, gossip, cliques, but we grew up in the same neighborhood in Lancaster on Golf Course Road." She tapped the photo. "Nora—Noreen—moved away her sophomore year when her dad reenlisted. And when my grandma got sick, we moved back to Philly. Took turns caring for her as she wasted away: breast cancer."

"I'm sorry about your grandmother. When was that?" Mac asked. "Did you have any contact with Roy or Reading prior to the Woolworth documentary?

"Nineteen-ninety-five. Yes, Irene and I roomed together at NYU our freshman year. After that, she moved into an apartment with acting majors. I stayed in the dorm; it was closer to the Drama Department, and I didn't have a car then."

"No hard feelings because she moved out?" Fields asked.

"No. Why would I?" Her eyes contacted Fields'. "We went our separate ways until JJ hired her same time as Lance."

"How long have you been Reynolds' assistant?"

"Three years. Our first doc featured Ulysses S. Grant."

Fields switched back to her attack. "You had a close call. Lucky that your family checked on you."

Her face blanched, her head fell back against the pillows. She shut her eyes. "I'm tired."

As if on cue, her day nurse breezed in, gray hair coiled into a topknot. "That's enough. You've tired my patient. What's that smell?" She looked around, stepped over, peered into the waste bin. "Why didn't you ring for me?" She made shooing motions. "Ms. Stein needs rest to recuperate."

The detectives filed out of the room, nodding at the uniform by the door.

"She knows more than she's telling," Mac said as she made a note of the officer's badge number to check with Fleisher.

"She's afraid," Fields concluded, as they walked down the bland corridor to the grey elevator doors. When the doors parted, a portly man, his dark hair threaded with grey, emerged. A salt and pepper beard obscured his chin. His bright blue eyes met hers. "Thanks for the courtesy call."

"SAC William Fleisher." Mac extended her hand.

"How's our survivor?" He gave Fields a solid, single shake, nodding to the empty seating area; vinyl chairs huddled together around a cheap coffee table with magazines fanned neatly across the surface.

"Shaken. Seemed she stirred up a hornet's nest by fighting back," Fields said, "but it bought her time until her relatives arrived. She survived."

"Lucky woman. Her brother Sam said she didn't answer her cell. Said she always answers their calls when she works nights. Her cousin Rueben works the docks, and he'd come around to check on her about the same time. Woman working alone at that time—"

"Did they describe the assailants?" Mac asked.

The Special Agent shrugged his shoulders. "Hooded, dressed in black, wearing ski masks. Around five-ten and six feet. The six-footer could match the size-ten shoe print we found. Could also match thousands of other people in the area."

"But the MO is distinctive," Mac said. "We're looking for someone with a grudge that may trace back to their childhood. The killers are punishing their victims. I first thought jealousy was the motive." Mac shared the pool photo. Pointing to Stein, Roy, and Frost, "These girls are cast or crew members of The Frank Woolworth documentary. Our homicide Vic," Mac's forefinger rested on Roy, "was the main target. She was engaged to the first Vic."

"Yes, I saw the Bible verse and 'Fornicator,'" Fleisher commented. "You're assuming that because the others survived? That doesn't necessarily follow. Stein's family scared off her attackers."

"Neither Reading nor Stein was strangled," Mac countered.

"Plus, they *survived*," added Fields. He crossed an ankle over the opposite knee. Brushed one hand over his crew cut.

"Oh, I think they would've killed Stein," Fleisher said. "Granted, the MO is similar, so they're linked. We're waiting on DNA results culled off the boat; no prints but we have a blood type, skin tissue, and piece of black knit fabric. Plus the murder kit. We're tracing those items to retailers, but they're generic—every Wal-Mart, hardware or Lowe's sells the stuff. Good news, if we can find a match, we can trace items to the buyer if he used a credit card. My staff is reviewing surveillance videos of the retailers." He stood, signaling the interview had concluded, extending his meaty hand. "Thanks for sharing your files. We'll keep in touch. I'll fax you the lab results when they arrive on my desk."

Mac stood and shook the agent's proffered hand. "And thanks for cooperating with our investigation. My partners are interviewing the other women in that photo as we speak. If news breaks, I'll call or email."

Threading their way through a field of cars and SUVs, Fields called HQ to check in. "Ten-nineteen, ETA, two o'clock." He thumbed the fob; the locks popped. Then they climbed into the vehicle.

Mac raised her eyes at the time differential; her watch read 11:35. She extracted her cell to update Chris and listened to his terse voicemail comment. "You know what to do. I'll call back." She left a brief message. Dialed Fleisher, requested a sketch artist for Stein. "She might remember more. Thanks. Over, out."

"We're stopping for lunch," Fields explained as his stomach gurgled "My treat. I'm hungry for a Philly cheesesteak."

Mac ended her call. "Let's look for a deli; I could eat a brat with sauerkraut."

The Murano crossed the South 26th Bridge, threaded its way through Philly traffic, past old brick buildings in the historical district check to jowl with skyscrapers. A city bus wheezed to a stop. Litter lined the downtown streets. People scurried along. Here the punk, Goth, and the tatty ripped-jeans looks dominated. The homeless huddled over heat vents. Stray newspapers and a plastic bag somersaulted across their path. They stopped at a corner deli for sandwiches, eating in the vehicle. They made better time on the Turnpike where Fields ramped up the speed.

"I guess Chris and Savage are in the box with Frost. Let's review what we found out." She opened Roy's file, paging through notes, photos, witness statements and Roy's lab prelims.

14

Snow tilted his chair back on its rear legs. Savage pushed the photo across the table to Jackie Frost. Her blond-tipped shaggy pixie had darker roots; her ears were double-pierced with diamond or crystal studs. The costume designer toyed with an infinity charm on a silver necklace. She blinked, leaned forward and smiled at the photo. Studied it, pausing at each face. The smile vanished when her eyes rested on Irene Roy.

"Why didn't you tell us you knew Roy and Stein since childhood when we first interviewed you?" Savage flipped the NYU graduation photo over, pushed it forward. Followed by the ballerina photo.

"You didn't ask." She said, her eyes on the photos. "Besides, how would that have helped?"

"Just answer our questions. It's our job to piece it all together." Snow let his chair fall back on all four legs, jolting their witness. "Any reason to hide that you knew Roy as a teen?"

Frost shrugged, her scoop-neck tunic top dropping off one shoulder. She tugged it back in place. "We grew up together: same neighborhood, same bus, same schools. Community pool. We weren't cliquey because we had different classes. When we all started dating, we spent more time with our boyfriends, except for Cassie, who didn't date. She's athletic. Think she intimidated most guys; she was the first female kicker on our football team. Also lettered on the swim and softball teams. She went to Penn State. And Nora moved away."

Snow frowned. "Nora?"

"Noreen Ahmed moved when the Army deployed her father to Iraq as an interpreter."

"Anyone closer to one more than the others?" Savage asked. "Any hidden secrets or animosities? Fight over boyfriends or—?"

Frost's grey eyes studied Reese for a long minute. "You could be in movies. You look a little like an actor what's his name." Her attention drifted off trying to recall. Her fingers raked her ragged bangs back. "Rufus?"

"Ms. Frost, did you hear the questions?" Snow asked, ignoring her question, tapping the table between them.

"Yes. No, you mean like 'I know what you did last summer?' We're not hiding any deep, dark secrets. Well, we toked a few joints, tipped back a few beers. No, make that a lot of drinks after the plays. Played a few pranks. Irene and I fought over one grad assistant, but he slept with us both—at once! Rachel was such a stick-in-the-mud, especially at NYU—always studying, taking it all seriously and graduated summa cum laude. What a nasty, moody, bossy bitch. She barks out orders: 'Get your script! Move to your mark! Offstage—silence! No donuts for the women!' No please or thank you from her. Look at me! I weigh one-ten. I eat what I please. But she gets the job done, and she's good at it. Does her research, and gives me copies of archival photos on costumes—always overbearingly helpful."

"So who would want to hurt Reading, Roy, and Stein?" Snow inquired.

She shrugged. "Maybe Rachel's aggressiveness pissed someone off, but JJ gave her the authority, so we couldn't say anything to him."

"Did you know Reading and Roy were engaged?" Savage asked.

"Yes and no. They acted like lovers but denied it. Still, that's no reason to kill someone." Frost dropped her charming smile. She gazed at the photos.

"Could someone be trying to sabotage the documentary?" Savage asked.

"Why would they? The cast and crew wouldn't; we need our paychecks. Once the documentary airs, we'll all have cache—and stability because JJ's doing another doc on Thomas Jefferson and Sally Hemings. He wants Halle Berry. If so, the crew stays with JJ. Maybe he'll keep some of the actors."

"Would Reynolds do this for the publicity?" Snow wondered aloud.

"No! He doesn't have a violent bone in his body. Wouldn't occur to him to do such a vile thing. He's just trying to keep us on track and under budget. This is a good documentary. Frank W. Woolworth worked hard building his franchise, living the American dream. He changed the way Americans shop."

"Can you remember seeing anyone on the set during rehearsals, at the house or the restaurants watching you? Following you?" Savage pinched the bridge of his nose and glanced at the humming fluorescent light.

"No, we're self-absorbed, detective. We don't usually mix with locals." She licked her dry lips. "Could I please have something to drink?"

Savage pushed from the table and to his feet. "Sure. What'll you have?"

"A bottle of water's fine. Or diet soda if you have Coke products."

The door sighed open, clicked shut after Savage exited.

"Have you heard from Cassidy Kline or Noreen Ahmed?"

"Cassie attended Irene's funeral. Said hello, goodbye—nothing profound or earth-shattering. No, I haven't seen Nora since high school. Think she studied abroad." Her eyes glanced over Snow while they waited. She sank back against the chair. "Irene's parents are devastated; they could hardly hold it together at the funeral. Can't believe Irene is gone. She was quiet—read a lot—but fun too, after two drinks." She smiled. "Irene ordered Sex in the City at the pub—the waiter asked, "Is that a drink?" He was incredulous.

"I meant Sex on the Beach," she said, blushing. "The slip-up cracked us up." She shook her head.

Savage reentered, sat a bottle of cold water in front of Frost.

"Thanks so much." She popped the lid and drank; a few drops spilled, dripping onto her skin, into her tunic. She shivered and wiped off the water with her top.

"Don't mention it." Savage stood a minute longer, sighed and resumed his seat. "What about the crew? Are you all tight as well? No suspicious characters?"

She shook her head. "Banks and Rogers are married—not to each other. They go home every weekend—opposite coasts. The sisters in make-up keep to themselves. JJ spends a lot of time on the set and the phone. Rachel does our schedules or scouts ahead, staging the next scene. Lance and Irene spent a lot of time together. Hell, Larissa and I spend a lot of time on the set getting the costumes, sewing, shopping vintage stores, etc. She handles props. None of us has time for intrigue or murder." She spread her palms over the photos, then pushed them away. Tilting the bottle, she quaffed the rest. Blew her breathe out, ballooning her cheeks.

Snow dropped his card in front of Frost. "That's all for now. You're free to go. If you see or think of anything helpful, please call anytime."

"Really?" She jumped up smiled at Reese, and pocketed Snow's card. "Guess I'll see you at the set later. We're getting ready to film the Grand Opening!" She scooted out of the room.

Snow checked his watch. "I need caffeine. Let's take a break before we bring in the next one."

Reese snapped off the overhead light. "Damned light's buzzing is getting on my nerves. I'm gonna shut that off and bring in a damn lamp."

Snow's cell chirped. He checked the number. "Talk, Castle."

"We can't locate the Kline woman." The uniform's cell faded, emitted static. Accompanied by Tanya Storm, the officer had sped to her house, then to her employer's business—a lopsided A-frame rustic cabin with the name and logo running across frothing water in blue resin.

"Why not?" Snow responded.

"She's an Outdoor Adventure guide at Harper's Ferry. We're standing in the office looking at the schedule. Her boss tells us she has a group kayaking on the Shenandoah or the Potomac, in Maryland, West Virginia or Virginia. Vehicle's parked in the lot behind the building—locked, empty as far as we can see."

"Find her. We need to question her in a homicide investigation."

"You mean go out on the river and track her down?" Castle clarified.

"Whatever it takes. She's known Irene Roy since childhood. I want her in this office by tomorrow afternoon. You have twenty-four hours."

"Roger that." Castle disconnected.

Reese located an ivory ceramic lamp with a flared shade, parked it on the table.

Snow shook his head. "Won't work. It's a possible weapon."

"There's nothing else in the room to set it on." Savage inspected the corners.

"Find a stand or crate. Better yet, get a lamp you can hang on the wall. Or get maintenance to replace the fluorescent tube." He pointed to the outlet below the moon-faced clock on the back wall in the interview room. "Besides, Castle and Storm can't locate the Kline woman, so we're done here."

"We've talked to everyone else except Ahmed. Located her parents; they said their daughter's in Kuwait visiting her grandparents for two weeks." Savage blinked several times. He dug in his pocket for eye drops, squirting some into each eye. Blinked again and then screwed the top back on the bottle.

"Get a phone number?" Snow shuffled the crime scene photos back into Roy's folder.

Savage nodded, picking up the lamp. Handed his boss a post-it note.

"She has a 717 area code? Does she live in Carlisle? Must be a cell. Let's go to the conference room, call her."

"That can be our first question," Savage said.

"Okay. Lead with that."

Ahmed answered on the first ring.

"We're Detectives Christopher Snow and Reese Savage," he began the conference call, reciting the time, place, case number, and other relevant information. "We have questions for you concerning Irene Roy."

15

Mac and Janelle stood in the front of the Woolworth
store among a crowd of Carlisle residents dressed in
early twentieth-century clothing: women in gaily-colored
ankle-length dresses wore hats decorated with flowers
or feathers. The dark plain garments of the Amish
provided a sharp contrast, their horse and buggies
parked along the street. A mustached man dressed
in twill, cuffed slacks, a collarless white dress shirt,
suspenders, and a straw boater tickled the ivories on
an upright piano. Red, white and blue bunting sailed
above the Woolworth Five Cent sign. With Elizabeth
Banks by his side, Lance Reading, a megaphone to his
mouth, called, "What a lovely Memorial Day weekend!
Welcome to the Grand Opening of the first Woolworth
five-cent store in Lancaster, Pennsylvania! I'm Frank
W. Woolworth. This is my lovely wife, Jennie. My clerk,
Charles, is handing out flyers with a list of our wares!
My brother, Sumner, on the piano." He paused while the
pianist ran the keyboard. "Come in, folks! You'll find all
your household needs here—for a nickel each.

"Yes, you heard right: a nickel, a dime at the most!
If you don't find what you need, tell us, and we'll
find it, order it, stock it and sell it here! Don't be shy.
Step forward. Come inside! You'll find watering tins,
hammers, biscuit cutters, skimmers, purses and
red jewelry for the ladies! I have apple-corers for Fall
canning! Fire shovels for the hearth, school straps and
pencil charms for the kids." He stepped aside, threw
open the door and gestured for them to enter.

In the cordoned-off road, cameraman Ken Rogers
rode along on a dolly, capturing the scene. Sumner
Woolworth switched to a rousing Sousa march. Hair
tucked under a white *kapp*, Janelle, in a plain black
cotton dress, stepped forward with one line, "I need
a hammer!" and disappeared into the store. Others
trickled in, curious, while several spectators peered into
the display windows at the wares displayed in willow
baskets. Two men stood aside conversing, clipping and
lighting cigars. At the opposite corner, a lad called, "Get
your hot peanuts here: a nickel a bag! Pretzels, two for
five cents!"

Mac sighed. On this cloudless September morning,
a breeze skipped along the straw-covered sidewalk. A
young woman in a long, print dress with bishop sleeves,
a basket in the crook of her arm, wove among the crowd
handing out penny candy to the children. For the film,
the girls, their hair pulled back and topped with large
ribbon bows wore shin-length dresses with leggings, and
the boys—knickers and shirts with suspenders.

Parked in the shade at the vegetable stand across
the street, Mac climbed behind the wheel. The windows
were cranked open an inch for Shadow. The dog sat up,
sniffed the air.

"You smell the peanuts, girl?" She keyed the ignition,
steered through the dogleg to the light. "Well, sorry, we
gotta go to work. They're filming and we're not dressed
appropriately." When the light turned green, she made a
left on High and drove through town to HQ.

Ducking into her office to catch any calls left on
her voicemail while pouring water into Shadow's dish,
she draped her jacket over the back of her desk chair,
dropped her purse and Glock into the bottom desk
drawer. "Stay, girl." She rummaged for a rare rawhide
bone, laid it on Shadow's bed. The dog sniffed at it,
licked it. Then settled down chewing. Mac grabbed

Roy's file and aimed for the Murder Room to check the whiteboards.

Sonja parceled out the list of interviews. Mac reached for the top tape labeled 'Frost,' slotted it into a CPD recorder, plugged in earbuds and listened, notepad and Sharpie in hand.

"Coffee?" Sonja pantomimed.

Mac nodded. "Please." She jotted down bits of information. Then moved on to the next labeled 'Stein.' Listening to the tone of voice, she wrote Stein's description of her assailants. Flipped her pad over, wrote *call Fleisher* about any evidence found in the murder kit or cap they left behind.

Chief March filed in with LT Stuart, whose long spider legs reached the boards in three steps. March dropped a stack of papers, pens, and a clipboard on the table, standing while the other detectives filed in. Fields entered with a cinnamon twist stacked on his coffee mug, Savage—a chocolate glazed donut stuck in his mouth, and Chris held two mugs, one he sat in front his wife, easing down beside her. Next, Huddleston ambled over to the computer, booted it up. Mac assumed Lee Jeffers was at the Woolworth site.

Greg Castle and Tanya Storm, she guessed, were still searching for Cassidy Kline.

"Okay, people, report," Chief turned to Snow. "Interviews?"

"We've interviewed all the childhood chums except Cassidy Kline. She's a whitewater-rafting guide out on the Shenandoah or Potomac. Couldn't pry any secrets or scare out any skeletons from the others. Either they don't remember or refuse to tell, but I don't sense anyone withholding info."

Mac cleared her throat. Set her mug down. "Except Rachel Stein. She's withholding info but was in no shape for us to interrogate her. Roy and Stein roomed together at NYU for a year but parted company after that. She claimed separate majors and interests. That's possible but there could be more to it."

"She did, however, describe her assailants like her family members did," Fields added. "Black clothes, ski masks, etc. When Fleisher faxes us the artist's sketches, we can give them to the media. Someone may notice the eyes, a mustache—some telling detail. And something may come back from the murder kit. We could get lucky if they left any DNA."

A curt knock sounded, Officer Castle shouldered the door aside. "Sorry to interrupt, sirs, but we're putting Ms. Kline in the box."

Snow, Savage, and Mac stood.

"If you'll excuse us, Cassidy Kline is our last childhood friend to interview."Mac strode to the door.

Chief March nodded, waving Reese back to his seat as pagers buzzed. Dispatch. "DV on South Street. Ten thirty-three." *Shots fired.* "Wife injured. Kid called 911."

"Dismissed. Fields and Storm, take the call. See if the doc's available in case you need a hostage negotiator. Savage, stay. I'll like a word."

Down the hall, the couple paused, observing Kline through the window. Seated and angled away from the table with one bare ankle crossed over the opposite knee, Kline waited. Her wheat-hued Dutch-boy razor-cut hair framed a square face with blunt features. Alert eyes watched the door. A faded blue tee revealed broad shoulders and defined biceps. She wore tan cargo shorts and canvas sneakers.

"We brought her party ashore three hours ago." Castle offered.

"Where did they spend the night?" Snow asked.

"Found them camping along the Shenandoah."

"Where's your partner?" Mac wondered.

"Writing our report. I'm whipped. My first and last time white-water rafting." Castle's baggy eyes bore signs of fatigue.

"Thanks, man. Go on home, get some shut-eye," Snow opened the door; Mac strode into the interview room, Roy's file in hand.

"Tell us about your friendship with Irene Roy, Ms. Kline." Mac started after Snow recited the essentials for the video.

"Call me Cassie. Yes, what a terrible thing to happen. Irene was on the verge of success. Though I haven't seen her for two years, I see her parents when I go Lancaster to visit. We've been friends since grade school; my family lived down the block from hers."

"Yes, Roy's parents have already provided us with some background," Mac said. "We'd like you to fill in the details. Any bullying at school? Fights? Secret grudges in Roy's history?"

"The usual. She was small for her age, petite. Wore glasses. The boys sometimes made fun of her, called her bug-eyes, but she ignored them."

"But not always?" Snow prodded.

"Once. Senior prom. She refused to spend the night with her date, Stan Cooper. He roughed her up, tore her dress, tried to force her into his car."

"What happened then?" Mac asked.

"I cold-cocked him. One punch. Then took her home."

"Was her brother there?" Snow asked.

"No. He was a freshman."

"Did this Cooper fellow hold a grudge? Would he retaliate?" Mac asked.

"No. He'd been drinking. I think he apologized later. He married his college sweetheart. Three kids now. They live in upstate New York."

"Anything else you can add about Roy's timeline?" Mac scooted a paper across the table with a record of their victim's history.

Ms. Kline put her finger on 'Shakespeare.' "She stayed two months with me until she left for London. I live in Leesburg—closer to the Reagan airport."

"So you were roommates? What can you tell us about that experience?" Mac leaned back to avoid crowding the woman.

Kline shrugged. "She didn't want to live at home after college graduation. She had a lot to do—getting ready to go abroad. Bought a passport, obtained health records, and made accommodations—" She smiled. "Plus working part-time, saving money. Her suitcase lay open for a month while she deliberated what to pack, what to leave."

"Did she and her parents have a falling out?" Snow asked.

"No, you know how it is when you're first out of college. You're not quite independent but want to be. Unsure about that next big step—more education or work? I chose work. When the Royal Shakespeare Company accepted her, she was thrilled.

"Irene also suffered a huge disappointment before that. She'd auditioned with the NYCB, then the San Francisco Ballet. Didn't make the cut. So . . ." she shrugged. "Didn't take the failure lightly."

"To your knowledge, did she have any enemies?" Mac said.

"She didn't have *any* enemies," Kline stated.

"Someone killed her," Snow remarked. "And attacked her fiancé, Lance Reading."

Kline's eyes shifted away, and then back. "Yes, well, it must be someone from that Woolworth project. I saw the news report on Rachel's attack too."

"The news didn't release her name," Mac noted.

"I recognized her; we grew up together, remember?" Kline countered.

Mac's eyes locked onto Kline's. "Yes." She wanted to keep Kline on track.

"Didn't you say you hadn't seen her lately? How did you know her whereabouts?"

"The *Lancaster Times* did a lengthy feature on the film cast and crew when they arrived there to film Woolworth's first *successful* store. There's a commemorative plaque on North Queen Street. Her mom sent me the article on the documentary that lists the cast."

The detectives nodded. "Did you call or text her?"

Kline shook her head. "I work seven days a week during the summer and fall. You know how it is; you're busy with the demands of your own life."

"Do you live alone?" asked Snow.

Kline's eyes widened. "I'm single if that's what you're asking."

"No roommates?" Mac clarified.

"To verify my movements? Just my brother Kerry. Just check with my boss. I'm always working."

"And during the offseason?" Snow asked.

"Doing maintenance, ordering supplies, updating brochures, mailings, shooting commercials for Outdoor Adventures. I work year around."

Kline checked her watch. "I have a trip scheduled at two, and your cops broke up our camp at 4 A.M. I need at least five hours sleep."

Mac nodded. "Sure. We need a DNA sample to eliminate you." She pulled a swab kit from her pocket. Kline shrugged and complied. "We're done for the time being. If you could give us your cell number," pushing a pink post-it notepad across the table, "in case we have more questions."

Kline jotted down the digits and then slid the pad back across the table.

"Or if you think of something, anything helpful about Roy's past. Did you know she was engaged?" Snow asked.

Color crept up her neck. "Yes, her parents told my mother and stepdad."

"You weren't pleased for her?" Mac stood, handed Kline a business card.

Her eyes skewed left. "It was none of my business. Like I said, we haven't been in touch. I knew she was acting, and work is my life."

"Thanks for coming in." Snow extended his hand, which Kline gripped with a solid shake.

"Did I have a choice?" Nodding with a wry smile, she walked out when he opened the door and then closed it behind her.

"She's lying about something," Mac said. "Why?"

"Guess we dig deeper. Interview her parents, her brother and her boss."

"How's her grip?" Mac led the way back to the empty Incident Room. Turned to her office as Shadow met her in the hallway, tail wagging, whining and nudging her knee. Wanting to go out.

"As you'd expect. Let's take a trip to Harper's Ferry. I'll make the calls."

"I have to walk Shadow first. See you in fifteen, then we take her home." Mac grabbed the dog's leash from its peg inside the door, snapped it on Shadow's halter, and led her out.

16

The detectives parked at the curb a block from 1130 Chantilly Avenue, the DMV address listed under Kline's name. Dew wiggled off the grass. Their footfalls echoed off the pavements, quiet at this hour. Identical red brick shotgun townhouses circa the 1950s lined the street, save for the yews flanking the front of number eleven thirty. Others had wrought-iron fences; some a white picket. A mature neighborhood, the trees looked over fifty, their lacy leaves providing shade as sunlight peppered shadows on the sidewalks.

The doorbell bonged deep in the house, which sat back from the three-foot front yard.

The detectives displayed their shields as a bare-chested, barefoot man in his thirties zipping his fly flung open the door. A whiff of sweet smoke greeted them. "Whoa, cops! Hey!" He held up both hands, surrendering. "Swear to God! I only bought an ounce." He peered up and down the streets. "What? Smoke in the clouds, empty concrete jungle. The animals are all caged. I don't know anything." He scratched his scruffy goatee and then combed fingers through rumpled brown hair.

"We're not Narcotics. Carlisle Homicide. We're looking for Cassie Kline," Mac said. "Is this the correct address?" She and Chris exchanged confused glances. iPhone in hand, she touched the camera icon, lowered her hand, carried it out to record.

"Don't know addresses. Kline, yes, Cass lives here on occasion. Spends most of the time at work. Work, work, work! Leaves Post-it notes of stuff to do. Drives me crazy! No time for life. Eat, mail, work, and mow. Tend flowers." He fidgeted with the loops on his jeans, tugging them up to cover his boxers.

"And who are you? asked Snow. "May we come in?"

"KK. Kerry, my sister's brother. Come in but don't stay. Stuff to do."

He backed against the wall. At right, a wood staircase rose behind him. Downstairs three rooms lined up in a row: living, dining, and kitchen. In the dining room, an open laptop sat on a round oak table beside a mug of coffee and half-eaten pbj sandwich. Florescent pink, orange, and green Post-it Notes stuck to the computer, doorframes, and kitchen cupboards read in order 'Work.' 'Eat.' "Take meds." 'Mail.' 'Mow.' 'Water flowers.'

Someone had converted a former porch to a small sunroom. Through the windows, they could see heads of orange poppies peeping back in the postage-stamp backyard. "Oh, how beautiful," Mac breathed. She walked to the door, poked her head out. Window boxes held rosemary and parsley in one, basil and thyme in the other. St. Johns Wort bushes dotted with yellow stars anchored the corners of the house. Fireworks of color and profusion lined the wire fence: Valerian, mint, and chamomile interspaced with lavender, feathery plants and rosebushes. The grass needed a mower.

"See? Water flowers," Kline pointed to another note.

"So many medicinal herbs," she said.

"Not rue. Mint crowded it out," he responded, his head down, despondent at the loss. "But there's basil, thyme, and rosemary."

"Know when Cassidy will be home?" Mac tried again while Chris ambled around, canvassing without touching. Kline didn't appear to be listening.

"Home. Where's that? This house? Not now." Kline's eyes followed Snow. "Don't search. Need warren. I need work." He pointed at the computer, the monitor, its screen black, resting.

"We don't need a warrant to talk. What do you do?" asked Mac.

"WORK! See?" Voice and motor ramping up, he pointed to all the Post-it Notes. To illustrate, he picked up the sandwich, took a huge bite, chewed. Swallowed. Pulled the 'Eat' Post-it off the computer. Wadded it up, tossed it in the trashcan under the table. "One down, fifteen to go. Day's done; gone the sun. Sister comes, sometimes not alone. Then I go to my room."

"OK." Mac sighed. She was getting the picture. "What about this one?" She tapped 'Take meds.'

Kline opened top cabinet over the fridge. Pulled a prescription bottle from a box with vitamins. Took out a blue and green capsule. Swallowed it, chased it with tap water. *Dulox*—a serotonin reuptake inhibitor. She noticed a bottle of Xanax. She suspected ADHD for starters. Pupils dilated, so stoned—marijuana. Throw in anxiety at their arrival and his diction. Perhaps Asperger's Syndrome.

Kline slotted the medicine container back in with the vitamins. Took out a multi-vitamin. Popped it. Jerked the faucet on, ran more tap water, and repeated.

Snow shook his head. No help, no clues, nada.

Mac nodded. Still, she pulled out Roy's headshot. "Do you know this person?"

"Irene. She lived here before. Friend. Sweet mouse in the house."

"Yes, Cassie told us," Mac added. "When did you last see her?"

"When? Dunno. Time is liquid, bleeds into today until it's today again. Then she cried. Yelled at us. Not friends anymore."

"Why? What happened?" Snow stopped in front of the computer, slid out his handkerchief, refreshed it. Up popped a graphic novel site.

"Can't touch. Prints. Wear gloves." Kline reached across, snapped the laptop closed. "Private. No warren, no peeking. Private business, my work. Please go." Spit spewed out that landed on Snow's cheek. While Kline swiped his mouth with the back of his hand, Snow turned his back, pulled a glassine out and collected the saliva with a Q-tip. Dropped it in. Pocketed it.

"Why don't you like Irene anymore?" Mac rephrased.

"Didn't say that. Not friends because she's not here." He pointed down emphatically, the other hand clenched into a fist.

"She left?" Snow asked.

Kline shooed them to the door. "Go away." He drummed his fingers along the doorframe. "Yes. Left for her work; she acts. Well, not anymore."

"What was she acting in?" They paused in the doorway.

"*A Midsummer's Night's Dream.*" He posed, head cocked to one side. "Maidens call it love in idleness. Fetch me that herb, the flower I showed you once.'" He dropped his arms. "I was Puck. Irene—Tatiana."

Snow stepped to the sidewalk. "Thanks for your time."

"You're an actor, too?" Mac stood her ground. Then pulled out a photo of Lance. "Then do you know this man?"

He shook his head. "No, we only make-believe. We beg your pardon to have deceived." He bowed, inches from the picture, and nodded. "That's Lance Railroad. Get it?" He laughed. "A joke! Reading! He's the reason for the play. Plays the Merchant Prince. Now, go!" He opened the door.

"Just one more question, Mac insisted. She handed him a scrap of paper that read '. . . *abstain from pollutions and idols and from fornication and from things strangled and from blood.*' "Are you familiar with this?"

"Acts 15:20," Kline responded. "But that's not the entire verse. It begins, 'But that we write unto them.' That's Paul, writing to the Gentiles in Antioch and Syria.

Trying to convert them to Christianity. But Christ was Jewish." He returned the note to Mac. "That's called irony."

"Thanks for your help." Mac snapped her cell off and left. They strode back to the vehicle in silence. "Well, can you believe that? Knows the verse by heart. That's no coincidence. I'm telling you, this guy knows something."

In the vehicle, Snow threaded down, back and around Leesburg. Chris sighed. "What were you doing back there?"

"Mirroring his language to keep him talking. He Puckish." She smiled.

Chris frowned. "What do you think?"

"One, he looks nothing like his sister; he's all angles, angst, and energy. Two, he has a disability; I'd like to show Dr. Drummer the video." She held up her phone. "Three, he knows more than he's telling, which could explain some of his anxiety."

"Maybe cops make him nervous. Are you kidding? Can you see that guy on the stand? A green DA would make mincemeat of him within ten minutes."

"Read between the lines," Mac said. "What he says connotes meaning."

"He doesn't even know they're filming the Frank W. Woolworth documentary."

"He said Merchant Prince—that's Woolworth. I think he was talking about something else, but I need to look it up. He's quoting Shakespeare. Told us several key things," Mac replied.

"Yes, I got that, Sherlock. But it's not germane to our case. Let's track down Cassie Kline while we're here. Lean on her."

Mac shook her head. "No, Watson, let's see if she'll come to us."

"You think? She'll be pissed we talked to her brother."

"Exactly. Let's stop for some Krispy Kremes and coffee."

They stopped at the donut factory where they watched glaze raining on yeasty donuts moving along a rack. Gloved workers caught and packed a dozen to a box. Each detective had two warm ones, and Snow bought two dozen to take home and to work. They drove to Harper's Ferry to Outdoor Adventures. "I want to find out what her boss will tell us. See if you can get a warrant for her work and phone records," Snow said.

"Probable cause?" she queried. "Based on our interpretation of the brother's interview? You're kidding!"

Chris sipped his coffee. Pulled a third glazed donut out of the box.

"Leave some for the rest of us!" Erin protested. She closed the lid and moved the box to the back seat—out of her husband's reach.

"OK. We'll try without one."

* * *

Outdoor Adventures—a cedar-shake shingle A-frame with the logo over the door sat on a tongue of land between the road and the Potomac against a backdrop of feathery white pines. Prolific deciduous trees, bushes, and weeds crowded to the water's edge. A paved parking lot to the right held twenty vehicles. Snow pulled over a striped no-parking area between the building and a large, open shed where kayaks and canoes were stored.

Inside, a lean guy with a weathered tan and wavy brown hair wore a blue t-shirt with the OA logo emblazoned across the chest with tan cargo shorts. An athletic build and ropy muscles suggested outdoor labor. He was hanging supplies on hooks. When the bell tinkled, he turned, smiled and skirted the counter to greet them. His hazel eyes assessed them. "May I help you? We have five attractive Intermediate Level Whitewater—"

Both detectives flashed their creds, interrupting him mid-pitch. "Detective Christopher Snow and my partner, Detective Erin McCoy. We'd like to ask a few questions about one of your employees, Cassie Kline."

"I'm Eddie Webb. Cassie's my *best* employee. She's guiding a trio of teenage-girls treating their dad to a birthday trip." He returned to his spot behind the glass counter beside the cash register, flipped through a calendar at the schedule. "They should return by dinner time."

"Does she work full-time or is the work seasonal?" Mac started easy.

"Well, we're not on the water in winter, but we offer hiking and other activities. We're open for business from May through November. Rest of the time, Cassie helps with inventory, maintaining the equipment, ordering supplies. She puts in 40-50-hour weeks during summers, cuts back a bit in winter, but she's full-time, though some of the guides are part-time."

"Do they each have schedules?" Snow asked.

"Yes, I book the parties as the reservations come in," He tapped the oversized calendar on the counter by the cash register.

"How many trips does Kline guide a week on average?" Mac leaned over to peruse the scribbles.

"A week? It varies." Webb studied the calendar as a minute ticked by. "See, various runs take different times, and a lot depends on the weather and whether participants are experienced or novices." He tapped his finger against his lower lip. Let's say ten to twelve, counting weekends during our busy season."

"Does she have any time off?" Mac turned toward the row of orange life vests in graduating sizes hanging on the end wall.

"Depends on the schedule. If we have no trips scheduled, she can take off. Mondays and Tuesdays tend to be light days."

"So she doesn't have a definite schedule?" Snow clarified.

"Like I said, it varies. I have three full-time guides and three part-time. May I ask why you're interested in Cassie's schedule?"

Snow palmed his hand. "Routine in a homicide investigation. We're looking into all of our vic's known associates. So could you copy her schedule for this month?"

"Not without a court order." Webb smiled and crossed his arms.

"We can obtain a subpoena," Snow smiled too but backed away. "Do you have a fax number?" He took out his spiral notepad to write it down.

He handed them a business card and then returned to the task they'd interrupted. "I'll wait for it. Good day, detectives."

"One more thing. Do your guides ever cover for each other? Take the other's party out?" Mac asked.

He nodded. "Sure, depends on who's here. I don't care who guides which party, as long as a guide covers every booked trip, though Cassie's my most experienced kayaker."

On their way out, Mac lifted a brochure that listed the different runs like Mad Dog and White Horse. The front photo featured a raft with the guide in the back, smiling kids in life jackets lined the sides—all with paddles, water sudsing all around them.

"Looks like fun. Should we book a day trip?" Erin wondered.

Chris shot her a look. "Figure out a way to get her schedule."

"I'll call her, ask her to fax us one." She drew out her cell.

"Did we learn anything helpful just now?"

"I'm not sure, Chris. Let me do some research, see if that play's listed in Irene's repertoire."

"And if it's not? I don't remember it being listed in the playbills, but I didn't read all of them. Did you?"

Erin shook her head, leaving a message for Cassie Kline.

17

As they pulled into the drive at Lisburn Avenue,
people jumped out from behind the new fence, yelling
"SURPRISE!" hoisting wine glasses. Balloons anchored
the corners of a canopy in the spacious back yard,
with tables lined up beneath it. CPD Detectives, Jay
Huddleston; Lee Jeffers and daughter Leah; Sonja and
her husband Ozzie, their kids Olivia and Oren, Danelle
holding Ian with Sydney beside her, standing next to
Savage. Then John Bowie, Mac's CI, stood behind Tanya
Storm, her white shorts and red tee contrasting with her
caramel skin, revealing a toned figure. Erin's sister-in-
law Dreena with her kids Kyle and Kayla standing next
to Debra Stone and her granddaughter, Tamara Bender,
who'd witnessed her mother's murder.

As they climbed out of the car, Erin whispered, "Did
you plan this?"

Chris smiled without comment. "Happy Birthday,
dear." He kissed her forehead.

Hand over her heart, Erin swallowed, eyes filmed as
she scanned the faces of colleagues, family, and friends.
"I'm speechless!"

"HAPPY BIRTHDAY!" The group sang.

"Don't just stand there with your mouth open, let's go
eat," Savage said, propelling everyone toward the tables.

Janelle and Ethan McCoy waited at the buffet under
the covered patio. "Grab a plate, napkin, and silverware,
serve yourselves! Happy birthday, babe." He leaned
over to plant a kiss on his daughter's cheek. Danelle
surrendered Ian to his mother. His pudgy fingers

latched onto her hair. She stood aside, waved her guests through first. Savage grabbed a plate, Danelle and Sydney behind him.

"Ma-ma," Ian chirped. He smelled of baby powder and sunshine. His auburn waves curled in damp wisps at his neck. "Da-da!" Ian lunged for Chris, who tossed him gently in the air.

"Hey, little guy! How's Ian?" He nestled his nose into his son's neck.

"Thank you! You went all out! You shouldn't have! I didn't expect a party." Erin's stomach rumbled. "All I've had today are Krispy Kremes!"

"Nonsense," Janelle returned. "The last year in your twenties? Trust me, you need to celebrate. Come to Nana, baby, let your parents eat!"

"Me eat," Ian said.

"You've already eaten, little stinker! Let's go change your diaper." She whisked him away.

Erica Snow bumped the screen door open with her bottom, carrying a pan of wings. "The hot ones are in the back. Middle ones are BBQ. Front are mild. Be careful!" She sat them down gingerly. "I'll leave the hot pads here to remind you the pan is hot." She placed them beside the mac and cheese.

Chris's dad followed with a stainless-steel condiment server with triple bowls, placing them in a bowl of ice. "Caesar, Blue Cheese, and light ranch." He set a clear platter of raw veggies beside the condiments. "Drinks are in the coolers between the tables."

Ethan returned to the grill and ladled hamburgers, brats, and hot dogs into another warming pan, hauling it to the table beside the plate of sliced American, cheddar, and provolone. Condiments sat next to the cheese.

"I'll have one of everything," Ozzie said.

"Kids, only get what you'll eat," Sonja said. "You can come back for more later." She ladled baked beans and salad onto their plates. "Don't touch that pan. Here, use the tongs." She handed Olivia the utensils to select her own wings.

"I want mac 'n cheese," her brother said, holding his plate out. His sister spooned out a serving. "Here." She dribbled ranch dressing over their greens.

"Think I'll try the pasta salad," Tanya dished out the tri-color spirals with grape tomatoes, olives, chopped cucumbers, cubed salami, and cheese.

"May I have a cheese dog? And a deviled egg?" Sydney asked Danelle, who wrapped a slice of American around a fat, crusted hot dog, snuggled it into a bun and laid it on her daughter's plate.

"OK. Just this once. I'll pretend I don't know what's in them! Please eat your salad too," Danelle responded.

Chief March and Lieutenant Stuart arrived in an unmarked, parked along the drive. March carried a small box over to the gift table, tucked it out of sight.

"You're just in time," Christopher Snow senior called out. "Come eat."

Zachery Fields helped himself to wings, a burger, both pastas, and salad. "What a spread! Happy birthday, partner!" he called out to Erin, who took a seat next to Danelle, with Sydney between her mother and Savage.

Reese looked relaxed for the first time in months, the crow's feet nearly fading in his tan. Smiling at something Sydney said, he gave her a bite of pasta.

She frowned. "What's on it?"

He said, "You mean the dressing? Caesar."

Erin wiggled her eyebrows at Danelle, nodding toward Reese. Yes, her friend nodded in response, smiling. Others joined them beneath the canopy as they filled their plates. Zach pulled a wine cooler from ice and set it before Erin, who nodded her thanks. Then he hefted a bottle of Bud for himself.

Music wafted from a Bose radio on the patio. A covered sheet cake and a dozen cupcakes waited in the shade, candles at ready.

The folks tossed introductions, greetings, questions, and responses around the tables. Murmurs of content and "Um, delicious" rose from time to time. After eating, the kids tumbled away to inspect the games: a wood tic-tac-toe and beanbag toss, jump rope, badminton. A soccer goal stood at the far end of the yard. The girls made a beeline for the swings. Sydney found a child-sized picnic table with wands and bubbles.

"I'll help you open the bubbles," Tamara offered, unscrewing the cap, dipping in the wand, and then handing it to the smaller girl.

"Thanks." Sydney took the green stick and blew at the circle.

Bubbles rode out on the air and burst as they landed. She giggled. Tamara picked up another wand with a longer handle and a compact-size circle, poured the soap into the pan provided and blew one big bubble. "Rainbows in the bubbles!"

Kyle kicked a soccer ball to Oren, who returned the kick. Down the field they sailed, passing it back and forth.

"There's plenty of food. Come back, get seconds!" Ethan ordered. The men rose as one to converge on the buffet line.

"Would you like seconds?" Chris asked the birthday woman.

Erin shook her head. "No thanks. I'm saving room for cake and ice cream."

Chris and Erin's parents served themselves, sat on the patio chairs to keep an eye on Ian and Leah, both exploring the soft blocks and stuffed animals in his playpen.

After devouring cake and ice cream, Chief March stood, clinked his fork against his beer bottle. The adults in the crowd settled as Jeffers slid away to check on her daughter and keep an eye on the kids. Ozzie jogged down the yard to find the boys. September light was draining from the sky, staining the western horizon salmon and dappling blue-grey shadows on the clouds' underbellies.

The Chief toasted Mac's birthday, ambled over to the gift table, and plucked his from the pile. "We will do this officially in dress blues on Monday during a press conference, but this award is long overdue." Opening the box, he withdrew a medal with a ribbon. "Mac, if you'll step forward."

Surprised and nonplussed, she rose to stand beside her boss. "For valor and execution of your job, risking your life and sustaining bodily injury in the line of duty, I commend you for your bravery and commitment to the Carlisle Police force, naming you Policewoman of the Year." He handed her the medal and shook her hand. "The mayor will give you and Officer Castle a plaque on Monday." Cameras and cell phones flashed.

"Thank you," Mac looked at the brass medallion, taken aback. Then to the assembled guests, she said, "I'll share this with my colleagues; this is for you too 'cause we all work hard! The Hawthorne and Sims cases were tough. I'm proud of CPD and humbled. We stop and acknowledge why we leap into the chaos of crime— blood, guts, and bones. We do this because we must protect the innocent, decent citizens. So they and we all can enjoy the sights, scents, and sounds of life like this in relative safety. Thank you." She swallowed and blinked back tears.

Someone started a round of "For She's a Jolly Good Fellow."

Chris, holding Ian, beamed and joined her, as did her informant, John Bowie, formerly Jean du Bourbon, pumping her hand.

Leah on her hip, Jeffers congratulated Mac. "Happy birthday." Turning to Snow, she added, "Thanks for inviting me. Now I have to go to the Woolworth set to mind Reading."

From the patio, Mac's parents rose from their chairs, applauding. Ethan beamed at his daughter's affirmation, which she—or everyone—needed: recognition for a job well done. That someone noticed and appreciated the effort, the toil, and toll on the body and psyche. Police officers courted doubt and battled darkness in themselves and others on the street every day. That anxious catch in the throat, eyes raking over the back seat, assessing the occupants, their states of mind. Making split-second decisions when the driver reached for the glove box or under the seat. Each traffic stop, every confrontation, and takedown spelled danger, perhaps even death. So for cops, suicide and divorce rates were high.

"No, don't get up," Mac said. "I'll come around to you all."

Reese planted a quick kiss on Danelle's lips. His eyes and smile promised more. He passed her his house key. "Shadow and I guard the Woolworth set at night. I'll be home by midnight. You'll be up?"

"Sydney will be sound asleep then." Danelle smiled back, her blue eyes bright with promise. "Yes, and so will you!" she teased as she pocketed his key.

Kyle and Kayla led the perspiring kids back to the table. "We want cake and ice cream too."

"Please," Dreena corrected her daughter. "I'll get it. Come along up to the patio. There are cupcakes, too."

"I'll have a cupcake please," Tamara requested.

"Me, too," Sydney echoed, her cheeks pink with exertion.

Olivia Hamilton waited patiently while the Snow children barged ahead.

Frowning and gesturing for her kids to step back, Dreena served the little ones first, asking, "Olivia, what do you prefer, vanilla, chocolate or strawberry ice cream?"

The girl smiled and proffered her plate, selecting a cupcake capped with chocolate icing. "Strawberry, please."

Oren grabbed a cupcake, "Thanks, ma'am," and streaked past the garden, disappearing into the yard.

"I can serve myself," Kyle helped himself to a cupcake, and then joined Oren.

"Thank you, mom," a chastened Kayla said.

"We serve guests first, ourselves last," Dreena reminded her. "Now go play while the light lasts." She picked up her bottle of green tea, eased onto a patio chair to watch the children.

18

At HQ, Chris balanced the bakery box containing the left-over birthday cupcakes and his lunch bag, leaving the sweets on the conference table in the Murder Room and carried his sandwich and apple to the fridge in the break room. Pouring coffee, Savage turned, bright eyes on his partner. His khakis ironed into knife pleats, his tan windowpane dress shirt starched; his tie matched his espresso eyes. He raised the pot in question.

"Yes, please." Snow thumbed his occipital ridges. He added creamer and one packet of sweetener, stirred with a wooden swizzle stick, and tossed it in the trash. He blew the steam, sipped. "Don't you look like the cat who had the canary."

"*Ate* the canary. Or both! Long night, man?" Reese propped open the door.

Fields swung past, aimed for the coffee pot. "Ah, a fresh pot!" He poured two, ripped open a packet of Swiss cocoa, stirred a third into the second, folded the envelope closed and slid out the door ahead of the other two. "I've got Mac's."

Snow said, "Yeah, Ian's teething, so we take turns walking the floor. Mac finally got him settled around 2 A.M. How about you and Danelle? Got a thing goin'? Did she iron your clothes?"

"I don't kiss and tell. It's been too long." Savage winked. They strode to the incident room where the team gathered for a briefing. "But boy is she limber! She does Yoga."

LT Stuart stood. "The chief's with the mayor at the press conference. He and Mac will join us shortly. Snow, if you and Savage will report on our vic's friends, then we'll move to lab reports." He tapped a stack of faxed copies at his seat. "Special Agent Fleisher sent lab reports from the Stein attack. Fields, join in with your observations. Jeffers is on the Woolworth doc set. When Mac arrives, she can delineate her plans, and the Chief will weigh in."

Snow cleared his throat. "Help yourselves to cupcakes." He pushed the box toward Fields, who peered through the cello. He chose an all-chocolate one, slid the box on. "We brought the tapes, except Ahmed's, so everyone can listen to the interviews. We learned: one, she's abroad, so has an alibi. Two, Cassie Kline has a brother, but I'll let Mac field that one, other than to say I collected his spit and sent it to our lab. (The comment raised eyebrows; no one interrupted.) Ms. Kline told us that Roy lived with her after college graduation before our vic left for London. Third, Frost hinted at the cast's animosity toward Stein's bossiness but offered no concrete evidence." He glanced at his notes.

"However, Ahmed encountered Roy and Kline in the same john at their senior prom," Savage added. "'Lip-smacking,' she said. "But they'd been drinking. Blushing, Roy had squeezed out the door, refreshed her make-up and returned to the dance floor." He let that info settle.

"Roy was a switch-hitter?" asked Fields, sensing a new angle.

"A high-school senior prom over fifteen years ago?" Snow snorted. "Let's verify the facts before we jump to conclusions."

"That explains a lot. Did Kline admit to being a lesbian?" Stuart asked Snow.

"No, she didn't; the subject didn't come up. And none of them mentioned the Bible, religion or any censure or condemnation of anyone." Snow said.

"Well," Savage said, "One, we all experimented in high school. Two, actors experience gay and lesbian relationships; and we should also be accustomed to lesbian and gay couples as they've been with us for eons. That's not news." He shrugged.

"But," Stuart countered, "it could be a motive for murder."

Mac and the Chief entered, both in dress blues with Mac wearing her medal.

March took a chair next to Stuart. Dr. Drummer followed with a stranger in a pink shell under a black jacket, slacks, and heels, a laptop case in one hand, a Starbucks cup in the other. A black purse and messenger bag were slung over her shoulder. Her sienna hair was twisted back from a stark oval face with wide fierce brown eyes, plucked, penciled-on eyebrows and a jutting chin.

"Let me introduce Dr. Cara Ladd. She's with the PA State Police CIAU here to observe and assist." Drummer sat beside her across from Mac, who sank into a chair by the door. Ladd eased her laptop from her bag and laid it on the table, shrugged her purse onto the chair back, nodded to all and leaned back in one fluid motion.

"Welcome. What does the Criminal Investigation Assessment Unit have to offer?" asked the Chief.

"The lab results from Irene Roy's clothes found in the trash barrel at the truck terminal next to the crime scene. We ran DNA samples through CODIS and one bloody print through AFIS and the Forensic Index. No hits, so your perps have no priors but we ID'ed two blood types, A and O. We found two different semen samples in the panties and traces of spermicide, which raises questions. She could've had consensual sex and also been raped because your photos reveal bruising—gloved hands exerting firm pressure on her thighs." She pantomimed the action—hands clutching, pushing. "Holding her in place." Extracting a stack of eight-by-tens, she pointed to the imprints spaced across each thigh.

"She bought her Ralph Lauren tee and Levis off the rack. Macy's, Boscov's, Bon Ton and Marshalls all carry them.

"A rusty, serrated knife was used to cut through her tee; see the hatching?" She stopped for a breath, eyes fixing on each person and slid the photo around.

"Could you ID the samples?" asked the Chief.

"Enough to get a court order for comparison." Ladd pulled a printed form out with a series of marks. At the top, a photo of Lance Reading stared out.

"No surprise there," Fields said. "He's the fiancé."

"Could he be both perp and victim?" asked Snow, pinching the bridge of his nose. "Though his grief felt real, and his injuries landed him in the hospital. Maybe he's not strong enough."

"Improbable but anything's possible," Ladd said.

"And would you agree that the Bible verse suggests judge, jury, and executioner?" Drummer sought a second opinion.

"Yes, it's exceedingly accurate as to the way she was killed—strangled and crucified. The killers are enraged over some perceived slight, jealousy or an Old Testament belief in an eye for an eye. 'Fornicator' is far more formal than 'slut,' so the judgmental, religious element could connote an older or conservative person. Paul addressed his epistle, *Acts,* to a Gentile audience, so . . ." Ladd's voice elided, letting the detectives draw their own inferences.

"And harder to spell. Or the verse could be a ruse to throw us off the real reason," Savage countered. "Despite media coverage of the Reading assault and the Roy homicide, no one has come forward to claim responsibility, send us letters or warnings for Roy's killing."

"Oh, I disagree. There's a strong religious connection here. The killer could suffer from a conduct disorder—a negative, hostile and defiant individual whose violence is escalating." She pointed her index finger into the air. "This behavior would have manifested in childhood as ADHD, but he or she is rebellious, destructive, and has few boundaries."

"Could this person's disability cause frustration, causing him to act out, display nervous tics and lack empathy?" Mac asked.

Snow nodded. "And hostile behavior like spitting?"

"Absolutely," answered Ladd. "That's why pediatricians often characterize conduct disorders as ADHD, prescribe Ritalin, and send the boys, mainly, home for parents and schools to contend with as best they can. There are also Autism and Aspergers Syndrome and Conduct and Oppositional Defiant Disorders to consider."

"All this psycho folderol is interesting," Savage noted, "but a killer's a killer because he had the means, motive, opportunity and wish or drive to kill. Someone pushed his buttons. He loses his temper. Then he gets off on the kill and repeats when the thrill wears off."

"And keeps souvenirs," added Fields.

Ladd shrugged, nodded. "Same difference. Only our semantics differ."

"For reasons unknown, our killers are targeting actors on the Woolworth documentary. We need to focus on the cast, staff, and crew," LT Stuart added. He capped, then dropped the marker and took his seat. "Or anyone who feels threatened and wants the documentary shut down."

"But our case could stem from a childhood or adolescent incident," Mac countered. She clicked her ballpoint. Then raked her curls back, held them in place while she rummaged in her pocket for a clip. Huffed out a sigh. "Frost, Kline, Stein and our vic, Irene Roy, grew up together."

"Well, did your interviews uncover anything new?" the Chief turned to Snow, as his eyes canted to Mac.

"We'll know more when lab results come back on Kerry Kline's saliva, Cassie's brother. He's an enigma: erratic speech, hyper, and anxious at our presence. His behavior shows parallels to Dr. Ladd's profile. He's hiding something. I captured part of our interview on my iPhone." She extracted her cell from her pocket and handed it to Dr. Drummer, who nodded.

He said, "Dr. Ladd, if you'd like to join me? Please excuse us for fifteen minutes while we look at this." Both rose in one accord and left the room. Pitched forward on stilettos, Ladd loped like a giraffe after Drummer.

"There's more. We also interviewed Kline's boss, Eddie Webb. He said she's an Outdoor Adventure Guide, a good employee but refused to give us her work schedule. I emailed her, requesting she fax it to us, which she did." Mac waved the single sheet of paper. "She was working the past three Fridays, but Webb admitted his guides can trade assignments if they have scheduling conflicts. So we need to question the other guides. Question is, do we have probable cause? I think we do, based on her brother's testimony, though we have to sift through it."

"Meaning what?" Savage emptied his mug, clunked it down on the table.

"You need to look at Mac's strange vid," Snow informed them. "I've never encountered anyone like him."

"He quoted phrases from *A Midsummer's Night Dream* that have an uncanny resemblance to Roy's death," Mac said. "He said, 'Maidens call it love in idleness. Fetch me that herb, the flower I showed you once.'"

"Meaning?" Fields glanced around the table. "Am I the only one in the dark?"

"That Roy was drugged with an opiate first. It explains no defensive wounds. If Kline knows that, he either witnessed or participated in her murder."

"Was that in her toxicology results?" Snow asked.

"Only if Dr. Chen asked the lab to test for drugs," Mac returned.

"I think that's routine," Stuart said, paging through the folder, trying to find Roy's tox screen results.

"Great. First the Bible, now Shakespeare." Savage tossed down his pen.

The detectives grumbled and growled.

"Yes, she did," The LT stated. "Traces of plant opiates."

"Poppies!" Fields and Mac piped together.

"All right, people. When Drs. Drummer and Ladd report back, we'll . . ." Stuart started.

"Sorry to interrupt." Sonja sailed into the Murder Room, picked up the remote, thumbed on the power button; the TV sprang to life, a reporter brandishing a mic. "First on the scene, this is Elena Michaels for WHTM. "Behind me, the set for the Frank Woolworth documentary has become a conflagration!" She paused, touching her earpiece. "No, we don't know exactly— perhaps a camera boom or spotlight, but it crashed onto the set, injuring the director JJ Reynolds and," she paused as she consulted her notes, "lead actor Lance Reading."

Pointing to the ambulance pulling away, Michaels exclaimed, "Someone is hurt! The building's going up in flames!" Lights flashed and sirens whined, a pumper weaving around three B &Ws at the scene. Firefighters on a hook and ladder truck peeled back part of the metal roof as plumes of black smoke and sparks shot skyward. An overhead sky cam showed the cast and crew members pouring from the exits where reporters waited.

"Nelson Daly here." He accosted a woman, face smudged, fair hair askew, her singed ankle-length dress hiked up in both hands. "Pardon me, ma'am. What happened in there?"

She shook her head, her lips a pinched line in a pale face, her feet tripping along the macadam.

"All hell broke loose! Elena, back to you." A red-faced Daley commented.

Michaels covered, continued breathily. "Is the cast cursed? This is the third incident that's bedeviled the documentary: first the assault on the actor Lance Reading; the second, the homicide of Irene Roy, who portrayed Jessie, Woolworth's sister. The third, the homicide on *The City Of Paris*. And now, the destruction of the Woolworth store replica." She stepped away from the camera as it panned across the carnage. "As you can see, police and fire crew are too busy to talk with us, so we'll give you a complete report on the six o'clock news. Back to you in the studio—-" Michaels' voice and image disappeared.

"Well, I'll be a son of a bitch." The Chief stood, but Mac and Fields had disappeared, the lead detective signaling for Snow and Savage to go to the hospital.

19

Shadow and Mac knifed through the bystanders, picked their way over the debris, soot and ashes raining down on them until they reached the pumper, waiting to catch Chief Lane Rusk's attention. "Fields, swing around back; snap photos of each person leaving. Help vacate the building if you can." Agonizing minutes ticked by until a firefighter exited the warehouse, pulling his facemask down and waving more men inside. Straining, Shadow surged forward, Mac followed.

Rusk noticed a woman with auburn hair and a K-9 officer near the entrance. Tilting up his face shield, he marched over to her. "Where do you think you're going? Get back—" He pointed, stepped toward her, backing her against his truck. Shiny as a candy apple, it was slewed against the curb. Uniforms plopped down orange cones and rerouted traffic. He reached into the cab, pulled out two bottles of water, sat down beside her on the running board. Handed one over. "The all-clear means people vacated the building. My men can enter— not you. Your dog would burn her paws, for one. Two, only firemen enter until I deem the structure safe."

Mac accepted it, closed her iPhone's camera and nodded her thanks. "Good point. Sit, Shadow. We can't go in yet." She sent the Chief and Sonja text messages, requesting fireproof booties for her K-9 officer.

"Not today at all," Rusk affirmed.

Police officers cordoned off the area with crime scene tape, climbing around hoses snaking everywhere. "Move back, folks. Don't get hurt by flying debris!" Inside, clanging metal collided and fell. The roof buckled in a thunderous din. Tongues of flame licked through a hole in the roof. Water shot from the pumper hose, arcing to meet the flames. Shouted commands, firefighters dragging equipment, showers of soot with smoke, rustling clothes and dramatic exclamations of the media assailed the ears.

"Arson or accident? Or too soon to tell?" Mac asked, knowing the question irritated him. "What can you tell me?"

"Nothing 'till we get inside to investigate, which we can't do until the hot spots are smothered." His face was charred with soot and hair soaked; he shook his head. "Not as bad as it could have been. The stage set's destroyed. The warehouse will need a new roof. At least everyone made it out. But it'll take several days to sift through all this rubble to determine the cause. But no dead bodies. Just let us do our job."

"I have a police officer here and an assault victim to protect," Mac said.

A blonde with a nest of frazzled hair collapsed onto the truck's back step, her long navy dress with pink roses piping the yoke was torn and singed along the hemline. A rip along the right sleeve revealed an angry burn.

"Lee!" Mac peered at her officer. "Are you OK? Do you need a doctor?"

Officer Jeffers waived her offer aside, leaned her head back. "Just a burn. Water?"

Mac pulled a bottle from her backpack and handed it to her. "Sorry, it's not cold."

"It's wet." Jeffers chugged, rivulets running down the corners of her mouth. She stopped when Rusk produced a first-aid kit, cleaned the area, located burn ointment, applying it to her arm. He wrapped sterile gauze around it, taped it. Dropped the tube into Jeffers' lap, nodded. Rusk stood up, replaced his oxygen mask, adjusted the air intake and trudged into the warehouse with a wave of his gloved hand.

"What happened in there?" Mac asked.

Lee picked up the tube. "Something fell from the catwalk or lighting grid, bounced onto the set, then tumbled down onto Reynolds who was running toward us to help. Sparks ignited the curtains then landed on Lance." She gulped more water, inhaled, then exhaled with a whosh.

"Where's Leah?" Mac asked, concerned that the baby might have been injured.

"Not here. Thank God! Mom has her. We'd just finished the birthing scene, the second daughter—Edna Woolworth. We used an anatomically correct robotic doll. JJ will dub in an actual newborn and then Leah later.

"I helped Lance down the steps and out the door; his arm was burned, maybe broken. Who knows what injuries JJ incurred? Smoke was smothering us. Most of the set was wood, so it was engulfed quickly. Rogers carried Banks out. Think everyone's OK." She smiled. "Jackie Frost and the Wells sisters pushed out three racks of costumes. Luckily, most of the film and disks, and editing equipment had been packed up and shipped out. Frost and Latch saved the props they could carry."

"Was anyone on the catwalk or nosing around the set?" Mac questioned. The shepherd jumped, shifted back and forth. "Shadow, sit." Turning baleful eyes on her handler, the canine dropped to her haunches. Mac gave her a treat. "Nothing to do yet, girl."

Jeffers was a police officer trained to notice, to observe, to canvass the area for strangers or danger. She had been through emergency scenarios, had even partnered with area EMT's, state police, HAZMAT, and fire companies in practicing similar incidents. She closed her eyes, concentrating. Opening them, she shook her head. "Not that I observed. We were easing off; today was the last day of shooting the Lancaster scenes. Next, the men are going to Philly to shoot *The City of Paris* for Woolworth's 1890 European tour. JJ will dub the New York harbor in later. I'll shadow Reading; we're to film the 'crossing.'" Her fingers air quoted the word. "JJ said a week should do it. But Leah stays here when the Woolworths move to New York because the girls are older then."

"Is the building being considered a crime scene?" Mac wondered.

Jeffers shrugged. "I need to go to the hospital." Yet she remained seated.

"Snow and Savage have that covered. Go home, get some rest."

Jeffers climbed to her feet. "All right, I'll go get a shower and a bite to eat and then go to the hospital."

"Let's go around back, girl." Shadow leaped to her feet, ready to move. "See what Fields found."

Ken Rogers had enlisted Fields to help move electronic equipment into the white van. Gaping rear doors revealed computers, cable, coiled cords, mics, monitors, modems, stacks of disks, and editing equipment. "Thanks, man." The bear of a man clapped Zach on the back, lumbered into the driver's seat with a wave. The vehicle coughed to life, sped away from the warehouse, its cargo intact.

"I got photos of everyone leaving but switched to video." He handed Mac's Powershot back to her but kept the camcorder.

"Let's go, see what we have," Mac suggested.

She picked up her cell, thumbed HQ. "Ten nineteen," returning to work, weaving past media trucks, reporters rapturous, their voices excitedly calling the plays, the camera panning the destruction.

20

Snow and Savage waited outside the ER's two rooms where nurses tended to Lance Reading and JJ Reynolds, hooked to monitors with oxygen masks covering their noses. One wrapped a BP cuff around Reading's bicep. Applied a wet compress to his left arm. In the second room, PA Patel probed the director's bruised wrist. The detectives observed from the hallway.

An attendant wheeled a bed to the door of Reynolds's room. Savage stopped him. "Where ya headed?"

"MRI." He waited, pushed aside his shaggy hair, met Savage's eyes but waited until the detective stepped aside.

"I'll just walk along," Reese remarked. "Got a few questions for the patient."

The man in the white jacket just shrugged. Both waited for Patel to open the door. She exited, her peach lab coat standing out against dark skin. "Detectives." She nodded, jotting a note, as aides lifted the director onto the mobile bed and wheeled him out. "Let's x-ray his wrist first. Then do a full-body scan. Need to check his ribs. How can I help you, Detective Snow?"

"I need to speak to these men, see if they can relate what happened, how they sustained their injuries."

"Well, Mr. Reading is available. He sustained a second-degree burn on one arm. He's getting oxygen for smoke inhalation. It could have been much worse. He claimed one of your officers saved him, led him out."

Snow, nodding, shouldered his way into the room.

Reading's eyes followed the nurse out of the room. Waited. Monitors beeped; his vitals normal. He coughed. Snow handed him water. Lance sucked slowly from the spiral plastic straw, letting the ice water coat his parched throat. He puffed out a breath. "Guess you want to know—"

Chris nodded. "I do. Spill."

Reading's shoulders hunched. "On the set, we were wrapping Edna's birth scene. I heard a creaking noise overhead and thought of *Phantom of the Opera*. A spotlight fell, bounded towards me. I ducked back. The bedroom curtains caught fire. My shirt was burning." He lifted his left arm. "Next thing, smoke billowed around us. Officer Jeffers batted at the flames, pulled me to the stairs, hustled me down, throwing a wet cloth around my arm. Slapped a wet hanky over her nose and mouth. Hauling me along, she missed the last step; we both fell to the stage. Jeffers dragged me outdoors and shoved me into an ambulance. EMTs went to work." Talking exhausted his reserves; he lay back against the pillows, breathing in shallow puffs.

Snow waited. "You didn't see any strangers? No one on the catwalks overhead?"

Reading's head moved back and forth—no. Savage slid into the room, back against the wall.

"All cast and crew accounted for—before the fire started?"

Reading shrugged. "We were focused on the birthing scene. But Banks rolled and skidded across the room first. I froze—the fire engulfed the stage, the smoke smothering. Your officer has lightning reflexes. Tell her thanks."

"You can tell her yourself. She's going with you; she's your shadow for the duration, and when you guys go back to New York. Or until we catch the killers. How's your arm?"

Reading nodded. "Hot. I'll live. If not for Lee, I'd be far worse. I might be dead. We're lucky to have escaped.

We're done here. Can't say I'll miss Carlisle. It feels like we're jinxed."

Snow nodded. "Most of the crew, staff, and actors have left, but we're still investigating assault and homicide cases. You saw nothing before the fire erupted?"

"No, well, yes, there was one thing. I looked up, saw a shadow. Then smelled smoke, the spotlight coming at me, and then Lee batting out the flames." He shifted his weight, resting his burned arm across his body. "Then a red dot."

Savage came off the wall. "You mean like a cigarette? Or flashlight or laser?"

Snow added, "Someone was up there."

"Unless it was a trick of the light careening toward me, shifting shadows."

"What's next on your agenda?" Snow wanted to know.

"We're to meet in Philly on the oceanliner tomorrow to film my first trip to Europe." His eyes lit. "*My* first trip to London. An advance team's securing the stalls in Piccadilly that will be converted to 1920s shops for our documentary. I'll buy porcelain and china cups and crockery. Then we'll sail across the channel and take a train to Germany where I'll purchase Dresden china, Christmas ornaments, and toys. Then fly back and shoot the New York City scenes. Buying our house and building the Woolworth Building—the only skyscraper in America fully financed by the owner's money."

"Well, thanks for your time. We appreciate your help." Snow left a card on the tray table. "Call if you remember anything that will assist our investigation." His pager vibrated. "Snow. Yes? We're on our way. Let's go." He tapped Reese's arm and strode out the ER entrance/exit. "Cassie Kline turned up at HQ, mad as a wasp."

Savage put in the ten-nineteen call, heading back to HQ where Mac, Shadow, and Fields were already in the box with a red-faced Kline who was breathing heavily in the interview chair facing the window. "Why are you going behind my back to interrogate my brother? Kerry's hyper enough as it is. He'll be wired for weeks because you dropped by unannounced. He follows a strict routine, which you upset." Her peripheral vision noted Shadow lying beside Mac.

"Actually, we were looking for you," Mac informed her. "He was very helpful, communicating in metaphors rather than facts." She leaned back, away from the suspect, crossing a leg over the opposite knee, her Dockers swishing—a non-threatening pose.

"You have my work schedule. Couldn't you see I was on the river?" She fisted her hands to her hips, arms akimbo, but her shoulders dropped slightly. Damp hair tied back in a stubby tail led credence to her words. Her breathing slowed; red faded from her cheeks. Then she propped her arms on the table. "What do you mean, he was very helpful?"

"He told us Roy lived with you before she flew to England to join the Royal Shakespearean Company."

Kline nodded. "That's no secret. I told you that. Yes, for about two months."

"And she slept with you?" Fields interjected, his fingers grazing his jaw.

Kline blushed, red creeping up her neck. She shrugged, eyebrows raised. "So what? Well, my brother has the only other bedroom; the third we converted to an office. Don't think there are any laws against that."

"Were you angry that she left you? That she met and was engaged to marry Lance Reading?" Fields followed up.

"No. Why should I be? I was happy for her. Last time we talked, she seemed more settled, more secure in her current setting. She took a minor part to be with Reading, but that's her business. I'm not her mother. My hands are full enough with my brother."

"Where are your parents? Do they help?" Mac wondered.

Kline puffed out a breath. "Mother's a Jekyll and Hyde when she's off her meds. A bi-polar dictator, a bitch on wheels. Think she's on husband number three; they moved to New York. Who knows where my father is; he left when we were tots. Can you imagine working all day and coming home to bedlam? He couldn't deal with her issues and Kerry's disabilities too."

"Do you resent that the responsibility for your brother falls on you?" Mac asked.

At that point, Kline leaned back, mirroring Mac's stance. She smiled. "Not at all. He's working, earning his keep; he's good company, if hyper, excitable and unpredictable. Moody, yes, but entertaining. And I won't institutionalize him; that would break his spirit. He already sees conspiracies everywhere. He said when the police came, it was two against one."

"What can you tell us about *A Midsummer's Night's Dream?* Did Roy every have a part in that play?" Fields tucked his thumbs in this back pocket.

"Yes, we did that our senior year in high school. Our English and Drama teachers had us modernize the language but keep the iambic pentameter. The Art Department designed the set—all ethereal and dreamy with dry ice. Kerry helped design and stage the woods scenes. They talked of nothing else for six weeks. Strolling around, he helped Irene memorize her lines."

"Did your brother play Puck?" Mac asked.

"No, he prompted the actors their lines when necessary, so he knew the lines. He worked on the set, went to rehearsals, and the whole school went to the play. Irene played Tatiana. Can't remember who played the duke. Maybe that's when the acting bug bit her. Why? What does that have to do with her death?"

Mac ignored the question. We're following all lines of inquiry. Your brother quoted several of Puck's lines. Did you do any Biblical miracle or morality plays?"

Kline shook her head, paused before answering. "No. But we saw several at the theater. Kerry liked *Joseph's Amazing Dream Coat.* He liked musicals; music calms him." Her eyes drifted away, then returned to the detectives. "Well, I think music has universal appeal; it lifts us up. It calms and centers us, eases our stress or lets our minds take a vacation from the routine."

"Anyone in your group religious?" Fields fiddled with his pen, his hand hovering over his notepad.

Again, Kline shrugged. "That was so long ago. We all went to neighborhood churches and synagogues. The Roys often invited Kerry and me to the Methodist Church. They were like a "Leave it to Beaver" family— normal, you know? Celebrating the holidays, going to school functions, making cookies and having birthday parties. We went to Dutch Wonderland, toured an Amish farm and attended the American Music Theater's Christmas show. For Kerry and me, getting a decent meal or having clean clothes for school were anomalies. We were elated to be invited and enjoyed occasional outings with the Roys. Still, I fail to see what this has to do with Irene's murder."

"So you weren't in Carlisle Friday, September fourth? Or the tenth?" Mac asked.

"No, I told you that already." Kline crossed her arms.

"Are you willing to strip?" asked Mac.

Kline and Fields blushed at the question. He stood up. "I'll leave you at this point and send in one of the female officers."

"Why?" Kline jumped up. Shadow shifted.

"Stay, girl. I'm looking for a tattoo." Mac rose, shut the door behind her partner. "Do you have any?"

Tanya Storm eased into the room.

"I do." Kline turned around and lowered her shorts. Right below her waist, a tiny kayak paddle was cresting three wavy blue lines.

She pulled her tee shirt over her head, eyes straying to the observation window. "Could I move to the corner?" Mac nodded. Kline unhooked her bra, turned around. Besides her freckled back, no other design inked her torso, except for one ankle, which had three more wavy blue lines.

McCoy signaled for Kline to dress. "Thanks for cooperating."

"Do you mind telling me what you're looking for?" Kline queried.

"Sorry, I can't relate information about an on-going case." Mac hated spouting the cliché, but she was following a hunch and had seen enough of Reading's body to know he wasn't wearing the tattoo she was looking for, the one that correlated to Roy's key tat.

Kline dressed. "Are we finished?" Her eyes canted to the dog, who watched her.

"One more question. Do you know why your brother would quote a line about giving a maiden a potion from a flower? I noticed poppies, St. John's Wort and lavender, among other plants in your back yard."

Kline laughed. "I wouldn't know. That's Kerry's bailiwick. He tends the yard, flowers, medicinal plants, and herbs. Then makes infusions and other concoctions. As long as it keeps him occupied, I have no objections. He's used mint to flavor our tea, drapes rosemary over pork loins, and thyme over nearly everything else. I doubt he knows how to harvest opiates. Wouldn't it take more than we have? And as you said, the poppies were in the yard, so not crushed or distilled—right?"

Mac handed her a card. "Yes, that sounds reasonable. Please call me if you or Kerry can remember anything pertinent to our investigation."

Kline glanced at the card, stuck it in her back pocket of her cargo shorts. "Am I free to leave?" She glanced at the shepherd, hesitating.

Mac opened the door and motioned her out. "Thanks for cooperating. Shadow, stay."

"Like I have a choice. Next time, call first if you need to talk to us," Kline said as she strode through the door and out of the building.

Fields walked back in. "So, you buy her answers?" He parked his hip against the scarred wood table and braced himself, his arms on either side, palms down.

"No reason not to," Mac responded.

"But?" he countered.

"That's not the whole story. She knows more than she's telling. Did you note the hesitations?"

"About her brother?"

"About everything. Like she was censoring her thoughts or sifting and sorting out what to tell, what to keep to herself."

"But you said she didn't have a heart tat," Zach observed. "But she could be protecting her brother."

"Yes, she has two tattoos but not the one I'm looking for. I could be wrong about that hunch. Good point about Kerry Kline. So we keep searching. Let's go over the fire footage you shot."

Zach righted himself and followed her to Murder One.

21

They watched the ten-minute fire footage on the camcorder a dozen times. Individuals stumbled out of the rear exit, coughing, fanning smoke away and squinting against the sun's glare. Smoke snaked out the open warehouse door. Water and fire retardant spewed over and down the metal building, leaving a dirty charcoal residue in their wake. Fields identified each person as he or she exited, though Mac recognized most of them. The white van blocked the view momentarily, so Fields backed his vehicle up to get out of the way. Rogers opened the van's rear door. The camera wobbled as Fields, one-handed, helped Rogers load the video equipment. Her flame-red hair a beacon, the props-buyer Latch and costume-designer Frost pulled a rack of clothes clear. The Wells sisters pushed a dolly stacked with hatboxes and one labeled make-up. Legs scurried from the yawning black mouth, a raincoat covering the person's head and shoulders.

"Stop! Who's that?" asked Mac.

"Haven't a clue. Can't see her, can we?" Fields rubbed his tired, dry eyes. "Got any eye drops? My eyes feel gritty. You saw who came out the front?"

"How do you know it's a her? Oh, knit pants and narrow ankles. Yeah, Banks flew out first, and then Jeffers, Reading, and Reynolds. Then Rusk exited and his men rushed in. Who's unaccounted for?"

Fields ran down the list of crew, actors and director. "That's all."

"Doesn't explain that extra person. What's that on her ankle?" The hair on Mac's neck rose; goosebumps prickled her scalp.

"Could be a tat." Fields zoomed in but the resolution wasn't good enough to show the ankle. "Or maybe an anklet of some sort."

"Then it would gleam, wouldn't it?" Mac stood, rolled her shoulders to ease the tension and paced. "It's dark. Like ink. This could be our killer."

"Do you think a woman could have lifted, held and tied our Vics to trees and a ship's door? I don't." Fields stood and stretched. "I don't know about you, but—" His stomach rumbled.

"If she had help. You're hungry." Mac checked her watch. "All right. Go grab sandwiches and bring them back. I want Huddleston to look at this video, see if he can blow up this frame and get a better view of the woman's ankle. "I'll take turkey on whole wheat with mayo or a veggie wrap and green tea." She pulled a ten out of her pocket, handed it over. Huddleston?"

"BLT club and a regular fountain Coke. You're buying. I'll rewind and run this again," the computer guru offered. Mac tried to give Zach another ten, but he waved her off.

Fields hustled back twenty minutes later, drinks in a cardboard tray, sandwiches, fries and condiments in bags. Shadow crowded in, sniffing. Zach fed her a fry. Then another.

"Enough," Mac said. "Shadow, sit." The shepherd sat, and then lowered herself to the floor, eying Fields for another morsel.

Over lunch, they crowded around Huddleston's computer and watched the video. At the last, upper body hidden by a black raincoat thrown over the head, legs garbed in black knit ran out and past the camera.

"There, stop!" Mac cried, forgetting lunch. "Can you zoom in on the ankle?"

"No need to yell." Huddleston rubbed his ear, his pink scalp showing through thinning strands of platinum hair and pale skin. He zoomed, enlarged the ankle.

"Sorry. We're just desperate for a clue," Mac whispered.

"Definitely a tat," Fields observed. "But it's too fuzzy to make out."

"Can you sharpen the image?" Mac asked. Sipped her tea.

"It could be a blotch of burnt debris from the fire stuck to her skin," Huddleston observed.

"Wouldn't she have brushed that off? Could be a burn." Fields munched on his fries.

"Then she'd be hopping up and down. Who's unaccounted for?" Again, Mac identified cast members, ticking them off her fingers. "Reading, Banks, Jeffers, Whelan, the teenager Charles . . . Her, you said her."

"That's it—the cast and the crew." Fields said. "The Wells sisters, Latch, Frost . . ."

"And the other suspects," Huddleston added, stroking his goatee. "The Klines, the other girls in the photo, except the one who's abroad."

Savage leaned against the doorjamb, chewing a toothpick. "Rachel Stein."

Mac grabbed her phone, dialed William Fleisher, the FBI Agent in charge of the Docks, who picked up on the first ring. "We need to talk to Rachel Stein. Is she still at the Naval Hospital?"

"No, she's been discharged," Fleisher, answered. "I can arrange a meeting but not at the shipyard; it's too dangerous."

"She didn't go home?" Mac asked, writing as she spoke.

"Negative. Too risky. The assailants are still on the streets. We have a safe house near Media—a ranch in a suburban neighborhood. I'll email you the address. Let's say 3 P.M. Can you make it then?"

Mac checked her watch. "We'll be there." Thumbed 'end.' "Let's go. Fields, drop in March's office, let him know where we're headed, and I'll call Snow. You drive. She collected the folder and stuffed it in her tote. "Need to stop by my office for my recorder and weapon and take Shadow home. Come, girl."

"If you're done, may I finish your sandwich?" Savage ambled over, picked up half of the turkey sandwich; half of it disappeared in one bite.

"Sure," Mac rolled her eyes but scooted back for her drink.

Once on the Turnpike, Fields popped the bubble on the dash, and the vehicle's lights strobed, "Just for shits and giggles." He smiled as vehicles peeled off onto the shoulder to give them room.

Mac frowned. "Just stay in the left lane then." She keyed the address into the GPS. When finished, she dialed Chris, left a message on voicemail about their ten-twenty. "We're doing a follow-up interview with Rachel Stein for a complete timeline of her activities, a better description of her assailants and movements in the last two weeks. May be home late. Can you see to Ian? Shadow's at home too."

The ranch crouched thirty feet off the bend in the cul-de-sac in an older neighborhood that had seen better days. Blinds were drawn. Broad, leafy oaks and maples shaded the red brick house; shadows played along the drive and sidewalk—humped and cracking in places by overgrown tree roots. Fields eased the unmarked Ford into the crumbling drive behind an old Chevy sedan. Bird dropping sprayed across one of the black shutters. A clump of Indian corn hung on the faded black door.

Mac rang the doorbell. A man in a dark suit looked out the middle rectangle in the door. Eyes panned across the front lawn. The door opened the length of the chain, weapon down by his side. "Let's see some ID."

Both detectives hiked their shields to eye level, waiting.

"Not that this looks suspicious," Fields buzzed in her ear.

Mac smiled tightly but said nothing until they entered. They stood on a square of tan linoleum. Beige carpet covered the living room floor; a table lamp separated flowered arms chairs at the front of the bay window with magazines in the rack underneath. Over a worn saddle sofa, a wooded landscape with a meandering stream was the only art on the wall. The trees' leaves flamed red, gold and pumpkin. To the left, an arch led to a kitchen/dining area. Bedroom doors opened along the narrow hallway.

"It's clear. Carlisle detectives here to see you." The man in the suit called down the hall. A woman in black leggings and a black belted tunic stepped out and eased toward them. A stylist had straightened, layered and threaded caramel highlights through Stein's hair. She'd lost at least twenty pounds. The bump in her nose had been smoothed out. Her make-up applied to widen her eyes. In her pierced ears, she wore simple silver hoops, and three bangle bracelets circled her left wrist.

"Rachel Stein?" Mac asked. The woman had had a complete makeover. But she recognized brown-black eyes with no pupil demarcation—flat orbs set close together, giving her a stern, pinched look.

"The changes were Agent Fleisher's idea. Thought I'd be harder to recognize if I looked different. What do you think?" she turned out her palms in question, revealing nail scars.

"Why don't we all have a seat?" asked the stranger in black.

"We'd like to ask you a few questions about your whereabouts the last two weeks. When did you leave the hospital?" Mac withdrew her recorder, entered the required data for an interview.

"Don't answer that." The man said. He'd holstered his Sig.

Mac turned to him. "Mister, I don't know who you are, but I'd suggest you not impede a homicide investigation. Ms. Stein is not only a victim but also a material witness who might have some significant information that may help us with our case. Are you her lawyer?"

He shook his head no. His chin jutted out, and his head was stippled with dark hair—as if he'd shaved it but let it grow back.

Mac faced Stein as she asked, "Are you willing to answer questions about your assault and our homicide?"

"Yes." Stein slid back against the sofa and asked her guard, "Would you mind getting us water?" Her eyes switched to Mac and Fields. "Or would you all prefer coffee or tea?"

"Water's fine, thanks," Mac answered.

Hesitating, his eyes roved to the detectives.

"I'll be fine. I know them. They're homicide detectives." Stein responded. The stranger acquiesced with a slight nod.

"OK. Will you return to the Woolworth's documentary crew?" Fields tried another tact.

"Agent Fleisher thinks it's too risky to appear on the set, given the recent attacks and the fact that the killer is still at large, but I sent Ken Rogers, Jackie and Larissa to London to hire extras and line up the shops where Frank will buy the pottery and glassware. Besides, Fleisher wants me to stay under the media's radar." She stood, stepped over to a computer on the dining room table. She tapped 'return;' the computer-animated storyboards popped up on the computer.

"Here, you can see Lance sailing on the ocean liner to England." She stood, refreshed her computer. *The City of Paris* plowed through rough seas, while Lance hovered over the commode in his cabin's bathroom. "In the next scene, wearing a wine robe over pajama bottoms, he's writing letters to his managers in the states by the light of an oil lamp bolted to the table."

"Reminds me of *The Titanic*. What happened before this?" Mac asked.

Stein waited while her bodyguard handed bottled water to the detectives, who nodded their thanks, eyes still on her computer. "The servants packed three trunks while three little girls 'help' Papa pack. Here, back it up. And before that, he started his candy line. Met with a Mr. Arnould to taste test the ones the candy maker made for a nickel a quarter-pound. The family had moved to Brooklyn by then." Mac and Fields watched as Lance promised his blonde beauties, Lena, twelve, Edna, seven and Jessie, four, to bring back dolls for them.

Then you'll go home?" Mac asked.

Again, a negative headshake. "I need to book a flight to Germany where Lance goes next to buy china, toys— the dolls and glass balls, the Christmas ornaments, a first for his dime stores. The others will join me to find an historical village or convert one to JJ's specs."

"Thanks for the water," McCoy said, Fields nodded.

Stein smiled thinly, her thin crooked lips more of a grimace.

"Can you remember anything more from the night you were attacked?" Mac pitched a softball to bring Stein's attention back to focus.

"Nothing besides what I told you guys before. There were two masked men dressed all in black carrying a black gym bag with them. Surprised me coming out of the captain's cabin. I'd just finished decorating, turned to lock the door. It was dark, late, maybe eleven-thirty. I'm trying to forget the rest." She shuddered.

"We understand it's traumatic. But they rushed you? Made no noise?"

"No, I didn't hear them until their feet hit the deck. So they must have had a boat because the ship was anchored offshore. They rushed at me, fists swinging. I fought back, and then WHAM—the thin one socked me in the face; the other punched me in the back. I must have passed out."

"And when you awoke?" Fields asked.

"My brother, cousin yelling. Dialing 911. The Coast Guard boarded the ship. Cop car sirens were wailing, tires screeching at the dock. Felt like they hammered me. I fainted again when they took the door off its hinges." She shook her head, sipped water, her eyes gazing out the window. "Then woke up in a strange hospital disoriented, wondering what the hell happened."

"Do you know why you were targeted?" Mac queried.

Stein brought her eyes back in. "Someone is sabotaging the Woolworth documentary—that's obvious. First Lance, then Irene . . ."

"Were you aware of the fire that burned the set?" Zach asked.

"Yes. It was on the news. Did everyone get out? Was everything destroyed?" Concerned eyes locked on Mac's.

"Everyone evacuated safely. Everything along the right side of the warehouse survived. Why would someone sabotage the documentary? From what I've seen of the outtakes, it looks very interesting, especially the historical detail."

Stein shrugged. "Maybe he or she doesn't want it aired. Or someone has something to hide."

"Or someone had a personal agenda—getting rid of Irene Roy," Fields interjected.

"How do you figure? Three of us were attacked." Stein frowned, her attention focused on a loose thread. She picked at it, snapped it off.

"Roy's the only one dead," Fields stated. "She was the target. And now we're looking into her background. We found out you and she roomed together at NYU. So you have a history with her you hadn't mentioned. Why hide it?"

"No one asked. We roomed together for one semester freshman year because we knew each other. But she was unorganized—messy, gone all hours, unfocused and needy. She wanted my help with difficult assignments. And asked me to read others' lines so she could practice hers. Or she wanted help to interpret her character. Walk her through the sets first. Could I do her laundry with mine? Buy her a sandwich? Loan her twenty bucks? Borrow my necklace? It became too much. So I asked her to move out."

"Did you have a relationship with her?" Mac wondered. The guard coughed, shook his head while a blush crept up Stein's neck.

"We were roommates. Period." Her eyes roved to her guard.

"So you shared jewelry? Anything in particular?" Mac zeroed in.

Stein blinked, eyes widening. "What? No, I don't think so."

"Where were you Thursday, September tenth?"

"With the crew—at dinner in the hotel. Then we went to Market Cross Pub for a while. Then I returned to the set with Larissa to go over the props we needed for the next's day's shoot. We're—the cast and crew were on a strict timetable."

"Did you sleep at the house on Pomfret Street that Reynolds rented?" Fields' pen hovered over his spiral-bound notebook.

"No. I slept on a couch at the Warehouse; we finished late and I like to start early." Her mouth curled into a crooked smile. "It has a nice enough bathroom."

"You saw or heard no commotion either inside or out back of the warehouse?" Fields followed up. Stein shook her head side to side.

"Do you know anyone who had personal animus toward Irene Roy?" Mac asked.

Stein shook her head no again. She sipped water. She caught stray drops with the back of her hand. Rolled her shoulders. Mac laid an 8 X 10 photo of the girls by the pool on the coffee table, turned it around for Stein to see. "Do you think it's a coincidence—you, Irene, Jackie Frost and Cassie Kline are together? Childhood friends? And three of you are together again on this project?"

"Well, I hired Jackie, so that's no surprise. JJ hired Irene when he brought Lance on board. I've worked with JJ on his last three projects, though this has the biggest budget—and it's the best, seeing as it'll be aired on TV. Look, I'm getting tired . . ." Her eyes beseeched her guard's.

He moved forward. "We're done here. Call her lawyer if you have any more questions."

Mac thumbed the recorder off and the detectives stood. "One more thing." She took a folded paper and thrust it toward Stein. "We have a subpoena to search you."

The guard seized the document, opened it. Then nodded. "Let me call Agent Fleisher." He stepped into the kitchen.

"No, that's OK." Stein peeled her leggings off. "My tat's gone."

"I'll step outside." Fields trotted out the front door, waited with his back to the women while scanning the neighborhood, which had a fifties vibe. No children played in the fenced-in yard. He heard a dog bark. A breeze lifted the leaves. A lone jogger, head down, passed the house.

Mac took out her camera, but once Stein had bared her legs and then her tee, there was nothing to photograph. "What happened to your ankle?" She pointed to the faded blue marks that resembled a hashtag.

"Oh, I had an old tattoo removed—an old college flame."

"What was it?" Mac wondered.

Stein pulled her tunic and legging back on with some difficulty. "Initials of a married college professor. You said one more question. That's it. I'm exhausted." She gained her feet, retreated down the hall.

Mac laid another subpoena on the glass end table. "We're also searching your apartment and your parents' home for evidence linking you to Roy. Thanks for your time." Stein froze in place. For the moment, Mac kept mum about her suspicions regarding the Warehouse fire.

The guard approached, muscling into Mac's personal space.

Mac put her palm up. "We're just leaving. Please tell Agent Fleisher thanks for cooperating."

On the way to the unmarked vehicle, Mac leaned close to her partner and whispered. "How did she know we were looking for an ankle tattoo?"

"And?" Fields asked.

"She had it removed. Must have been incriminating." She thumped the door with her fist as Fields slipped behind the wheel.

"Or she's telling the truth. Another dead end." Zach keyed the ignition, backed out, and turned the SUV west, toward home. Signs led them to the turnpike.

"Not necessarily. She froze when I left the other subpoena."

"So she's worried we'll find something?" he asked.

"Maybe." Mac checked her watch and then speed-dialed Chris to tell him she'd be home for dinner, left a message on voicemail.

WHAM! With no warning, an F150 truck slammed against the CPD Escape, the grating of metal, the screech of tires, the sudden bombardment of bass from its radio thundering. The gunning engine growled.

"What the hell?" yelled Mac. "Did you cut him off?" She craned her neck to see the driver as Zach fought the wheel, hand over hand, trying to keep the vehicle straight. The truck rammed them again, jamming the smaller vehicle against the railing, the scraping metal sparking and crunching.

"BRAKE! BRAKE!" she yelled. Punching nine-one-one, she exclaimed, "Officers down. Road rage incident on the PA Turnpike just outside of Media. Near mile marker—" She didn't see one. "Black F150, Pennsylvania plates, Bravo, Delta, Waco—thirteen ten."

Fields stood on the brake pedal; the truck veered into their path and slowed as another vehicle rammed them from behind. The Escape broke through the guardrail, hovered airborne, then bumped down the embankment; the front wheels caught, and the vehicle rolled. The windshield spidered; the driver's window shattered; a thousand shards spewed over them. Mac's arm flew up to guard her face; then her hand shot to the roof as they rolled. Her cell slipped away. Zach's head snapped against the headrest, banged against the grab bar, then tipped forward. Front and side airbags aimed a one-two punch in their faces first and then their sides, knocking them out.

Cars slowed but then drove on. Another vehicle stopped, a soldier in desert camo scrambled to see if he could help the upside-down, unconscious occupants. He pulled a knife to cut the jammed seatbelt, catching the auburn-haired woman and carrying her from immediate danger. Smoke billowed from the engine. EMT's pulled along the shoulder. One EMT got a pulse on the driver while another pulled a stretcher out of the ambulance.

"Gotta get them out before the fire catches the engine or gas tank," a bystander yelled across the road.

Fire trucks, another ambulance, and black and whites materialized, sirens wailing, lights whirring and blinking. Orange cones marked the accident scene. A uniform lit flares. Firemen doused the smoking vehicle with fire retardant as EMT's loaded their cargo and tore away, siren blasting.

22

Erin woke in a quiet, white familiar world where
monitors beeped, computers recording her blood
pressure and other vitals. Tethered to an IV, she
moaned, "Not again." Her body ached; her head pulsed,
pain tattooed along her neck and drummed into her
temples. Swollen eyes squinted at a fading opaque light,
though a considerate person had drawn the shade.
Overhead fluorescent rods hummed. To her right, a grey
curtain blocked her view. Eyes slid left, her husband
stared in the distance, his fingers worrying his chin.
He swiveled, noticed her squinting and dragged a silver
chair to her bedside. Put a chocolate shake in her right
hand. A cast enclosed her left wrist.

Snow pushed the button on the recorder in his
shirt pocket."Thank God, you're OK. Well, besides the
concussion, bruised ribs, lacerations, and a broken
wrist. Your nine-one-one call came through. A soldier,
firefighters, and EMTs got to you first. We're scanning
security cams; we'll find the driver who ran you off the
road! A Good Samaritan also called in his classic car
plates, but they were stolen. Still, we have an APB out
on the F150—photos out to all media. Notified garages
in the tri-state area to report right front fender and
bumper damage when the driver tries to get it repaired.
Plus, you have full media coverage."

She drew the velvety goodness through the straw.
"Thanks for this. Feels good on my raw throat. How's
Zach?"

"Good, good. He has staples in his crown from hitting the headrest and grab bar, a busted ankle and slipped disc, but he'll live."

"Where's Ian?"

"Ian's fine. He's with my parents." He pulled her into a hug. "Brand new Escape's totaled, so March is fuming, but he's not mad at you this time. What happened? Was it road rage?"

"I thought so at first, but when I got a peek of the driver, I'm not sure." Mac eased back against the pillows. Her free hand massaged her temple, then neck—muscles pulled taut. A thread of heat stitched down her right side. She felt hands on her trapezius, massaging gently. Her shoulders relaxed a little.

"Can you identify him?" Snow dropped to the seat.

"He was wearing a light brown wig and had painted oversized freckles across his face and the bridge of his nose; they were too big to be natural. Dark eyes alive with adrenaline or high on something." She shut her eyes to visualize the incident. "He came alongside, then steered into us. Once, twice—pushing us against the guardrail. I yelled to Zach to brake. He did, but the trucker pulled in front of us. Can't remember the rest. Then a guy rammed us from behind." She thumbed the orbicular ridge of her eyes. Bright rods flickered across her vision. "And then we went airborne, rolled when we landed. Airbags exploded."

"I've got a sketch artist coming. Between you and Zach, we should get a visual likeness we can give the media—even if he's disguised."

Mac nodded without comment. *The man's physical features would be the same: that aquiline nose, long face, and scruffy facial hair. Kind of like the kid in the 'Scooby Do' cartoon.*

The door swung open, an aide pulled back the curtain. "Good morning people. Rise and shine. Another day, another dime." He smiled. His brown hair was corralled with netting. "I've got breakfast." His eyebrows arched at her milkshake then pivoted, trotting to the hall where a dolly of trays waited.

"Zach!" Mac squealed.

"Mac!" her partner returned. The ER doctor had shaved Zach's head; his eyes were purple bruises, and his cheeks were scraped raw. Mean metal clips closed the exposed scalp, which was red and swollen.

"The Chief wanted you together so we could guard you easier, though CRMC raised a stink. There's a bed vacant across the hall now. We'll have you moved later." Snow breached the divide to shake Fields' hand. "Can you remember what happened? I want to record your version of events." He tapped the recorder in his pocket.

The aide slid the trays laden with scrambled eggs, toast, jelly, and coffee with creamer and a packet of sweetener onto their tables. "Happy trails." A perfunctory smile tipped his lips. Away he flew on his rounds to the patients capable of eating—their aches, stitches, broken, bandaged limbs and diseases a reminder of both human frailty and the body's strength to repair itself with medical intervention. And time. They were the lucky ones—still breathing.

Mac picked at her eggs as she listened to her partner's recitation of events. Panic froze his limbs as he tried to keep the vehicle on the road. How the impact jarred him; how the airbags erupted as they rolled, blood blinding him. Yes, he thought it was road rage. No, the other driver didn't know they were cops. No, he didn't stop.

A sketch artist arrived, a passable likeness emerging as both detectives described the assailant, though Mac provided more detail. "No, the nose is longer, thinner—straight as a knife. Eyes are wider, set farther apart. The wig had a shaggy cut with straight bangs kind of like John Denver's."

"Detective Fields?"

"I only remember wild eyes, white-knuckled hands on the steering wheel."

"Any tats on the knuckles?" The pencil hovered. "Wearing rings?"

"No, just large pale white hands."

"Ears have lobes?" The artist asked Mac. He wiggled his own.

"I don't know. The wig covered the tops." She touched her own ears, connected to her neck; she had no detached earlobes! She shut her eyes and turned her head. "His head swiveled toward us. An earring glinted in his left ear." Shrugging, Mac sighed. "That's all I remember. No, wait. He wore black—a long-sleeve knit tee."

"That's good!" The artist widened the eyes, added shading. Changed pencils, colored in the top black. "Crewneck?"

Fields added, "And strings hanging down, so it had a hood; he wore a light knit sweatshirt instead of a tee."

"That it?" Both detectives nodded. "Did this top have a zipper? Both detectives shrugged.

"Thanks, Chuck." Snow said. "Get it on the air before the noon news cycle. With luck, someone may recognize him or the F150. Any idea how many of those vehicles are on the road?"

Chuck strode out the door, his artist pad tucked under his arm.

Zach volunteered, "We can limit those to the tri-state area with recent right front fender damaged. If I had my laptop, I could look it up. It's on my desk."

"Great work, guys!" Snow nodded, smiled at his injured detectives with a thumb up. He kissed his wife's forehead. I've gotta get on this. Oh, how did your interview with Stein go?"

"She's changed—lost weight, new hairdo, clingy black knit clothing. Big improvement, if you ask me," Fields commented.

"Yeah, I wouldn't have recognized her on the street. Didn't want to talk about Roy—seemed defensive, and her guard muscled his way into the conversation. I recorded—wait, did anyone get my purse? What happened to my iPhone and recorder? And my tote with the files and photos?"

"Here. An EMT brought your purse along on the stretcher; guess we'll find the phone smashed. Don't know about the files. You should be able to recover them if they're still in the vehicle. We had the Escape towed to Impound; McKenna's team is examining it. And the highway patrol has men on the crime scene, collecting evidence. The lab's analyzing the black paint. They'll send us a report by tomorrow morning."

"OK. Let's get on it." Mac tossed back the thin blanket, swung her legs down. The room spun; hands gently pushed her back, hoisted her legs back onto the bed. Covered her. "Oh, the plates were 'BDW thirteen ten.'"

"Yeah, they were stolen. And you're not going anywhere until the doctor discharges you. Stay put; watch the twelve o'clock news on Channel Eight; they're more likely to cover it unless the other crews identified you as CPD detectives. Officer Storm's outside. Call me this afternoon. We'll see. Fields, we'll give you a lift home. You're both on medical leave until further notice."

"I'm fine." Zach fingered his staples and winced. "Scalp's a little tender." He patted his arms, moved his legs and rotated his ankles. "Ah left ankle smarts." He lifted the covers, swung his leg out. "Definitely sprained, maybe worse. But I think I'm in one piece." Wincing and leaning left, he put a hand to his side. "Ah, my ribs."

"Like I said, stay put. That's an order. Mac, I'll see if McKenna recovered your cell and files and swing by later after work unless you call first. You sure as hell yanked somebody's chain." Snow pivoted, shoes tapping against the linoleum.

Thoughts flitted like little fireflies everywhere, winging the air, winking briefly, and then blacking out. Mac put her head in her hands, moved them back to massage her neck muscles. Her wrist cast knocked her forehead, which telegraphed pain from her wrist, along her arms and up to her neck and head. "Let's brainstorm this case from the beginning. All the pieces keep flitting inside my mind."

Zach turned raccoon eyes and hatched cheeks toward his partner. He smiled. "OK. Number one, unknown suspects assaulted and trussed Lance Reading to a tree. Two, they killed Irene Roy. And three, they attacked Rachel Stein but she survived."

"Let's focus on our homicide for now. Irene was strangled and nailed to a tree. Naked, with 'FORNICATOR' printed across her abdomen and inside, a note from Acts 15:20: ". . . *Abstain from pollution of idols, and from fornication, and from things strangled, and from blood.*"

"A lot of 'ands.' Whatever that means," Zach mumbled, frowning.

"Didn't you read the chapter?" asked Mac.

"Yeah, but words and *meaning* are two different animals. So a religious vendetta?"

She shrugged. "As I understand it, Paul and some other disciples wrote letters and then visited the Gentiles in Antioch, Syria and other sites to convert them to Christianity. Meaning, let's not throw a lot of Jewish rules at them but focus on three things: worshipping idols, avoiding adultery, but 'things strangled'—hmm—could be the sacrifices. But the message is clear: the killer punished Roy for that perceived transgression."

"Idols are easy enough. So fornication?" Fields asked.

"Technically, it means singles having sex. Adultery refers to—"

"Married people humping others besides their spouses. "*From blood*" could be meat or women's monthlies. So that means our killers—"

"That's an assumption, but likely accurate. This scenario suggests the killers punished Roy for sleeping with Reading—because they were engaged." She smiled but waved away her partner' objection. "Let's assume."

"Reading said she wore her engagement ring on a necklace." Fields noted. "We need to find it. That's concrete."

"Ken Rogers stated that she never took it off. Plus, According to Reading, it's engraved, but we haven't found it. We found a broken necklace at the murder scene. Along with the vic's shredded underwear."

"So, the killer's angry and his accomplice just goes along with the idea, or the religious angle's there to throw us off—to send us down a dead-end trail."

"Maybe, maybe not." Outside the yellow yolk dipped below the horizon, left dusk in its wake—the time between light and darkness, a soft golden afterglow. Time for a hundred unremembered things, one deadly decision.

"Dr. Drummer and the State police profiler Dr. Cara Ladd agreed. 'Enraged,' they said. Now, we found blood types A, the vic's and O, the killer's at scene, but a partial print is not in AFIS, so the killer has no priors."

"And Reading's semen, so that implicates him." Fields added. "And spermicide, which represents birth control or someone else?"

"He has a solid alibi—in the hospital recuperating from his own attack. If they were engaged, that would've been consensual." She shook her head, then regretted it: pain tapped her temples. She rubbed them with the pads of her fingertips. "And Savage found the rest of her clothes in a drum at the next warehouse over."

"So her belongings were scattered across a large area. The perps wanted them to be found? I'd carry them off or burn them," Fields said.

"They were in a hurry. Or maybe someone startled them. So from the pool of suspects, we can eliminate Reading, Banks—in fact, most of the cast and crew of the Woolworth doc, except for Rachel Stein—as she was in Philly—and a victim."

"What evidence did that FBI agent send about *The City of Paris* site? I can't remember what all's in the duffel bag." Her partner admitted. He fingered his scalp. Winced. "Rope, nails?"

"This time AB and O blood types, a partial print on the duct tape matching the one found at Roy's crime scene, so they're connected. Bleached hair and fiber from a black knit fabric. Nylon rope, a knife and duffel bag available at any local big box or online retailer."

"If we could narrow that down, we could trace the supplies to their source, and if they used a credit card, track the killers that way," Zach repeated Fleisher's observation.

Mac reviewed. "Fleisher's people are working that angle, but follow up on that. Go through Rachel's file again and call Philly to nail that info down. Now, from the list of childhood suspects, we've cleared Noreen, who's still abroad and Larissa has a solid alibi, which leaves Rachel Stein and Cassie Kline. Perhaps even her brother, Kerry. He knows the basics of the murder, which he related under the guise of *A Midsummer's Night's Dream.* He alluded to Roy being sedated, and the lab found a trace of opiates and alcohol in her system. Problem is, he's bright but learning-disabled. Snow says he's unreliable, would muddle a jury."

"But you disagree? You're making assumptions based on a play?"

"Yes. I think his opinion has merit because it fills in the blanks; he speaks in metaphors and symbols, and the evidence backs him up, but it requires reading between the lines, so . . ." Her right hand wobbled to indicate shaky ground.

"So Cassie Kline had opportunity, means, but what's—oh, yeah, Roy was a switch-hitter. So she slept with Kline, and jealousy is the motive."

Mac nodded. "And she has holes in her schedule but no tattoo to correspond with Roy's.

"Again, that's an assumption," Fields observed.

A rolling cart lumbered down the hall. The door swung open interrupting their conversation.

23

"Supper!" The kitchen aide set a green tray on each table. A slab of turkey, steamed carrots and peas crowded a mound of mashed potatoes. He dropped plastic utensils wrapped in a napkin in a cello sleeve. He shuffled out to deliver the meal to other patients. Fields wolfed his down while Mac picked at hers, spearing the carrot cubes one at a time, chewing gingerly.

Five minutes later, Snow treaded into the room with the doctor on his heels, a stethoscope looped around his neck. Tongue depressors peeped from his white coat pocket. He frowned as he perused Mac's chart. "Why do we have a male and female together?" He pulled the privacy curtain, the 's' hooks screeching.

Snow responded. "Easier to guard. This way, one officer can cover both. Some fool ran my detectives off the road. Could be road rage, but we're investigating a homicide, and the killer's still at large, so there could be a connection." His head canted out toward Tanya Storm, the uniformed officer outside the door.

The doctor was examining Mac's pupils for dilation, the forehead contusion, moving to her limbs, inspected her cast. "Other than your wrist, your MRI shows no internal injuries. Flex your fingers. Wiggle your toes." He palpitated her abdomen. OK.

"Follow-up with your primary caregiver and see a PT for your wrist once the cast comes off, but otherwise, you seem sound. Headache?" She nodded.

Chris laid a change of clean clothes on her bed. She nodded her thanks.

The doctor scribbled on a pre-printed pad. "A script for four days of pain pills." He tore it off, laid it on the table. "Rise slowly to avoid dizziness. You may leave when you're ready, but wait for aides to wheel you out." He moved across the aisle to Zach, drawing the privacy curtain. Snow followed with clean jeans, a long-sleeve tee, underwear and a lightweight jacket for him.

Mac sat, letting her legs dangle for a moment, listening to the doctor instruct Fields on caring for his injuries. Then she grabbed her things and wobbled barefooted to the bathroom to change. By the time she emerged, Fields had dressed and settled into a wheelchair, holding gauze packets and a roll of medical tape.

"Your chariot awaits," her husband bowed, gesturing. She lowered her butt into the second chair. Snow pushed her to the elevator; a volunteer wheeled Fields out to the Explorer parked at the ER doors.

"Could we stop for cokes? I'm parched," commented Fields. "Then would you mind dropping me at my parents?"

Snow drove through golden arches, ordered three. Handed them around. He punched straws in his and Erin's lids. "You guys feeling all right?"

"What's a break among friends?" Fields joked. "My ankle stings."

"My wrist itches," Mac attempted to get her pinky into the gap in the cast but failed. Then used her straw to scratch. "How's your scalp?"

"Pinched." Fields made a face at her then grinned. "I'll live." His shaved head, like a reverse Mohawk, revealed a pink scalp and scratched cheeks gave him a clownish look. He crossed his eyes at her, so she turned to face front.

After dropping Fields at his parents' domicile in a development off of Walnut Bottom, Snow aimed for home. The aroma of beef vegetable soup, simmering in the crockpot on the counter, filled their bungalow. Shadow, Erica, and Ian converged on the couple as they entered through the mudroom door. Chris took Ian after he escorted his wife to a dining-room chair. The baby lunged for his mother.

"Oh, baby, go glad to see you! I take it he's eaten?" Erin asked her mother-in-law, who nodded but wisely refrained from comment about her injuries.

Erica answered, "Blended veggie soup, crackers, and strained apricots."

Erin kissed the baby; he wormed down and nudged at her breast. "OK! OK! I get the message." She pulled up her blouse, let down the nursing bra flap. Ian latched on while Erica dished up soup for Chris and Erin—sliding hers out of Ian's reach. Homemade chunky applesauce waited in a clear glass bowl.

"All right, I'm headed home, see what Christopher made for our dinner." Erica kissed her son, patted Erin on the shoulder. "Get better, Erin. Holler if you need anything. Erin, your Dad called about tomorrow."

"Thanks for the soup, mom!" Chris smiled.

"I'll give him a buzz then. Thanks for dinner and minding Ian," Erin added. Shadow plopped down beside Erin's chair and nudged her foot. Her fingers stroked her shepherd's neck. She slipped her a tiny piece of beef. Shadow laid her paw on Erin's foot.

"We like to help—makes us feel useful!" Donning a heavy sweater and hefting her knitting tote over her shoulder, Erica nodded and slipped out the front door, trekking up to the farmhouse.

"This is perfect." Erin spooned up the soup. "I'm starved!" While they ate, she shared what they learned from Stein's interview.

Chris listened, his brown eyes shifting from his wife to his son.

"Let's not talk shop tonight. You're tired and sore; I'm just plain beat." His eyes looked smudged; the tracks between his brows permanently etched. He collected their bowls, rinsed them out and racked them in the dishwasher as Erin spooned down the homemade applesauce, giving Ian some.

He kicked his feet and thrashed his fists. "Uhm, yum."

"Okay, buster, finish mama's milk and then to bed with you." Erin rose. "If you could put his 'jammies on, I'll slip into mine, wash up." Pain anchored at the base of her skull. Her wrist itched and burned, so she slid a bamboo back scratcher between the cast and her skin. "Ah, that helps." Laying a blue knit tee on the bed, she slipped into the matching bottoms and crawled between the sheets. Chris laid Ian in her arms, bolstered him with a pillow. While he nursed, Erin combed her fingers through his soft auburn waves. His lake blue eyes locked onto hers. She snuggled him closer. The mudroom door eased open as Chris let Shadow out for the final time that night. A glass of water and a lone white Oxi lay on the nightstand.

* * *

Erin reached for the other side of the bed. Empty. Cool sheets. She felt wrapped in a fugue—hazy light sliced between the blinds. Her eyes refused to open. An arousing dream about her, Chris and Savage lingered. Swimming up to consciousness through the fog of the dissipating dream, she remembered her injuries. *Don't shake your head.* Pain camped out behind her eyes. Her breasts were leaking. She heard garbled cooing sounds, and then Ian's tryout words—sounds without meaning. A door opened, closed. She tried to flip back the covers, but fatigue bore down. Questions penetrated the fog: *Where's Ian? Why could she hear footfalls? Or was someone letting Shadow out?*

Kitchen sounds: the Keurig thrummed to life: the plunk, drip and aroma of coffee. The microwave hummed. More sounds: the tinkling of dry dog food cascading into the dish. The swish of running water. A low voice crooned. *Dad. Forgot to call him.* Erin blinked, rolled her shoulders. Urging her body to move, she straightened to a sitting position.

Ethan strolled in, a tray in one hand, Ian cradled on his left hip. Shadow trailed behind, her tail thumping in greeting. "How about a mocha and toast?" He'd slathered a skim of peanut butter and swirled jelly, melted, on the toast. "I brought strawberries and late black raspberries too for a smoothie unless you feel up to an egg."

Erin smiled. "No, thanks, Dad. Toast is fine. I meant to call you last night to tell you not to come today. That I have off." She reached for the toast and took a bite, chewing with care. "Hey, baby."

"'S OK. You need rest, and I'd rather not miss face time with my grandson. I lost a few years of your childhood in a fog. That's not gonna happen with Ian. Chris called. Think he knew you'd be under the weather. Good thing, too 'cause it's going on eleven."

"Mama." The baby lurched for her but Ethan held firm.

"Let you mama eat a bite, Ian."

"Good lord." Erin sniffed and sipped her café mocha, its rich chocolatey goodness comforting. Then set it down to take Ian. "I've got 'im. Thanks, Dad, for being so dedicated. I overslept, but that's the Oxi."

"I'll run Shadow through her course and bathe her. She smells a little gamey. Remember, it's September; her training session's on the calendar next week. Be back in fifteen. Come on, girl, let's get your gear on and let's go out for a run." Shadow trotted after the big man wagging her tail.

"Another item on the agenda I forgot." Her chores, duties, caseload, K-9 training and host of other things yammered for attention. "Not to mention you and

Chris." Tears of frustration leaked from her eyes. "It's all so overwhelming. It's like my life is living me!" Bruises purpled wherever her body had hit when the SUV rolled. Her head felt heavy; her wrist stung.

Ian's mouth turned down; his chin trembled—so attuned to his mother's moods was he.

"It's Ok, baby, Mama's having a weak moment. I'll stop." She smiled and he continued his work. "I'm lucky to have you, Daddy and your grandparents helping. We're lucky to be alive." She shivered, remembering the burning tanker sliding toward them the night Ian was born. Propping him up to burp, she grabbed another bite of toast. Switched him to the other side. His head connected with her cast; he frowned. "That's my cast. Pretty hard, huh? Well, get used to it, kiddo. The ER doc said at least six weeks."

Their landline trilled but she let it go to voicemail.

Her husband's voice vibrated. "We found the F150 that ran you off the road at a Park 'n Ride along Route 15 just this side of the Pennsylvania state line! We're having it towed to Impound. Fields and I are working the crime scene. Will fill you in later. Get some rest."

After bathing the baby, she handed him over to her dad for his lunch. Taking a quick shower, Erin slipped into comfortable knits, booted up her laptop, and sent Captain McKenna an email requesting his full report on the F150 when he completed it. Then she emailed Sonja, asking her to funnel any new information on the Roy homicide case to her ASAP. Opening the file and studying the notes, she tried to assimilate all the pieces into a coherent timeline.

"Hey, if you can work, you can eat." Ethan set an oversized cup of the beef vegetable soup beside her, a collar of crackers circling the saucer. He handed her a spoon and napkin. Shadow moseyed in behind him, her tail slapping the duvet. She heard Ian in his highchair, banging a utensil against the tray. "You know the sun's shining; a high of seventy-five today. A perfect day to be outside."

Erin stopped. "You're right." She dipped the spoon into the soup and sipped. "I'll join you in the kitchen. Let's go to the lake and feed the ducks and get Massey's frozen custard!" After lunch, they crumbed stale bread into a bag, leashed Shadow, tucked and secured Ian in his infant seat and motored to the Children's Lake in Boiling Springs. As they arrived, a flock of quacking ducks glided in formation, touching down on the glassy water and paddled toward them. The water rippled in their wake, radiating light in glistening little winks.

24

The next morning, Fields picked up Mac in his
spotless Murano, the bronze gleaming in the morning
sunshine. "Another beautiful day in the neighborhood,"
he sing-songed as he pushed the passenger door open
for her. "Think you're up to working?"

"Well, if you are." A steaming mocha sat in a cup on
the console. "We're supposed to be on medical leave.
For me?" Mac asked, smiling. "Thanks, Zach. You're so
thoughtful, but I'm not sure I should ride with you after
our 'accident.' I'm surprised you can work with a broken
ankle. How about I drive?"

"I won't tell if you don't. Nah, I got it. Your wrist
is broken." He grinned at her. "Nothing's wrong with
my right leg. I promise to drive safely." He held up
three fingers in a Scout's salute. His bruised eyes had
mellowed to yellow; scratches still hatched his cheeks.
"We're headed south." He handed over a scrap of paper.
"DMV got a fix on the license plates for a vintage '66
Mustang. The owner has a car lot south of Littlestown."

A rusty chain-link fence squared off the lot about the
size of a football field with "Beware of Dog" sign looped
over it. The privately owned car lot by the side of the
road held maybe fifty vehicles; two more were parked
in the garage, one on the lift. Looked like the concrete
block building had been standing since the fifties, the
white paint chipped and faded. A wide, dusty plate-glass
window faced the highway. A gray-haired man in khaki
shirt and slacks lumbered toward them, wiping his
grimy hands on a towel. "I'm Carl Campbell. You're the

detectives on the phone?" His eyes flicked to the stapled stitches on Fields's shorn scalp. He winced.

"Detective Zach Fields and Erin McCoy," Fields reiterated. He showed Campbell a photo of the plates in question. "These belong to you?"

"They do. They were stolen." He returned the photo. "Where are they now?" He scratched his temple. "Are you returning them?"

"No. Sorry," Mac said. "They're evidence in a road rage incident. When did you notice them missing?" She tapped the warning sign. "Where's your dog?"

Campbell's calloused fingers rubbed his chin. "Let's see. Before Labor Day weekend. She's inside." As if called, a Rottweiler nosed the dusty window.

"Did you report it to the police?" Fields asked.

"Yes, I called the locals. Not much they could do. Funny thing, though."

"What's that?" Fields eyes scanned the lot for a Mustang.

"They didn't take the Mustang. It's worth a lot more."

"Where's the vehicle in question? I'd like to see it." Mac said.

"I own it. Now, it's parked in my garage at the house."

"Where's that?" Fields turned his eyes back to the car owner, whose head motioned down the road a hundred feet. Mac and Campbell walked and talked.

Fields hobbled to his vehicle. "I'll drive." He pointed to his air boot.

"Where was it parked last month?" Mac wanted to know.

"In my carport, under a tarp. Give me a minute to get my door opener." He strode over to a small black pickup and pulled if from the visor. "I moved it into the garage in case the guy came back for the car. It was my first car; I bought it my senior year in high school. It was fifteen years old with rusted fenders. I restored her." He approached a white three-bay detached garage down the lane from an older Cape Cod and thumbed the opener. Pulled off the tarp to reveal a pristine, shiny red Mustang convertible with a sleek racing stripe slicing along each side.

"O, she's a beauty." Zach whistled low. He limped around the sports car, leaning on his cane. "Do you drive it? What's under the hood?"

"A V6. Not without plates. I wanted to take it to the Carlisle Car show this month but couldn't. I'd like the plates returned."

Mac nodded. "In time. Do you have security tapes?" Her eyes roved over the eaves of the garage, the white clapboard house, and the telephone pole along the road.

"No security cameras, ma'am. We're a little community, pun intended. Thieves are rare around here. After my plates went missing, I put in an alarm system, a camera over the front door of the business and two spotlights out front."

"When was the car last washed?" Fields asked. Taking a small flashlight out of his pocket, he rounded the car, leaned down to inspect the plate area.

"Why? My boy detailed it after the plates were stolen."

"He's looking for latent prints. Was your son working then? Did he or your wife see any strangers?" Mac said.

Campbell looked at Mac, startled by curious jade eyes studying him or the rapid-fire questions. He shook his head no. "Nobody mentioned anything like that."

"So one day the plates were missing?" Fields' brows quirked up.

"Yep. Overnight. That's what happened." Campbell asserted.

"Why the Mustang plates?" Mac waved her hand over the lot, as they walked back. "When there were so many others to choose from?"

"None on the lot have plates. I keep temporary tags in the office. Put them on if anybody wants to test drive one. I always lock up at night." He pointed to the thick bulky chain and heavy-duty lock attached to the open gate at the lot.

"Any vehicles missing?" Fields queried as the man returned the garage door opener to his truck's visor, then flipped it up. Again, he shook his head.

"Do you own a black Ford 150?" Mac asked. Campbell escorted them back to the Nissan. "Did you sell one to anyone recently?"

"No. Most owners hold on to those. They're the most popular truck on the road. Too pricey for my blood. Wait! Did the thief put classic car plates on a truck? What an idiot!" Campbell shook his head. "I've heard it all now!" A car pulled onto the lot, the gravel crunching beneath the tires. Parking near the building, a man and woman in an old two-toned Chevy climbed out, looking around.

"Well, I got customers." He pulled a card from his shirt pocket as Fields took one from his. They exchanged them. "When will you return my plates?"

"As soon as we solve our crime," Mac answered. "Thanks for your time."

Campbell turned away and approached his customers.

Disappointed, Mac rounded the Murano, ducked into the passenger's seat, as her cell pinged.

"McCoy. You what? You did? We're on our way." She turned to her partner. "Let's go. McKenna's found a partial print on the gas cap. And the paint scrapes match the Escape we totaled!"

"Hot damn! Finally, a friggin' break. Now we're getting somewhere." He pointed his SUV north.

At the Impound, McKenna's team had dismantled the truck. McKenna greeted them.

"Look at this." He waved them over to the smashed right front fender, fingered the deep gouges along the side. He pointed to the wear on the tires. "One, the paint scrapes match your vehicle. Two, the truck's right front tire is worn; it matches the rubber pattern laid on the road at the site of impact." He gestured to the tire mold beside the tire and held up the smashed side rear-view mirror. "Picked up shards of glass from the Escape." He set the half-globe on the plain paper on the bench that stretched the width of the garage under the windows. "Found a bag of marijuana in the spare tire well. Registration's in the car." He waved the papers in a clear glassine.

Mac took it, read the owner's name. "Who in the hell is Herbert Lindberg?

Fields, beside her, was shaking his head. "No idea."

"Let's find out."

McKenna swiped his black hair from his forehead, handing them a headshot. "The print belongs to Lindberg. He was arrested for possession and a DUI in 2005." The man in the mug shoot looked sixtyish. Thinning hair framed a square face with a florid complexion exacerbated by broken capillaries mapping his nose. His squinting eyes were either compensating for missing glasses or the light glaring in his face.

"Wait, there's more." McKenna shifted back to the bench, picked up another glassine which contained a single strand of strawberry blonde hair, root attached.

"That seals it. Bet it's Irene Roy's! Please send that for DNA typing to the Harrisburg lab ASAP." Mac withdrew her cell from its pocket in her purse. "Sonja, Fields and I are headed to HQ. I'm faxing you a mug shot of the F150 owner we're hunting. Will you check the DMV in Pennsylvania, Ohio, Maryland, Virginia and New York for an address and phone number? Thanks."

When Zach wheeled his vehicle into the CPD parking lot, Mac said, "Boot the computer in the Murder Room. Let's get this guy on the horn, find out why he forced us off the road."

Mac thumbed her cell, requesting an arrest warrant from Judge Acorn for one Herbert Lindberg for assault on police detectives with a deadly weapon, withholding evidence, leaving the scene and failing to report a crime.

"Lind . . . berg residence."A woman's shaky voice answered.

Fields put her on speakerphone.

"This is the Carlisle Police, Homicide. We need to speak to Herbert Lindberg."

"Why?" the woman asked.

"Are you Mrs. Lindberg?" Mac asked.

"Yes. I'm Sarah Lindberg." They could hear subdued hubbub in the background. People talking. Mac heard swishing movements like paper rustling and murmured conversations.

"Please put your husband on the phone," Mac said.

"I can't. Here you talk to them." The phone exchanged hands.

"NYPD. Detective Davis. How can I help you?"

"Tell him you want to speak to Commissioner Frank Reagan," Zach quipped.

Mac waved him off. "We're trying to locate the owner of a black Ford 150 that ran us off the road. DMV records show that Mr. Herbert Lindberg owns the vehicle.

"You're a day late. Lindberg's en route to the hospital. Wife came home, found the door ajar and her husband unconscious. Bludgeoned from behind. Looks like a B&E and assault. But nothing seems missing. Did you send an officer to arrest him?"

"No, I've just requested a warrant."

"A black Ford truck is not on the premises," the detective determined.

"No, we found and impounded it," Mac said.

"Wait a minute. The wife wants to speak to you."

"My husband gave that truck to my son last month."

"So you're saying Lindberg is no longer in possession of that vehicle? What's your son's name? Does he live with you?"

"Kerry Kline. No, he lives with his sister, Cassidy. I told Herb not to give it to Kerry because of his disabilities, but Kerry wheedled until Herb gave in. Said it'd save him paying the parking fees, which are outlandish here—"

Mac cut in. "Does your son have a license to drive? Did your husband transfer ownership?"

"Yes, but I won't get in a car with him. See, he's bright—a computer geek—but has Asperberger's Syndrome with ADHD and has a hard time concentrating. He's with Cassidy in Virginia. She's an outdoor adventure—"

Fields cut in brusquely. "We're acquainted with Cassidy and Kerry Kline. Thank you. You've been most helpful. Hope your husband improves."

"Have you seen your children lately?" Mac cut her eyes to Zach, brows quirked. Shoulders shrugged.

"No. I assume they're at their townhouse outside of Leesburg. Or maybe it's in Lexington. I get them confused. Actually, I've never visited them because we don't travel outside the city much, and they've never invited us because Cassie holds a grudge against me. It's not my fault their father left; I did my best as a single parent until I met Herb. He's kind as the day is long, but the kids never bonded with him.

"Any idea who assaulted your husband? Or why?" Mac asked.

"No. Look I have to go to the hospital." The receiver clunked into its base.

"Thanks for your time," Mac spoke to dead air.

"It's not worth the trip to The Big Apple," Fields answered her unspoken question. "We've got the vehicle and enough evidence to arrest Kline."

"Which one?" Mac intoned as she punched in the judge's numbers on the CPD replacement cell to request a warrant. "I miss my iPhone. This one's chunky and slow."

"The driver was male." Fields glanced at the older model and nodded. "Not sure we can subpoena a Virginian. We need to find out if Leesburg has its own force or call the state police for extradition forms."

"And the FBI. He crossed state lines." Mac made the call and then sat back. "Now we wait."

The phone pinged. But instead of a judge, Sonja's voice informed Mac she had a call on line four.

Mac picked up the receiver, punched the blinking button.

"Kauffman here. Please report to the Carlisle High School tomorrow at 8 A.M. for K-9 Training in the mock attack on the school. We've coordinated it with CPD, Fire, Cumberland County EMT's and HAZMAT."

25

When Mac and Shadow arrived a few minutes late, the operation had already begun. She snapped on the dog's Kevlar vest, then shrugged into hers, tugging the Velcro straps tight. Two Black and Whites were parked crosswise, blocking the semi-circular drive to prevent vehicles from coming or going. A fire truck idled at the curb, Chief Rusk and his assistant awaiting instructions. The white HAZMAT van disgorged white-suited praying manteses, heads and faces covered. Hemmer parked a Cumberland county EMT van close to the building; uniformed technicians unloaded stretchers to bring out the 'victims.' On one a tall beefy teen moaned while an anxious EMT clamped a compress over a stomach wound. He and his partner hustled toward the ambulance. It looked awfully realistic.

Shadow's neck ruffled, her senses on alert, curious eyes taking in the bustling activity. Again, Kauffman held the black Lab Inky on a leash. Several other K-9 officers and their handlers circled the red brick high school, stopping at the exits. "Easy, girl. Heel." Trembling, Shadow circled to Mac's right side, her shoulders brushing her handler's knee. They approached Kauffman for their assignment.

"The situation is a teen with multiple weapons wearing a vest. Don't know if he's a lone shooter or what his beef is or what's in his vest," he said. "We weren't briefed on the whole scenario to make it more realistic. You and Shadow go around back, cover the rear exit in case the kid makes a run for it."

Mac nodded. Rounding the east end of the building to locate the rear exit, she halted when she heard shouting. Shadow growled low in her throat, stopped, turned toward the bank of windows. Giving her shepherd the 'heel' signal, they approached and leaned against the brick, listening.

"I'll kill her if you take another step!" A voice yelled.

"Look, son, you don't want to do that. Your teacher—"

"Stood by and did nothing when that asshole jock bullied me. I'm sick of his bullshit! I'm not taking it anymore. Be a long time before that asshole picks on somebody else again."

"What happened in the classroom?" the principal asked.

"Almost every day, he shoved me, pushed my books to the floor, stole my homework, or knocked my glasses off my face. Smashed my fingers in my locker yesterday." The boy lifted his right hand, swollen and purpled along the knuckles.

Mac angled along the building until she found a door. Patted her pocket to check if the Taser was in place. Left her weapon holstered but unsnapped the strap that secured it. Wondered if an alarm would sound when she opened the door. A siren whined as an ambulance tore down the road. The metal door yielded with a click. She and Shadow slipped in. Mac unleashed her. The kid and the principal were still exchanging words. In the hall outside the classroom door, the boy held his teacher in an arm lock, a knife at her throat. Blood splattered his black vest and tee, blotting out the "T" and "F" of the popular band. She'd intended to approach from behind, but—

The kid's head swung around. "I SAID NO COPS!"

Mac and Shadow approached.

"We can handle this," the principal said.

Mac gave her shepherd a sit signal. She sat. "Just here to talk. What's your name?" From what she could see, his vest pockets were slack—empty.

"Gavin O'Brien. Keep that dog back, or I swear this teacher's history." He chuckled. "Get it? Oh, this is my *history* and homeroom teacher, Mrs. Grant." He laughed. Glancing at Shadow, the teen's left hand pushed the knife against Grant's throat, piercing the skin. Blood bloomed and tiny droplets beetled down her throat. Her eyes wide, she tried to inch away from the knife. Gavin gripped her tighter.

"Gavin. You've already threatened and assaulted your teacher with a deadly weapon. How old are you? Sixteen? Seventeen?" He nodded.

Mac continued, "Mrs. Grant is not the source of your pain. Let her go and come with me. We can work this out. Should we call your parents?" His uneven, lanky bangs nearly covered his eyes, which shifted to Shadow again. "Won't do any good. They're not home."

"Achtung," Mac said softly. Shadow bared her teeth and barked. Usually, the 'attention' demand scared the attacker into submission—or at least distracted him for the second she needed.

"Call off that damned dog!" Gavin demanded.

"Do you have any idea what Shadow can do? Her bite exerts thirteen hundred pounds of pressure. If I give her the command, she'll shred your arm."

"Not if I kill her first," the disturbed teen retorted. Racing blood pulsed through his carotids, adrenaline fueling his rage.

"Look, this violence isn't necessary. Gavin, please, just put the knife down." The principal paled. "We have a zero tolerance for bullying. We'll file a complaint against Ward. Suspend him for starters. He may lose his athletic scholarship."

Mac added, "I'm sorry you suffered bullying, but life is not a nest for you to thrive but a competition to survive. Surrender your weapon before you do any real damage." She edged closer. "Come on, Gavin. Mrs. Grant is injured and losing blood. She's looking faint." Her face had leeched of all color. Mac was hinting that Grant go limp to throw Gavin off balance.

Shadow growled louder, stepped closer. Gavin's eyed the dog, then the detective as he shifted the knife from the teacher's throat to aim it at the shepherd. In that second, Mac aimed and shot the Taser; the wires snaked out, bit into his chest. He crumpled to the floor. The knife skittered across the linoleum. The teacher staggered away, the principal offering her his handkerchief to press against her wound and led her down the hall.

"Good job, girl." Mac handed her K-9 officer a treat, hooked the leash onto her halter. Unhooked her cell, thumbed her partner on speed dial. "Fields, we need another stretcher in here. I Tasered and disarmed the teen. Name's Gavin O'Brien. Stay with him, and then arrest him for assaulting his teacher when he's coherent. Get photos of his bruised knuckles. Then book him—we may have to send him through the juvie system. And call his parents." She ended the call, extracted a paper bag from her pack, and donned latex. Dropped the knife in. Dated and labeled it.

When Fields appeared, Mac motioned to Gavin, who leaned against the wall, dazed, his eyes unfocused, his hands cuffed behind him.

"Thought this was supposed to be a drill," Fields observed as he helped the teenager to his feet; the gurney arrived. The detective uncuffed the kid's right hand, cuffed it to the gurney as Gavin lay back, his free hand rubbing his chest. They exited together.

"Just keeping it real," Gavin muttered. "Damn jocks think they own the place."

Mac and Shadow strode toward the principal's office to get Gavin's story. The secretary directed them toward the teacher's lounge, where a shaken Mrs. Grant stirred, then sipped a cup of hot tea. The school nurse bandaged her wound while the principal paced between the women and the door.

"I'll need your statements," the detective stated. She swiped a blank composition book off a shelf, shoved it in front of Grant. "And the history of this Ward kid with Gavin. Is he a bully? I'll need his parents' address. And what's his last name?"

Grant looked up from her writing. "Williams. I didn't witness bullying in my classroom, but Ward is a big guy, plays football. You know how teens are—wouldn't rat out each other."

Mac frowned. "Adults need to enforce this zero tolerance policy then." She called HQ, asked for a uniform. "Head to the med center, find Ward Williams— and question him about his behavior toward Gavin. Then arrest him for simple assault and put him under guard until CRMC releases him. Inform his parents."

Turns out, Williams had closed the locker door on Gavin's hand, the nurse reported. Plus verbally abused the younger boy by name-calling and shaming. Another teacher witnessed Williams shoulder-butting other kids in the hall between classes.

Mac bought a bottle of cold water from the vending machine in the lounge, pulled Shadow's collapsible cup off her belt with a shaking hand, poured a third in for the dog. She chugged the refreshing liquid herself, trying to gain control of her adrenaline-fueled body. The shepherd sensed her anxiety, shifted her weight but lapped the water. Her cell pinged. "Detective McCoy." She listened as she collapsed the cup and clipped it to her belt. "On my way." She collected the comp book.

"Come on, girl, let's report this to Kauffman." Mac reached down to pat her K-9 officer, then righted herself and aimed for the K-9 instructor, who was outside talking with the HAZMAT team. They were peeling off white protective coveralls while they compared notes. Other K-9 Units clustered around.

"Excuse me," Mac intervened. "Sorry to interrupt. I have to leave to bring in a person of interest in our homicide. You forgot to tell us this was a real incident. A teen threatened and attacked his teacher; he must have knifed his bully. Blood all over him."

"It's news to us too, but thanks for averting disaster," Kauffman said.

"I had to Taser him," she admitted.

Kauffman nodded, pointed to an iPad propped at the rear of the HAZMAT van. "You're on the news."

"Damnation!" Mac swore. "I didn't notice a news camera."

"Cameraman was filming through the window." The same windows she'd observed the standoff between the teen and the principal, in the hall right outside the classroom door. The K-9 trainer returned to his discussion with the other dog handlers.

In route to HQ, Mac called in her ten-twenty. "Leaving Carlisle High School, Fields and I are going to Virginia to pick of a suspect."

"Roger that," replied Sonja.

Fields was waiting at HQ in his Murano, its motor running.

She shook her head. "I'll drive. We may need Shadow."

Fields shrugged, parked his vehicle and hopped into the passenger seat of the K-9 unit.

26

By the time they arrived in Leesburg, the Virginia State police had Kerry Kline holed up in an interrogation room, cuffed and chained to a bolt in the floor. Watching through the two-way mirror, the Carlisle detectives listened to the rundown and then strode into the room. Mac dropped a file folder onto the table. Kline's eyes darted to them, then to the window, his fingers drumming against the scratched wood table. Shadow stood at her handler's knee. Fields set the recorder out.

"Detectives McCoy and Fields interviewing suspect Kerry Kline." Fields noted the case number, date time, and listed personnel present.

Mac began. "You're under arrest for assaulting police officers with a deadly weapon, leaving the scene of a crime, and withholding information and evidence. You have the right to remain silent. If you'—"

". . . give up that right, anything you say may be used against me in a court of law. I have the right to an attorney present. If I cannot afford an attorney . . . yadda, yadda, yadda," parroted Kline. "I waive rights to an attorney, but I want my phone call. Carrie should know; she'll be worried. How did you find out? The truck, right? Sorry, a dumb thing to do." He combed back his bangs with his fingers, flipped into theatrical mode. "If we shadows have offended; think on this—"

"Did you know it's a felony to attack police officers or prohibit them from doing their sworn duty?" Mac interrupted. "Shadow, sit." The shepherd obeyed, so Mac handed her a treat, which the suspect noted. The dog's head and amber eyes moved from Mac to Kline as if following their conversation or reading the suspect's behavior.

Kline shook his head no. "I haven't studied law yet, but you're getting too close. Shakespeare wanted to kill all the lawyers. Why, do ya think?"

"Too close to what?" Mac asked, leaning back in her seat, giving the suspect some room, toying with the dog's leash.

Kline's fingers crawled along the table. "May I pet your dog?"

"No, she's a K-9 officer. Focus on the questions. What are we too close to?"

"A devil in a private brawl. Souls and bodies we've dispatched three and satisfaction can be naught but death!' No, not 'dispatched' but it will do." Kline's voice rose in the stifling air.

Shadow growled a warning.

"Lower your voice." Mac cocked her head. "Quoting Shakespeare again? But butchering it. Is this about—"?

"Yes, the character was a butcher—Jack." Kline, in actor mode, finger-combed his bangs back and then tapped the table as he studied the shepherd.

Fields leaned into Kline's personal space. "This is nonsense. As soon as the extradition papers are ready, we're taking you to Carlisle to arraign and incarcerate you there. Any clever response to that?"

"You got in my private space." Kline leaned away, putting distance between him and Fields. "First I meant to pass you. Then I recognized you, so I bumped you, shake you up. But then I got carried away. How did I know you'd wreck? Thought cops knew how to drive. Why, on *Criminal Minds*, the agents all maneuver—"

"That's TV! Why were you disguised?" Fields interrupted. "That suggests premeditation, not a spur of the moment road-rage incident."

"No, I was in costume. Our Little Theater does matinees for elementary school kids. I'm Shaggy in a Scooby-Doo mystery. To encourage kids to read. We hand out Scholastic books. Talk about acting."

"Why did you abandon the F150?" asked Mac.

"I didn't. It had a flat," Kline didn't grasp the severity of the charges. "And I didn't want Carrie to find out I dented the fender." He dropped his head into his hands. "My mother won't ever let me forget this. She didn't want me to have it. Woman's so stingy. But I drove it a whole month without incid—"

"Is that the reason for the stolen plates? And why steal classic car plates for a truck? Duh! What else are you hiding? That's another count against you." Fields peppered him with questions. "You're going to jail, buddy."

Kline blinked. "Classic car? Not for my first offense. I'll plead not guilty."

Fields shook his head. "You just admitted on tape that you bumped us off the road. Plus your print's on the gas cap, and your mother told us your stepfather gave you the truck. And the paint transfer from our vehicle matches the scrapes on your fender. It's a slam-dunk. Who knows what may come back from the lab?"

"But I have no prints. You guys got my juvie file! No fair! You cheated! That's supposed to be sealed!" Kline protested, popping up and down as far as his shackles allowed.

"Found out you have a DUI and Possession of an Illegal Substance," Mac opened the file and scanned the judgment.

"*Post hoc, ergo propter hoc,*" retorted Kline.

"We're not suggesting cause and effect, only that we have a match on your prints," Mac explained. "Thought you haven't studied the law."

"I learned that in Comp II: Writing Argument. We studied fallacies, forming a hypothesis, logical deductions and all that. Didn't know I have a degree, huh? I changed my mind; I want that lawyer now." He clamped his lips shut, crossed his arms across his chest and stared ahead.

Mac's phone pinged. The TM said extradition papers were ready. "Enough talking. Let's go, buddy. You're going to Carlisle."

"What about my phone call?" he whined.

"All in good time. After we arraign, print and book you, we also have that other issue to discuss with you— Irene Roy's homicide."

"Dirty pool. You trumped up these charges to get even. That's it. Nothing more. My lips are sealed." He 'zipped' them shut. Kline remained silent the entire two hours home, even during their brief stop for burgers and Cokes at Wendy's. They bought him a Frosty.

At HQ, Fields booked Kline, printed and jailed him until arraignment while Mac walked Shadow around the block, mulling over Kline's words. Her husband was holding the side door open for her, so she updated him on the interview. She ushered Shadow into her office, poured a bottle of water into her dish. For a few moments, the only sound was the shepherd lapping. Mac fished a dream bone out of her bottom drawer and gave it to the dog. "Good girl, you earned it. Scared Kline into admitting bumping us off the road." The dog took her treat to the corner and dropped unto her blanket, gnawing.

"Savage and I'll take it from here," Snow commented as entered the observation room.

"Wait! He admitted to running us off the road. And I think his last quotation from Shakespeare related to the Roy's murder," Mac said.

"Quoting Shakespeare won't hold up in court," Snow countered. "Let's see what Savage and I can do."

Mac frowned, as she watched from the observation room. Denise Wilhelm sat beside Kline facing the mirror conferring with her client. That swoosh of white hair against the black as startling now as when Mac met her last year. "That was quick," Mac commented about the attorney's presence. Unclipping her cell, she called Fields. "Savage and Snow are taking over the interview. Would you write up our road rage incident? Thanks."

Savage Mirandized Kline, who nodded his understanding.

"Say yes, that you understand these rights for the recording," he instructed.

"Yes."

"And you admitted to running Detectives McCoy and Fields off the road?"

"Not in so many words."

"We have your admission on tape," Snow reminded the defendant.

"Let's start from the beginning. He'll plead not guilty at arraignment," Wilhelm said.

"And waste time with a trial when we hand the DA a taped confession? Don't think so." Savage commented. "It'd be better to be honest, or perhaps we can offer a plea deal if he can help us with another matter."

"Was the confession coerced?" the lawyer asked her client. He shrugged his shoulders.

"We can play the tape," Savage commented.

"Which other matter are you referring to?" inquired Wilhelm.

"He's connected to our open case, Irene Roy's homicide. They grew up together. The victim lived with Kline and his sister a decade ago before she left to study abroad."

"Not guilty," Kline stated unequivocally. "By reason of temporary insanity."

"That's not a viable defense in Pennsylvania," Snow shook his head, his brows furrowed in concern. "Try again."

"*Non compos mentis* means not legally competent," Wilhelm countered.

"Let the defendant answer; he seemed loquacious enough with Detectives McCoy and Fields," Savage commented. He stared at Kline.

"It was her fault," volunteered Kline. "I fell into those mesmerizing jade eyes. Like diving into a pool and being buoyed by water." He shook himself as if waking from a dream.

"Wipe that smile off your face," Savage ordered, his jaws working to tamp down his temper. "Focus. We have evidence, namely the Ford 150, your prints on the steering wheel and gas cap, paint exchange from your truck to our unmarked vehicle and Mrs. Herbert Lindberg's statement you were in possession of said vehicle, which you were driving with stolen plates. One last chance to come clean."

Wilhelm raised her brows and turned to her client as if to give him consent to respond.

"And I said I was sorry. *Mea culpa.* 'O cursed spite. Time is out of joint—

"Two can play this game, Savage retorted. "Tomorrow and tomorrow creeps' into our todays at a steady pace, casting all our yesterdays into the dustbin of time and all our tomorrows into dust in the end. Cut the theatrics. What we need are facts."

"You're misquoting Macbeth." Kline frowned, his face questioning—an educated cop—one that could improvise!

"Well, butter my butt and call me a biscuit!" Savage grinned. "So were you—misquoting, dancing around the truth, couching answers in symbols."

Snow leaned toward Kline. "And what's with quoting Shakespeare? Let's focus on your plight. The Prosecution will seek no bail on this charge. We're holding all the cards. You might as well admit—-"

Kline lunged forward and bit the detective's ear, growling and tearing with strong teeth. Snow reached for his throat, but Savage had already rounded the table, gripped the defendant in a headlock, applying pressure to both carotid arteries until his eyes rolled back in his head, and he passed out. Chris fumbled for a handkerchief, pressed it against his bleeding ear. He lunged back, blood dripping onto his dress shirt while Savage called for back up to hold the now struggling prisoner.

"You're baiting him!" Wilhelm leaped to her feet. "You know he's mentally challenged, yet you deliberately pushed his buttons."

"Tasty," Kline said, blood dripping from his mouth. "Perhaps better with a few fava beans." He grinned manically.

With his hand on the doorknob, Snow added—hand pressed to his damaged ear. "And a third assault! No deals. You're going to prison for sure. For Roy's murder, we'll seek the death penalty."

Fields and Castle entered with chains and duct tape. Mac followed them.

Wilhelm followed Snow out, closed the door. "Can't you see he needs a psychiatric evaluation? If anywhere, he should be in a mental institution."

"So order him one. Our psychologist, Dr. Drummer, will evaluate him for the Prosecution before going to trial. I'm going to the ER."Snow growled.

"But this is his first offense." Wilhelm's heels clicked along behind Snow.

"Hardly," Snow barked.

"Does it hurt? Do you need me to drive you to the med center?" Mac interjected. She trotted along beside them.

"No thanks. Get him to talk." Snow strode through the door to the parking lot. Fobbed the lock on his Explorer, motioning Savage into the driver's seat, rounded the SUV and climbed into the passenger's seat—all the while holding his hanky to his throbbing ear. Savage keyed the ignition and peeled off.

"Boy, he's pissed." Mac returned to the box. Savage had bound the defendant's arms and chest to the chair with chains, which threaded through his cuffed hands and feet. He was going nowhere. Fields and Castle were standing guard. The tape rested on the two-way's sill. "That's OK. I got this." She turned toward the door. Castle left, but Fields sat beside her. "I'm good. Kline and I are going to have a heart to heart. Maybe bring him some water."

Fields wavered. Stood but stayed.

"Make that a Dr. Pepper," Kline requested. Though he'd wiped his mouth, her husband's blood colored Kline's teeth. Her partner raised his eyes in question but complied, closed the door with a final click.

"Now, it's just you and me. I need to know if you have something to bargain with. If you do and can answer my questions, I'll ask the DA for a lighter sentence in the road rage incident. Can you tell me anything about Irene Roy's death?"

"Where's my lawyer?" Kline turned to the empty chair. He blinked.

"Probably waiting for your sister to arrive. We don't have much time." She glanced at her watch. "What's it going to be? Tell me about that Biblical verse: *Avoid idols, blood and all things strangled.* If you know anything, spill it. This deal on the table—It's now or never."

"Isn't that a song? 'Give your heart . . .'" He hummed.

Mac jumped up, slid her chair in and stated, "So long. See you in the next life." Laid her hand on the knob. The knob turned, Fields walked in, set the bottle of water in front Kline. Sat down again.

"Wait! It was an accident. I got carried away." Kline reached for the bottle. "This isn't Dr. Pepper."

Mac backtracked. Eased the chair back but remained standing, waiting for more. Waited until the silence stretched out and filled the room. Until silence became sound: the fluorescent lights hummed. Her cell pinged a text message. Slipping it from her pocket, she read Chris's message. *Five stitches.* Returned it to her pocket. She tapped the daisy recorder that Agent Howard had given to her, counting to herself. Rapping twice, Sonja entered carrying a mug of coffee and mocha in one hand. "Thanks." The admin nodded, backed out, closing the door. Mac slid the coffee to Fields.

Kline gulped a long drink of water. "It was a play. We wanted to scare her—that's all. And you're misquoting the Bible. The verse is *'But we write unto them, Abstain from pollution of idols, from fornication, from things strangled and from blood. (Acts* 15:20)*"* He tried to cup his hand over his mouth—but his restraints rendered that impossible. Too late, the words spilled from his mouth. His face registered worry and guilt.

"So you know about that. Start at the beginning— that night. Were you at the bar?"

Kline chewed on his lip and then blew out a breath. He scrunched his lips, slid them side-to-side as if deliberating with himself how much to divulge. Shook his head no. The internal dialogue continued as his face contorted.

Dr. Drummer knocked and opened the door. "My eval will take at least two hours." He checked his watch. "Three o'clock now. See you at five."

Mac stood. "Fine. I have to go see about Chris anyhow." She whistled for Shadow, who bounded out of her office. "Wait. Sit. I need to get your leash. Good girl." She ducked in, grabbed the braided leash off its hook, and latched it onto the shepherd's harness. Once outdoors, Mac led her to the verge of grass beyond the parking lot so she could tinkle.

"Good girl!" This time she produced a dog biscuit for Shadow. "Let's take you home. Then I have to run to the hospital."

27

Cassie Kline screeched to a halt in the CPD's parking lot, her face flushed from speeding from work, Outdoor Adventures in Harper's Ferry—her boss Eddie Webb had to take her clients out on the Shenandoah's mile-long Staircase, named for its descending levels of whitewater. She looked down at her sweatshirt and khaki cargo shorts. Shifting from work to worrying mode, she muttered to herself, "I knew this would happen one day. And I can't always work and worry about Kerry. Lord knows I've tried my best. Talk about stressful!"

She entered through the front portico and faced the glass-walled reception area where an attractive African-American sat, wearing headphones and transcribing something into her computer. But she looked up and smiled. Clear, unblemished caramel skin, her hair tamed into a topknot of curls, she wore a rose cardigan with a navy skirt. Amethyst studs and a sunburst necklace winked in the light. She removed her earbuds, stood, and slid back the glass panel. "How may I help you?"

Kline had had a moment to get her breath. "I understand my brother is here, that's he's been arrested and detained."

Sonja Hamilton shook her head. "You can't see him now. Our psychologist is evaluating his mental state. His lawyer is waiting in the conference room. Perhaps she can fill you in." The admin assistant backed away from her desk and moved toward the door to accompany the sister to defense counsel.

"Do they know Kerry's learning disabled? That he has ADHD and—"

"I'm sure the detectives apprised our psychologist, Dr. Drummer, of the facts," Sonja answered.

"What did Kerry do this time?" Kline asked.

"He's accused of a road rage incident; he ran two detectives off the road on the Pennsylvania Turnpike. Totaled their vehicle and sent them to the hospital. CPD located the truck and found evidence linking him to the incident. And he left the scene of the crime. During today's interrogation, he bit a senior detective's ear. He'll be incarcerated at the Cumberland County prison until trial." Hamilton opened the second door on the left along the hallway. The smell of coffee wafted from the break room. "Would you like coffee or tea while you wait?"

"Oh, how kind. Yes, coffee would be great. I'm at sixes and sevens—not knowing what's going on with Kerry. You see, I've been his legal guardian since I was eighteen, so—" her voice drifted off as Denise Wilhelm stood and offered her hand, the white swoosh in her black hair arresting Kline's attention.

"I'm Denise Wilhelm. I assume you're Cassidy Kline. Let's talk about Kerry's current situation. It's quite serious."

Cassie took the padded folding chair opposite Wilhelm, whose cell phone lay beside a sleek, silver laptop and a file folder labeled *Kline, Kerry*. She waited. "They said I couldn't see him. Is he distraught? Where is he? Can I post bail?"

"You know, it's hard to say. Looked like he was enjoying the attention until the questioning went south, and he bit Detective Snow's ear, quoting Shakespeare and Hannibal Lecter. That earned him a third assault charge on a police officer. The CPD impounded Kerry's vehicle, found his prints and enough evidence to go to trial. It's ironclad. He'll go to jail or a mental institution if he's deemed mentally incompetent to stand trial. The detectives also offered to plea bargain if he assisted with Irene Roy's homicide investigation. Seems there's a connection? You all lived together at one time?"

Kline nodded.

The counselor continued, "I have to admit I'm just getting up to speed on the case. Perhaps you can fill me in on the homicide case. I'm not sure how it connects to the current case, but if he knows something, he should cooperate to gain leniency with the court. As it stands, he's in deep *shite,* pardon my German."

"I don't even know where to start. Why was Kerry following the cops? Did he know they were cops? What earthly reason could he have for road rage? Did they cut him off or pull him over? Sometimes he displays a temper, especially if he forgets to take his meds, but I can usually talk him down by giving him a dose of Lorazepam. He also takes a serotonin reuptake inhibitor—for his ADHD."

"I can't answer your questions. They hustled him into the interrogation room for questioning." Wilhelm turned to her notes as Hamilton returned with two mugs of coffee on a tray with individual creamers and packets of sugar and artificial sweeteners.

"Thank you," Wilhelm and Kline intoned in unison.

"You're welcome." She nodded and left, pulling the door shut.

"In the road-rage incident, one detective incurred a broken wrist; the driver sustained head injuries, bruised ribs, and a broken ankle when the car rolled. Since your brother did not stop, it's a hit and run—considered an aggravated assault and battery with a deadly weapon, leaving the scene of an accident and withholding evidence because he abandoned the truck. And it had stolen plates, so that speaks to intent or premeditation."

"Oh, my God! Why on Earth would he do that?" Kline dropped her head her shaking hands, trying to steady both. "I'm not sure I can do this. Seems like he's getting worse. And he doesn't belong in jail."

"Here. How do you take your coffee?" Wilhelm peeled off the lid and poured creamer in hers. "The psychologist may suggest incarceration in a mental institution." She repeated for emphasis.

"Sugar and cream. I can do that much." Kline focused on her task. Took a sip. "My, this is good coffee." She took another appreciative sip, letting the rich, aromatic coffee warm her inside and the caffeine wake her from the tedious two-hour drive. "He'd probably go crazy there. I thought Pennsylvania closed all its state institutions several years ago and released the mental patients to fend for themselves. Except for the ones lucky enough to land in a halfway house with supervision. Look how well that turned out. How many thousands became homeless and languished on the streets? It's a travesty. And how many of those are learning or mentally disabled?"

While she doctored her coffee, Wilhelm opened her laptop to check the date the Harrisburg State Mental Hospital closed: January 27, 2005. Others followed suit. "You're right about the closings. However, Allentown is still open."

The attorney tried a different tact. "Can you tell me about Irene Roy? The detectives claim your bother is connected to her homicide. If he has any information on her case, that may be our leverage and Kerry's ticket out of jail. He says it's his first offense, so if he cooperates, maybe, just maybe—" Wilhelm let the sentence trail.

"Did he admit to anything?"

"I can't reveal anything because of attorney-client privilege, but I'll just say, he's said nothing helpful. Quoting Shakespeare. Is he an actor?"

"More or less. He does skits for kids in schools. Plays Shaggy in *Scooby Doo* mysteries.

"But that's not Shakespeare."

"He's directed many plays for our Little Theater." Kline frowned, combing her straw-like hair back off her forehead. She rolled her shoulders, attempting to work out the knots. "He knew her, yes. Irene stayed with us the summer before she studied abroad. Actually, we grew up together. She had the Beaver-Cleaver type family: her mother's a well-adjusted homemaker happy in her role. We spent a few holidays with them when my mother allowed us to. Her dad *liked* kids, so he set up croquet wickets, volleyball nets and installed an aboveground pool for his kids and their friends. So Kerry knows a lot about Irene, but we haven't seen her since she moved to New York. Oh, except when we saw her in *Cats*."

"Does your brother work?"

"Yes, he works on-line—drawing and inking graphic novels for Marvel and DC Comics. I work for Outdoor Adventures, so I'm away a lot. I leave Post-it notes for Kerry to remind him to mow, eat lunch, and tend to the flowers and garden—which he does—and take his meds. I can't imagine what he knows about Irene's death. We were friends. Hell, I spoke at her funeral."

While Kline talked, Wilhelm opened the file, paging through documents, stopping at the lab reports on the F150. While this looked like the truck involved in the road-rage incident, she didn't see any connection to Roy's homicide. "Well, I need to talk to him fast, find out. Otherwise, he'll have to plead no contest and go to jail for assaulting police officers."

"Can he claim diminished capacity?" Kline asked.

"Is he?" countered Wilhelm.

"He has ADHD and a form of Asperger's Syndrome, but he's functional. Sometimes he confuses reality with the world he works in. He's comfortable alone, but while in school, he needed behavior-modification therapy and counseling, which my stepfather paid for. Funny as a toddler, he rarely spoke. As an adult, he speaks, but social conventions are lost on him. He perceives things differently than most—through a literary scope. But he's not destructive." She rubbed the tension building in her neck.

"He has a juvie record." Wilhelm pointed out, turned the report around so Kline could see it.

"One DUI and one assault. I know about both. They occurred the night of his high-school graduation, and there were mitigating circumstances where a guy bullied him into a fistfight. Kerry has a brown belt in Taekwondo, so he won. So then the bully's parents brought charges against the victim! Because there were witnesses, the judge dismissed the assault but the DUI stuck. Surely they can't use that! I thought juvie records were sealed."

Wilhelm nodded. "Usually, but the police—"

The door opened. Dr. Drummer and an officer entered with a subdued, crestfallen Kerry, papers in hand. Once the introductions concluded, both men sat. The policeman cuffed Kerry's clasped hands and then his feet. The defendant's lips drew taut. He looked sloppy with his shaggy hair and scruffy goatee. Coffee drops stained his flannel shirt, and his ripped jeans looked juvenile.

An awkward moment followed, while the psychologist adjusted his wire-rim glasses and opened his notes. He swept his sandy hair to the side. Took a deep breath, blew it out. Opened his folder.

"What are your findings?" Wilhelm queried.

"As far as *mens rea*—his mental state, Mr. Kline clearly knows right from wrong. He admits forcing the CPD vehicle off the road and driving off, fleeing the scene and then dumping the truck."

"And I apologized for that. I had a flat and thumbed a ride home," Kerry corrected.

His sister shook her head and threw him a warning glance. "Let's hear what Dr. Drummer has to say, OK?"

Her brother nodded, clasping his hands together, clamping his lips shut.

"Impairment includes hyperactivity and its attendant characteristics: inability to follow a series of instructions, impulsivity, lack of concentration and easily distracted and frustrated, as you know. However the ADHD—

"I take meds—just don't have 'em with me," Kerry interjected.

"Kerry, please, let the man finish," Kline insisted. Again, her brother's lips clamped together.

"However," Dr. Drummer continued, "his disabilities do not enter into my assessment: he knowingly and willfully caused a car crash that left two CPD Homicide detectives hospitalized with serious injuries. So, you cannot claim diminished capacity, and temporary insanity is not a credible defense in Pennsylvania. I find him sane and able to stand trial, or he can plead—well, that's within your purview, counselor. Any questions?"

"You'll testify for the Prosecution?" asked Wilhelm.

Dr. Drummer nodded, shuffled his papers into the file folder, leaving her a copy. He consulted his watch. "If you excuse me, I have another appointment."

As he closed the door, Wilhelm said, "We'll get another opinion." She turned to Cassie. "I need to confer with my client in private."

"But I'm his guardian," Kline protested. She pulled a prescription cylinder out of her pocket, uncapped the lid, and laid one white pill and one green and black capsule on the table. "Take your meds."

"Nevertheless, what we say is privileged. Please, just wait in the lobby or go grab sandwiches and come back in an hour," suggested the lawyer.

Kline nodded grimly, pushed herself up and left the box.

Wilhelm turned to her client. "Now, tell me, do you know anything about Irene Roy's death? The Carlisle Police think you do. If so, maybe we can parlay the information for a lesser sentence."

"I won't rat on my friends." Kline crossed his arms across his chest. "Besides, it was really an accident."

"Then why not tell the detectives? Were you a witness? Who else was present? You used the plural—*friends.*" The defense attorney stood and stretched her back—thumbs massaging her lower back. "So do you know who killed Irene Roy?" Wilhelm thumbed her recorder off.

"They can just send me to jail. I'd get three squares and a cot. Work out. Maybe take courses. Study law." His chin lowered; his hooded eyes telegraphed defiance. "And I haven't read *Henry V* yet."

"You've watched too many movies. After biting that detective's ear, they'll send you to Allentown, one of the few state mental institutions still open. I'm prepared to bring in a psychiatrist to evaluate your mental state. He may offer another opinion. Your disabilities *may* have been a mitigating factor if you were off your meds. That's a defensible reason for your outlandish behavior.

"I'd think hard on the notion that jail is some kind of summer camp. Believe me, it's not. And I can't defend you if you won't talk, so I'll just leave you here." She slid her business card across the table toward Kline. "Call me if you change your mind. Otherwise, just plead 'no contest' to three assaults. I'll be at your arraignment tomorrow. And clean yourself up before then—get a haircut, shower and shave. Brush your teeth!"

"I'll talk to Cassie." His rigid posture remained unchanged, but he was biting his lower lip, thinking.

"I'll send her in when she returns. Let's hope she brings food; it's going to be a long day's night. Meanwhile, I'll call a psychiatrist. Maybe we can find an expert on ADHD and Asperger's Syndrome."

"I don't want my disabilities aired in court," he retorted.

"Then plea bargain. See you tomorrow at 10 A.M."

28

At Carlisle Regional, the ER doctor had stitched
Snow's ear back to his head after shaving the area and
applying a local anesthetic, then swathed it with iodine.
She covered the injury with a gauze bandage, taped it
and smiled. "Return here or see you primary-care giver
to remove the stitches in twelve days. Keep it dry for
twenty-four hours, so wear a shower cap and change
the bandage daily."

She pulled a script pad from her pocket and wrote
one for a painkiller. "And try to avoid ear-splitting
prisoners." She chuckled and winked at Mac, unable to
contain her amusement. A physician's aide with Patel on
her pocket label handed Chris a small paper container
with two pills and a glass of water, which he tossed back
and chased with water. Crushed both and threw in the
trashcan. Stood up, motioned for them to leave.

Patel put a can of cold ginger ale in his hand. "Stay
hydrated too."

He nodded his thanks.

"I'll drive home," Mac offered. "Does it hurt much?"

"Hell with that. We're going back to finish our
interrogation of that son of a bitch. You can take over
awhile. He seems to like you. Beat back his defensive
shield. Get him to talk about Roy's homicide. He knows
something."

"I agree. He told us as much the first day we
interviewed him by quoting *A Midsummer's Night's
Dream*. Both Reading and Roy were drugged, then
dragged and lifted onto a tree. He bit—sorry about the

pun—when I mentioned the Bible verse. He corrected me when I said 'Avoid idols . . .' OK, we'll go back if you feel up to it, but let's go home when the pain bothers you. We'll grab lunch on the way." Thumbing her cell phone's home button, Mac called HQ. "Sonja, we're returning to question Kerry Kline. Is he still with his lawyer?"

"No, she stalked out of here a bee in her bouffant," the admin said. "Don't think she likes the odds. Kline's sister was here but left, said she'd be back with lunch."

At HQ, Mac reentered the interrogation box, which smelled of sweat and fear, the prisoner still chained. Kline looked wilted, the empty water bottle smashed flat on the table. She tossed it in the trash. Perspiration beetled down his brows. She made a show of settling in, laid two folders on the table, and opened the one with the truck and accident photos. For the moment, she left Irene Roy's underneath.

"Now, where were we? Oh, you'd just quoted *Acts* 15:20. How are you familiar with that Bible verse? It's relatively obscure, except to priests, preachers, and Biblical scholars."

"Paul wrote epistles to the Gentiles in Antioch, Samaria and other places to try to convert them to Christianity. Most people know that."

"I'd agree, but most people cannot quote the verses verbatim. Have you seen it recently? Are you a missionary, too? Trying to convert people?"

He snorted. "Hardly. Eidetic memory." He looked down at his hands.

"Can you recite any more?" Mac inquired.

"Sure. Psalm twenty-three, but everybody knows that. The Beatitudes. *Ecclesiastes* Three: verses one and two: "'*To everything, there is a season and a time to every purpose under heaven: a time to be born and a time to die.*' Turn, turn . . . you know the song? Why?"

"How prescient! Just curious. If you know more, then we need to talk about your relationship with Irene Roy."

His fingers drummed a tattoo on the table. He blinked several times. His eyes skittered around the room. "We didn't have a *relationship.*"

"Yet you knew her well. She lived with you and your sister for three months. What was she like?"

His eyes settled on Mac's. "She was quiet, slow to laugh or cry but quick to aid others in need or see neediness in others." He gazed beyond the detectives. "Too pale to be pretty but her ballet skills took her as far as NYCB tryouts. Didn't make the cut. An elitist troupe," he spat, "She took flight on dance floors. Defied gravity! Cassie urged her to try others, but Irene went to Royal Shakespeare Academy—more suited to her talents. Anyway . . ." His voice strayed down remembrance path.

Mac noted the man's first lucid statement. "What about the evening of September tenth? Did you see her then?"

He nodded, "I stayed in my truck—didn't go to the bar. Drinking makes people unpredictable. She came out tipsy, singing and leaning on somebody's arm."

An impatient rap tapped the door, which flew open to admit Counselor Denise Wilhelm, her face stormy. "What makes you think you can interrogate my client without my presence? Please leave us. And I want to see the video when I'm done here." Another knock, knock, knock!

This time, Cassie entered carrying paper bags and a cup carrier. "I've brought sandwiches. Time to chow down, fuel up and develop a defense!" She dropped the bag but lowered the drink tray more gingerly to avoid spilling them.

Mac nodded without a word, conceding Wilhelm her space and huffed out to the counter inside the reception area behind bulletproof glass. CHIRP, CHIRP a cell phone sounded. She glanced around, seeking and found the phone in an unsealed evidence bag along with Kline's wallet, watch and loose change. Donning gloves, she picked it up. Without waiting for a greeting, a female voice rasped, "Well, did you get rid of the cops? Why didn't you answer your phone?"

"Hello," Mac answered. "Carlisle Police Department. How can I help you?"

Silence, then a hang-up. Too late. Mac thought she recognized the voice.

Her own cell tolled like cathedral bells. Her finger swiped. "Hello?"

"Mac, this is Lee. I'm sending you a TM—a photo of a letter mailed to Lance from the States. I had to surrender it to the authorities here but just faxed HQ a copy. I can't talk because the police want to question and detain Lance, so I'm going along with him to explain the situation. They're putting two Bobbies on us for the duration. If we're lucky, two more days here, then we're off to Sonneberg. Expect to return home in a week. Over."

"Where's the envelope? Where was it posted from?" Mac asked.

"They took that too. Philadelphia. Gotta go. Out."

"Roger that." The one-page letter, cut from magazine words pasted haphazardly on a plain piece of paper read: *So you think your out of the woods? Look behind you.*" The error stood out—'your' instead of 'you're.' That could be intentional or a mistake made in haste. She hustled down to Snow's office—empty. Then accosted the Chief. "Request permission to go to Philly."

"For what?" Chief March frowned, pulling his head up from review of the budget and adjusting his attention to Mac—who was standing at the door to his office, one hand clutching the frame.

"To interview and perhaps arrest a person of interest—the leader in the Roy homicide and the suspect bedeviling the theatre group. Said person is already a flight risk, and I may've just warned her off. I'll take Fields, as I can't find Snow."

March nodded, making a shooing gesture. "Apprise me of the situation when you return to HQ."

She stuffed Kline's cell back into the glassine, dated and labeled it. Peeked into the Murder Room where Fields and Huddleston huddled over a computer, watching with rapt interest. "Fields, with me; you drive. I'm entering Kline's phone in Evidence. Huddleston, can you get his phone records? See if you can trace that last call." She rattled off the digits. Punched her own, hit speed dial and left a voicemail message for her husband. "Fields and I are trekking to Philly. Can you get an arrest warrant for Rachel Stein? Zach and I may need backup if we have to chase the suspect." She called Special Agent Fleisher's phone and repeated the message.

"Won't the Special Agent be pissed?" Zach quirked one eyebrow at her. "Or just move her to a more secure location?"

Mac shrugged. "Let's go." She slid her holster over her shoulder, grabbed her Glock and Kevlar, and raced outside. The Murano was parked near the front door. "Let's go get Shadow. We'll need her to track. Our suspect may rabbit. Code two."

Fields hobbled out, fobbed the door and popped locks. Parked the bubble on the dash, keyed the ignition, hit the accelerator, and sped out of the parking lot. Vehicles slid out of the way, clearing a path. The Nissan hit Rt-74S doing eighty, slowed slightly, and veered left at the intersection. Palming right, then left, he tore down the Lisburn driveway and halted at the Snows' bungalow.

Mac hopped out, reappeared with Shadow bounding beside her. She jerked open the back door; the shepherd leaped onto the seat. "Sit." She clipped the seatbelt around the dog. "Stay." She rewarded Shadow with a dog biscuit. Then climbed back into the passenger seat, nodded.

"Does the suspect know we're coming?" Fields queried.

"Maybe, if she recognized my voice. I'm guessing yes. But, she'll have already prepared to split, may book when we get to her hideaway."

"What about her guard?" Fields asked.

"She either ditched him, or he's with her. No good scenario comes to mind." Mac called the Philly and BWI airports, advising them of a BOLO—Be on the lookout for Rachel Stein, aka Rebecca Strayer—a five-seven female fugitive, chestnut bob with caramel highlights—leaving her name with personnel to check with every airline to see if that name or alias was on any of the commercial flight manifests leaving the country for London or Germany today or tomorrow. "If she's already flown the coop, then we hold Kline and charge him as an accessory in Roy's murder, though I know he didn't act alone—and I mean that literally. *Act*. In his mind, Irene's death was an act in a play—a modern morality play."

Fields left Route 15 for the PA Turnpike. Stomped on the accelerator, the vehicle surged ahead. The blue light flayed the air; cars peeled out of the way. "There's another possibility. Is *The City of Paris* still anchored on the Schuylkill or is it Delaware Bay? Remember, Woolworth has to return by that oceanliner, so they'll shoot their return there. You should call Lee—"

"Jeffers said they're going to Sonneburg in a couple. I'm on it." Mac dialed Officer Jeffers number, but it went to voicemail, so Mac left a message asking her how and when she and Reading were returning to the states. "If that threat came from our suspect, they could be in danger."

"We're still going to the house in Media?" He punched the address into the GPS on the dash. The map appeared on the screen, their vehicle moving toward heavier traffic. Still, Fields sped past vehicles. Mac fielded return calls from the airports—negative. No such name(s) on any out-going flight.

Her cell pealed. "McCoy."

Fields commented, "You changed your ring tone."

"Bill Fleisher here. What the hell's going on? You called a BOLO on my witness? Are you out of your mind? Her ID's changed, her appearance altered. You're putting her in danger. Do you have a reason for trooping in like a cowboy?"

Mac related the information gleaned from Kerry Kline—whom CPD now had in custody and outlined the bare bones of her theory: he was a subordinate, and the ringleader sent a threatening letter to Lance Reading in London. By taunting authorities, the killer was warning authorities she wasn't finished.

"What physical evidence do you have for this theory?" Fleisher demanded.

"Blood evidence from both crime scenes, a grainy photo at the Woolworth warehouse fire, and scraps from victim's clothes and hair in Kline's F150 toolbox."

"Which fingers Kline, not my witness. Let me call my man with her first. Don't go all Dirty Harry yet. I'll meet you at the house. Twenty minutes."

"OK. Over and out." Mac buzzed Snow again. "I need you and Savage to cover *The City of Paris.* Stein may be hiding on the boat or planning to blow it up, burn it or sink it once Reading appears.

"That's the suspects' other avenue of escape. I suspect she'll be in the vicinity—maybe track down Stein's family and cousin's residences. Or she may have already booked a flight to Sonneberg, so have someone check the airports. They're supposed to shoot his return to the states next week."

"I'll have Huddleston send a photo out," Snow said.

"Well, she's changed, so that headshot Reynolds gave us is dated."

"Do you have a more recent one?" he asked.

"Yes, on my cell, I'll email it to you. Oh, and her name's now Rebecca Strayer." Thumbed end call. Tapped camera, found the close-up of Stein and emailed it.

Cathedral bells caroled. "Yes?" She released her seatbelt to tug on her Kevlar.

"Jeffers here. We have booked a flight to Sonneberg tomorrow."

"Cancel it. Take the Chunnel to France, then go to the nearest airport; go as a courier or on standby, so there's no official documentation of your travel plans for anyone to sabotage. The killer may come after you or already be in Sonneberg, for all I know. Or waiting on *The City of Paris*. Too bad you can't use assumed names. We're on her trail now, but I'm trying to anticipate her movements—it's like herding kittens. At her last interview, she mentioned she planned to go to Germany to line up the stores where Woolworth will buy Christmas ornaments and toys."

"Yes. Reynolds sent Latch and Frost ahead to get a B&B for the cast and crew. Three days . . ." static corrupted her words. "And we then we head back to Philly to film his . . . (Words faded out), where Banks, the girls and I will meet the boat.

Fields cut the pulsing light, slowed as he turned into the cul-de-sac.

"Find other means of travel to Germany and then home. Flash your badge. Show the threatening letter on your cell—do whatever you need to do—"

"To keep Lance safe. Roger that. I'll get my weapon back too. Should I explain to JJ what we're doing?"

"Not if you can avoid it. The fewer people who know your movements, the better. We're at the target site. Thanks. Over and out." Thumbed off. Climbed out of the SUV, let Shadow out, signaled *Quiet,* then *Heel!*

Silent as her name, the shepherd hugged Mac's knee as they approached the ranch. Fields slid his Glock from the paddle holster at his back, held it down at his side, hidden.

Mac made a circling motion. She gestured at the motion-sensor lights at the corner under the eaves. They approached, hugging the house, stooping beneath windows. She pointed Fields left; she and Shadow crept right. No perceived movement inside. Desiccated leaves dropped and drifted down to the sidewalks and lawns. No children played in the yards. No walkers shuffled up and down the lane. No dogs barked.

A BMW loomed in her peripheral vision, so she halted. Retreated to confer with Special Agent Fleisher. The man strode up to the front door, rang the doorbell. Three other agents followed, moved on cat feet, surrounding the house. After a minute, Fleisher slid left to peer in the front bay window. Sheer panels blocked his view—except for the slit where they met. Fleisher shaded his eyes and yelled. "Stand down, officers! My man's in there."

Mac joined the rotund agent, who stepped aside. Fields leaned on his cane at the far edge of the covered porch, his weight on his right foot, his broken left clad in an air boot.

In stocking feet, standing on a slippery wooden stool in the middle of the living room, his agent had his hands tied behind his back, a noose around his neck. Panic in his eyes, sweat dripped from his forehead. He shook his head back and forth, and then glanced at the front entrance. *Don't storm the door.*

Agent Fleisher pointed to the bay window, his brow quirking up. The man inside shook his head. "OK, Stein rigged the door and windows to the noose or to blow up all points of entrance." He shook his head. "And I thought she was a nice person. All right, we gotta find another way in."

His agents—all topping six feet, two hundred pounds—returned to the front of the house. The one with a rust-colored buzz cut with a strong, square jaw reported, "The basement doors are locked. Same with back door and windows."

"Anyone bring bolt-cutters?"

"I did!" Fields hobbled to the vehicle for it.

Fleisher held up his index finger for the agent inside to wait a moment. "Dog entrance?" Another negative. Shadow nodded, her face turned to Fleisher, rear legs dancing—ready to go.

Mac stared at the brick chimney on the west side of the house, circa 1950s, that loomed five feet beyond the roofline and spanned six feet. "What about the chimney? Anybody got any rope?"

"You're not thinking of going down the chimney?" Fields frowned.

"No other option. I'm the smallest one here. Provided I can get up there and get the wire cap off. And climb down with one good hand." She glanced dubiously at her cast. Flexed her fingers. "Doable."

"What if she's waiting for you inside?" asked Fields. "Not a good idea—going in alone without back-up and with a broken wrist. Someone needs to clear the domicile first." He stepped up to the window, peered in. "Guy's distressed but otherwise unharmed."

"Begging your pardon," said another of Fleisher's men. "We don't know that. Besides, Duck's vehicle is missing."

"Duck?" Mac peeled off her khaki jacket, slipped the holster over her head, laid them on the porch rail. "I need a ladder, too. Let's go. Time's a wasting. Fields, call Snow, apprise him of our situation. She did this to buy time to get away."

"Duckworth—the man in the noose." Fleisher took his cell from his belt, called in an APB on a 2000 Chevy Impala. "No, I don't. Check DMV for the plates or look in his file. Thanks." Ended call.

By this time, several elderly neighbors had dribbled out of their homes, observing. One man in his seventies was lugging an extension ladder. Two agents jogged to take it, thanked him and tilted it against the chimney. The square-jawed agent retrieved a nylon rope, tied a sliding knot that formed a loop, slid it over Mac's head and shoulders. She situated it to fit snugly under her bust line and armpits. Someone slapped a wire cutter in her hand, a small flashlight in the other.

"Shadow, sit. Stay." Mac handed her dog a treat, then swallowed her anxiety. The aluminum creaked and swayed with the slight breeze. Her cast clunked awkwardly against it—telegraphing a frisson of pain. Shadow whined but kept her seat. At the top, the detective scrabbled onto the roof and crawled to the chimney. A sharper breeze sliced through her turtleneck. She gripped the chimney; some of the chinking gave way beneath her fingers. The wire mesh had been bent to cap the chimney. It lifted right off.She tossed the wire cutters down. Mac let out a breath. "If Duckworth's OK, I'll open the back door; Shadow and Fields can clear the house."

"All right up there?" called Fleisher. "Need help? Neal will keep the rope taut. Tug when you want to come up."

Mac nodded, then shook her head. "I'll come out through the door." She peered into the dark recess. *Closed in.* About every three feet, bricks stuck out at random intervals—*a foothold for the chimney cleaners, perhaps.* Gripping the top, she swung one leg up and over. The second followed. She flicked the flashlight on, stuck it in her mouth. Its bright cone stabbed the darkness, lighting her way. She lowered herself, hooking her left arm over the chimney's rim. Sweeping her right foot, she found an extended brick. Tested her weight on it. Looked for another foothold. Her little light found another just beyond reach. She lunged, caught it, slipped down several more feet and repeated the process, groping her way until her feet hit bottom. Her boots stirred up the ashes, making her cough. She pulled the rope off, tugged it, and parted the mesh grate, scanning for a trip wire. Nothing. She leaned into the room, eyes roving. Eased her Beretta out of her ankle strap, held it up—pointing with the flashlight.

"Anybody here besides you?" she whispered to Duckworth.

Negative headshake. His body relaxed a smidgen.

Her eyes followed the rope, snaking to the opposite wall, anchored to the doorknob. C-4 plastique with red and blue wires was mounted on the doorframe and every visible window. A cell phone timer read fifteen minutes. Mac slipped through the dated kitchen, examined the back door, her fingers reaching overhead, around the frame. Bolted top and bottom but otherwise clear. Once she opened the door, Shadow and Fields breached the gap and cleared each room: dining, kitchen, hall, and closets, down the hallway. Three bedrooms, two baths. The basement door was bolted shut from inside too. Fleisher's team followed. Cut through the outside padlock. Two rammed the inside basement door, wood splintering, clambered down, descending into the darkness.

The Special Agent took charge of his man and the crime scene, calling for CSU. Another agent fetched water for Duckworth. Neal called for an ambulance. Fields stretched crime scene tape around the perimeter, using the trees as posts.

"Eleven minutes," one commented.

"Step back," the square-jawed agent ordered. He studied the timer connected with three wires to the plastique and a burner phone. "Find a bucket; fill it with water." He used his army knife to pry it away from the doorframe.

Mac hurried back to the bound man, dragged a kitchen stool over, holstered her weapon, climbed up, and drew her knife from its sheath, cut through the zip ties at his wrists. Hands tugged at the noose. "Stay still." Slowly, she sawed through the rope above the knot—snug against the man's red-rimmed neck. Lifted it away and dropped in in an evidence bag. Once freed, he stepped down on wobbly legs and then collapsed onto the stool.

"When did Stein leave?" she asked.

"Fifty minutes ago." Duckworth rubbed his hands together, then massaged his wrists, trying to get his blood circulating. Trembling fingers on chafed wrists went to touch his bruised throat.

Neal thrust a glass of water into the man's hand. "Go easy."

Duckworth emptied the glass, handed it back to his colleague, lowered his head onto his hands. "Another, please," he rasped, fingers tracing the rope burn.

"How did this happen?" Agent Fleisher demanded.

Mac didn't wait for the answer but excused herself as another agent brought out a carpenter's bucket filled with water.

28

Officer Lee Jeffers and Lance Reading arrived
in Sonneberg, Germany, checked into an A-frame
chalet B&B and met the cast and JJ Reynolds at the
Deutsches Spielzeungmuseum. The toy museum
displayed toys available in 1890 when Frank Woolworth
bought merchandise for his new franchise—The
Woolworth five and dime stores in Lancaster, Reading
and Harrisburg and his brother's in Scranton and
others in New Jersey and New York.

"There's so much to see! How clever the German
toymakers were!" Reading exclaimed, his enthusiasm
contagious. "Would Lena, I mean Leah, like any of
these?" He waved his hand across the expanse of
the dioramas where miniature paper mache figures
clustered around a pile of straw braiding cloth while one
worked an old sewing machine—a cottage industry—
making dolls.

Jeffers said, "That reminds me of Rapunzel. Yes,
she'd like the dolls and the hobbyhorse. The sign says
this museum opened in 1904, so Woolworth wouldn't
have seen it." She still felt jet-lagged from the flight
from France—or maybe she was just hungry. Dressed
in jeans, boots and a gold cotton sweater with her
long, wheat-colored haired braided into a rope hanging
midway down her back, she scanned the tourists.
Looking for anomalies—anyone who stood out.

"But not the toy soldiers." He pointed at the stiff
symmetrical lines of metal army figures, circa Napoleon
Bonaparte's era. "Though Frank would have. He

admired Napoleon. I think he even went to France to tour Napoleon's summer palace. JJ mentioned dubbing that in later."

"Yes, he'd buy those for boys. Hmm." They moved along—passed Nutcrackers, stopped at a table model of a Circus in winter—cottony snow under the performers' feet. Three clowns in jester costumes stood beside an animal trainer leading a muzzled bear. A carousel took the central space. Four sets of railroad tracks separated the town from the display. Toy trains thrummed along the tracks, under and over arched bridges and past miniature three-story red brick and stucco Tudor homes. Tiny fir trees dotted the landscape.

"Ooo! Sorry." Jackie Frost collided with Reading, who'd stopped to admire the wooden toys. "Is this nineteenth century Sonneberg?" "Look—Noah's ark!" Twin sets of animals marched up the plank in another diorama: elephants, horses, giraffes, zebras, lions, sheep, pigs, chickens, squirrels, and mice. "Oh, gosh! Just look at the detail! Amazing. I had no idea children had so many toys back then."

Reynolds backed up as he spoke, "This'll give you some idea of the German ingenuity in the toy industry in the 1890s; the carved wooden toys are intricate, the porcelain dolls beautifully detailed. But, according to his letters, Frank bought mainly dolls and Christmas ornaments."

"Bet he bought more than that. These are adorable." Frost studied the cars.

A woman with spiky black hair, sharp features and a weak chin wearing a black dress coat and knee-length boots strode toward them. Her right hand was buried in an oversized patent leather purse. Jeffers stepped forward, jerked the purse straps around the stranger's arm, twisted, stepped behind and jerked up, quick and hard, right hand pressing the woman's elbow—forcing her to her knees. Pamphlets scattered; a compact, lipstick, a pack of tissues, wallet, and other detritus clattered to the floor.

"Ow!" yelped the woman on her knees. "What the hell?" Others approached. Jeffers showed her badge and ordered, "*Polizei*! Police! Back off."Spectators backed up, hands up but held their ground, muttering in German. A young girl collected the scattered items and offered them to their owner.

Jeffers searched the woman one-handed while she held her stance but found no weapon. She assisted the woman up. "Carlisle Police. You presented a clear and present danger, ma'am." Jeffers stepped back—giving the woman space and shielding Reading, who wore a bemused expression during the incident.

"Hrump!" She dusted off her brocade coat, turned to the girl, and opened the patent leather purse. The girl dumped the articles in. "Danka." The woman gave her a coin. The girl curtsied and returned to her family. The lady dipped into her purse and extracted a brochure— extending it to Reynolds.

"Thanks," The director opened he tri-fold color pamphlet labeled "Der Weihnachten Haus" to study the photos.On the left panel, porcelain dolls were standing on shelves, sitting in child-sized rockers and posed on carousels. The middle panel featured trains and a model city with tiny houses nestled against the mountain among the trees. In the center, a locomotive hauling milk tanks crossed an arched bridge while a passenger train ran beneath. The third panel showed various wooden toys: tops, jointed dolls, a rocking horse, and blocks. While perusing the pamphlet, JJ and his cast let the museum security guard, the docent and Jeffers work out their differences.

"I'm Verna Dittenhaufer, proprietor of The Christmas House. An article in our local newspaper reported you're filming a documentary with the Dime-store Merchant buying merchandise for a documentary. As you can see, my store would be perfect for that. If you turn it over . . ." She flipped the final panel over to reveal *Der Tannenbaum*—trees decorated with colorful, ornate glass balls; one held simple wooden ornaments; another was dotted with marzipan and lacy crocheted snowflakes. "You're free to use my store if I can take a few photos for ads. It's right down the road, at the end of this plaza. My number is on the back."

Intrigued, Reynolds folded the brochure and said. "What luck! If we could come look now, I'll accept your offer because Frank Woolworth—"

". . . bought dolls and Christmas ornaments in Sonneberg in 1890. I have a picture of him with my great-grandfather behind the cash register." She smiled, mission accomplished, her sharp features softening, satisfied. "Follow me."

"I didn't know you had so many skills," Lance whispered, following Lee down the wide plaza to see the dolls.

"And you haven't seen half of them," she returned, blushing. "You need to stay alert. The person who assaulted you, threatened your life, and killed Irene is still at large." She looked up to catch his crestfallen features, which a minute before had been friendly and impressed. "Sorry to be so blunt, but Detective McCoy just called to warn me that Rachel Stein may appear."

"Well, she's late. I know, you're right. Let me buy Leah a doll. Pick one out that looks like her." He stood before the shelves, searching for a soft, jointed baby doll with blue eyes, a button nose, and Cupid's bow mouth.

At Weihnachten Haus, Dittenhaufer showed them the dolls with their histories printed on placards mounted along the walls. Germany was the first country to mass-produce dolls in the 1600s: porcelain, bisque, and even paper mache. "I'll leave you to explore. Just let me know when you're filming and I'll close the store." She turned toward the sales counter where a clerk was waiting on

American tourists buying a dollhouse and miniature wooden furniture. The grandparents gushed, the elder gent claiming, "I can't make these for this price. And the people are so realistic. Look, there's even a dog and cat."

"Mackenzie will love it!" His wife decked out an elegant gray pantsuit agreed.

"If you know anyone who has period clothing and wants to be an extra, I'll pay them fifty dollars for a day of shooting. I need two men about my size and several women. One who resembles your ancestor and one to represent Woolworth's traveling companion, B.F. Hunt. And a few customers." Reynolds tapped the frame of Woolworth with the toy proprietor. Frank's hair looked lighter—receding on top—bushy eyebrows and the darker rogue mustache.

"Of course. My pleasure. Let's see, day after tomorrow?" she asked.

"Yes. We'll need a day to rehearse. We start filming at 8 A.M. Will that work?"

"Yes. And I'll have lunch catered for your people if you let me know of any dietary restrictions." They moved to the counter so they could confer and she could take notes.

Reading selected a baby doll with pale blue eyes, blonde wavy hair and a bow mouth. "Or would she rather have a Mama Doll?" He pointed to the talking dolls. "Or one that wets?"

"The first one's perfect. I had one like that called Tiny Tears, but diapering one baby's enough, thank you very much." Jeffers cell phone vibrated. "Excuse me, I have to take this call." She stepped outside. "Hello?"

"McCoy here. Have you spotted Rachel Stein in your vicinity? We haven't located her, but her name wasn't listed on any flight manifest departing Philly, Baltimore or New York either."

"No, but we had an incident in the toy museum." Jeffers relayed the day's events.

"Stay alert. We have a BOLO out on Stein as a person of interest. Her looks have changed, so I'm sending you a recent photo. Sent one to Interpol too. Her name is now Rebecca Sterner or Strayer—I've heard both."

"Wait a minute, I thought she was an assault victim."

"She was, but she ran from her safe house, trussed up her bodyguard. Just be on the lookout. We're pursuing every avenue here. How's it going there?"

"Good. They're filming the day after tomorrow. Then Lance and I will return to Philly to film Woolworth's arrival on *The City of Paris*. And I miss Leah."

"Leah's fine. Your parents dote on her. And you'll be home soon." Mac reassured her officer. "How's Lance?"

"I know. Yes. He bought Leah a doll that could pass for her twin!"

"Hmm. Stay close to your charge. Again, take a different route. Snow, Savage, and Agent Fleisher's people will cover the docks and search the luxury liner. Over. Out." The connection ended.

Lance appeared at her side carrying a box. Took her hand and smiled. "Let's stop at that Biergarten we passed for lunch." He consulted his watch, moved to her left. "Feel like a German bratwurst and a beer?"

"Sure, but no beer. I'm on duty. I'll walk on the outside," she said. They strolled down the Sonneberg Plaza, the sun overhead on a clear breezy day. Shoppers strolled past, parcels and hatboxes in hand. Jeffers cast her eyes about, seeking threats, but people seemed intent on their own errands or business on this sunny September day.

He stopped, looked into her eyes, and then nodded. "Then I'll buy lunch."

29

Three days later, at the Philadelphia dock, Detectives
Snow and Savage watched as Fleisher's divers swam
out to *The City of Paris* to inspect the hull below waters
while Fields joined the Special Agent searching the boat
for clues or traces of his former victim/witness. Pewter
clouds churned overhead while seagulls soared on wind
currents, cawed and scrabbled for scraps along the
dingy dock. Raucous clanging—longshoremen unloading
cargo—ripped through the air, screeching of steel on
steel. Tugs pulled huge cargo ships out to the bay, and
the oily, fishy smell of the river permeated all.

Savage buried his nose in his CPD windbreaker. "She
wouldn't dare show up here."

Snow shrugged. "We've searched her parents'
domicile, her apartment, and her cousin's place. Got a
better idea?"

"Yeah. Go back to Cumberland County jail; squeeze
Kline. Get him to spill the whereabouts of his partner—if
she is or he has one."

"Well, everybody else in the cast and crew has been
accounted for. They're returning today, will likely film
Woolworth's arrival day after tomorrow, so . . ."

"So what're we doing here now?" Savage shivered as
the wind off the ocean flew at them, spattering the men
with cold spray. "Let's at least go get coffee and lunch."

"Wait until Agent Fleisher and Zach come off the
boat. I want to hear the divers' report, too. We need to
anticipate what Stein might do to get even."

"So that's her scheme, you think?" Savage fingered the cigarette pack in his shirt pocket but left it there because Snow would lambast him for returning to his pacifiers. He preferred nicotine and alcohol to addictive drugs the doc prescribed.

Snow shrugged. "If we're on the right track, I think she's already accomplished her goal."

"Then why run? Why stage a hostage near-hanging at the safe house?" Savage asked. "Waiting for another stab at Reading? Where's Mac?"

"And that's why we're here." Snow paced up and down the worn, wooden planks. "She's at BWI if Stein flies in or out of there."

"And what about Reagan airport?"

"FBI. Agent Howard and his people have that covered."

His partner shook his head; his dark curls damp with mist, obsidian eyes scanning the distant hazy horizon. "But the cast and crew are flying into Philly." Then he nodded. "Reading and Jeffers must be flying under the radar; they're not on the passenger manifest." He studied the list while the wind tried to tug it away. "Harder to find."

Snow nodded, hopped up and down to warm his feet. "Let's hope."

* * *

The lady in question was hiding in the ladies' restroom, tugging on a blonde wig and changing into worn jeans, a cowl sweater, and denim jacket, stuffing her black dress into her tote bag. She tugged her boots back on but pulled the jean legs down over them. Donned a pair of sunglasses. "Okay!" She huffed, slinging her hobo bag across her body and tote straps over her left shoulder to leave her hands free. She had pepper spray on her key ring, "But why would I be carrying my keys to get on a plane? If I see Agent Fleisher, I'll turn myself in, but those Carlisle cops . . ." She let the sentence trail as she straightened, took a deep breath and glanced once more in the mirror. "Yes, I may get away."

Stein/Strayer walked out of the ladies' room, striding unhurriedly yet with determination to her gate. "Plenty of time: ten minutes before boarding time." She passed waiting passengers who quaffed down deli sandwiches or snacks. A teen picked over a salad. Kids over by the windows plastered their palm prints on the glass— exclaiming over departing and arriving jets.

"I wish I could fly!" the little girl said wistfully.

"I'm going pilot one of those 737s someday," the boy boasted.

Others peered into their cell phones or typed on their laptops. Young men paced, checked their cell phones or talked into them. One lady, her white hair in finger waves framing a creased face, sat in a wheelchair, knitting. An aide leaned over and whispered in her ear. She nodded, rolled up her project around the needles, and motioned for her wheelie. The aide obliged, moving it within reach. The zipper slid open; the woman pushed the needlepoints into a sponge; plunged the needles into the pocket and zipped the front flap closed.

Strayer wanted to object. "How did you get those knitting needles past the screeners?" The lady and her aide ignored her. So absorbed was she in observing, she forgot to canvass the steady stream of passengers, pilots, airline stewards, and other personnel. She didn't notice the auburn-haired detective until the cop stood right behind her. She felt a zip tie pinch her right wrist. Stein's tote slid to the floor. McCoy clipped the tie onto the woman's left wrist. Picked up Stein's bag and said. "Come, Shadow."

"How did you recognize me?" Stein asked.

"I didn't. Shadow nosed you out. Let's go." McCoy guided her prisoner down the aisle from behind with her right hand, keeping the cast on her left out of the way. "Shadow, guard. *Vamos.*" The shepherd's throat hummed as she padded beside Stein. "You are under arrest for fleeing the scene of a crime, obstructing justice, assaulting a federal agent, making terroristic threats and withholding evidence from a homicide investigation. You have the right to remain silent . . ." She Mirandized her prisoner, patted her down as spectators stopped to stare. "Homicide detective, please stand aside and go about your business," she advised, displaying her shield. Mac piloted Rachel out through the EXIT, down the sidewalk to the street, her eyes sweeping the crowd for Agent Fleisher's men.

"How did you know I was here?" Stein shuffled along. "You don't have jurisdiction here."

"I have a warrant for your arrest because you booked. Makes you a flight risk. Pick up your feet. Don't try anything stupid. Shadow can take you down in seconds. She will hurt you," she warned. "We have officers stationed at all the major airports, watching and waiting. Where were you headed? Sonneburg?"

Stein nodded. "I wanted to intercept JJ before they returned to the states. Is your Officer Jeffers still guarding Lance? What happened to your wrist?"

Why are you so interested in Jeffers and Reading?" countered Mac.

"I told you. Frank bought Dresden china cups, dolls, and Christmas ornaments. Since I still work for JJ, I wanted to check the inventory. They'll be wrapping up the documentary soon. We have just two more shoots— when Frank disembarks in Philly—standing in for the New York harbor, which we'll dub in later—and then the family's move from Lancaster to Brooklyn. The girls are older; JJ won't need Leah anymore. Then I need to go to Virginia to scout out Monticello."

"Jennie just had Edna." Mac corrected.

"Yeah, that's the beauty of film. Edna was born in 1883, Jessy in 1886—both in Lancaster. JJ may use the same footage for both. All three girls were born before Woolworth's first European trip. And he booked his return on the *Etruria* from Liverpool to Ireland to see if anyone knew his grandparents, but we skipped that in the doc because of the budget."

"Why did you run?" asked McCoy. Her white K-9 SUV stood at the curb, its lights strobing blue and white. "Watch your head." She helped her prisoner into the back seat, attached a chain to her waist, threaded it down and around her feet, fastened her seatbelt, shut and locked the door. "Good girl." Mac rewarded Shadow with a pat and a dog chew for the trip home. Opened the cargo bay, Shadow jumped in; Mac secured the dog's special seatbelt. "Stay." She fobbed open the driver's door and lugged Stein's bags and her own into the front passenger's seat. Reached for the bottled water on the console, poured a cup for Shadow, who lapped it greedily.

"Because you CPD cops have a hard-on for me. Don't know why. I was assaulted too. Remember, I'm a victim, not a criminal. Hey, I want my stuff!" Stein objected through the metal mesh grill. Shadow growled.

"Not a chance. You'll get them back when you're released, which should be in about ten years if you plea, fifteen or more if you go to trial."

"I want a lawyer. This damn wig's giving me a headache. Can you take it off?"

"Sorry, no. You've uttered the words that mean we don't speak again until your lawyer is present." She shut off the blue bubble, stored it on the floor.

"Where's that boy officer—your partner Fields? I assumed he was following us." Stein looked around. "You wouldn't want to drop me off at Special Agent Fleisher's office, would you? Is agent Duckworth OK?"

Mac remained silent even though she wondered how Stein subdued and trussed up Fleisher's man. She smiled and looked back at her canine partner. The dog's head rested on the back seat a foot from the prisoner's head—which meant that the woman would behave. She palmed the vehicle out into traffic, punched home on the GPS screen, and headed west. Picked up her cell and called HQ, "Bringing in the prisoner Rachel Stein, aka Rebecca Starner/Strayer. Where's Fields?"

"On his way back from Philly. The boat's clear." Sonja related.

"He can interview Stein when I return. ETA 3:30 P.M. DST. Over. Out." She wanted to take Shadow home and grab a late lunch. Her stomach ached with hunger. She gulped the rest of the bottle of water. Rummaged in her bag for a granola bar, chewing and savoring the chocolate coating. Two hours later, she swung her K-9 SUV into HQ's parking lot.

After perp walking and processing her prisoner, Mac drove home where her Dad was watching Ian. Letting Shadow out of the vehicle, the shepherd patrolled the property's perimeter. Resetting the security alarm with flying fingers, Mac slung her gear on the hall table, strode into the empty but aromatic kitchen. Sniffed— clam or potato chowder in the Crockpot. "Dad! Ian!" The house was silent. She ladled a bowl of soup, grabbed a spoon and carried the bowl with her to the backyard through the mudroom. Shadow greeted the burly man, who was swinging Ian. The boy squealed at the height of the swing. Ethan stopped it on its return and scooped the baby out of the bucket swing. "'gin!" Ian yelled. Shadow loped up to them. "'Adow!"

"Look, mommy's here!" her dad said. He hefted Ian to his left arm and hugged his daughter, greeting Shadow by ruffling her neck. "Busy day? You look beat. I see you found the soup. Ian ate but hasn't napped yet."

"Not clam chowder, I hope," she teased, leading the way back inside.

"He'd like it. No, he ate turkey and veggies. Then strained apricots."

Ethan dished up a bowl for himself and motioned for Mac to sit. Packets of oyster crackers nested in a glass dish.

She finished her soup. "Another great concoction, Dad. Did you make this clam chowder with chicken broth?"

"But with just enough cream to stick to your ribs until supper. Still hungry?" He uncapped the cake lid, which hid a spicy apple cake glazed with a burnt sugar icing.

"Hmm. OK, a small slice. Come on, buster, you need a diaper change. I'll nurse him, then with any luck, he'll sleep for a couple of hours."

"I'm going to head home. Janelle and I are going out to eat and then a show at The Majestic."

"What're you going to see?" she asked as she settled in an armchair with Ian.

"Damned if I know. I'm just going along for the ride. Oh, wait. I'm lying: 'Mama Mia." He scooped up the bowls, rinsed them out and upended them into the dishwasher. He sliced a piece of the cake onto a dessert plate. Then the doorbell chimed. He frowned. "I'll get it. Expecting anyone?"

"No, but . . ." Mac was thinking about interviewing her material witness, thus was planning on returning to work. She heard voices murmuring.

"No, thanks, Mr. McCoy, she's fine. I'll just put her on the couch. Sorry for barging in like this. No, sir, she's not heavy. There. Oh, am I interrupting? OK, goodbye, sir. What's the code again?"

"022908, Ian's conception date but keep that secret."

Danelle Markley, Mac's college roommate, had returned to the states when she divorced her Italian prince with a toddler in tow last year. She knocked lightly on the doorframe to the bedroom and entered, bussing her friend's cheeks and patting the baby before perching on the edge of the bed. "I'm going over to Reese's, but didn't want to wear work clothes." She wore a Chanel black shift with a fitted beige jacket, black heels and carried an oversized tote. "Tomorrow's demo day—he's taking out the wall between the dining room and the kitchen. Remember we talked about it at your birthday party? Is it OK if I change and hang out here for an hour or two until he gets home? Give him some downtime to unwind first. You know how . . ."

Mac smiled. "Yes, I do know—he's hyper. Is Sydney asleep?"

Markley nodded.

Mac hefted Ian up to her shoulder to burp out of force of habit. Patted and rubbed his back until an air bubble escaped. "Sure. Once I get him down, I need to go back into work and interview a prisoner. Can you keep an eye or ear on Ian?

"Chris should be home for dinner soon. There's soup in the Crockpot if—"

"No, thanks, we ate on the way, and I stopped at Sandoe's for produce. If I can borrow your kitchen, I'll make a potato salad and stick it in there for tomorrow. I have the stuff in the car: spuds, rolls, pickles, and chips. Can you make something green—hey, even bagged salad will do—tomorrow morning? Snow can bring it along unless you and Ian are coming too?"

Mac shook her head. "I don't know. No one invited me. The kids might be in the way or get hurt by flying debris."

"I brought my laptop and a movie for Syd to watch, plus Playdoh and puzzles."

"Why don't you leave her here with me? She can spend the night and play with Ian and Shadow."

"Oh, I wouldn't want to burden you—you have so little time to yourself. And look, a cast on your wrist. What happened?" Danelle shrugged out of her jacket, hung it on a hanger she's pulled from her tote. Kicked off her heels and wiggled her toes. "Oh, the urge to kill whoever invented high heels—" She peeled off nylons, wadded them together, and dropped them in the tote. Pulled on jeans and a long-sleeve teal tee.

"Long story for later. I think I just invited her to stay. Ask her when she wakes up." Mac laid her son on his back in the crib in the blue room across the hall. Though the crib seemed out of place in the corner of the guest room, and he seemed so small. She watched as he flipped to his right side and tucked a balled fist under his chin. She rolled up a receiving blanket to brace his back. Danelle observed from the doorway. "I can toss a salad together tomorrow. I'll bring it around noon. But now, I have to run. If Chris isn't here when you're ready to go, call me, and I'll come home. Thanks a lot. We'll talk tomorrow. You and Reese got something going on?"

"We take care of each other's needs." Danelle shrugged, smiled and blushed.

Erin blurted out, "Well, take care. He can be unpredictable—moody, angry and cynical—though that's at work."

"Why don't you tell me what you really think?He's very different in bed." Her cheeks bloomed."Uh, I meant at home. He's handsome, spontaneous, funny and kind—doesn't pressure me and doesn't make demands. And a big plus: he's very attentive to Sydney. And he cooks!" She sighed. "He's so different from Tony. Reese's honed by another Vulcan altogether. With Antonio, everything had to be ordered, organized, and spotless. He's a social butterfly, debonair—a model of decorum in public but very different in private. He's remarried now. They have a baby boy, so I wonder . . . Anyway, Erin, I'm a big girl, so don't worry about me."

"Sorry I brought it up. And what're *you* doing tomorrow? Can't see all 100 pounds of you tearing down a wall. You bring a hammer?" They strolled along the hall to the living room where pajama-clad Sydney was snoozing on the leather sofa, a fleece throw tucked around her.

"One–twenty pounds. Not just a hammer—my entire pink tool case. But he asked me to help pick out stain and paint. Since his furniture is dark brown leather and his new cabinets are hickory, maybe we'll do the walls in champagne and a Belgium chocolate accent on the fireplace wall. Or maybe I'll match the colors to the quartz in the island. Let me run out to the car for the groceries, then you can go," she whispered. "What's the code again?"

"022908. Go ahead. I can get it." Mac followed her friend out to the living room. A golden oblique sun washed the room in a warm half-light from sunroom windows, throwing a cross pattern on the opposite wall. She punched in the digits. Grabbed a bottle of water from the fridge. Stopped, stared at the slice of cake. Cut it in half, forked it down and savored the apple, cinnamon, and nutmeg flavors. That caramel glaze kept it moist! Dropped her holster down over her shoulder, slid the Glock in. Donned her jacket and met Danelle at the doorway. Gave Shadow the 'come' signal. They scooted out the door as it closed. Mac hopped into the K-9 vehicle to pay the mysterious Ms. Stein a visit.

Pausing outside the interrogation box, Mac observed Stein and Swoozie Rusk—her defense counsel, with their heads together over cartons of Chinese takeout. Stein's wrists and feet were shackled. Fields hobbled down the hall, stopped beside Mac, Shadow at her side, and wiggled his eyebrows. She nodded. He flicked on the video and then opened the door. The trio strode in.

"How cozy," Mac jumped right in. "Who said you could eat in here?"

Rusk waited for a beat, arched an eyebrow, and glanced at the detective. "Nobody said we couldn't."

Mac grabbed a waste can and swept the remnants into the trash. Fields stepped out of the way and settled into a chair opposite the attorney and Stein, her eyes darting from Rusk to Fields and McCoy and then back.

"Shadow, sit." The dog parked herself at the end of the table, midway between the opposing sides. Mac handed her a treat, picked up her chair, swung it around and straddled it, her arms across the chair back. "Not our policy or goal to make the prisoner comfortable. Detectives Zachary Fields and Erin McCoy interviewing Ms. Rachel Stein with attorney Swoozie Rusk present, September 25, 2009, citing the Roy case number and time. Nodded at her partner.

"Let's start at the beginning. What was your relationship with the deceased, Irene Roy?" he asked, his tone easy, conversational.

"We didn't have a relationship," Stein snapped back.

"We have it on record you roomed together at NYU; you admitted to a falling out, and you're the only member of the Woolworth crew who had a beef with her," Mac countered.

"I said that?" Stein queried. Her brows furrowed.

Mac pulled out her notes. "You said she was needy, always wanting something from you—from borrowing clothes to money."

"Oh, that. Yes, that's why she moved out of our dorm and into an apartment. That's not exactly 'a beef.'"

"Sometimes it's the little things that piss us off, crawl under our skin and itch until we scratch it." Fields commented. "Sometimes it's the people we know best that irritate us the most—to the point of us wanting to squeeze the living shit out of them."

"I didn't kill her, if that's what you're getting at!" she insisted. Rusk patted her arm.

"Au *contraire*. Your partner is already in the Cumberland County Prison awaiting trial. He's admitted to being at the crime scene." Here Mac fudged, as he'd quoted lines from *A Midsummer's Night Dream* about the sleeping potion but had not admitted anything else.

"You don't have to respond to that," Rusk said. "You on a fishing expedition or do you have evidence to back up that assertion? And who's incarcerated in CCP?

"Kerry Kline." Fields flipped open the folder, revealing the crime scene photos and lab reports. "We have her blood type, saliva, underwear, and hair fibers, nylon rope from Reading's, Roy's, and *The City of Paris* crime scenes that correspond to our homicide," Fields stated. "Should I continue?"

"I was the victim! I staged *The City of Paris*," Stein said. "I fought back, was injured—hospitalized. They left their toolbox there when my brother and cousin scared them off. That's how my blood or DNA got there. I'm sure that's all in Agent Fleisher's reports. How could I be both victim and assailant?"

Mac nodded, rubbed her chin with her thumb and forefinger."Good question. You've heard of transfer of evidence? The criminal takes away evidence from one scene, transfers it to another."

Rusk nodded. "It's clear the same person or persons who assaulted Roy also attacked Stein."

Mac responded, "That's one conclusion you can deduce."

"And the other is I'm responsible for my own assault? That's absurd," Stein claimed. "I didn't nail myself to a door!"

"Do you deny you were in the Carlisle area on September fourth and tenth—the dates of the Reading assault and the Roy homicide?" Mac shot back.

Stein shook her head. "No, I was here. We were filming at the Warehouse that entire week—both the home and grand opening of the store scenes. Most nights I slept at the Warehouse to prep the next day's shoot."

"As Reynolds assistant, you're responsible for what exactly?" Fields wondered.

"Everything! Overseeing the set-up of the house and store, making sure the cast and crew have what they need. Checking Jackie's props and costumes for historical authenticity—you name it. Lining up sites, staging scenes so they could rehearse and film. Hiring caterers to deliver breakfast and lunch. Collecting and paying invoices. Assuring that everything's historically and biographically accurate, down to the dialogue, ink well or merchandise for the dime store." She stopped to catch her breath.

"So you didn't resent that Irene had a part in front of the camera or was engaged to Lance?" Mac probed. A pink blush flushed Stein's neck.

"Or that she studied at The Royal Shakespeare Academy or had a two-year run with *Cats?*" Fields added.

"No, I've been working with JJ for three years. We did a doc on Ulysses S. Grant and assisted with *Gettysburg.* The Woolworth doc will be aired on TV! And next, we have a Jefferson/Hemming docudrama. My degree is in stage management. I'm not an actor. Why should I resent her career? I enjoy my own." Here, Stein made direct eye contact with both detectives, proud of her own merits.

"And you never slept with Roy yourself?" Mac guessed.

Stein colored from her neck to her cheeks, as she bristled at the innuendo. "Who told you that?"

Rusk interjected, "Don't see the relevance to your current investigation."

"Jealousy. Roy was a switch-hitter," Fields provided. "How about Cassidy Kline?"

"Well, she should know!" retorted Stein.

"How so?" Fields shot back.

"Irene lived with the Klines before she left for England," Stein stated.

"And how did you know that? You claimed you hadn't seen Roy for years." Again, Mac consulted her notes.

"We're from the same hometown. Word gets around."

Rusk cleared her throat. "Looks like we're going nowhere fast. Let me propose that you either arrest my client or release her."

Mac looked surprised. "We've already arrested her on dodging a subpoena, leaving the scene of a crime, assaulting a federal officer, and making terroristic threats. There's also the matter of the arson at the Warehouse we'd like to review and—"

"Duck wasn't in danger!" Stein claimed. "The chandelier wouldn't have held his weight. And they weren't real bombs!"

"STOP! You just admitted to two felonies!" Rusk admonished her client. "Wait a sec! Who the hell is Duck?" Rusk demanded. "How does any of this relate to your homicide? You're talking pine trees and apple orchards!"

"Trust me, they're connected. We have solid evidence of her blood, fibers, and hair at both scenes. Ms. Stein was there all right—as a witness or participant. And she stays in jail during the interim because she's a flight risk," Fields stated unequivocally.

"The one piece of evidence we withheld from the press that we found at Roy's crime scene matches the paper from your printer at the Warehouse." Mac tried to broach the Bible verse without mentioning it. "Your partner also mentioned a phrase about avoiding idols . . ."

"What the hell are you talking about? Partner? Paper? We all use the fax and computers."

A quick rap on the door, then it snapped open, Fleisher filling the frame.

Shadow stood to alert, barked at the intruder, then sat at attention, waiting a command. Mac signaled OK, *friend* to her shepherd. "Down girl."

"I have to admit, Mac, you're adroit, but a federal case preempts a state, so we're taking Ms. Stein in custody." He frowned. "Your BOLO on her new name wasn't helpful, so now we have to start over."

"Why are you here? An open homicide case has no preemptions," Mac countered. "And what about your agent, Duckworth? Stein racked up a whole list of charges—"

"He's not pressing charges. He wasn't in any real danger. Fake explosives."

"Didn't look fake. Your agent's sweat and anxiety were real enough," replied Fields. His finger tapped the table for emphasis.

"But she willfully held up our investigation, intentionally fled the scene. She disguised herself in a blonde wig at BWI ready to flee the country," Mac explained.

"I was going to Queensland to trace Woolworth's grandparents, but JJ cut that scene anyway," Stein offered.

"Another lie," Mac countered, flipping back through her notebook. "You said you were going to Sonneburg to clear or check the toy inventory."

"OK, you have any physical evidence?" Fleisher kept his hand on the doorknob, motioned Stein up with his left hand. Then held his hand out, making a gimme motion to Mac. She dropped keys into it.

"This is my lawyer, Swoozie Rusk," Stein said. "And this is Special Agent William Fleisher." Each nodded at the other.

"We've met," Mac acknowledged. "We have conclusive evidence. And her partner's in jail, awaiting trial," Mac said. "Why do you keep coming to her rescue? Is something else going on here? Like drug running or human trafficking?"

"Something like that. Let's go get your things." Fleisher said to Stein. She jumped up, held her wrists out to him. She smiled in relief while he unshackled her. "Thank you, Ms. Rusk. We're done here. Send me a bill." He dropped his card on the table. Then he and Stein walked out, flanked by two of his men.

"Well, we might as well go home." Fields sighed, pushing himself up from the table, easing his left foot encased in the awkward air boot out from under the table and collected his cane from the corner.

"Shit like this always happens! Just once, I'd like a clean, straight case!" Mac complained.

"Another day, another fifty cents." Fields shrugged, gestured toward the door.

"I need to stop by the office to get my stuff. Come, Shadow. And drop by Giant for cheese, salami, bagged lettuce, and . . ." Now talking to herself. Then her phone vibrated. "McCoy."

"The Spear has landed. We'll stay the night, drive to the docks tomorrow to rehearse Woolworth's return on *The City of Paris*." Lee spoke quietly. "Then on to NYC for the move to their house and opening of the Brooklyn store. I think the documentary ends there—with Woolworth, on the brink of fame and fortune, meeting an architect to design the Woolworth skyscraper. He explained that, while the credits run, the skeleton of the skyscraper takes shape and then the building overlays that. Over. Out."

30

The next morning dawned cool but clear, the air
crisp and clean. The pecans, walnuts, and apples were
ready to harvest. Except for the apple, the fruit trees
lining the woods had shed their fruit. Snow had propped
ladders against a walnut and an apple tree. Maple
leaves were leaching sugar, exploding into gold, orange,
and crimson. Shadow bounded around the lush lawn,
chasing squirrels that leaped up the tree trunks and
chittered from high limbs. Knee deep in her in-law's
garden, Erin plucked grape tomatoes, tugged cukes
from the vines and pulled several green onions.

"Shadow, come." Once inside, Erin fed and watered
the dog. Then washed and drained the romaine,
chopped the veggies for the salad, added cubed cheese
and meat—tossed all the ingredients together.

Chris came out of their bedroom and powered up the
Keurig. "What? No coffee?"

"I wanted to throw the salads together before the
kids wake up. Would you fix me a cup? And then I need
about six apples for a Waldorf salad."

He got creamer from the fridge, popped a cup in the
holder, lowered the top, and depressed the mug button.
"Hint. Hint. Shall I add nuts to that?"But he smiled
and kissed her, setting her Smiley Face mug on the
island beside her. "Ian's stirring. Sydney's still asleep."
He pulled bread slices from the bag, slid them into the
toaster. When they popped out, he lathered peanut
butter on one, fruit spread on the other, slapped them
together and munched, heading for the door.

"Here's a bag for the apples and nuts." Erin hooked the plastic handle over his pinky. She smiled at his jeans and Penn State sweatshirt, the scent of sandalwood wafting her way. Kissed his lips. "I can fix you eggs."

"I'm good. Mom's bringing down pans of mac 'n cheese and apple crisp for you to bring over to Savage's." He eased the door shut behind him. "Please, when you bring the food, stay for lunch."

Next, Erin scooped Ian up to change his diaper and then let him nurse. Syd stirred, one arm hugging Eeyore. Her blonde curls tousled, one leg poked out from the duvet; pink pj's hiked up to her knee. She blinked, sat up, trying to orient herself, twisted around and turned glacial blue eyes on Erin. "I have to pee."

"Go ahead, sweetie." She pointed to the bathroom. Listened as the four-year-old lifted the lid. After she flushed, running water in the sink. "You found the stool, then. Good job, Syd. What would you like for breakfast?" She burped her son; his chin dug into her shoulder as his eyes followed the little girl. Erin heard the front door open and close.

"Hot cocoa and peanut butter toast. I smell it." Sydney straightened her pajama bottoms and then used both hands to push her blonde waves off her face. "I need a brush. Where's my backpack?" Her eyes cast about until they spied her pink pack with Ariel on the front. Rummaged around until her fingers latched onto a small brush and proffered it to Erin, turning around. With her free hand, Erin brushed the girl's shoulder-length hair, marveling at the sandy colored strands threading through the lighter strands. "Women pay hundreds to have hair like this."

"Huh?" The little girl turned to watch Erin's face.

"Oh, nothing. Come on to the kitchen." She helped her scoot in the island stool. While Syd chewed her toast, Erin fixed Ian's breakfast. Snapped him into his highchair next to Syd's stool. "Open up, buster." Ian's mouth popped open.

"Oh, let me!" Sydney took the baby spoon, dipped it into the oatmeal and spooned a portion gently into his mouth. "Chew, chew. How about some yummy applesauce? It's good for you." She scooped it up, spooned it in. Ian's wide eyes followed her motions. Then she sipped her Swiss Miss. "Now another bite of cereal."

"C-c," burbled Ian as Erin slipped to the door and back with her bag of apples.

"Is he trying to say my name?" She asked Erin. "Aren't you a smart baby?" She kept feeding him until both custard cups were empty.

"Uhm. Maybe." Erin sat opposite them, drinking her coffee while coring apples.

"What's that?" Syd pointed to the cylinder steel tool in Erin's hand.

"An apple corer. See I push it through the middle, and it takes out the seeds and core." She showed her again, plunging the corer through the middle. Chopped both halves first lengthwise, then across, dumped the cubes in a bowl of cold water and squeezed in some lemon juice.

The doorbell pealed, Shadow charged toward it. Mac hurried to tap the security code. In strode Danelle in tan Capri's and a long-sleeve black tee under a zippered knit sweatshirt. She backed against the door, shutting it, kneeling to hug her daughter. "Were you a good girl?"

"Yes, ma'am. I fed Ian! He ate it all up!" Her palms turned out for emphasis.

"Good! Now go get dressed. Remember to brush your teeth. I'll be in then." She stood, hugged Erin as they made their way to the kitchen. Danelle made herself a cup of coffee, added a drop of her daughter's drink to it. "Hi, Ian. All finished? Let's get you out of that highchair." She unhooked the belt, gathered the baby in her arms. "Oh, we need a damp cloth. Thanks for keeping Syd overnight." She picked up Ian's washcloth, wiped his mouth and hands. He grunted and leaned down, trying to grab a Cheerio. She sat so he could reach his tray. "Wall's out. The space has transformed into a great room! Greg Castle, Les Stuart, and Chris are installing the beam as we speak. Others are putting down the hardwood floor. Are you coming?"

Erin shook her head, taking celery from the fridge. "No, Ian might get in the way or get hurt toddling around, and besides, I have work to do. I have to type a report and file papers to bring a suspect back to Carlisle. But I'll bring lunch. Oh, I have to finish this salad before the apples turn." She returned to her task, draining the apples, shelling walnuts and tossing them together. She fished the mayo from the fridge.

Danelle parked Ian on her hip. "Let's get dressed, big boy. If they're ready, I can take the salads, so you can bring Erica's dishes."

Erin squirted light mayo over the apples and tossed in currants and miniature marshmallows, chopped celery, and folded them into a large plastic container. Stacked it on the salad container. "OK." Shadow bumped her knees, cast her amber eyes at Erin, beseeching. "Since when do you like apples? How about a chewy instead?" She opened the pantry, gave her dog a kabob stick. Shadow took it and then fled to the mudroom with it.

"Here's your little guy. Want to walk?" Danelle put the jean and tee-clad baby on the floor but held his hands while he balanced precariously.

"Come, Ian," Syd kneeled about three feet away and thrust out her arms. Ian hesitated, his eyes on the four-year-old. "Come on!" She beckoned with her fingers. "I'll catch you!"

He took a step, then another, a grin spreading across his face until he reached Sydney.

"Yay! Ian." She took him in her arms, smiling too. "He's so cute."

"Thank you. And you're so pretty too," Erin said. "You've grown so!"

"OK, Syd. Get your stuff. Let's go to Reese's house. You can help me stain the cabinet doors. They're outside, lying across trestle tables." Sydney disappeared into the guest bedroom; Shadow followed, curious about this other small person. They could hear her talking and cooing to the shepherd. "At least come eat with us. You need to eat. We're doing burgers, dogs, and brats on the grill. And I don't want to be the only female there. Well, the blonde biker cop is there, but she's nailing. Or I'll bring lunch back; we can eat here."

Mac extracted the salad containers from the fridge, lowered them into a Styrofoam cooler, and dropped ice packs on either side. "If there's no room in his fridge, they can stay in the cooler until lunch. All right, I'll stop by around noon for an hour."

Syd and Shadow emerged together. Danelle and Erin hugged again.

"What do you say to Aunt Erin?" she asked her daughter.

Sydney thought for a minute. "Thanks for the overnight and making me breakfast. And brushing my hair. Bye, baby." She tugged at Ian's sneakers.

Erin lowered him to Sydney's level so she could hug him, and then hoisted him again to her hip. "I'll bring Erica's dishes at noon."

Mac took Ian and Shadow for a walk in the woods so the dog could run through her obstacle course. Ian wanted to swing, so she pushed while Shadow toured the perimeter—a two-hundred-foot round trip to the farmhouse and back—an initiative the dog took on her own. Trotting back to her handler. "Good dog!"

Back at the bungalow, Erin deposited Ian into his playpen with his toys. She turned to her laptop, booted it up, typed and filed her report on the Duckworth rescue and the aborted interrogation of Rachel Stein. By the time she hit send, she looked up—eleven o'clock! Her eyes roved to the playpen; Ian was sound asleep. Shadow watched over him.

Quickly showering and dressing, Erin was tugging on jeans and a green cotton pullover when the bell pealed again, waking Ian. Startled, he sat up, crying. Erin plucked him up and ran to the door.

Erica lifted two sturdy sheet pans with lids from the little Radio flyer, bussed Erin's cheeks and set her dishes on the island. "Warm from the oven. Why don't you let me take Ian? Feels like I haven't seen him for days! We'll feed him lunch and then go feed the ducks at Children's Lake." She beamed. "Come to Grandma, Ian." Tears dried, he lunged for Erica.

"Well, if you're sure." Erin tried not to sound disappointed that her son was just as happy with her mother-in-law. She sighed. "Thanks for making the food." *Once a mother, always a mother. Be grateful she's such a doting grandmother.*

"My pleasure. Let's get a sweatshirt on him. If you'll pack a change of clothing, a bottle and some snacks, we'll get going. I have diapers. Want a ride in the little red wagon, Ian?" She zipped up his little sweatshirt and pulled up the hood, waiting until Erin tucked two bottles—milk and water—and a pack of goldfish into an insulated holder, then in his diaper bag.

"Enjoy your lunch." Erica took Ian, shouldered his diaper bag and eased out the door.

"Shadow, bed—mudroom. Stay." She checked to make sure the dog had water, loaded the food into Silver, punched the security code, locked the door and drove across Middlesex Road to Lisburn—the little gray raised ranch on a third-acre corner parcel. Woods stretched behind the house. Other houses marched right along the road until Lisburn met Trindle. On the left, soybean bushes swayed in a farmer's field. She turned into the gravel drive, parked behind Chris's Explorer. Fields, Stuart and Castle's vehicles lined the drive. Three motorcycles huddled between two towering firs.

Danelle jogged down to greet her, taking the top pan from Mac. "Thanks for coming. Let's put these in the oven to keep warm until we set up the buffet. I'm famished!"

Right behind her, Sydney held a stained rag. "We just finished! And the doors are beau-ti-ful! Come see!" The sun spun the cabinets a honey gold, the delicate grain like veins shining through.

On the raised deck, smoke floated from the gas grill, where Reese flipped the burgers. On the lawn in the shade, three picnic tables butted up against one another, clad in red and blue checked tablecloths, clipped at the corners to keep them in place. Somewhere out of sight, a saw buzzed, a nail hammer spit, a soda or beer can fizzed and the raised voices of the cops' camaraderie met her ears. Together, the women and girl mounted the stairs.

Gabriel Summers and Chase Rivers, two members of the motorcycle unit CPD had dubbed *The Three Musketeers* slouched over the balcony rail. They tipped their beers toward Danelle and Erin. "Afternoon, ladies bearing food. Just in time for lunch."

"Where's Shannon?" Erin asked about the third Musketeer.

"Manning the nail gun," Chase supplied.

"And what are you guys doing?" asked Danelle, skirting around them to the kitchen door that opened onto the raised deck.

"Holding up the porch." Gabe smiled, slow and easy. "Here, I'll help." He opened the screen door. "Smells great!"

Erin smiled. "Don't break a sweat." She eased into the kitchen, following Danelle to the new stainless-steel range and slid the foil-covered pan into the oven beside the mac 'n cheese. "You guys have KP duty after."

Chase smiled and shook his head at their banter.

Straddling a stepladder, Chris was holding an ancient, distressed oak beam in place while Shannon angled nails into the frame and Greg Castle steadied the twelve-foot beam at the other end. At the far end of the room, the Chief and Les were knee-kicking hardwood boards into grooves. Zach was loading a basket with plastic plates, napkins, and condiments for the picnic tables. Reese sent her an OK signal from the deck.

"All right, guys, let's eat! Grab something and carry it out!" Danelle opened the fridge, handing Erin one salad while she took the other. She reached back for bottles of salad dressing and ducked out the screen door. The men and Mahoney followed their noses to the picnic—the feast arrayed on platters down the middle. Erin opened the buns while Zach stacked the plates and utensils on the end and Danelle unscrewed the pickle jar, stuck a fork in it. The guys grabbed plates and tucked into the food talking about the progress they'd made.

"We'll finish this project by nightfall," Chief March beamed.

"Nothing like a physical workout to whet the appetite," Les added. He spooned Waldorf salad onto his plate next to a hot dog and brat. "And take our minds off of work."

"And thanks for assisting," Reese said as he doctored his burger. "It would have taken me several weekends to get this done. And thanks to the ladies for the food." He turned to Chris. "And to your mom for her mac 'n cheese. It's always delicious."

"And the apple crisp," Danelle added to Erin.

Conversation lagged as they chowed down.

31

Chris and Erin had just tucked Ian in his crib and given Shadow her last romp around the yard for the evening. The couple parked their tired bodies on the living room sofa—plates with leftovers from the picnic on the coffee table. She wore a nightshirt; Chris wore boxers and a tee. The muted TV televised images, while Chris was sipping a Dubliner and Erin a glass of Woodbridge Zinfandel. Shadow gnawed on a rare treat, a real bone, on her kitchen mat.

"What a productive day." Chris tilted his head back and rolled his shoulders.

"Did you hang the cabinet doors?" Erin asked, her feet tucked beneath her. She reached for a handful of dark-chocolate-covered almonds. Sipped her wine, savoring the fruitiness.

"No. They need a coat of polymer yet. Guess Reese and Danelle will do that tomorrow morning."

"Did she mention work?" Erin asked.

"No. But she did say she and Syd would head home around noon tomorrow. Why?"

She shrugged one shoulder, frowning. "Just wondered."

"She seems happy with Reese. I haven't seen him this mellow since, well . . . before his deployment overseas. What's wrong?"

"It's complicated." She turned to her husband. "Well, Reese has major issues, his PTSD episodes are unpredictable; he's still in counseling—"

"They seem content with things as they are; they enjoy each other's company. Everyone has issues, Erin. Besides, it's none of our business."

Erin bristled. "Easy for you to say." She sat her glass on the coffee table. "What if he has a PTSD flashback when she and Syd are around?"

"Well, didn't your dad go through that? And you were six? Give me your feet." He pulled them into his lap, rubbing and wiggling her bare toes. Ran this thumb up and down her instep as his left hand massaged her calves. "You seem a bit touchy tonight. Are you worried about our case?"

She didn't answer. Her head sagged against the sofa; she closed her eyes, enjoying his touch—his hands radiating heat, her muscles yielding, relaxing. Each time his hand reached higher, his fingers digging in from the back of her knee to her foot. Massaging up her calf to her thigh, down the back of her leg. Switching to her left leg, he repeated the process while watching her face. Her frown lines and crow's feet melted away.

She smiled. "You're wandering into dangerous territory."

Chris smiled. "Wandering my ass." He leaned over. When their lips met, his hands found their goal until Erin moaned—her ready signal; then he moved on in.

The landline jangled. They jumped.

"Oh, shit, not now." Chris groaned. He stumbled to the phone, grabbed the receiver before a second ring would wake Ian. "Hello? What's happening?"

Erin sat up as Shadow nosed her hand, the dog's signal for 'Let's go.'

"Who? CCP? Now?" He rolled his eyes. "Yes, sir. We're on our way." He speed-dialed his parents. "Can you come stay with Ian? He's asleep. Yes, we both have to go—all detectives dispatched to Cumberland County Prison."

Erin stole into their bedroom to dress. Pulled on underwear, jeans and a pullover, socks, sheathed her knife, and then tugged on boots. "I have to get my and Shadow's Kevlar out of the SUV." She dashed out, returned in minutes. Strapped herself and Shadow in, dropped her shoulder holster over her head, and slipped in her Glock.

Chris nodded as he dressed and went to the front door.

Christopher Senior and Erica Snow materialized out of the darkness. Nodded as the couple slipped out the front door. They took the K-9 vehicle, sped code two, to the CCP while Snow filled McCoy in. "Seems Kerry Kline collapsed in the visitor's center after some kind of altercation with his sister."

"Between them or with others?" Mac asked.

Snow shrugged. "The Chief ordered all detectives to CCP. State cops en route. Prison guards are locking the facility down."

"Shadow, stay." The shepherd, alert, snapped her head back and forth but remain seated, peering into the darkness.

Sirens and lights strobing, the state police arrived, braking along the outside perimeter. Glistening concertina wire topped the fence; its razor-sharp thorns circled the prison under a curdled moon.

When they arrived inside, the detectives had to show their shields, ID and surrender all weapons. Mac unleashed her K-9; Shadow led the way, parting traffic. Stepping through the metal detector, they were escorted to the Visitor's room, vacant except for Kerry Kline, who lay on the floor, breathing shallowly, eyes rolling back in his head. Limbs thrashed feebly, as a paramedic was trying vainly to slip an oxygen mask over Kline's mouth and nose. The shepherd skirted around and stepped through the open door, sniffed the prone victim's mouth and sat by Kline's head.

"Is there a doctor on the way?" Mac asked, standing on the visitor's side of the Plexiglas. She whistled for the shepherd and gave her a dog biscuit. "He's OD'd! Shadow's trained to recognize drugs. My guess—opioids."

Snow shoved his way through, past an objecting guard. "He's my prisoner."

Savage and Fields entered through the front doors, assessing the situation. Reese addressed the guard at the desk. "What's the situation?"

The beefy guy shrugged. "Trouble in the visitor's room. You need to talk to Gary Wilder; he escorts prisoners from their cells to the Visitor's room.

Fields limped up to the bars, waved his shield. "Where's Gary Wilder?"

"Yer talkin' to him." A uniformed guard with a buzz cut and pencil mustache stood on the other side of the bars, his uniform blotched with sweat.

"What just happened in the Visitor's room?" Savage asked.

"The visitors were talking to the inmates. Suddenly, this Kline guy pushes away, yelling something like 'Liar' or maybe 'Fire!' Twisted in his chair toward me—standing. He lunged forward, falling to his knees and clutching his throat. Then dropped sideways onto the floor. Flipped to his back."

"Did he say anything else?" Fields asked as Mac walked up beside the guard.

"Nothing sensible. Think he was quoting—something about witch's or maybe bitch's brew."

What happened just before that?" Mac asked. "Was his sister visiting?"

The guard turned to McCoy. He checked the sign-in sheet. "Yes. Big girl—six foot with sandy hair like straw. Dutch boy haircut."

"Did she give her brother anything?" Mac wondered.

Wilder shook his head. "No, that's not permitted."

"Not even meds?" Fields interjected.

"Especially meds. Who knows what could be in it?" Wilder ventured.

"Where is she? We'd like to question her." Mac had been scanning the rooms for Cassie Kline.

"Why, I don't know. In all the commotion—" Wilder looked around. "Surely she didn't leave!"

Growing concerned, Mac shot back. "Did she get past the lockdown?"

Fields limped back to the guard at the desk. "Did a large-boned blonde pass by here?"

"The Amazon?" The man looked like he needed a shower. Sweat half-moons stained his grey uniform. "Yeah! Walked out right before lockdown. Why?"

"She's an accessory to a crime. I don't think her brother's having a heart attack." She strode back through the barred door, Wilder swinging it open and shut and tracked down Snow. "How is he?"

"The paramedics just left—in an ambulance. They're taking him to CRMC. What did Shadow find? Shall we head over there? What's up?"

Mac said, "Coke, heroin, or opioids." She leashed the shepherd. "Cassidy Kline booked. We need to find her. Stat!" once they'd collected their weapons and belongings, she waited while a guard unlocked the door, pushed through it, motioning for Fields and Savage to follow her and Snow. Her eyes scanned the parking lot. Two guards stood several feet away, smoking.

"Excuse me. Did a tall, athletic-looking blonde woman come this way?" she asked. They both nodded, dropped their cigarette butts and turned to go.

"Did you notice her vehicle? Get the plates?"

"Yeah," the first one answered. "One of those utility crossovers. It's white with a blue logo on the driver's door. Outdoors something. Didn't see the plates."

"Outdoor Adventures," said the second.

"Anything on the carriage rack?" she asked.

"A kayak." The guards hurried back inside.

She repeated her questions to the uniforms guarding the perimeter. Negative. No one saw Kline or her vehicle. "If she gets to water, she's gone. What's the closest stream?"

"Letort?" Fields asked as if Mac were giving a test.

"An exit?" Savage nodded. "I'd bet The Yellow Breeches; it dumps into the Susquehanna and flows south."

"Let's assume she panicked and goes for the closest getaway," Snow said.

"How do you figure? She's got a vehicle." Savage replied.

"Because she'll think we'll put out a BOLO on the vehicle." She unhooked her cell to call Dispatch to do just that. "Let's hope that's the only SUV that Outdoor Adventures owns." She gave instructions to search the DMV under Eddie Webb, the Outdoor Adventure Owner. "Just Harper's Ferry; I don't have a street address." Ended call.

"We'll go to Messiah, look for the vehicle or her. What's the next closest point?" she asked, jogging to the Explorer, her shepherd heeling.

"Plenty of places along those forty-odd miles to disembark and camp."

"Camp? In the dead of night? She's running," Mac asserted. "What's your best guess?"

"Don't people sleep at night? Where the creek meets the Susquehanna in New Cumberland. What if she just keeps on going?" Savage asked. He slid into his Bronco. "She's already had a head start, so Fields and I'll head for New Cumberland."

Shadow leaped in the back seat when Mac opened the rear door, then Mac belted the dog in.

"OK. Let's go!" Snow jumped into the driver's seat. Fired the ignition and gunned the engine before Mac had secured her own seatbelt.

"Why Messiah? Why not Allenberry or South Middleton Park? More cars and she'd be inconspicuous." He detached his radio and alerted Dispatch of their destination. A moment later, Dispatch alerted all police, "Be on the Lookout for a white Honda Pilot, Virginia plates Alpha, Waco, zero, seven niner—an APB ordered for fugitive Cassidy Kline of Leesburg, Virginia. Last seen at Cumberland County Prison. Suspect likely heading north or south. Repeat . . ."

"Why would she backtrack? They're good spots where other parked cars can disguise her van, but locals would notice that kayak. Besides, I don't think the water's deep enough at the Park for it." Mac kept her eyes on the road.

Snow sped under the Route 15 overpass, turning into the back entrance of Messiah College, flicking off the strobing lights and siren. They approached the covered red bridge, pulling the vehicle over to the verge. Mac grabbed her Canon from her backpack. The trio exited with the lumens of the moon, Snow and McCoy drawing weapons, holding them down, their eyes scanning the shadows. All quiet except the crickets clicking. Each trekked the opposite direction looking for the Pilot among other parked vehicles. Shadow led Mac right to it. Tucked between two student vehicles adjacent to the building across the road from the covered bridge. She scanned the plates. "Yep." Unhooking her phone, she called it in. "McKenna, we need a tow," giving directions, plus the make and model of Kline's vehicle. Gloved up, tried the door. Locked. "No kayak. Let's look along the creek," she said. She gloved up, snapped her flashlight on.

Shadow put her nose to the ground and led Mac across the road and under the bridge. Snow dropped from the bridge to the far bank. His Maglite bobbed over the dark rippling water and along the bank. Mac trod along the edge to avoid disturbing any evidence. A silver key ring glinted in the mud. Mac breathed, "She dropped her keys!" She shot a photo of the keys, then marked the spot, took another of the imprint and one footprint. She picked up the key ring containing a SUV fob, house keys, and an engagement ring.

"Good girl. Really good girl!" Mac ruffled her neck, slipped her a treat. Took out a glassine. "Look! This seals it!"

Snow joined her, looked down. "Kline's keys? I'll make casts; tell McKenna to pick them up when he tows her vehicle." He ran back for the plaster carton, cupped water from the stream, stirred with a stick and poured it over the footprint and key imprint.

Mac nodded, unable to speak because her breath caught in her throat, adrenaline quickening her pulse. "I can't believe this!" She took a breath; expired with a whoosh. "Look—here's Irene's ring!"

Snow flashed light on the inscription: LR Heart IR

He dropped the keyring in the glassine Mac held open. She sealed, labeled and dated it. "Get a few shots of the bridge and her SUV for context. Let's book to New Cumberland."

Mac lugged the back door open. "Shadow, up."

In the Explorer, he dialed Dispatch with their twenty. "Headed to New Cumberland. Tell McKenna to collect the two casts under the covered bridge. Over. Out." Flipped the lights on, met little traffic on Rt-15, so they made good time, pulling off the road next to the tan Bronco. Fields sat in the passenger's seat, door open—left leg propped on a guardrail. "She's on the river. Heading south. Savage is commandeering a boat." He nodded toward the boats moored along the river. A motor growled out of the silence and pulled alongside, Savage at the helm. "Hop in, Chris. Fields' ankle might slow us down. Fields, you and McCoy follow the river. Go down Water Street past the Capital City Airport and HIA until you come up behind the Defense Distribution grounds. There's a landing at Marsh Run Road. If she's not there, go on to Goldsboro to Railroad Street."

Shadow sniffed the air, her curious face casing this new scene—alive with possibilities. She leaned on the leash, aiming for the rippling river swishing against the bank. Frogs croaked and crickets clicked among the cattails.

"Shadow, sit. Did you see Kline?" Mac asked Fields as he rounded the Bronco to the Explorer driver's seat, its front doors hanging open.

'We saw the kayak shoot out into the river. That chartreuse glows in the dark," he said.

"You're thinking of heading—where?" she asked. Shadow nosed into the fleece throw piled in the back seat.

"South to intercept her." Snow climbed into the motorboat.

Fields and Mac returned to the K-9 vehicle, headed south about five miles, following the Susquehanna to the spot Savage directed; Mac drove down a graveled lane to the wooden dock where moored boats rocked at the water's edge. The moon illuminated patches of the shore but trees cast the rest in deep shadow.

The trio burst from the vehicle. "That's Hoak Island." Fields said.

Shouldering her backpack, Mac's eyes peered across the boats. "We need to find something like a net to stretch across the river to stop her. Look in these boats."

Fields inspected the first three. "They're locked. This pontoon has a coil of rope, but that won't work. And she's just paddle around the island, down that far side of the river."

"She may not realize there's a far side. Grab that bolt cutter from the cargo bay." Mac liked to carry enough tools for any contingency, a trick she learned from the Musketeers during their Amber Alert case.

He nodded, turning back to the hulk of the SUV. Minutes later, he hobbled to each boat, snapping the locks. Mac jumped into the second, hauled up the anchor, maneuvered the second boat to the stern of the first, and together they hooked the anchor to the first boat. Working quickly, they lined the boats across the river until they tied the rope to the last anchor around a tree on the island. "Here, I found more rope!"

"Look! Look!" he cried, spying several fallen trees—one's desiccated upper branches hidden in the darkness. Shadow loped alongside sniffing the damp fallen leaves. Portions of the bark had sloughed off. "Must be forty feet. It's hollow!" Taking that coil of rope off the pontoon, he tied it around the trunk. Together they lugged it to the opposite side. Then pushed and pulled end over end, until it splashed into the river, brittle, arthritic branches brushing the opposite shore, blocking egress.

Winded, they returned to the row of boats. "Got your vest?" Mac pulled her holster off, donned her Kevlar and pulled Shadow's out of her backpack and snapped it onto the dog. "Shadow, up." She motioned the motorboat.

"Kline packs a weapon?" He rummaged around in the open bay, tugging it over his head, attaching the Velcro straps with a ripping sound. Hefted the roll of rope across his shoulder. "Life jackets would make more sense."

"We don't know that. A desperate suspect may have several weapons." Mac climbed over boats until she hit the center Pontoon, pulled out her Glock, checked it.

"You can't shoot her!" Fields insisted. "The bullet could ricochet, maybe hit one of us. Besides, don't you want—" He stopped at the sound of swish, swish cutting through the water—the bow gliding within view. He dropped to his knees, tugging off his shoe and air boot in case he had to go in. He formed a sliding loop along the end of the rope.

Mac dropped behind the pontoon seat, waiting. Shadow hunched down.

Too late, the kayaker saw the boat barrier, paddling madly to backwater, brake and turn the single seater around. She muscled hard but her forward momentum and the current were too strong. She rammed the small cabin cruiser that Fields occupied, but he'd braced for impact. Standing, he looped the lasso overhead. Kline swung her weight left. The kayak rolled and then Kline reappeared, her helmet dented and scratched, swinging the bow around the opposite direction. Water sluicing from her helmet, body, and boat. From six feet, the lasso sailed neatly over her. Fields jerked hard, then hauled her in. Kline struggled as blood slipped down one cheek. Water ran in rivulets from her hair, smelling of fish and laced with foam. Her soaking clothes clung to her. She pushed the detectives off, slapped at their hands, and head-butted Fields, who fell hard on the deck but held fast to the rope, feet braced against the boat. He tugged harder, tightening the rope.

"God, she must weigh as much as I do!" He groaned, teeth clenched.

"Kline, I'm going to Taze you if you continue to resist!" Mac leveled at her. "It could electrocute you! Shadow, hold. Or you could lose an arm." The shepherd's mouth closed on one muscular arm. Kline stilled.

Together, Mac and Fields freed their prisoner from the kayak; zip-tied her wrists behind her back and her feet. Then they hooked the kayak, pulling the slippery green banana on board, water sloshing over them in the process.

A breeze kicked up; the boats knocked into one another, swaying in the current. The luminous rock overhead ghosted over them. Mac called in their position. Dialed Chris, but the motorboat drew up alongside, rocking the chain of boats. Savage shaking his head, Snow beaming. He boarded. "Let's take her in."

Fields tugged off a wet sock and his ankle compression, donned air boot and shoe, Velcroed and tied them. Stuffed his socks into his pockets.

"Cassidy Kline, you are under arrest for the murder of Irene Roy and an assault on Kerry Kline, fleeing the scene of a crime and resisting arrest. You have the right to remain silent, but if you give up that right, anything you say can be held against you in a court of law. You have the right to an attorney—" Mac quoted while Snow used cuffs and chains, severing the zip ties at Kline's feet so she could walk. She stumbled, but Snow grabbed her elbow, kept her upright. Shadow assisted. Savage turned his motorboat around to head back upstream where he'd parked his Bronco.

Snow belted Kline in the backseat. "Fields, let's untangle these boats. Return them to their berths."

"Shadow, guard." The shepherd sat and growled at the prisoner.

Mac collapsed in the driver's seat to keep an eye on the prisoner. "Want me to look at that wound?" she offered.

Kline glared at her, seething but silent, her square face a statue of discontent. The woman's face bloomed blotchy red patches as her muscular shoulders hunched forward. Mac shook out an aluminum blanket and laid it across the prisoner's shoulders.

"We'll get you into an orange jumpsuit and then take your statement when we get back to HQ," Mac stated.

"Hell, let her stew," Fields said. "We need some shut-eye." He rubbed the goose egg forming on his forehead as Mac tried to scratch her wrist under a sodden cast.

32

The next morning, booked and seated in the chair bolted to the floor, their prisoner sat alone fuming over a cup of coffee. Fields and Snow stayed in the observation room. Savage and Mac entered interrogation. They took their time settling, laying Roy's folder on the scarred wood table. Mac set her recorder beside her pad and pencil, even though the video camera aimed its eye on them.

Kline's key ring jingled in Mac's pocket as she sat.

"Good mooring, I mean morning. Sleep well?" asked Savage.

"You being a smart ass?" Kline's straw hair had matted blood under her bandaged forehead. It hadn't seen a comb, but her jumpsuit was clean. Her face was no longer blotchy; she'd calmed somewhat.

"Tell us about Acts 15:20," Mac finally made eye contact with flat, stormy eyes. "Let me read it." She flipped open the file and read from the facsimile: "'But that we write unto them, that they abstain from pollution of idols, and from fornication and—'"

"'. . . from things strangled and from blood.' Yes, I know it. The verse begins with 'But' because it's a continuation of the previous verse." Kline stopped. Sipped her coffee. "How'd you know I'd be on the Susquehanna?" she queried.

"We didn't," Mac answered. "We had the Conodoguinet covered by chopper, but we were closer to Messiah and the Yellow Breeches so assumed you'd escape by the most direct . . ." She let the sentence tail, shrugged one shoulder.

"So what does the verse mean?" Savage asked.

Kline nodded, her thin lips quirking at the allusion. "Why? Don't you understand English?"

"Now who's being a smart ass?" Savage returned.

Mac said nothing, waiting. She tapped Savage's knee with hers.

He cupped his chin in his palm. "I spend most of my time trying to keep my shit together," he admitted. His fingers migrated to his temples, signaling his mental state.

"Funny, most other people try to get rid of theirs," Kline quipped.

Mac said, "Can we focus? The Biblical verse?"

Savage smiled. "Yeah, I get that the disciples were traveling in the Middle East, converting Gentiles to Christianity but returned to Jerusalem to check with the Pharisees on the Jewish rule of circumcision and other laws. Should those be required of the Christains?"

Kline studied Savage for a minute, debating with herself. She nodded. "James decided no; Gentiles needn't follow our rules—only accept Christ as their savior. Remember, Jesus was a Jew, grew up in Galilee, attended the synagogue—perhaps read the Torah, had an epiphany and some say became a Christian when baptized. Gentile converts were not to worship false gods, have sex outside of marriage and avoid—" she stopped. Hesitated. Another sip. Heat crept up her neck.

"And *'from blood'*? We talking road kill, women's monthlies?" Savage asked. "The society was a stern patriarchy. What about *'things strangled?* Help us out here. I can only think of killing chickens; aren't they strangled? Or slang for masturbation—choking the chicken. Or does it mean animal sacrifices?"

Kline shook her head. "It's open to interpretation. "*Abstain . . . from blood*" means do not drink animals' blood because it holds their spirit. For Jews, that was taboo. Can't understand why Christ would've said, 'Drink; this [wine], it is my blood.' We assume most humans wouldn't drink blood, but some hunters drink animal's blood.

"But you won't trick me into admitting anything. I plead the fifth. I want a lawyer." She tried to cross her arms, but the shackles restrained her.

"The magic words." Savage turned toward the new two-way and gestured 'phone' with his thumb to his finger and pinky to his mouth. "Tough one, all right."

"Over a Bible verse?" Mac's brow arched. "Wow, and we haven't even mentioned Irene." She pulled the key ring in its evidence glassine from her pocket, slapped them against the table.

"MY KEYS! How did you get my keys?" Kline's eyes bulged. Blood pulsed through her carotids. Hands patted her pockets, chains clanking.

"You dropped them under the covered bridge at Messiah," Mac stated. "How did you obtain Irene's engagement ring? I can deduce only one answer since she wore it on a chain around her neck. We found the broken chain at the crime scene."

"You bitch! Another know-it-all Gentile! You're nothing! Understand? You're beneath us. We are the chosen! And the nerve; she had the cojones to leave after she returned from the London after all I'd done for her. On stage, she flaunted herself in skimpy ballerina tights and those slinky cat costumes. Paraded around in her bikini undies and push-up bras in front of Kerry. Then climbed into my bed every night. Then she had the nerve to run to Lance's bed in New York. She's a cat, all right—guilty of all. Breaking all the rules. Did she think she could walk away? Worshipping idols, fornicating? Getting engaged to a man?" Kline jingled her chains. Tried to push away. Her anger egged her on, her voice shaking.

"My brother drooled over her from a distance. She thought him cute and funny, but he was serious. He wanted her but was too shy to say so. She would've laughed at him anyway. Yeah, he was there. I insisted—no witnesses! But there he was, ruining her punishment—her carnal fornication! Pumping into her. How's Kerry doing, by the way? Is he OK?"

"We haven't heard since they took him to Carlisle Regional." Savage offered but withheld the detail that he'd survived. "So this was about retribution?"

"NO! Redemption. I was saving her soul! Are you so dense—"

A hard knock sounded. The door swung open, slamming against the wall. A lawyer strode in. "Stop talking!" she admonished Kline. "You have the right to remain silent. Use it! I'm your defense counselor, Swoozie Rusk." Rusk turned to the detectives, who stood and gathered their evidence. "You cannot use anything she said in court after she asked for a lawyer."

"Where's Denise Wilhelm?" Kline asked; Rusk was a stranger.

"She's representing your brother." Rusk stared at McCoy and Savage.

Savage saluted Rusk, then turned on his heel. "She's all yours." His face-hardened into tight lines. "This isn't about religion at all, is it? A green dragon rears its ugly head. You're guilty as blood."

Mac smiled tightly and nodded. "We have all the evidence we need. Kline's blood at all three crime scenes, Irene's hair entwined in the rope in the F150." She dangled the key ring. "Here's the clincher! Roy's engagement ring in plain sight in Cassidy Kline's possession, until she dropped it while fleeing another crime scene." Mac pocketed the key ring that held the most damning piece of evidence upon which they would seal their case.

"I need a copy of that file," Rusk said. "Like yesterday."

"Arraignment's Monday the twenty-eighth." On the way back to the Murder Room, Mac felt relieved, deflated and world-weary—tired to her marrow. Her shriveled wrist smarted; she'd removed the wet cast the night before. Chris set it with Popsicle sticks and wrapped it in purple duct tape. She returned the glassine to Evidence. Collapsing at the table, she watched Huddleston peer into his computer. She needed to go to her office to type a report. "I'll just bring my laptop in here, so I can see the whiteboards. Whatcha doin'?" Mac asked.

"Just got the video feed." He turned the monitor toward Mac. Driving a red Audi, a woman wearing a blonde pixie wig and plum pullover glanced over her shoulder waiting in line.

"Zoom in," Mac said.

Visible on Stein's neck was a heart-shaped locket tattoo with a slot in the middle. She passed beneath the camera, turning her head at the last second to see if she were being followed. Rachel Stein, aka Rebecca Strayer, smirked.

"That looks like JJ Reynolds' vehicle! Where's the feed coming from?" Mac leaned forward, trying to place the environs, and then recognized the border crossing gates, guard house and guards. "Canada."

"Yep. Is she still a person of interest?" Huddleston wondered.

Mac shrugged. "Early days. We just captured our killer. We thought Kline's brother was an accomplice, but his sister said 'witness.' She drugged him for ruining Roy's 'punishment.' I need to call CRMC to see how he's doing. They'll both go to jail. But Stein was a question mark; she's an accomplice."

"So did Kline admit to killing Roy?" Huddleston turned to look at Mac.

Mac nodded. "Well, she couched it amidst a Biblical lesson about Jews converting Gentiles and Roy's punishment for switching to men."

"Good job, Mac. Fields went for sandwiches and cake!" Jay smiled. Leaning forward on his elbow, he pulled his glasses off, pinched the bridge of his nose. "This has been a long and winding road."

Her phone vibrated. She unhooked it and answered, "McCoy" as she padded back to her office for her laptop.

"We'll be at the Philly docks tomorrow to film Frank Woolworth's landing," Jeffers informed her. "Can you make it or send someone? I need to come home to see Leah. We don't leave for New York until Monday to shoot the family's move to Brooklyn, so I'll have a free weekend if someone can guard Reading."

"I think he's home free. We've finally caught Irene Roy's killer."

"Who?"

"Cassidy Kline. Yeah, one of us can be there. Thanks, Lee. You did well."

"Just doing my job. Thanks, sir. Over and out."

Mac could hear the smile in her voice. She reviewed the evidence scrawled over two whiteboards to write up her report. Flipped open the folder, laid out the evidence: photos across the table, lab reports spread out to peruse all again. She blinked, held the last page closer. The other semen contribution in Irene matched Kerry Kline's spit sample.

She climbed out of her chair to flip the board and study the timeline. Returned to her seat. Rifled through the pages until she found the DNA sheets with marks like UPC symbols. Laid one over the other, walked to her office, taped one over the other against the window and studied them.

She heard Zach enter with lunch, the rustle of take-out bags. Aromas of toasted buns, burgers and fries carried across the room. Shadow beat a path into the

Murder Room where the squad swooped in. Savage dealt out paper plates and napkins. Snow carried a tray of drinks in one hand, balanced a cake on the other, which he scooted to the middle of the table.

Mac picked a hunk of turkey off her deli sandwich, "Come, Shadow." The shepherd turned her head but remained beside Reese, sniffing.

"Aw, let her stay. She's one of us." Savage took turkey from McCoy's sandwich and fed it to the dog. Chief March and LT Stuart joined them. Mac shrugged, turned toward the interrogation room, knocked once, and poked her head in the door where defendant and lawyer were conferring. "Sorry to interrupt. But what's your mother's maiden name?"

Kline answered without hesitation, "Stein."

Mac nodded."Then why would Rachel *play* the victim?

Kline studied her for a minute. "Think about it."

"Thanks." Mac closed the door quietly and returned to the celebration, mental tumblers clicking as the puzzle pieces started falling into place.

33

"**Time to** go home." Snow stood in Mac's office doorway, Shadow following, moseying over to her bed for her bone.

"My report's not done. I need to list the evidence and marshal all of it together before court convenes. We were looking at cockeyed. I just figured out that Kline and Stein are related. And Kerry Kline is the other semen donor. He wasn't even supposed to be there.And Jeffers called in; she wants to come home. We need someone to cover Woolworth's landing."

Chris cocked his head, his brows knitted."Why?"

"Because Rachel Stein's still at large." She explained her findings to him. "She played the victim to throw us off the course or maybe because she wanted to assuage her role in Roy's death. Or feel her pain. She was at the murder scene. And she just crossed into Canada, so I need to order an arrest warrant and file extradition papers based on this new evidence." She didn't mention the tattoo.

"Hey, Shadow." He rubbed behind her ears. "Good girl." To his wife, he said, "But there's a reason Agent Fleisher keeps springing her. Apprise him of your findings, see what the feds are up to. Anyway, you have the weekend to file. Cassidy Kline will be formally arraigned Monday. Her brother's also in custody for the three assaults on police officers.He may plea bargain, but Cassidy's trial won't start until October.

"It's dinnertime and I'm hungry." He rounded the desk, pulled her up and planted a kiss on her lips. "In more ways than one." He held her hand, gently leading her toward the door.

"Come, Shadow." Mac dialed her partner, directed him and Savage to Philly to cover Woolworth's homecoming on Saturday. "I'm so tired, even though I wanted to watch Woolworth disembark from his ship," Mac sighed and finger-combed the hair off her forehead.

"Disembark?" Snow guided her to the Explorer. "We can watch it on TV when they air the documentary."

She opened the back door for Shadow, anchored her in, shut the door and slid into the passenger's seat. "You know when it'll be aired?"

"Think Reynolds said December 31st on *American Icons*."

"Wow. And to think one of our own will be on it. Lee looks good in period clothing. Puffed sleeves and her hair crimped and pinned up. Lance, too, with those muttonchop sideburns and handlebar mustache, looks the part."

Snow turned the ignition, drove out of the parking lot. "And Janelle's in it too. Could you go for a pizza?"

"That's right! As long as I can pair it with a salad." Her stomach rumbled.

"Want to stop at Massey's too?"

"Sure, why not? We've already gorged on cake at lunch." She smiled at Chris and rolled her shoulders to loosen the tension.

"You're due for a rubdown." His right hand reached over, massaged her neck. She leaned into his touch.

"Full body?" she asked.

"Whatever you want." He pulled his cell off its dash dock, ordered the pie and salad. Wheeling the SUV into the frozen custard lot. "Look, they have mudpie!" He climbed out and returned with a quart. They arrived home as the pizza arrived. His dad paid the driver and took the pizza inside. Erica greeted them at the door,

Ian on her hip. She kissed them both, surrendered the baby to his mother. "He's eaten and bathed."

Mac could smell lavender powder and baby shampoo. Her son's hair was settling in damp auburn waves, his blue eyes wide and happy at seeing his parents.

"'Addo," he pointed at the dog, wanting to pet her, so Mac kneeled down. Shadow had a lick in greeting for Ian too. Chris's parents bustled about, collecting their pads, cell phones, magazines, and Erica's knitting. "See you tomorrow. Bye. Love you." Erica waved.

"Love you too," Chris said. Erin added, "Thanks for watching Ian."

"Our pleasure, dear. That's what grandparents are for." Her father-in-law eased the door shut. The elder couple ambled up the drive to the limestone farmhouse.

The setting sun threw oblique golden light through the sunroom, forming a shadow cross on the wall opposite the mullioned windows. "Now there's a symbolic statement to end the day," Chris said while he kicked off his shoes, emptied his pockets into the leather valet on his chest of drawers.

Erin ate while Ian nursed and occasionally batted at the slice just out of his reach. Then tried to kick at it, grunting. "You're not old enough, baby. I don't want you to choke on the cheese. And besides, you're getting old enough to drink from a bottle. Or maybe skip the bottle and go to a sippy cup." She balanced the crust on her paper plate. Picked up her fork to spear a cherry tomato with lettuce dripping Italian dressing.

"And the pepperoni is too chewy and spicy," Chris added. They'd reclined in the living room—Erin and Ian on the rocker, Chris across the room on the leather sofa. His stocking feet crossed on the coffee table next to the pizza box. "Wine?"

Erin shook her head. "Not with ice cream. Later."

"We have raspberry Sparkletini, coconut rum, and Zinfandel. I can make Margaritas. What's your preference?"

"Later, light wine, heavy sex." She winked at him. His amber eyes melted from warm to an inviting come on.

"Want another piece?" He reached for the box, dislodged another slice.

She smiled. "Of course. Then ice cream. And then you."

The landline trilled. Snow lunged for it. "Chris Snow. What? Why? Shit! OK. Savage said turn on the news, channel eight."

QUESTIONS FOR
BOOK CLUB DISCUSSIONS

1. Does Christopher Snow working with his wife pose any problems for the CPD?

2. What does Reese Savage contribute to the CPD?

3. How does Savage's PTSD affect his job?

4. What themes thread through the novel?

5.What's the title's significance?

6. How are Shakespeare and The *Holy Bible* clues to the mystery?

7. How does the Woolworth sub-plot affect the main characters?

8. What memories does the Woolworth subplot stimulate in readers?

9. Why do police procedurals appeal to mystery buffs?

10. *Things Strangled* is the fifth mystery in this series; what's the cumulative effect of the cases on the Homicide Squad? On the readers?

11. What motivates the main characters to persevere?

12. Can you guess what's on the Channel Eight News at the end?

FREQUENTLY ASKED QUESTIONS: (FAQS)

Why do you write police procedurals?

I write to keep the dragons subdued and hope for a better tomorrow. I admire those intrepid souls who risk (and many lose) their lives to protect the rest of us. Plus keeping company with my characters is far more interesting for me than watching the news on TV.

Why do you write novels?

As a former Professor of Composition and Literature, I read to learn, to enjoy, to engage my mind and become educated about other people, professions and cultures. I research and write novels for the same reasons. They allow me more flexibility and freedom than other genres. I also write poetry, my first love; I've had twelve published in literary journals but need to compile them and find a publisher.

What novelists do you read?

My favorites include the following series: Diana Gabaldon's The Outlander, Beverly Connor's Lindsay Chamberlain, Deborah Crombie's Gemma James and Duncan Kincaid, Lisa Gardner's D.D. Warren, Julia Spencer-Fleming's Clare Fergusson and Russ Van Alstyne, Jacqueline Winespear's Maisie Dobbs, Louise Penny's Three Pines mysteries, Charles Todd's Inspector Ian Rutledge, William Kent Krueger's Cork

O'Connor, Robert Dugoni's Tracy Crosswithe, P.B. and Patricia Ryan's Nell Sweeney, and Thomas Perry's Jane Whitefield. And so many others like Susana Kearsley's novels, especially *The Winter Sea*!

Where do you get your ideas?

Most of my ideas for plots originate from the news, Internet, police blogs, overhead conversations, court records, research, people and a vivid imagining of 'what ifs.' *Things Strangled,* as are all my mysteries, is based upon an actual crime.

ACKNOWLEDGMENTS

I thank all at Sunbury Press for giving my stories a chance, for the Knorr's patience and support, especially to LK for designing my book covers and Crystal Devine for editing this book. Gratis to the Charles Bruce Foundation for underwriting the cost of my review books and for supporting struggling artists! Thanks also to my booksellers in the Carlisle Area: Barb Bui, The Bookery manager; P.J. Heyman, proprietor of the Village Artisans Gallery & Studios in Boiling Springs; Kim Laidner, manager of History on High Shop (Cumberland County Historical Society) and Cindy Thrush. To my police consultants: my detectives owe you too!

For research, I used biographies of Frank W. Woolworth, online articles, maps, and the televised series "The Alienist" for visuals. For those interested, Karen Plunkett-Powell's history *Remembering Woolworth's* is informative and nostalgic. Descriptions of the store replica are based on my experience working the candy counter at Woolworth's in Cincinnati during high school and college. I also studied the Lancaster and NYC sites. *It Happened in Pennsylvania* by Fran Capo and Scot Bruce described Frank W. Woolworth's first *successful* store in Lancaster, PA. For crime specifics, Dr. D.P. Lyles's *Forensics, a Guide for Writers and* Val McDermid's *What Bugs, Burns, Prints DNA, and More Tell Us About Crime* are excellent resources. Other excellent resources include *Really Useful: The Origins of Everyday Things* by Joel Levy and *The Macmillan Visual Dictionary. Down Range* by Dr. Bridget C. Cantrell and

Chuck Dean provides a vivid portrayal of the struggle of service members suffering PTSD. And, to paraphrase former Supreme Court Justice Thurgood Marshall, "The Bible and Shakespeare" are forever a source of inspiration.

I thank my readers for following my detectives as they solve crimes; I am forever shocked at criminals' audacity—their lies and evasions, and the excuses they give when caught. Their harm to victims—whatever the crime—is irreparable. So the case, chase, the struggle, and the journey in my cases are as realistic as I can render them. Thank you, Mike and Jarod West, for your computer expertise and assistance for all you do. Thanks, Alida Hodgson, for designing and providing my business cards. Thanks, Terry, for understanding and proofreading this one. And I'm thankful for my writing group: Alma, Pat, Phyllis and Sherry for valuable feedback, critiques, and support.

All errors are mine alone.

I am grateful for the enthusiastic people I meet at book signings for their kind words and encouragement, for recognizing the hard work involved in the writing process, the journey from idea to completion. I'm indebted to readers for asking so many provocative questions and offering suggestions. And to friends like Judy Martin, Sandy Kearns, and Jim Schlichter, who send kind affirmation and positive feedback. To Thomas Law III, Dr. Alma Bond and others for writing affirming reviews. And to my cousin, Beverly Connor, for her support in posting the Sunbury Press "Milford House Mysteries" blog podcasts to hers and the Phillips' Facebook pages.

Please like me on Facebook.com/Carlisle Crime Cases by J M West and listen to our blogs at wwwblogtalkradio.com/bookspeak/milford-house-mysteries where my co-host, Sherry Knowlton and I discuss mysteries, interview authors, and provide podcasts on writing for aspiring writers. You can also visit my website **www.carlislecrimecases.com** for more information on all the mysteries in the Erin McCoy and Christopher Snow police procedurals.

www.ingramcontent.com/pod-product-compliance
Lightning Source LLC
Chambersburg PA
CBHW030647020726
47493CB00006B/1904